FOUR SECONDS
TO LOSE

ALSO BY K.A. TUCKER

Ten Tiny Breaths
One Tiny Lie

FOUR SECONDS TO LOSE

TO LOSE

a novel

K.A. TUCKER

ATRIA PAPERBACK

NEW YORK   LONDON   TORONTO   SYDNEY   NEW DELHI

ATRIA PAPERBACK

A Division of Simon & Schuster, Inc.
1230 Avenue of the Americas
New York, NY 10020

First Atria Paperback edition April 2014

ATRIA PAPERBACK and colophon are trademarks of Simon & Schuster, Inc.

For information about special discounts for bulk purchases, please contact Simon & Schuster Special Sales at 1-866-506-1949 or business@simonandschuster.com.

The Simon & Schuster Speakers Bureau can bring authors to your live event. For more information or to book an event, contact the Simon & Schuster Speakers Bureau at 1-866-248-3049 or visit our website at www.simonspeakers.com.

Manufactured in the United States of America

10 9 8 7 6 5 4

Library of Congress Cataloging-in-Publication Data

Tucker, K.A. (Kathleen A.).
  Four seconds to lose : a novel / K.A. Tucker.—First Atria Paperback edition.
    pages cm
1. Stripteasers—Fiction. I. Title.
  PR9199.4.T834F68 2014
  813'.6—dc23

                              2013036474

ISBN 978-1-4767-4049-2
ISBN 978-1-4767-4050-8 (ebook)

I believe some people are inherently evil.
I believe guilt is a powerful motivator.
I believe redemption is something you can strive for but never
*   fully achieve.*
I believe second chances exist only in dreams, never in reality.
I believe you don't have years, or months, or weeks to impact a
*   person's life.*
You have seconds.
Seconds to win them over,
And seconds to lose them.

—Cᴀɪɴ

chapter one

. . .

CAIN

10 years ago

Blood drops decorate the dusty gray concrete like an abstract piece of art. The stocky brute facing me—his bottom lip split open, an angry cut across his cheekbone—can account for some of that. But given the colossal beating I'm taking at the hands of this recently paroled rapist, most of that blood is probably mine.

Holding my left elbow tight against the ribs that he just splintered with a series of powerful blows, I struggle not to wince as my feet shuffle back toward the ropes of the makeshift ring. Screams and shouts bombard me from all angles, echoing through the underground parking lot of the downtown business building. Normally I have a decent crowd of rich bitches throwing their names, numbers, and "pretty boy" comments at me. Not tonight, though. All of these people took the twenty-to-one odds against me and they're no doubt picturing sandy beaches and shiny BMWs.

Hell, *I* almost bet against me. But, there's not a person in the world that I trust with that kind of money to place it for me. Except maybe Nate. But he's fourteen and a known associate of mine, so I might as well have painted a target on his head if I sent him to the bookie.

"Come on, pansy ass!" Jones bellows, slamming his meaty fists together, a wicked grin on his face.

I remain silent as Nate splashes my face with cool water and I swig some back, trying to rinse the coppery taste out of my mouth. I've heard this guy likes to draw his beatings out, so I'm not worried about him charging me like a bull. I *am* worried about the crowd shoving me in, though. I can feel their impatience swelling in the air over my pause. They want to see my skull hit the ground. Now. This is *real* underground fighting. The kind that brings the high-rolling criminal element and thrill-seekers together like family at Christmas. There are no weight classes here. No drug tests. No rules. No true refereeing. The match doesn't end until one fighter's broken body is collected off the ground.

Not exactly the world a loving father would introduce his son into. But I don't have a loving father. I have a mean wannabe-mobster prick of a dad, who—after pounding on me enough to teach me how to hold my own and harden my muscles beyond their years—decided he could make some real cash by throwing me into L.A.'s illegal fighting scene at the age of seventeen, when my body wasn't even fully developed but was solid on account of the grueling workouts my dad insisted on. I can't say that I went unwillingly. I've even enjoyed it, most times. It's always my dad's face I'm bashing in, his bones I'm snapping, every time I raise my fists.

Every time I pulverize my opponent.

And now, at nineteen years old, I've ended up fighting for my life in the upper echelon of this illicit world. I could win *big* on this one with what I put down. Or I could end up in a body bag. As I gaze at the goon in front of me—steroid-enhanced pecs twitching with anticipation, ugly veins protruding from his neck, his face a hideous mess of blood and ink—I accept that I probably won't be the last one standing here, tonight. I'm a fucking moron for showing up to this fight. Jones is likely high on meth. Nothing short of two shots of fentanyl is going to bring the animal to his knees, and I don't have elephant tranquilizers in my back pocket.

"Zee!" Nate's voice cracks behind me, using my fighter name. I glance over my shoulder at the scrawny kid in my corner. My only reliable confidante, the one by my side through every single fight. He's holding his cell phone to his ear, his ebony skin turned a sickly ashen tinge. "Somethin' big is going down at Wilcox." *Wilcox. My parents' street.* Nate's wide molasses eyes flicker to my waiting opponent before returning to my mangled face.

"They fighting again?" I ask. It wouldn't be the first time.

Nate's head shakes slowly, somberly. "Nah, something different. Benny saw two guys show up about twenty minutes ago." Benny's a fifteen-year-old kid who lives across the street from my parents and goes to Nate's school with him. He's a shithead, but he worships Nate because Nate is connected to me.

"For him or her?" As disturbing as the question is, it's valid. Both of my parents took entrepreneurial paths down the wrong side of morality—my dad venturing into the drug trade, my mother running a quaint bookkeeping business/brothel out of my late grandmother's house. And now one of them has clearly pissed someone off enough to track them down on their doorstep.

Normally, I wouldn't give a shit. I'd be ecstatic. Maybe, if my dad pissed off the right people, they'd get rid of my problem for me. Only it's one in the morning on a Tuesday, and Lizzy, my sixteen-year-old sister, *could* be asleep in her bed. And, if these guys came looking for money and my dad goes to the hollowed-out armchair to pay them off, he's going to find it empty.

Because I stole every last bill earlier today to put down on this fight.

A new visual blazes in my head. One of these guys collecting their payment on Lizzy.

That's all it takes for my adrenaline to kick in. The crippling pain in my side instantly vanishes as I look at my opponent through new eyes. If I bury the odometer needle, I can get to their house in under fifteen minutes. It may be enough time. It may not. This goon is the only thing stopping me from leaving *right now*.

"Nate, tell Benny to call the cops."

I toss my water bottle to the ground and charge forward.

It's over so fast, no one watching seems to know what the hell happened. Silence fills the vast parking lot as everyone waits for Jones to get up. Everyone except me. I know he's not getting up for a while. I felt the bones crack as his head snapped to the side with the venomous blows that I delivered in quick succession.

He still hasn't moved as my peeling tires screech up the underground ramp.

■ ■ ■

"Stay here," I bark at Nate as I pull my GTO to a stop in the middle of the street. I'm not sure how I didn't crash, given that one eye is swollen shut. I jump out, running past the crowd of curious onlookers, toward the throng of emergency vehicles and police officers, lights flashing, cops running with radios in their hands. They couldn't have beaten us by more than ten minutes.

It takes four police officers, a gun aimed at my forehead, and a set of handcuffs to stop me. They won't let me go in. They won't answer the one damn question I ask over and over again. *Is Lizzy okay?* Instead, they hammer me with an onslaught of words that don't register, that I don't care to acknowledge.

"What happened to you, son?"

"Who did this to you, son?"

"You need medical attention."

"How do you know the occupants of this home?"

"Where have you been since midnight until your arrival here?"

Despite my warning, Nate ventures out of my car and somehow slips through the police tape. Like a silent shadow, he waits with me as a young paramedic tapes the gash above my eyebrow and informs me that I have three broken ribs.

I barely hear her as I watch a parade march in and out of my parents' front door.

As I watch the coroner show up.

The beginning of dawn lights the sky when one . . . two . . . three gurneys finally roll out.

All topped with black bags.

"I'm sorry for your loss, son," a stocky police officer with a gruff voice offers. I didn't catch his name. I don't care about his name. "Things like this shouldn't happen."

He's right. They shouldn't. Lizzy shouldn't have been there in the first place. If I hadn't given up on her, if I hadn't kicked her out of my apartment, she wouldn't have.

I could have saved her.

But now I'm too late.

■ ■ ■

Present Day

"What do you mean you can't deliver until *after* the weekend?" Despite every effort to keep my cool, my tone is biting.

"Sir, I'm sorry. As I've already explained, we're experiencing labor shortages. We're working as fast as we can to cover orders. We're sorry for the inconvenience," the customer service rep recites evenly, sounding like she has said it a hundred times today. Because I'm sure she has.

Pinching the bridge of my nose to dull the sudden headache forming, I fight the urge to slam the receiver against the desk. This conversation is a complete waste of time. It's the same one I've had every day for two weeks. "Tell your management that 'inconvenient' isn't the right word." I hang up before she has a chance to spew the prewritten response for that.

With a groan, I lean back in my leather chair and fold my arms behind my head. I survey the walls of my office—lined floor-to-ceiling with shelves, doubling as supply room overflow. Five weeks of abnormally busy nights at Penny's coupled with sporadic beer deliveries means I'm out of our top brands for the coming weekend. That means I'll have to spend yet another Saturday night explaining to customers why being out of Heineken doesn't entitle them to a free lap dance.

I hate this business, some days.

Lately, I hate this business *all* days.

Cracking open a fresh bottle of high-end Rémy Martin, I pour the deep golden liquid into my tumbler. It's my vice—a glass before the club opens to take the edge off and one to close the place down. Unfortunately, the edge doesn't come off so easily anymore and I find myself topping up the glass a lot. It's a good thing our hours are limited or I'd have a drinking problem. At two hundred bucks a bottle, I'd also have a money problem.

My office door cracks open just as the comforting burn slides down my throat.

"Cain?" Nate's deep voice rumbles a second before his six-foot-six, 280-pound frame eases through the doorway. I'm still in awe of how that twiggy little kid turned into the giant now standing before me, almost overnight, too. It shouldn't surprise me, though, given that I was the one footing the steep grocery bill through his teenage growth spurts. "Just got a text from Cherry. She's sick."

"She texted *you*?"

He nods slowly, his dark eyes never leaving mine.

"That's the third time she's called in sick in two weeks."

"Yup," he agrees, and I know his thoughts are on the same wavelength as mine. No one knows me better than Nate. In fact, no one *really* knows me *but* Nate.

Cherry has worked for me for three and a half years. She has the immune system of a shark. The last time she started missing shifts because she was "sick," we found her battered and strung out on blow, thanks to her douchebag boyfriend.

"Do you think he's back?"

I shove my fingers through my hair, gritting my teeth with rising frustration. "He'd be the world's biggest moron if he is, after what happened the last time." Nate put him in the hospital with a broken femur and two dislocated shoulders as a warning. I have to think that was an effective deterrent.

"Unless Cherry invited him over."

I roll my eyes. She's a good girl with low self-esteem and terrible taste in men. Though I'd be surprised, I wouldn't put it past her. I've seen it happen before. Many times.

"I think I'll just swing by her place to make sure this isn't something more than a bug or chick issues." Nate grabs his keys from the rack.

With a sigh, I grumble, "Thanks, Nate." We've helped her stay clean and idiot-boyfriend free for a year. The last thing I want to see is a repeat. "And, here." I pull a twenty-dollar bill out of my wallet and toss it across my desk. "Her kid loves Big Macs."

Nate scowls at my money, leaving it where it lays. I should know better. "And if he's there?"

"If he's back in the picture . . ." I run my tongue over my teeth. "Don't do anything yet. Call me. Immediately."

With a lazy salute, Nate exits my office, leaving me with my elbows on my desk and my folded hands against my clenched mouth, wondering what I'm going to do if Cherry has taken a turn for the worse. I can't fire her. Not when she needs our help. But . . . *fuck*. If we have to go through this with her *again* . . .

And I had to convince Delyla to go back to counseling just last week because she started cutting again. And two weeks before that, we were rushing Marisa to the hospital with complications after the back-street abortion that her asshole boyfriend convinced her to undergo. She hasn't even made it back to work yet. And the week before that—

A knock on my door only seconds later makes my temper flare unexpectedly. "What!"

Ginger's face pokes in.

Taking a deep breath, I gesture her in with a "sorry," silently chastising myself for barking at her.

"Hey, Cain, my friend is coming in to meet you tonight," she reminds me in that low, husky voice suitable for phone sex companies. The customers here love it. They love everything else about her, too, including those naturally large breasts and that sharp-witted tongue. "Remember? The one I mentioned earlier this week."

I groan. I *completely* forgot. Ginger sprung it on me last Friday as I was refereeing an argument between Kinsley and China in the hallway. I never did agree to meet with this person but I didn't say no. Ginger is clearly taking advantage of that. "Right. And she wants a job as what again? A dancer?"

Ginger's head bobs up and down, her wild short hair—colored in chunks of platinum blond, honey, and pink—in styled disarray. "I think you'll like her, Cain. She's different."

"Different, how?"

Ginger's hot pink lips twist. "Hard to explain. You'll see when you meet her. You'll like her."

My hand finds its way to the back of my neck, trying to rub the permanent tension out. It won't work. Weekly trips to a massage therapist do nothing for the kind of knots this place creates. "It's not about liking her, Ginger. It's about being overstaffed. I don't need any more dancers or bartenders right now." Given Penny's reputation, this place has basically become the crème de la crème of adult entertainment clubs. I don't take walk-ins or random applications. Employment is by referral only and turnover is low. Aside from Kinsley, I haven't hired anyone new in almost a year. Too many dancers means catfights over money.

"I know, Cain, but . . . I think you're *really* going to like her." Ginger has been bartending for me for years, longer than anyone

else. I trust her opinion of people. The three others she recom-
mended turned out to be outstanding employees who are now on
healthy life paths, leading far away from the sex trade business.
Hell, she's the one who introduced me to Storm—my shining
success story!

After a long pause, I ask, "And her preferences? Is she . . . ?
Not that it matters, of course."

Teal-green cat eyes sparkle as she smiles at me. "I'm pretty
sure she's into dudes. Haven't seen the proof yet, but that's what
my vibe tells me. Unfortunate for me." I've come to truly appreciate Ginger's sexual orientation. There's never been that awkward
moment with her, where she's decided that I would welcome her
hand on my cock. She's one of the *very* few female employees I
can say that about. It's one of the reasons why I get along with
her so well.

"Her name?"

"Charlie."

"Real or stage?"

She shrugs. "Real, I think. 'Charlie' is the only name she's ever
given me."

I pause to take another sip of my drink. "You vetted her?"
Ginger knows the requirements. No track marks. No pimps. No
prostitution. I have zero tolerance for drugs and prostitution. I'd
get shut down in a heartbeat if the cops caught on, and too many
people rely on Penny's to let that happen. Plus, there's no need for
it here. I make sure the girls can rake in the money safely, without
selling the last shreds of their dignity.

Her curt nod answers me.

"Experience?"

"Vegas. She had a couple of interviews here, including one at
Sin City." Ginger's brow arches meaningfully. "You know what
Rick makes them do."

I lean back in my chair. Yeah, I've heard what Rick's requirements are for getting and keeping a job in his club. The fact

that the guy's a fat, sweaty tub of hair doesn't help. "She didn't comply?"

Ginger giggles. "She barely made it out of there without puking, from what she told me."

I nod slowly. That definitely earns her a few points with me. I want to help out every woman who feels she needs to take her clothes off to survive but I'm only one man, and not every woman is strong enough to avoid the pitfalls of this industry.

I've seen too many of them fall fast.

And trying to catch them over and over again is so very exhausting.

Taking in Ginger's exotically beautiful face, I finally ask the big question. "What's her deal, Ginger? Why strip?" With a finger, I slowly trace the rim of my glass. There's usually a good reason. Or a bad reason, depending on how you look at it. As far as ratios of completely normal to fucked-up employees go, the numbers generally weigh in heavy for the latter. "High school dropout with no future? History of abuse? Douchebag boyfriend wanting extra cash? Daddy issues? Or is she just looking for attention?"

Ginger's head tilts as she murmurs in a dry tone, "Jaded much?"

I throw my hands up in the air. "You're the exception, Ginger. You know that." Since the day Ginger walked into my office—on her eighteenth birthday—I've never had to worry about her. She comes from a stable, abuse-free home and she has never even batted an eye at the stage. Her purpose is straightforward and honest: save enough money to open an inn in Napa Valley. With the kind of money she rakes in here, I'd say she's getting close to that dream.

After a pause, she shrugs. "All I know is she wants to make good money. But she seems to have her head on straight, since she didn't take the other jobs."

Because she probably figured out she'd be sucking cock in the pri-

vate room . . . With a deep exhale and my hand pressed against my forehead, rubbing the frown smooth, I mutter, "All right. We'll see." *Am I really going to do this right now? What if she's another Cherry? Or Marisa? Or China? Or Shaylen? Or—*

"Great. Thanks, Cain." She pauses, her curvy frame—dressed in cut-off shorts and a tank top for setting up the bar—leaning against the door frame. "You okay? You seem worn out lately."

Worn out. That's a good way to describe it. Worn out by week after week, month after month of brazen customers, everyday ownership issues, and employees who can't seem to straighten out their lives without someone running interference. Throw in police attention—because they assume, based on my past and my current business, that I'm following in the footsteps of my parents—and you've summarized my life for the past decade.

It's enough to make any rational person quit.

And I have considered quitting. I've considered selling Penny's and walking away. And then I look at my employees' faces—the ones who I know *will* end up at a place like Sin City without me—and the metal teeth of the trap around my chest dig in tighter.

I can't abandon them. Not yet. If I could just get this lot out and safe, without adding any more problems to my plate, I could live out my life somewhere quietly. A remote beach in Fiji is sounding pretty damn good.

None of those thoughts ever gets spoken out loud, though. "Just haven't been sleeping well," I say to Ginger, pulling on the fake smile that I've mastered. It's beginning to feel like a suffocating iron mask.

By the way Ginger's brow pulls together, I know she doesn't believe me. "Okay, well, you know you always have my ears if you want 'em," she offers, grinning playfully as she rolls her hips and winks. "And *nothing* else."

Her soft laughter follows her out the door, temporarily lifting my dour mood as I set to preparing payroll for the small army of dancers, security, kitchen, and wait staff I have under my employ. Serge—a forty-eight-year-old retired Italian opera singer—manages my kitchen as if it were his own, but I handle everything else.

Unfortunately, the dour mood returns with a vengeance twenty minutes later when Nate's call comes through. "His blue Dodge is here."

My fist slams down against the desk, rattling everything. "You're kidding me, right?" I take a moment to gain control of the rage bubbling inside me. Nate doesn't bother to answer. The two of us have always had an easy back-and-forth banter, but he knows what not to joke with me about. Fuckheads taking advantage of women is one of those things.

"You want me to go in?" Nate offers.

"No, wait outside. If he's back, he's probably carrying." As stupid as this guy is, he must have learned after the last time. "I'm on my way. Don't go inside, Nate." I throw that last warning in with a stern voice. I couldn't bear to lose Nate over this. I shouldn't even have let him get involved. I should have made him go to college and lead a normal life. But I didn't, because he's all I have and I like having him around.

I'm out of my seat and crouched in the corner in seconds, dialing the safe combination. My fingers wrap tightly around the biting steel of my Glock. I despise myself for touching it. It represents violence, illegality . . . the life and the choices that I've left behind, that I would never let consume me again. But if it means keeping Nate and Cherry and her eight-year-old son—the one who dialed my number on Cherry's cell phone for help when he found his mother unconscious on the couch the last time—safe, then I will jam the barrel right into the scumbag's temple.

I'm about to slip on the holster when the door creaks open. "Cain?"

I need to start locking my damn office door again, I tell myself. Stifling a curse, I slide the gun back into the safe and stand, struggling to keep the venom from my voice as I growl, "Ginger, you really need to learn—" *How to knock* is how that sentence is supposed to end.

But instead it ends in a sharp hiss, as I find myself staring at my past.

At Penny.

chapter two

■ ■ ■

CHARLIE

Plan A—Turn myself in and beg for immunity in exchange for information.

I don't have enough concrete information to nail him. I'll probably end up in jail for the next twenty-five years. If I even make it there, alive.

Plan A — Turn myself in and beg for immunity in exchange for information.

Plan B—Lose all my identification and fake amnesia so the government will be forced to create new documentation for me . . . eventually.

What if they put my picture up on the news? He'll find me. Plus, I could end up locked in a psych ward for an indefinite length of time. And I don't know that my acting abilities are quite that convincing.

Plan B—Lose all my identification and fake amnesia so the government will be forced to create new documentation for me . . . eventually.

Plan C—Buy a new identity and make Charlie Rourke disappear.

He's just standing there, boring holes into my face.

Given that I've never laid eyes on him before, I don't know what his normal complexion looks like, but I'll bet it's not the sickly white pallor that I see now.

As if he's seen a ghost.

I try to catch Ginger's eye, to see if she thinks his reaction is strange, but I can't.

"Sorry. I knocked but you didn't answer," she offers in apology. It's true, she did knock, and we waited for close to a minute before entering. I don't know what he was doing in his office—behind the closed door with a sign that reads "boss man" and a pair of lacy underwear pinned to it—but, by the stunned expression on his face, we've interrupted *something*. A glance down confirms that his belt is at least buckled.

"This is my friend, Charlie, who I told you about." Ginger's long, slender fingers point to me and I force a bright smile. "Friend" sounds a bit misleading, seeing as everything I've ever told Ginger about me is a deliberate lie.

I met her only three weeks ago. Her beginner pole-dancing class was just finishing up and she stayed on to watch the advanced class. I guess I impressed her, because she sat through the entire hour and then talked my ear off in the change room afterward about how good I am. I took her proffered number with no intentions to call. The next week, Ginger cornered me after class and wouldn't leave until I went out to lunch with her. Last week, she coerced me into shopping. There's nothing wrong with her. She's twenty-six, but she doesn't act like it most of the time. She has an easy, genuine laugh and a sarcastic sense of humor. She's persistent, too. I just didn't plan on getting to know people, seeing as I won't be in Miami long. But I guess you could say that we've become friends—lies and all.

It's ironic that we met when we did, actually. By my pole-dancing skills and looks, Ginger automatically assumed I was a stripper. There was no judgment in those bright green eyes when she asked which club I worked at. That's why I admitted to the few unappealing adult clubs I had applied to and the appalling "interview" at one called Sin City. The one I had run out of. Her pixie-like face lit up, which was not the reaction I was expecting. Then she explained that she bartended at the best club in Miami and offered to get me a job. She asked about my experience and I, of course, lied. I told her that I had worked in Vegas.

I left Vegas when I was six. I have certainly never stripped there.

After my experience with Sin City, I wasn't sure if I could go through with it. But when I saw the unusually elegant sign out front—void of any big-breasted caricatures or flashing lights, just the name, *Penny's Palace*—I knew instantly that this was the place for me. And Ginger promised me that the owner, Cain, is like none other. The way she talks about him, I'd think he holds some sort of "boss of the millennium" award.

But he's still staring me down.

He hasn't blinked once.

I catch the almost indiscernible shake of his head before he offers in a clipped tone, "Charlie. Right. Hi."

"Hi." I was cool and confident coming in here, leveraging countless hours of acting classes to ready my wide, friendly smile. Now, though, under this man's steely gaze, I hear the wobble with that one tiny word. I step forward and hold my hand out.

His coffee-colored eyes finally pry themselves from my face to glare down at my hand—without moving—and I fight the urge to retract it. Ginger swore that this guy was first class, but he still makes his money off the sex trade. A lot of things get shaken under this roof and hands are probably not one of them. I never did shake the hand of that slimeball at Sin City—Rick—before he instructed me to climb onto his lap two minutes into my interview. I shouldn't be surprised by this guy's reaction.

These owners are all the same.

I take a deep breath, reminding myself that I've handled my fair share of degenerates and can do this.

Hell, *I'm* a degenerate.

As if snapping out of a daze, Cain finally accepts my hand in his, his eyes locked on mine. "Hi, Charlie. I'm sorry. You just . . . startled me. You look a lot like someone I know." There's a pause. "Like someone I knew," he corrects himself softly. His voice carries with it a smooth, educated sound, which surprises me, given our surroundings.

"Okay, well, I'll just be at the bar, getting things set up." Ginger scoots out of the office, closing the door behind her, leaving me alone with this man. I take a few calming breaths. I'm going to throttle her.

I don't know what to expect now. Ginger didn't tell me much about Cain, other than that he's really nice and honest, he treats his employees very well, and if I'm going to dance in Miami, then Penny's is the place to work. She did say that he sometimes comes off as intimidating but he's just reserved. And he's got a lot on his plate, running this club.

She certainly left out details about his physical appearance, I realize, as my gaze skates over his frame to see the well-defined curves beneath a fitted button-down black dress shirt and black dress pants. As if that body isn't enough, his face is flawless—angular cheekbones and a sharp jaw combine to give him a masculine yet almost pretty look. He's like a sculpture—and about as opposite to Sin City Rick as you can get.

Basically, Cain is panty-dropping hot.

That your boss is panty-dropping hot is an odd thing to leave out of the equation. Cain's the type of guy that makes women lose their words and their train of thought when he walks by. Except Ginger, it would seem.

But attractive or not, I'm feeling all kinds of uncomfortable right now, as Cain's hard, intelligent gaze slowly rolls over my body, appraising me. Taking a deep breath, I pull my shoulders back. I hold my chin up. I look him straight in the eye. I do all the things I know to appear confident. I will not cower under the intense scrutiny. If I'm going to be up on his stage, taking my clothes off for his customers, I can't be unnerved by this.

And so I stand and let him pass silent judgment while I survey his office, taking in all the shelves, crammed with boxes. Aside from the large desk on one end and a black leather couch tucked into a corner, it seems like a storage room. By his appearance, I'd expect something sleek and tidy.

"Ginger said you have experience?" His tone is gentler than it was when we first stepped in.

I answer without hesitation. "Yes, one year in Vegas. At The Playhouse." I fight the urge to start twirling one of my loose blond curls. I know my tells, and that's one that says I'm lying. Ginger warned me, under no circumstances, to lie to Cain Ford, because he always finds out anyway and it pisses him off when he does. It's kind of impossible to heed that warning, though, given my situation.

Plus, I am a very proficient liar.

And I'm banking on him not doing an in-depth reference check. Short of divine intervention, he won't find a Charlie Rourke that worked at The Playhouse in Vegas.

Because Charlie Rourke doesn't exist.

Cain leans back against his desk and folds his arms over his chest, only accentuating the defined muscles in his shoulders and biceps. "Do you have a preference?"

I keep my face composed—I'm an expert at stone-cold— while I struggle to decipher his question. *Preference* with what exactly? The desk? The floor? That couch? Is he seconds away from undoing his zipper?

Either Cain interprets my long pause as confusion or he replayed the question in his head and realized how it could be taken because he adds very clearly, "On the stage. When you're dancing."

I exhale and silently admonish myself. "I'm pretty good on a pole." That isn't a lie. That's actually a discredit to my talent. I've been in gymnastics since I was five, so my body is strong and limber. Then, two years ago, I needed an excuse to visit a specific dance studio in Queens once a week so I enrolled in a pole-dancing class. Not under my real name, of course.

It turns out I took to pole-dancing naturally. I just haven't worked up to the move where I drop my clothes.

"Okay," Cain says slowly, his jaw shifting, appearing as if in thought. He hesitates for a second. "Full nude or topless?"

"Topless." I shouldn't be so eager. I've heard what these girls wear as bottoms and they may as well be completely naked.

Cain's eyes automatically drop to my chest when I say that, and they seem to settle there. His entire form is frozen in place.

As if he's waiting.

Of course he is. He wants to know what he's putting up on his stage.

A quiver runs through my stomach. *I can do this.* This will be way less mortifying than the last time. Trying to pace my breathing before my heart explodes out of my chest, I quickly slip my thumbs beneath the spaghetti straps of my lemon-yellow sundress and pull on them until they pass the balls of my shoulders. With a sharp inhale, I let my arms drop and the dress goes with it. I intentionally didn't wear a bra today. I figured that would make this uncomfortable process quick and a tiny bit less embarrassing. The last thing I wanted to do was fumble with bra hooks . . .

Because that would make standing in this man's storage-room office in my white thong that much more awkward than it is already.

Cain's lips part but not a sound comes out of him as his eyes widen for one, two, three, four seconds. And then it's as if he wakes up, because he's suddenly moving. Standing, unfolding his arms, and taking steps forward to reach me quickly, I watch with my lungs constricting as he crouches down in front of me and grasps the straps of the dress pooled around my ankles. He pulls my dress back up, his fingertips leaving hot trails against my skin as he affixes the straps. If my body weren't already as stiff as a corpse, his touch probably would have made me shudder.

Locking eyes on me that look wise beyond his years, he says in a strained voice, as if he's holding his breath, "You don't have to do that for me. In fact, I ask that you please don't do that for me again. Ever."

I swallow and nod, my cheeks flaming, somehow more humiliated by his reaction than had he groped my breasts like that other pig. Spinning on his heels, he marches over behind his desk, a grimace on his handsome features. I don't know if I've done something wrong or if I have the job.

I need *this* job.

Cain speaks up again. "Just stage dancing? What about private dances?" I see his gaze on me from beneath a fringe of thick lashes. "I don't charge any stage fees, so what you earn up there, you take home."

The small exhale escapes my lips before I can stop it. When I came up with this plan two weeks ago, I wasn't fully aware of the inner workings at these clubs. But you can find anything on the internet. I found out that many owners charge a high stage fee, so the girls actually earn their money working hard on the floor and in the private rooms. Rumor has it that, though illegal, many of them do "extras," on top of the lap dances. The idea of stripping on a stage in front of people is a giant pill for me to swallow. But lap dances . . .

I'll do it.

I have to do it, I remind myself.

When I ran out of Sin City that day, I was sure that my plan was dead in the water. I mean, how was I going to perform daily lap dances when I couldn't even get through my interview!

But Ginger told me that Penny's is different. That Cain is different. That no one in the private rooms will be taking their pants off, and that doing "extras" is one of the only ways that you get fired at Penny's.

Cain sounded too good to be true.

Setting my chin with steely determination, I say, "Both, please." Swallowing the revulsion bubbling up in my throat, I clarify with a struggle, "I want to work the private rooms as well as the stage."

Cain blows air out of his mouth, one hand on his hip while the other pushes through perfectly styled, slightly wavy dark hair as he stares hard at me. There's an inexplicable look in his eyes, but I know he's trying to read me. I wonder if he's deciding whether to ask me for a demonstration. My gaze drifts to the couch again and my stomach tightens. Somehow I think giving this guy an interview lap dance might be harder than doing one for a sleazeball.

Because if I could get past the embarrassment and nerves, I might enjoy it.

But he doesn't ask me to demonstrate. Instead, he asks me, "Have you ever bartended before?"

I shake my head, frowning.

"I have too many girls working the private rooms right now. But working behind the bar would bring your earnings up significantly. It's what another stage dancer of mine used to do." He continues, more to himself, "Maybe we'll see how that works out first."

I came in here expecting the worst—that I'd be grinding on guys' laps by the weekend because I have to. And yet, now, the relief is pouring out of me.

"Why are you in this profession?" he suddenly asks, lifting his eyes to bore into me once again.

One question I did expect. I meet his stare and hold it as I explain, "Because I'm good at it, I've got a decent body, and have no interest in serving French fries for minimum wage while I figure out what I want to do with the rest of my life." I deliver that as I practiced it—calmly, clearly, convincingly. It's a good answer. One that creates no doubt. And so far from the truth. I know exactly what I want to do with my life.

End it and begin a new one.

He nods slowly, his lips pressed together in a grimace. I don't know if that means I'm hired or not, so I bite my tongue and wait for a concrete verdict. I'm still waiting for Cain's decision when his cell phone rings. I watch with fingers laced together in front of me while he answers with a gruff, "Yup." He listens, his free hand absently rubbing a small tattoo behind his ear. A second later he barks, "No! I'm on my way." Hanging up, he digs into a drawer and comes out with a handful of papers. "Fill these out, please. Bring a copy of your driver's license with you tomorrow night." Whatever gentleness crept into his voice before has vanished. It's all business now, as he slides the sheets across his desk with hands that look strong and muscular but incapable to soothe. "If the crowd likes you, you've got a job." Turning those eyes my way once more and pausing for a moment, he adds, "Fair?"

"Absolutely. Thank you," I say with a nod and what I hope is a courteous smile as I collect the forms.

With that, he turns and crouches down behind his desk. I hear something metal slam that reminds me of my stepdad's safe door. When Cain stands again, it's to fit a holster and gun on him, startling me. It's not the first time I've seen a gun. I have a gun. I've used a gun. But seeing Cain with one right here, right now, was unexpected. Why does he even need one?

Throwing a light jacket over himself to conceal it—he'll die wearing that in the summer heat, but concealing your weapon is a law in Florida and I guess Cain is a law-abiding citizen—he walks over and, with one hand on the small of my back, ushers me toward the door. It's not exactly rude, but it's also far from polite. With me in the hall, he pulls his office door shut and marches out the back exit, not turning once.

I'm left standing alone, inhaling the faint scent of beer, my ears catching someone testing the sound system. The one that will play music that I strip to tomorrow night.

I take a deep breath as a rash of butterflies swirl through my stomach, the sudden urge to let loose my bladder overwhelming.

It's not a big deal.

Mom did this.

I can do this.

After everything I've done, that I've been an accomplice to, taking my top off in front of a bunch of drunks is nothing. I deserve to suffer a bit.

I glance down at the paperwork in my hand. He said he wants a copy of my license. That's fine. The only accurate thing on it is my picture.

chapter three

...

CAIN

"Hi, Cain."

She pushes one of those big, blond curls back over her bare shoulder, drawing my attention to her neck. It's such a flirtatious move but, with Penny, I don't believe she does it intentionally. "How are you, tonight?" She closes the distance and a delicate hand skates over my arm, as it does every time she greets me before her shift. Shivers run along my skin, as they do every time she touches me.

"I'm good, Penny." I'm so much taller than her that, when she stands directly in front of me, she needs to dip her head back to peer at me. It gives me the best view of that wide mouth that I came so close to kissing last night. So close to giving in to a selfish urge.

I wish things could be different between us, but they can't.

She deserves so much better than me.

Knowing that is what stopped me from kissing her last night, though she was obviously hoping for it.

I force myself to sound like I care when I ask, "How is Roger doing? I hope you two have plans for the holidays?" He'll give her a good life. He's a quiet plumber in his thirties who follows her around the club and desperately wants her to quit. They could have a nice life together. She'd be away from this world.

I can't give her any of that. This is where I belong.

I catch the slightest furrow cross her brow before it's gone. She tucks her hair behind her ear and steps back, swallowing before she speaks. "Oh . . . good. He's good. Yes, we're going to meet his mother." Nodding her head as if to confirm her words, she tucks the same strand in a second time. "I should go and get dressed."

I watch her walk away, drowning in my disappointment.

■ ■ ■

I know she's not Penny.

And yet, as I race my black Navigator down the street—with the air-conditioning cranked to max—toward Cherry's apartment, to deal with impending disaster, the name *Penny* plays over and over inside my head. Those blond curls, those full red lips, the eyes outlined in heavy black kohl that make me wonder what she looks like without makeup. *Decent body*, my ass! People pay thousands to have that beautiful hourglass figure. And those tits are fucking perfect. Plastic surgeons would use her as a design model. She doesn't even need a bra to keep them up. She obviously wasn't wearing one today when she slid her dress off.

Just like Penny that first day she walked into my dive of a club, asking for a job.

I don't fuck my staff. Ever. I'm here to help them get on their feet and away from the sex trade, not drag them down further by being the sleazy boss who treats them like whores. From that day almost nine years ago, when I laid down the payment for The Bank—the club I owned before opening up Penny's—I've maintained that code with stoic resolve. Of course, a young guy surrounded by strippers throwing themselves at him daily was a true test of willpower.

I had a lot of cold showers those first few months.

I figured I'd be fine. Then Penny walked in and, well, she was impossible to ignore.

Impossible not to love within seconds.

And if I had just stuck to my policy and stayed away from her in the first place, she wouldn't have ended up with her head bashed in just steps away from my office.

If Penny's death did anything, it stopped me from ever getting distracted from my purpose in this business. It sure as hell isn't love.

Here I was, thinking I had put that tragedy behind me and moved on. Until tonight, a Penny lookalike walks in and blows my recovery to smithereens.

What did I do? I gawked at her like a fucking pervert. I stared at her body, I avoided her polite handshake, I made her squirm under my gaze.

And then she dropped her dress and that spark—the strange concoction of intrigue, hope, and lust that's so much stronger than just a waiting naked body should provoke—hit me. The one I have felt only once before. When Penny walked into my office.

I went hard as a rock in an instant.

Ginger was right, though. She's different. Unreadable, for the most part. Not cold, but she's either very skilled at controlling her expressions or she's not expressive at all. Aside from that blush when I pulled her dress up, she seemed unfazed through the entire ordeal. And that's not normal. In all the years, in all the interviews, I've never seen a woman so calm as she asks for a job in my club. The women are always nervous. They're usually flirting heavily. Once in a while, I'll turn my back for a second and find them spread-eagled on my desk.

Not this woman, though . . .

She has never worked a private room. I caught that hard swallow when she stated that she'd like to work both. Either that or . . . she *has* worked a private room before and something bad happened. I'm keeping her out until I find out which it is.

I'll certainly be passing her paperwork on to my private investigator. The one who does the kind of in-depth background checks average employers don't bother with. I know it's not normal, but *I'm* not normal and I won't let any illicit shit get dragged into my place, derailing everything I've worked so hard to build.

Speaking of illicit . . . I pull into the parking lot outside Cherry's apartment complex, wondering how long before this goes sideways.

■ ■ ■

"You sure you're fine?" Nate's booming voice thunders over the Bluetooth speaker in my Nav.

"Yeah," I mutter. The passing streetlights cast enough light to reveal my swollen knuckles. I can't believe I injured my hand, but I guess it *has* been a while since I've cracked a jaw with my punch. Years, actually. Despite the multitude of close encounters in this business, I've rarely had to lay a finger on the lowlifes that my employees naturally draw to themselves. Nate's shadow passing over them typically has them running before there's a need.

But Cherry's ex is a special kind of scumbag—a small-time coke dealer with a penchant for slapping around pretty strippers. I guess he thought the "never so much as bat an eye at Cherry again" warning had a one-year expiration date. A more permanent removal from Cherry's life was necessary.

And I think we made sure of that tonight.

While waiting for me outside Cherry's apartment, Nate saw her son playing at the neighbor's place, so we knew he wasn't in imminent danger. A quick walk by Cherry's window found her bent over the couch, clearly not fighting him off, while the jerk-off plowed into her from behind, in prime view of anyone passing by.

It took everything in me not to kick the door in. I was livid. Livid with her for letting the guy in.

Livid with her for allowing him to use her like that.

Livid that he's still breathing.

As much as the idea of pummeling him into the ground appealed to me, there are better ways of getting rid of this cockroach. Nate stood guard while I ran back down to the parking lot. I popped the locks on the guy's truck—some talents you just never unlearn—and, once inside, planted a sizeable bag of coke in the glove compartment.

I may avoid the drug scene at all costs, but I have connections wherever I need them. Tonight, on my way out to Cherry's apartment, I needed them. For her and her son.

We waited for him to leave Cherry's. As I suspected, he was carrying, but it took nothing to disarm him and throw him up against the wall. I didn't even have to pull my own gun.

I had no intention of laying a hand on him. But then the stupid fuck went and called me a pimp. I shouldn't care what a degenerate like him says, but I do—because I know that, to anyone outside, it's exactly what I look like. I got a couple of good shots in on Cherry's "boyfriend" before Nate pulled me off. We let the jerk stumble away to his truck. I even gave him his gun back—unloaded and wiped clean of my fingerprints—and then we tailed him until the cops I'd notified of an intoxicated driver pulled him over.

He has a record, so I know they'll do a full search. When they do, they'll find the drugs and the gun.

He's as good as dead for the next twenty-five years.

I know it was a dirty thing to do. And I know I'd do it all over again if I had to. Still, dipping my hands back into that world leaves me cold.

"I'll be fine. You sure you can keep the bar up and running on your own?" I ask Nate as I turn onto the street leading up to my condo.

"Piece of cake. A chimp could run that place. Actually, a chimp *does* run that place," Nate jokes, earning my chuckle. "Take a break. You need it." It's funny that Nate—who is at Penny's almost as much as I am—would tell me that *I* need a break. Then again, Nate's not the one losing his cool lately.

"Yeah, okay. Check up on Cherry later, will you?"

"Already swung by. Had to get fresh food. The other stuff went cold. She's good. Clear-eyed. Looks like it was a straight booty call."

I roll my eyes but let the smallest breath escape me. One of small relief that she's not back into the blow and, that with that guy behind bars, his "booty calls" won't involve pretty girls like Cherry for a long time.

"See you tomorrow, Nate." After a long pause. "Thanks for your help."

"Yeah, boss. Try to keep out of trouble."

The second I hang up with him, I hit my speed dial.

■ ■ ■

"Unusually hot, even for July," Vicki croons, her four-inch heels clicking against the marble. My eyes follow her swaying hips as she struts through the foyer and into my spacious kitchen. She's a thirty-year-old platinum-blond stockbroker who thinks I'm a twenty-nine-year-old investment banker. Because that's what I told her. Women of her caliber want socially acceptable men.

Strip club owners are not socially acceptable men.

And I'm *clearly* successful in the field of investment banking—based on my spacious two-floor corner condo overlooking the Miami waterfront, in one of the most sought-after buildings by the bay. Really, it's *because of* a great investment banker that I have all that I have. Aside from that lie and my address, she knows nothing about me.

Well, she also knows my favorite positions.

There can be no doubt about what I want when my number shows up on her call display. There's never any guilt. Not on my part, anyway. Vicki is a smart, successful businesswoman who knows—and gets—what she wants. She probably devours male egos for breakfast. She made it clear from day one that she doesn't have time for a boyfriend or a husband; she's more focused on being the first female VP at her company. That's fine with me because I don't do relationships. In truth, I don't know *how* to do a relationship.

But I do know how to fuck.

And with Vicki, that's exactly what we do.

"Yeah . . ." I push a hand through my damp hair—fresh from a shower—as Vicki turns to settle green eyes on my bare chest. I didn't bother putting on a shirt. She likes to shamelessly stare at my body and the various tats that adorn my skin. I had them done years ago, in the thick of my other life. I'm just relieved that I opted for tribal designs rather than skulls and rabid animals.

"How was your day?" she asks with a coy smile. We both know that neither of us really cares how the other's day went. Her attention flitters over my injured hand for a brief moment, which is now wrapped within a bag of peas.

I hand her a glass of Chianti. "Been better." I'm not much of a talker. I think she likes that about me. She once made an offhand comment about wanting to gag her male co-workers because they loved to listen to their own voices.

Vicki doesn't ask me what happened. She makes a cute *tsk*ing sound and then offers, "Well, then . . . how about you relax and let me take care of you," as she leads the way out of the kitchen. I pick up my habitual glass of cognac and follow her to my sparse cream-and-gray-themed living room that overlooks the bay through a double-story window.

Taking a seat in my leather chair, I quietly examine her tall, fit body as she draws a long sip of her wine. She told me once that she's at the gym by five a.m. every day. Judging by those shapely mile-long legs that disappear into her dress and everything rock hard that I know is beneath it, I don't doubt her.

Setting her purse and wineglass down on the end table, she methodically pulls a strip of condoms from her purse and lays them out. She likes bringing her own. It's a control thing. I can't help but chuckle. "A little ambitious?"

"A girl can hope," she purrs as she reaches up to unfasten the strap around her neck. Her dress slides down, revealing small, firm breasts and the flawless dip of her tight stomach. I was already hard, in anticipation, but a new surge of blood rushes to my groin. With the windows uncovered and the lamp next to me on, I wouldn't doubt that anyone with binoculars in a nearby building is getting a good show. I'm sure Vicki has thought of that too, and she doesn't seem to mind. In fact, I think she enjoys the idea. She oozes confidence. Given how hard she works at it, she deserves to feel good about her body. I'm not sure how confident she'd be if she knew I was surrounded by naked mind-blowing twenty-something-year-old bodies every day, with the ability to have any and all of them if I wanted. That kind of knowledge knocks even the most assured women down a notch. But I have no reason to ever tell her that, so I don't. I just sit quietly and enjoy the view without a shred of guilt as she kicks off her heels. The dress follows closely.

And I'm hit with a flash of a yellow dress hitting my office floor and the perkiest round breasts in front of me.

Charlie Rourke.

Back to taunt me, hours later.

Vicki's hands move to the waist of my track pants. I help her by lifting my body up so she can tug them off. "It's been a while. I'm glad to see you've missed me," she teases seductively, her hand wrapping around my length as she begins to stroke.

"I've been busy." It *has* been a while. To be completely honest, I've been getting bored with these nights. There's nothing wrong with the woman. This all just feels so . . . vapid.

Either way, Vicki isn't the one eliciting this response, but if she wants to lay claim, so be it. It'll make us both happy. I tip my head back and close my eyes, a deep groan escaping my lips. And I recall the visual of the brown-eyed beauty in my office today. I let the memory consume me, figuring this is the best way to get Charlie Rourke out of my system before I have to watch her dance tomorrow.

I'll *have to* watch her dance tomorrow.

My eyes stay closed—the image of Charlie without her dress firmly in my mind's eye—as Vicki sheaths me, climbs onto my lap, and guides me into her.

We burn through her supply of condoms.

chapter four

■ ■ ■

CHARLIE

"Little mouse, you're perfect for this job," he says with a large hand squeezing my shoulder. *"No one will suspect you."*

"Are you sure?"

His warm smile speaks his promise. *"Of course. We make the perfect team, you and I."*

"I miss you."

"I miss you too."

"Things are good? You're enjoying Miami?"

I pick at a loose thread on my bedding. It's early, it's sunny, and I barely slept last night. I have yet to decide if I'm more worried about the act of pole-dancing topless on a stage in twelve hours or what will happen if I'm not any good at it.

I *need this* job. Sin City gave me a taste of what straight-out prostitution would be like and I can't bring myself to do it. So, this is it. And working at Penny's feels as right as it possibly could, under the circumstances.

"Yeah. Things are great." I keep my voice airy. Non-suspicious. Right now, I have his trust. I need to keep that.

"Spending a lot of time on the beach?"

"Yup. That and the gym."

"Good. I'm glad you're enjoying life. Any theater groups down there for you to join?"

"Yeah, maybe." Theater group . . . doesn't quite live up to Tisch School of the Arts, where I was supposed to be enrolled this fall. After what happened, my stepdad made me defer for a year and shipped me off to Miami to "be safe."

The reality is I'll never get to go, and that burns me with disappointment. "Good, good." There's a long pause. "Obviously, you've received the package."

"Yup." Like clockwork. Every Monday morning at nine o'clock a small parcel arrives at the extended-stay hotel where I'm supposed to be living. Kyle—the cute twenty-six-year-old security guy who has a thing for me—holds onto it in exchange for a coffee and a fifteen-minute flirt session.

Each package has a new phone with a new number. A new phone each week means no legal wiretaps, which means no incriminating evidence.

And Sam is all about no incriminating evidence.

Of course, my explanation to Kyle doesn't involve burner phones or why I might need them. Instead, I fabricated a lovely modern fairy tale—that my mom likes to send me care packages each week but they have to continue arriving at that address or my father, whom I'm now staying with, will go into a blind rage.

I had a hard time getting that lie out with ease. If Kyle's attention were on my face and not my breasts, he might have caught on. Mom can't send me care packages because she died ten years ago, due to rare complications during childbirth, along with my unborn half-brother. It's a sad story, really. As a high school dropout and mother by fifteen, Vegas stripper by eighteen, Jamie Miller was sure her luck had turned when she caught the eye of the *much* older, wealthy New York businessman Sam Arnoni.

Or, as some know him, Big Sam.

I was six when they got married—after a whirlwind three-month affair. We moved out of our two-bedroom Vegas apartment and into his sprawling Long Island house. The day we moved, my mom sat me down and told me to listen to Sam. That if I was a good little girl for him, he'd give us a good life.

I was eight when she died, leaving me alone with my stepdad. He's all I've had ever since. In truth, he didn't have to keep me. No one would have faulted him for hunting down my real father—who didn't want me—and dropping me off on his doorstep. I mean, why burden yourself? But he didn't. As long as I was an obedient little mouse, Sam told me that we'd be together.

So I was. And, in return, he gave me everything I could possibly ever want.

Knowing what I know now, I would have preferred my estranged father's doorstep.

"Good. I'm glad to hear that. I'll top up your account tomorrow."

"Great." As much as I've begun to detest taking money from him, the more money he sends, the faster I can save.

The sooner my plan can come to fruition.

The sooner I can run from him.

"Well, I've got to get back to work." Conversations with Sam never last more than a few minutes anymore. He's a busy guy. "Check your email, will you?"

Those are the magic words. "Okay." I know that my voice sounds strained and so I clear my throat to shake it loose. There's no sounding doubtful with Sam. He needs to think that I'm fully onboard with this.

"Love you, little mouse."

I swallow a painful knot. Maybe he does . . . in his own way. "Love you too." No real names. No reference to Dad or Sam. That's another rule, even with burner phones. Sam's a paranoid guy. With good reason.

Closing my eyes as I hang up, I heave a deep breath. I knew it was coming. It's been three weeks since the last one of *these* calls.

With icy dread creeping through my body, I reach over and flip open my laptop.

Logging in to the Gmail account—the one I share with Sam—I click on the drafts to find the unsent message. That's how Sam gives me his directives. No transmitted emails means no intercepting them. I stare at the message, containing the name and address of a café off Ocean Drive, along with a meet-up time for me and Jimmy, a hotel name, and a picture of the buyers—"Bob" and "Eddie."

My mouth instantly dries as the wave of nausea hits me.

■ ■ ■

"Hey, Uncle Jimmy!" I force the fake smile wider as I wrap my arms around the burly man in his mid-fifties.

"Hello, my dear. It's so good to see you." He chuckles softly, crushing my body against his round belly. To any innocent bystander, Uncle Jimmy could pass for a vacationing Santa Claus. Sure, his hair is more gray than white and I have a hard time picturing Santa in a yellow Hawaiian shirt and Birkenstocks at any time of year, but he's got that twinkle in his eyes and that easy, quiet laugh that puts you at ease.

Appearances can be deceptive.

Like me. Here I am, smiling and casually accepting an iced latte at a Miami café from a man who isn't really my uncle. My naturally straight blond hair is now chestnut brown and wavy—thanks to a wig. My eyes are olive-green and adorned with heavy brown kohl eyeliner, hidden behind dark sunglasses. A tight sports bra disguises my well-endowed chest beneath a casual T-shirt, topping off my spandex capri pants and sneakers. An effective illusion of a young woman meeting up with her loving uncle for a coffee on a Thursday morning, during errands.

We participate in idle chitchat for fifteen minutes—he asks me about the college English program I'm *not* enrolled in and I tell him how fantastic it is. I ask him about Aunt Beth, who *doesn't* exist, and he tells me that she's loving her new white Honda Accord. Man, he's good. So smooth. He and Sam have been "in business" for years. He lives in Manhattan but has a construction company down here, so he travels regularly. It's a "kill two birds with one stone" scenario. Aside from Sam's best friend, Dominic, Jimmy is the first "business" friend of Sam's that I've met. Sam keeps me on a need-to-know basis, and I don't need to know anything else besides what *I'm* doing for him. I don't know if that is to protect me or minimize his own vulnerability, should I ever betray him. That I'm now working directly with Jimmy speaks volumes. He obviously trusts Jimmy as much as he trusts me. Sam has never been to Miami and when he kissed me goodbye, he said he'd see me in a year. I'm not allowed to fly home and he won't be caught down here.

With a noisy slurp of my drink—I really did need that caffeine—I stand, give Uncle Jimmy a quick hug, grab the set of car keys lying next to mine on the table, and head off down the street, looking for the white Honda rental.

• • •

I may die of heatstroke before I get through this day. Even with the cold air of this rental car blasting on my face, several beads of sweat still trickle down my forehead. Though that could be due more to nerves than to the hundred-degree temperature. Either way, this wig certainly isn't helping matters.

Pulling up to the front of the hotel, I throw the car in park and hit the trunk release. And then I pretend to read something on my phone. Really, I'm taking a moment to collect myself while the valet unloads my bag.

This is my life, for now. I must do this. And in an hour, I can package the memory into a tiny ball, stuff it into a box, and pretend that it never really happened.

Until the next time.

When I climb out of the driver's seat with my empty camera

bag, I'm nothing but another smiling tourist. Every fiber in my body wants to grab the handle of that suitcase—which is much bigger than the last drop—but I don't. I simply show the valet and bellhops my pearly whites as my fist holds a death grip on the piece of paper with the number *1754* scribbled on it.

That's the hotel room I need to visit.

"I'm just going to drop my things off and then I'll be back to do some sightseeing. Fifteen minutes, tops. Should we park the car or can I leave it here?" I ask casually.

"Whichever you prefer, miss. We can even hold your luggage at the front desk until you check in later, if you'd like." He's a grandfatherly looking man with white hair and a kind smile. He probably has lovely grandchildren, whom he plays with and hugs.

I haven't seen or heard from my grandparents since I was three. All I know anymore is Sam.

"Oh, thank you so much. My boyfriend has already checked in, though. I'm just going to freshen up and then head back out while he's working." I fake a yawn, my quick thinking surprising even me sometimes. "Long flight and all."

"Of course."

We're walking into the main lobby when I hand him a ten-dollar bill and stealthily maneuver my hand around the handle of my suitcase. "I'll take it from here."

He begins to object but I flash him a grin. "It's okay. It's just one bag and it has wheels. Besides, I like the exercise." *And you don't want to be anywhere near this suitcase, grandpa.*

With a delayed nod of thanks, the kind man heads back outside.

And I release the smallest breath of relief. That was the easy part.

If I let myself think about it for one second, what I'm walking into is downright terrifying. So I don't think about it. I blank my mind and pretend I'm about to go onstage as I wheel the bag into

the elevator and hit the seventeenth-floor button. In a way, I am.
I'm certainly playing a role.

Leaning against the cool wall, I watch the buttons light up,
sure to keep my face angled down, away from the security cameras. And I wonder, for the thousandth time, how I got myself
into this mess. How could I have done things differently? What is
it about *me* that made this arrangement a wise bet for Sam? Was
this what I was always meant to be? Or was it meant to be my
mother? Some people might wonder what drew a smart, wealthy
New York businessman to a twenty-one-year-old stripper with a
child. Aside from her stunning beauty, of course. But, had she not
died, would *she* be standing in this elevator right now, instead of
me? Am I merely a delayed substitute?

And did she know what kind of world she was bringing her
daughter into?

Twelve years ago, I stepped into a fairy tale. My new stepdad
had taken my tiny hand and led me into a room doused in purple
and brimming with toys, books, and clothes. Everything needed
to win a six-year-old's love and devotion. And win it, he did. Sam
showered me with more affection, more gifts, and more attention
than I could ever possibly imagine. Everything I could want and
things I could never dream of.

Like the day Becky Taylor said her daddy loved her more
than mine loved me because he bought her a pony. The fact that
I never even met my real dad made that sting so much more than
it should have. I'm not the type of kid to cry, but that day I came
home crying.

A few weeks later, for my ninth birthday, I found a black
stallion with a yellow bow around his neck tied to a tree in our
backyard. It was the best birthday present I'd ever received, and
it solidified how much more Sam loved me because he didn't buy
me a measly pony. He bought me a racehorse.

I named him Black Jack. Not very original as far as racehorse
names go, but Sam said it was perfect. On the day that Black Jack

won at the Belmont, Sam was the one hoisting me up onto the horse's back. A photo of that still sits framed on Sam's desk at home, making him appear the proud, doting father.

An illusion. For outsiders, for me. Maybe even for himself.

I didn't notice for a long time that Sam might be "different." I mean, he was my dad and the only person I had. And besides, I was "different" too. Exceptionally intelligent, according to all of the aptitude tests. But with those results came reports that I was unusually inexpressive. "Morose," some jackass teacher called me in a parent-teacher interview, because I didn't gallop around, hooting and hollering and giggling, like every other kid around me. "Weird," I heard some kids whisper not so discreetly behind my back.

Sam said they were a bunch of idiots and I was perfect the way I was. But he also decided I should learn how to hoot and holler and giggle. So he signed me up for acting classes. He told me that sometimes you need to pretend to be something you're not. Turns out I'm a terrific actress. When I'm concentrating, I can mold myself into just about anything.

Maybe *that's* why Sam thought this would be a good fit.

I was ten the first time I witnessed something one might call "shady." Sam and I took a father-daughter trip down to Nicoll Bay one evening. On the way, we played a fun game of do-you-see-any-strange-cars-following-us, where I watched out the back window for any vehicle that kept making the same turns as we did. When we arrived, it was dark and quiet down by the water. We went for a walk, and he held my hand as I devoured a strawberry ice-cream cone. I remember us stopping at one point, him reaching into his coat pocket. A second later, he swung his arm back and launched something into the deep waters.

He took my hand again, winked at me, and we continued walking.

I didn't ask what he had thrown in. In fact, I didn't say a word. I just squeezed his hand and followed along.

I was twelve the time that I passed by the cellar in the middle of the night—on my way to grab a new box of Bagel Bites from the basement freezer—and heard the angry voices. I had to press my ear to the door. Sam and Dominic were in there arguing, something about the police and fingerprints and Dominic wanting "out" and Sam telling him there is no "out," that they were in this together. In a harsh tone that Sam never used on me, he accused his best friend of being fucking sloppy. Sam *never* swore. The stairs creaked loudly as I scurried back to the kitchen, where I pretended to heat up a glass of milk.

That's where Sam found me.

"What did you hear?" he had asked in that cool, even tone of his, his gray eyes severe. I never lied to Sam and my instincts told me not to start then. "You and Dominic talking about the police and fingerprints."

With a deep inhale, his hand lifted to his mouth to cover it with a rub, smothering a curse. "Sometimes you might hear things that you shouldn't hear."

I nodded slowly.

"It's important that you never repeat those things. Ever. Or everything that we have here—you, me, this house, your life—it's gone. You'll be taken away. You'll live in an orphanage, where people won't appreciate you for who you are. You'll have no one to love you. You won't be in gymnastics or acting. Do you want that?"

Pursing my lips tightly, I shook my head.

"*Never* talk about things you may hear or think, okay?" Sam warned.

I nodded again. "Just like that night at Nicoll Bay."

I remember his eyes widening, as if startled. As if he was surprised I noticed or remembered, or both. "Yes. Just like that. People will use information to hurt us. You don't want that, do you?"

"No." I leaned in to wrap my arms around him in a hug. Sam was the only dad I knew. He loved me, even though I didn't see him very much on account of his busy schedule. But he made sure to attend every gymnastics competition and every school play. He always sat in the front row and he was *always* the first one on his feet—his arms loaded with flowers—to tell me what an incredible little actor I was going to be. The idea of losing him pained me. I would do anything *not* to lose him.

When Dominic's wife came to our door a week later in hysterics, looking for her husband who'd been missing for days, I stood beside Sam and watched quietly as he hugged her and wiped her tears, as he shook his head, his face full of concern, telling her that we hadn't seen him since the Fourth of July party, three weeks earlier. When she hazarded a glance at me, I bobbed my head up and down in concurrence.

That was the first flat-out lie I'd ever told for Sam.

After she left, Sam patted me on the back and whispered, "That's my little mouse. Quiet as can be."

I beamed. Making Sam proud always made me feel warm inside back then.

A hiker found Dominic's body at a national park in Maine, months later. His gun lay next to him. The news report cited a suicide. All Sam said was, "It's a shame." No shock in his eyes, no tears down his cheeks. Not until the funeral, that is. That's where he let loose. Apparently, Sam has his own acting abilities.

Me? I said absolutely nothing.

And now I'm here.

The elevator dings as it reaches the seventeenth floor, and I need to clench my muscles to stop from peeing as I roll the suitcase out. *You can do this. The last time was fine.*

Yet something about this delivery feels different. The guys I delivered to before were different. That hotel wasn't as classy. And this bag is just too damn big. If it's completely full, then . . .

I try not to think about it, zoning in on the door numbers and the exit signs and camera at the end of the hall. By the time I reach 1754, my pep talk has lost all its worth and I'm back to clenching my muscles.

Two quick knocks followed by a long pause and a third knock, per Sam's directions. My stomach leaps into my throat as I see something pass behind the peephole. I'd had to take my sunglasses off in the lobby because walking through a hotel with them on is just plain suspicious. Thankfully, with heavy makeup and the hair, most people wouldn't recognize me if they passed me on the street.

The door opens to a tall, balding man in a tan golf shirt who matches the picture I found in the draft email. He goes by Bob. A very basic, very fake name. He doesn't even bother to conceal the Beretta strapped to his hip.

This is where I leverage the acting skills that got me into Tisch in the first place.

With a friendly smile, I offer, "It's so good to see you again!" That's the scripted line, and I'd made sure I memorized it to a tee. Big Sam relies on various forms of safeguards. That's why, even with burner phones, we never talk openly. That's why even his draft emails, never transmitted, are worded carefully. That's why there are several very specific stages to these exchanges.

That's why he continues doing what he does, smoothly defying the law.

Based on their appearances, these guys are the type to take precautions as well. I hold my head up as the man leads me through the spacious suite, past two little boys distracted with a boxing game on their Wii, and into a bedroom where a blond man in his mid-thirties lays on his king-sized bed, one arm resting behind his head while he surfs the channels.

Unremarkable green eyes finally peel themselves from the screen to take my face in and roll over my body. I want to shudder, but I smile instead and say, "Hello, Eddie." That's the name that went with the other picture. Not his real name either, of course.

"Hello, Jane. You a cop?" he asks.

"Isn't that a made-for-television line?" I shoot back smoothly. It's kind of disturbing, how easily I can fall into this role when I'm finally in it. I think it's my strength with improvisation-style acting, coupled with an instinctive need for self-preservation. Whatever it is, I come off as confident and experienced. The two things Sam said I must exude. The two things I am most definitely not. "But if it makes you feel any better . . . no, I'm not a cop. You know who my boss is, Eddie." Well, he knows who my boss is, but he doesn't know that my boss is also my stepdad. Under no circumstances does that kind of information *ever* get revealed, a rule Sam drilled into my head long ago.

Without preamble, Bob seizes my purse and begins his search, flipping through my wallet, past the cheap, dummy driver's license with the name "Jane," that I use for these occasions. A third identity. Another safeguard à la Sam. He doesn't bother reading the information because he knows as well as I do that it's a fake. Once done with my wallet, he empties the few other contents within my bag—a pack of gum, a pen, the Glock that Uncle Jimmy armed me with. *Just for show. It's expected,* he told me. All the same, Eddie's brow arches as Bob lays that on a side table. "You know how to use that?"

"What do you think?" Yes, I know how to use a gun. I've known since I was sixteen, when Sam casually suggested bringing me with him to the shooting range. As an avid hunter, he likes to keep up with his target practice and he goes every Saturday. I jumped at the chance to spend more time with him, likening it to a father-daughter bonding moment.

I'm an okay shot.

Sam is a killer shot.

Eddie doesn't answer me. Instead, he offers with a lazy smile, "If it makes you feel any better, we aren't cops either."

"Good. I'm glad we've settled that," I mutter dryly. "I hope you're enjoying your family vacation. It's quite lovely here. Hot though, this time of year."

A family vacation. I guess that's part of the big ruse. Take your family on a vacation. Send the innocent young woman in to deliver the goods. No one pays any attention.

That's Sam for you. Clever.

I'm wondering how many hotel rooms these poor kids see.

A crooked smirk curls Eddie's lip. "Yes, the wife is out spending my hard-earned money."

Satisfied that my purse isn't bugged, Bob now steps toward me and demands, "Arms up," in a firm voice. I comply swiftly, my stomach tightening in knots. I focus on a painting that hangs over the bed's headboard, on the woman dancing in the rain with a red umbrella lying on the sidewalk next to her. Thinking about how much nicer my life would be if *I* could be dancing in the rain right now.

That thought reminds me that only seven hours from now, I'll be using my pole-dancing lessons for the greater good of Miami horn dogs.

And for that strange club owner.

I wonder if that will churn my stomach worse than this.

I welcome the distraction that comes with those thoughts as Bob's hands take their time, working their way up and down my legs, making me take my shoes off. When his fingers start prodding my crotch area, I clench my teeth together tightly, wishing I were allowed to wear jeans. If I had, though, they'd make me take them right off.

I breathe.

Deep, long breaths.

I breathe through the rising discomfort, the panic, the nausea.

The harsh memory.

Sam promised me that these buyers aren't lowlifes. They're smart businessmen—just like him. Interested in nothing more than making money.

That nothing like *that* would ever happen again.

"Come on, hurry it up," Eddie barks. Bob's rough hands squeeze my ass on their way up to my shirt, then under my shirt, where they linger.

Deep breaths.

I am not really here.
This will be over soon.

Though I don't enjoy this any more than the attention to my lower region, it doesn't jog the same horrific memories. Still, when a fingertip digs under my bra and starts sliding back and forth over my nipple—the lascivious flicker of a smile touching Bob's lips—I decide I've had enough.

"Sal Pal liked doing that, too," I say in a low, calm voice, fighting the shiver that name still elicits as I level Bob with a meaningful stare.

I see the spark of recognition that comes with it and he pulls his hands away with haste and a sneer. Not surprising. Most people in this business have heard that name. How could they not? The gruesome discovery of Sal's body made the national news. Reports say that he was still alive when his hands and other vital extremities were cut off.

When Sal did what he did to me that day months ago, he had no idea who I was to Sam. I mean, how could he? He probably figured I was a hooker, looking to make some extra cash. No one in Sam's position would send his own stepdaughter—a girl he raised and supposedly loved to no end—into a drug transaction.

No one but a crazy man.

Sal certainly had no idea what kind of man Sam *really is*.

Neither did I. But we both found out rather quickly. That night was the second time I've ever run home crying to my stepdad. He remained calm while I, between ragged sobs that I couldn't control, explained in great detail how Sal felt the need to explore any and all possible—and highly improbable—places for a hidden wire.

Sam gritted his teeth and smoothed his hand over my hair, telling me that I did well, that I'd held up, that completing the drop and then coming to him was the right thing to do. He handed me sleeping pills and waited by my side until I passed out.

A week later, while forcing down a cold piece of pizza in the kitchen in a semi-catatonic state, I watched vacantly as Sal's ugly face streaked the news station with the taglines "drug-related" and "sending a clear message" making the headlines. The killers didn't even attempt to hide his remains. They left them strewn along the side of a major highway, with the word *respect* painted over his chest in his own blood.

Sam wrapped his arms around me and whispered into my ear, as if afraid of being overheard, "I caught him for you, little mouse. He tried to run. But you can't run from me." He kissed my forehead then, adding, "No one disrespects me like that. And no one will ever touch you again."

I remember sitting there, shaking within his arms, inhaling the scent of his Brut cologne—once comforting to me—and noting a few things: his reference to respect for himself, when *I* was the one who had been violated, and the word *again*. What "again"? I didn't want an again. I wanted no more! Like Dominic, his best friend and business partner.

Dominic, who turned up dead.

A few things clicked that day: that I was involved in something way over my head, and that it would be impossible to disentangle myself from it until Sam allowed it. *If* Sam ever allowed it.

But most importantly, that was the day I realized that I should be terrified of my stepdad.

■ ■ ■

The rental car is waiting for me as I walk out of the hotel with my camera bag—the one that's so heavy with the payoff that the strap is cutting into my shoulder—and that amazing fake smile plastered to my face.

I was right. This drop was something altogether different. Eddie must have an established network down here if he's going to move that much heroin. *Maybe that means I won't be called again for a while.* That hope makes me sag in my driver's seat with relief.

As much as I want to race to the exchange point and get rid

of all evidence, I can't risk being pulled over by the cops with a bag full of hundred-dollar bills. So I stick to the speed limit, making the distance to the exchange point—a semi-quiet residential street—unbearably long. My phone reveals a text from Jimmy, telling me it was great seeing me today. That's code for "the coast is clear."

I park the car, locking the keys and the money in the trunk. There's a public park across the road and in that park, I know I will find a Santa Claus–looking man in Birkenstocks, lounging on a bench, reading the paper. Waiting.

But I don't search for him because that is, under no circumstances, permitted. Following strict protocol, I walk a hundred feet ahead to where my navy-blue Sorento awaits. With my extra set of keys out to unlock it, I climb in and pull away, just as my phone begins ringing.

"Hello?"

"All good?"

I open my mouth but hesitate. Should I tell Sam what happened in there? No . . . Bob is a douchebag, but that was *nothing* compared to Sal. Plus, I don't want to be the reason for another brutal dismemberment and murder. I think I have Bob under control now and if he's the worst that I have to deal with, I can manage.

"All good. Everything went as planned."

"Good. You'll be dealing with them a lot more going forward. Eddie has big connections. Enjoy the rest of your day."

The phone goes dead.

A lot more going forward. "How could you do this to me, Sam!" I whisper into the silence. How could he? Even I know that you don't knowingly put people you love in danger.

It's in the parking lot outside my apartment that I finally start to shake, my nerves reacting to the mountain of tension that my willpower managed to suppress for far too long. I stopped counting the number of drops a year ago. They were all so small, so easy. But then they started getting bigger, and the thing with Sal happened . . . and now I'm dealing with major deliveries. I know in my gut that they'll only get harder, more risky.

There was a break from deliveries after the "incident," during which Sam showered me with Louboutins and pretty dresses and diamond earrings. I thought that was his way of saying he was sorry, that he acknowledged that involving me in his "business" was a bad idea.

I let myself believe that it was over.

Then a man cornered me coming out of the gym one night in May, just after finishing the last of my high school exams, asking all kinds of questions about Sal and Sam. I kept my cool, playing the clueless, normal eighteen-year-old girl to award-winning perfection.

I told Sam the second I got home and the next day, he handed me a manila envelope full of new documents and identification—birth certificate, driver's license, passport, credit cards. Everything needed to be twenty-two-year-old Charlie Rourke from Indianapolis. The package came with a one-way ticket to Miami leaving that night and a bank account with ten thousand dollars in it. With a heavy hand on my shoulder and a slow, even voice, Sam said that his little mouse needed to disappear for a little while. "This will keep you safe and hidden from guys like that. Just relax, lay low, and wait until all this blows over. We don't want anything pinned to us for Sal."

To us.

"But what about Tisch?" I had asked.

I got a regretful smile in return. "You're going to have to delay for a year. Too risky, otherwise. I'll take care of it." I remember the disappointment that flooded through me at that news.

Instructing me to hand over all of my real identification, right down to my bank card, Sam murmured, "You're not you anymore. You're Charlie Rourke and only Charlie Rourke. Be who you want to be but stay in character, my little actor. As long as you do that, no one will find you. No one will hurt you. Everything in this envelope is legit. It's a genuine ID." Muttering more to himself, "For a hundred G's, you should have no issues at all."

I remember my jaw dropping—a rare but unplanned reaction.

This wasn't a half-assed get-you-past-the-bouncer type of ID that you pick out from a bag of stolen drivers' licenses. Sam would have had to start making these arrangements for me long before yesterday, before anyone ever approached me.

That was my first clue that Sam wasn't telling me the truth.

And when the first drop request came a month after moving to Miami, I knew with certainty that this move had less to do with my safety and more to do with business.

Sam was looking to expand his enterprise into Miami.

And he'd decided to use me to do it.

That's when I started wondering if that guy who approached me outside the gym that day was ever a real threat. It was all too well timed to be a fluke. Perhaps he was a friend. Perhaps Sam hired him to give him an excuse to send me to Miami.

To scare me.

I've thought about just running. Packing my bags and disappearing into the night. But Sam's earlier words hang over me like an ominous cloud. *You can't run from me.* As long as Sam has a name, I'm afraid that he'll find me.

And when he does . . .

What's left? *The* plan. It's a good plan.

I've created an entirely new person, complete with big, bold curls and brown eyes and layers of makeup, with equal parts perfection and flaw. A *real* person in the eyes of the unsuspecting.

Just not really me.

I'll stay until I make enough money and arrange for a new identity. One that Sam doesn't know about. And then I'll run. I'll fly to the farthest corner of the world.

I'll disappear.

For real.

chapter five

●●●

CAIN

"We're fully stocked again, thanks to *moi*!" Ginger's husky voice hollers as I stroll past, on my way toward my office. The sound of clattering beer bottles stops and I drag my feet back to the walk-in fridge, where I find Ginger ass-up in her shorts, leaning over a keg, trying in vain to move it. The girl may be well toned, but she has no hope in hell of moving a 160-pound keg.

Without hesitation, I dive in and grab the other side. "You know Nate or one of the other guys will move all of these around, right?"

With a *phssst* sound, she smirks and mutters, "You know I don't need a man for *anything*."

I chuckle, shaking my head. "Yes, Ginger. You've made that *very* clear." Taking visual inventory of all the beer as I run a hand through the back of my hair, I mutter, "How did this happen?"

Ginger's grin is nothing short of triumphant as she folds her arms over her ample chest and leans against the cooler wall. Streaks of blue that weren't there yesterday color her hair. "We really need to work on your charm with customer service, Cain."

I wait for her to elaborate, knowing full well that it would take more than charm to get our fridges and shelves restocked that quickly, given the supposed shortage. Finally, Ginger confesses. "A small truck came by last night with sweet fuck-all. So . . ." The way she draws that word out, her pretty eyes averting to the ground, I know I'm not going to like what I hear. "Hannah and I gave the delivery guy a short *demonstration* of the private show he'd get if our supply room was somehow miraculously filled by tonight."

"Jesus Christ, Ginger," I groan as my forehead hits the door frame. I have a good idea of the kind of "show" those two could provide, given that they've been linked as an item in the past and are, at the very least, *close* friends. "You know I won't let anyone prostit—"

"Hey!" She snaps her manicured fingers inches from my nose. She's one of the few people who has the nerve to do that. "Don't you dare use that word with *me*. We offered *no such thing*. But, if letting the fucktard get off in his pants while Hannah and I round second base means we don't have to deal with angry customers all weekend, then I don't give a rat's ass who watches. I'll do her full-on, right up on the stage!"

Ginger rarely gets snippy with me and she's fairly private when it comes to her relationships, which means that the supply issues have started to wear on her. Unhappy customers generally mean shitty tips, and shitty tips means pissy staff. They work hard for their money.

I hold up my hands in surrender. Now that she's negotiated this deal, backing out would guarantee an irate deliveryman and even worse service for who knows how long. "Okay, fine. But don't *ever* offer anything like this again. And warn me so I can turn the cameras off, will you?" I don't want any evidence of . . . anything. "And make sure you've got Ben or Nate outside that door, for safety."

She winks. "You're welcome."

Shutting the cooler door on our way out, I add, "You know, I could use a full-time manager. You sure you don't want the job?"

"I'd rather have my scalp waxed," she says in a singsong voice, heading back toward the main bar to finish setting up. She comes up with a new clever retort each time I ask. "Oh," she slows and throws over her shoulder, "don't forget that Charlie's on at eleven. Try not to act so weird again, okay?"

"Did she say I acted weird?" Not surprising if she had.

"*I'm* saying you acted weird. Just . . . She really wants this job."

I nod slowly. "You okay with her on the main bar with you? I'm thinking we can use a third girl there, given how busy it's been."

Her full lips curve into a frown. "I thought she was looking for dancing."

I consider how to answer this. "Only stage for now."

Ginger narrows her eyes at me and I know she's trying to figure my motives out. "Sure, okay. I just thought you said you weren't hiring anyone else for the bar."

"Yeah. I thought a lot of things yesterday." And then Charlie strolled into my office.

Ginger shrugs. "If this busy run keeps up, we'll definitely need Charlie." Then those streaks of blue disappear around the corner, leaving that name hanging in the stale air between us.

Charlie.

No, I haven't forgotten about her. She was at the forefront of my night with Vicki, she plagued the four hours of sleep that I got, she hijacked my morning workout . . .

It's because she looks like Penny. That's all. But she's not Penny. She's just another young woman who needs to make money and she's looking to me for a job and *nothing else*. Whether her motives for stripping are true or not remains to be seen. The sooner I get accustomed to her, the sooner she'll become just like all the others. Hopefully she won't be here for too long.

And I need to keep my dick *far* away from her.

■ ■ ■

"The line-up's around the corner again," Nate says next to me, his eyes roaming the crowd.

"This is insane. I mean, it's great for business, but . . ." I rub the side of my neck as I take in the sea of heads. Penny's is a decent-sized club—fifteen thousand square feet of stage, V.I.P. rooms, and seating area—and we're at capacity. According to the front door, no one has left in the past hour. Most patrons are angled toward the stage, and Mercy—a petite platinum-blond girl with big blue eyes and an ultra-skinny waist who's real name is Annie. Some steal glances at one of a dozen flat screens showing the Marlins game. Others are busy trying to catch the eye of one of the many girls milling around the floor.

I've done my best to keep Penny's looking upscale versus sordid. I kept the neon lights to a minimum, opting for soft lighting to balance off the stage lights instead. The floors are all mahogany, as are the bars. On the south side of the club, there's a slightly raised V.I.P. lounge, complete with plush leather chairs and an unobstructed view of the entire stage.

Still, no matter how new and tasteful the décor is, no matter how hard the cleaning staff works, when I walk into this club, it always feels seedy to me.

"Thank God that delivery came in today or we'd be dealing with a small riot," I mutter, more to myself.

"By *God*, you mean Ginger, right?" Nate's deep laughter is a low rumble. For anyone who doesn't know the guy, he comes across as one scary-ass dude. The stuff gangster stereotypes are made of. He certainly plays the part perfectly when he needs to.

But I knew Nate when he was the underfed, grubby little neighborhood kid, running through the streets alone at night when a child his age had no business being out in South Central. I saw the angry bruises across his cheeks, earned when Nate didn't move fast enough to answer his strung-out mother's demands. I saw his rib cage when he hadn't eaten anything but a moldy loaf of bread in a week. I saw his tears on the nights when he sat confused on his back porch steps, wondering why his mom still didn't love him like she said she would after he fetched her a dime bag of crack.

Nate has been a fixture in my life for thirteen years now. I took him under my wing, making sure he was fed, bathed, clothed, and safe. In exchange, he gave me his unwavering trust. The kid idolized me. It was always a rather strange friendship—Nate was five years younger than me, after all—but in him, I found a level of co-dependence that kept me going through those dark years after my family was killed. Taking Nate with me when I left South Central for Miami was an easy decision.

Prince's "Cream" starts booming over the sound system. That's Cherry's signature song and the regular crowd knows it, exploding in a round of cheers as the exotic Asian struts out onto the stage in a silver sequined dress and heels that could gouge a person's eyes out.

"I made some calls. The guy's going away for a *long* time," Nate says, watching her begin her routine.

I see nothing but smiles and winks as Cherry rolls her hips. "Does she know that we know?"

Nate shakes his head. "Don't think so. She was in a good mood when she came in today."

"Good." Although I'm still bitter that the ass-wipe insinuated that I'm Cherry's pimp. My eyes drift over the crowd of horny men, each staring hungrily at her as she twists and turns her body to the music with unbelievable agility. That's her talent.

Extreme flexibility.

And that's all these guys picture in their heads—their greatest fantasies come alive with Cherry at the helm. What they don't see is the twenty-four-year-old who got pregnant at fifteen and who's been struggling to give her son a good upbringing since her very traditional parents booted her out of their home and their lives. Who is so insecure that she ends up with douchebags who use her for sex and get her hooked on drugs.

"Cain . . ." Nate just shakes his head as his eyes drift over the crowd. I know he's about to say the same thing that he always says. *You can't save everyone.* He doesn't, though, because a small commotion on the floor grabs his attention. Hannah, with a drunk patron's hand cupping her breast.

No amount of money buys that under my roof.

Nate is talking into his mike in seconds, ordering three bouncers over to remove the guy and his rowdy eight-person bachelor party through the side exit, by their necks if necessary. That's why I put Nate in charge of security. Aside from being one of the only people I trust, he's a natural at making fast judgment calls. He gets how important it is to overreact.

How critical it is to take nothing for granted.

I know he still blames himself for the night Penny was killed. But it wasn't his fault. Hell, he shouldn't even have been working in a club back then—he was too damn young, despite his size. If Penny's death was anyone's fault, it was mine. For waiting too long to tell her that I was in love with her.

For ever telling her.

For having my door locked, for not stopping the murder that happened mere steps away.

A hand slaps me over the shoulder, breaking through my dark thoughts. "I feel like I just had my balls x-rayed! When'd you have those new metal detectors installed?" I turn to find a tanned Ben standing next to me in his black bouncer uniform, fresh off a one-week celebratory vacation after taking the bar exam. Aside from Nate, Ben is the longest-standing bouncer at Penny's, working here while he put himself through law school.

I've always tried to keep a solid line of separation between myself and my employees. It helps maintain a level of respect when it comes to following the rules. It's worked with most of them. But Ben has managed to weasel his way over the line to become one of my closest friends. He's an easygoing guy and a fantastic employee, aside from a few rumors of taking late-night blow jobs in the stock room. But I've also heard through the grapevine that I enjoyed a threesome with Mercy and Ginger in that same room.

I think I'd remember that.

"Monday," I answer with a welcoming pat on his back.

Ben frowns. "Where was I?"

"Shit-faced in Mexico?" I offer, earning another one of Nate's deep chuckles.

A wide grin splits Ben's face. "Was I ever!" I see his eyes drift off somewhere in thought—likely to the numerous women he nailed while down there—before his attention comes back to me. "Why the beefed-up security?"

"Teasers is closed indefinitely." Teasers, a popular but sleazy club with a reputation for welcoming shady clientele, got shut down six weeks ago for running a prostitution ring. Now that clientele is looking for a new place to conduct "business" while receiving lap dances and, unfortunately, judging by the rise in men trying to get through my doors with weapons on them, Penny's seems to be their preferred locale. Frankly, I'm surprised. This isn't your typical adult entertainment club. We're only open in the evenings, and I shut the doors by two a.m. I've even started closing on Mondays. That, plus my connections to the police force through Dan Ryder—my former dancer Storm's fiancé—and my outright refusal to associate with any illicit activity, makes Penny's an unlikely place for them to congregate.

Ben nods in understanding. "Some idiot tried to come in with a samurai sword strapped to his leg two weeks ago."

Nate and I both shake our heads in dismay as Cherry's act comes to a close, earning a boisterous cry of approval from the crowd.

"You need to hire more Asian dancers, Cain," Ben murmurs. "This crowd loves Asians."

"They love *her*, dumbass," I correct with a wry grin and a shake of my head.

"Yeah. I had customers demanding free drinks and lap dances last night because she wasn't here," Nate offers with an incredulous look.

Damn customers. Always looking for a free ride. Or, in this case, to be ridden for free. I heave a sigh and pat Nate on the shoulder. "Thanks for covering here last night, Nate. How did things go?"

Nate falters with his answer, his steely gaze on a large cowboy whose arm is stretched out over the rail, reaching out to grab Cherry's ankle, to get her attention. The other bouncers are on him in a second, though, pulling him back. After the attack on Storm three years ago, they all know to toss first, question later. That strung-out guy should never have been in here to begin with. I fired the two bouncers watching the section for that.

Nate finally answers my question. "Fine. Except China and Kinsley were at it again."

I curse under my breath. "Those two are getting a bit too territorial for Penny's." That's what happens when dancers work here for too long. They start to stake claim to regulars and get testy when someone encroaches on their turf. And China can be especially testy with that sharp tongue of hers. That sharp tongue hides the fact that her father repeatedly assaulted her, physically and sexually. She's actually quite sensitive when you get under her Teflon exterior. I've had my work cut out with that one, helping her through a serious and undiagnosed case of dyslexia. She's ready to take her GED soon. If I fire her, she'll end up back in the hands of a slimeball like Rick Cassidy—where I found her to begin with—or some other guy who feeds off vulnerability like a piranha.

That's the thing with these girls. Yes, some of them are just here to put themselves through college and pay the bills. But many were dealt a really shitty hand that's left them with no self-esteem, a need for attention, and no idea how else to make their lives work. Even as young as sixteen, I knew my sister Lizzy was headed down that path. In some ways, China reminds me of her.

But I'll never know how my sister would have turned out because I didn't save her in time.

Terry the deejay's voice crackles over the speaker to announce, "Next up is Charlie . . . a new addition to Penny's. Make sure you give her a warm welcome!"

"New girl?" Ben's eyes immediately light up.

"Don't start, you jackass," I warn with a cutting tone. All of my bouncers know that they're gone if I catch them screwing the girls. Ben loves this job, so I'm pretty confident that he's never broken the rules under my roof. But I also know that controlling what he does outside of Penny's is too dictatorial and just plain impossible. I can only hope that Ben would treat them with some level of respect. Truth be told, if one of these girls could tame this tall blond's wild side, I think she'd have a happy life ahead of her.

He gives me a shrug. "We haven't had any new talent here for a while. Things were getting stale."

A grunt of agreement makes me turn to my left, to find Nate's normal scowl gone, replaced with the beginnings of a crooked smile.

"You too, Nate?"

"I think we could all use a change." There's something secretive in that look that I can't read.

"Is she any good?" Ben asks, adding with a sly smirk, "At dancing, I mean."

"Sure you did, Morris," I offer wryly. "Just keep your fucking hands off her."

chapter six

■ ■ ■

CHARLIE

I'm going to puke.

The fact that I can stroll into a hotel room and conduct a sizeable heroin trafficking transaction without my hands shaking doesn't matter right now.

Right now, as I stand behind a privacy screen in a pair of tiny black boy shorts, my ass cheeks hanging out, and a fitted snap-on vest covering a skimpy hot-pink bikini top—which is only barely covering even more flesh that is about to be exposed to a large crowd of jeering, judging men—my knees feel like they're about to buckle.

The three shots of tequila I pounded back in the dressing room did absolutely nothing for my nerves. They only made me more queasy.

I'm not sure that I can do this.

And why do those lights have to be so bright? It feels like there are a million spotlights out there, ready to beam down and highlight every square inch of my uncovered skin.

"You ready?" a husky voice calls into my ear.

With a startled jump, I turn to find Ginger behind me. I immediately throw my arms around her shoulders, surprising both of us. I'm not a hugger and we're not really on hugging terms but, clearly, I'm desperate.

She giggles. "Oh, come on. I'm sure this is nothing compared to Vegas, right?"

Sliding my arms away from her, my head bobs up and down and I swallow, releasing the lie smoothly out of my deceitful mouth. "I get bad stage fright. That's all. It's my thing."

With a gentle smile and a squeeze of my biceps, she winks and says, "Well, go spin your *thing* out there and I'll cheer you on. I've seen you do this. You'll be fantastic." She disappears down the steps as the deejay gestures to me.

Thirty seconds.

I take a deep breath and mutter under my breath, "Only a few months of this and then I'm free."

I didn't know what I was getting myself into when I dropped off that pencil-case-sized bag at a dance studio in Queens— besides a shiny silver Volvo. I mean, Sam was always sending me on little errands. Dry-cleaning, mail pickup, check deposits. I took care of all our grocery shopping. Errands were my way of "earning my keep," Sam cheerily told me. So when he asked me to drop off a package in the city . . . I dropped off a package.

Simple.

When Sam handed me an ID with my face and some other person's name and told me to sign up for a weekly dance class at that same dance studio in Queens, I figured it out pretty quickly. Still, I went along, not saying a word.

He rationalized it by saying we were giving people a good time and making a bit of money. It wasn't any different from selling booze during Prohibition. I bought that bullshit in the beginning. But, then again, I was only sixteen.

I was naïve.

I was stupid.

It really didn't seem like a big deal. I had watched my friends smoke a joint after school. I'd been to parties where someone brought an eight ball of coke or a handful of ecstasy pills. I'd heard the whole "say no to drugs" campaign loud and clear, but drugs seemed to be *everywhere* in high school. Everywhere people were having fun. And when something's everywhere people are having fun, it begins to feel less immoral. Almost . . . acceptable.

And when your own stepdad—the man who has raised you and given you everything—asks you to do something, the lines of right and wrong become more confusing, and it becomes easier to deny that little voice inside your head. I guess I didn't have the best moral guide growing up.

When I actually *saw* the inside of a suitcase on the first Miami drop, though . . . it finally hit me. Sam doesn't deal in eight balls and handfuls of party-time highs. He deals in hundred-dose vials of heroin. Bags of them.

Goddamn *suitcases*.

He deals in the stuff that turns people into junkies, ruins their lives, and eventually kills them.

And I'm helping him do it.

That's when I stopped ignoring that little voice. I finally realized that what Sam has me involved in is plain wrong and it doesn't matter how many cars and designer dresses he buys me. The wake-up call has brought a wave of guilt that I'm still learning how to deal with. Now I struggle to sleep, to eat. I've lost at least ten pounds off my already lean frame. Every morning I get up and feel the urge to walk out my door and never look back.

When I hear about another overdose on the news, I feel responsible. It's not the recreational overdoses that are making the headlines—it's the *really* addictive stuff, like heroin. It feels like the reporters are talking to me, judging me, condemning me. With *my* help, kids as young as fourteen have overdosed. Kids have been left orphaned because their parents overdosed. There really is no such thing as an occasional heroin user.

But I don't want to spend the rest of my life struggling financially, so I guess my feelings of guilt still aren't overwhelming enough. That, or I am just a truly bad person.

I deserve what happened to me with Sal, back in New York. I deserve to strip in front of a crowd of salivating men. I deserve a whole lot worse.

Sam also deserves to be punished for all that he's done—to countless, faceless victims, and to me. For giving me love and protection that seemed unconditional, but actually had strings attached.

But who's going to punish him?

I peek past the screen, through the crowd, and I see all the faces—waiting expectantly. All of those eyes will be on *me*. I don't think I've ever been on a stage that big before in my life. Then again, maybe it's just because I'll be on it alone—basically naked—that makes it seem all the bigger.

I watch as three girls climb down from the circular platforms that jut off from the main stage. In between the main shows, the girls take turns teasing the audience a bit. But they know to get off now.

To let all eyes fall on me.

My potential boss is there too, looking classy in a midnight-blue fitted button-down as he leans over a railing, talking with that gargantuan bouncer—Nate, I heard someone call him—who was guarding the back door earlier tonight. Even in the darkness and at this distance, I can see the cut of his arms. The guy must have an immaculate body beneath those clothes.

There was plenty of chatter about Cain in the dressing room as I was getting ready. Comments about him being overly moody, suggestions for how to cheer him up followed by wicked giggles. It's clear that any single one of them would give her left boob to sleep with him. I'm not at all surprised. Under different circumstances—both mine and his—I'd probably want the same. A dark-haired one named Kinsley made a comment about him "comforting" her last week in his office—in private. I wonder how many of them he's slept with. It's confusing, though. I mean, I had my dress on the ground. He could have tried something on me but he didn't. I guess I'm not his type. That's probably for the best.

I'm not sure what to think about the other dancers. I earned a few looks of surprise from them, but otherwise they pretty much ignored me. Ginger says it's because they haven't had a new girl in here in a while, other than Kinsley. And few people like her.

Terry taps on the glass window of his little booth and points toward the stage as the beginning chords of my chosen song—"Coming Undone," by Korn—blast over the speakers. I earned a delayed nod of approval when I requested that one. I know it's probably not the first choice for most dancers but I find it energizes me, and given that this is the song I work out to the most, I'm able to move fluidly to it, almost like in a routine.

And a strict routine is what I need.

With one last, deep breath, I manage to slip on that same coat of confidence I don through the drops.

And I remind myself that my mother did this.

That *I* can do this.

That I *will* do this so I can free myself from Sam's softly padded shackles one day very soon.

I emerge from my hiding spot, my adrenaline firing on all cylinders, my heart pounding in my stomach. I zero in on the brass pole ahead of me and I time my steps with the beat of the music—the chords distorted within my ears, competing with my thumping heart—in what I hope is a sexy strut. Unable to help myself, my eyes flicker in Cain's direction for just a moment, to see his dark gaze intently locked on me.

I want to run.

But I can't. I force my attention back to the pole, seizing it with one determined hand. My brain may be going haywire but my body knows what it needs to do.

I begin.

Years of competitive-level gymnastics has given me physical

strength, balance, and coordination to hit just about every move I learned in pole-dance classes, and I don't hold out now, executing the most complex spins, drops, and transitions with ease.

It feels surprisingly organic, the moves coming naturally to me. And if I keep my eyes glazed and my attention on the brass, the heavy beat of the music, and the soft blue hue of the stage lights, I can almost forget that I'm surrounded by leering men.

Almost.

But I can't shake the feel of their eyes on me. And Cain . . . Somehow, his attention is more nerve-wracking than that of the hundreds of others combined. Probably because his opinion is ultimately the one that matters. When I make the simple mistake of letting my eyes graze over him during a boomerang hold, I find that same steely expression on me, only heavier. Heavy enough to halt my racing heart for a beat. And unsettling enough that my grip slips. Luckily, I'm not in the midst of a nose-breaker drop or another dangerous move, and so I quickly recuperate.

I hear a couple of hoots and hollers of "come on!" I can't stall the inevitable any longer. Gritting my teeth, I reach up with my free hand to pull the snaps of the vest open. I let it fall from my shoulders and I toss it aside, exposing the stringy top beneath. The buzz from the crowd spikes with pleasure.

My stomach is no longer churning. The second those snaps popped open, numbness took over. I'll gladly take it, because I have another minute and a half of this song and that vest wasn't the last thing that needs to hit the stage if I want this job.

And so I push away the catcalls and shouts as I continue with my well-practiced moves and I let my mind drift elsewhere. To the valleys of Tuscany, where I could run a small vineyard. To the African hills, where I could watch lions bask in the hot sun; the Swiss Alps, where I could fly through the air on a snowboard. I don't know how to snowboard. But maybe one day, I'll learn.

By the time I reach up to tug the strings of my bikini top, to let the scrap of material drop, fully exposing my breasts to the cool, air-conditioned room and the cheers and whistles, I'm tanning on a private beach in the Maldives.

I'm anywhere but trafficking drugs. Or stripping on this stage. Anywhere but in my shameful life.

It isn't until I've escaped backstage—my body shaking as the rush of adrenaline fades—that I'm able to breathe again. I did it. I made it through my first strip show. I swallow the revulsion bubbling up. I just stripped on a stage. I just stripped in front of a club full of men. They may not have touched me, but . . .

I have the bikini top on in seconds and yet I feel the need to curl my arms around myself, to hug my own body. And I wish Ginger were here, because I sure could use her friendly comfort again right now.

By the looks of the black-haired woman in an electric-blue leather outfit glaring at me with a crooked smirk, I'm not going to get it from her. "You've never been on a stage before, have you?" Her eyes skim my body as I quickly do up the snaps on my vest.

I take a deep breath to steady the wobble in my voice and appear confident. "Not in Miami. Why?"

Raising one eyebrow at me, she mutters, "No reason."

A rare sting bites my eyes. I wasn't good. I was bad. I was up there, on the stage, thinking that I might be doing okay but I wasn't. I reeked of amateurism. If I don't get out of here right now, I'm going to burst out in mortified tears before I can control it.

I will not cry in front of her, or anyone else.

"Next up is . . . China!" Terry's voice calls out over the system as the first notes of "Like a Prayer" comes on. With a smirk, the woman—who I assume is China—brushes past me to take to the stage. I fight the urge to stick my foot out and trip her.

I'm fully dressed again, running down the steps, and making my way out into the bar area, when I realize that I didn't pick up a single bill off the tip rail. "Shit!" I curse, tears now scorching my eyeballs. I just stripped for free. A trip to hell . . . for nothing!

I blink several times to keep from bawling in the middle of

a strip club and, when I've refocused, clear-eyed, I see a fistful of money, attached to a tall, attractive, blond, smiling bouncer, in front of me. "Here . . . You may want this." I'm not sure if it's because I just stripped in front of a crowd or the conversation with that bitch—who is now stalking around the stage like she owns the place—or the way this guy is smiling at me, but I just stand and stare at him, utterly speechless.

"I'm Ben."

Ben is my knight in shining armor.

It takes me a few moments to gather my wits. Ben waits patiently while I do. "I'm sorry. That was stupid of me," I say behind red cheeks, muttering a "thanks" as I accept the wad of bills. "Wow."

"Yeah, you did well for your first night." He takes in my frown of confusion and asks, "What's wrong?"

"No, it's just . . ." I cast a sidelong glare at China in time to see her dress hit the ground as she blows a kiss at a short, bald man. *She doesn't waste any time.* "I didn't think I did very well. I didn't really interact with anyone." I did exactly *zero* interaction.

Ben's head nods in agreement. "You'd definitely make a lot more if you threw out a few winks and smiles. But Penny's isn't your typical club, and a lot of these guys will pay for a good show. That was a *good* show."

"Thanks, Ben." I like this guy already. Even though his attention has shifted from the stage to my chest, where it lingers with a small, knowing grin. I cross my arms over my chest and the grin only widens. I realize there's no point covering myself. He has probably committed to memory *exactly* what's beneath my clothes, as has most of the crowd. Mercifully, Ben turns and strolls toward the main bar. I trail him as he leads me to the area where Cain was standing, my head ducked slightly so as not to attract anyone's attention.

I think I'll collapse on the floor if someone says a single word to me.

I need a happy verdict tonight. If I'm going to do this, it has to be at Penny's. My gut tells me so.

Now that I'm off the stage, the place doesn't seem quite as threatening. The lights aren't as bright, the music isn't as distorted, and I'm no longer alone. There are girls *everywhere*. There must be forty girls on the floor right now. My eyes roam the club to take in the sleek, simple yet sophisticated furniture and fixtures that I didn't notice earlier. The style, the atmosphere, all exude the bit of Cain that I've seen. Classy, masculine, yet with an edge of something uncertain.

Speaking of Cain . . .

I glance around, looking for him in earnest, and catch Ginger's eye from behind the bar. She gestures at an empty glass and mouths, "Do you want a drink?"

I nod appreciatively. Charlie Rourke is twenty-two years old and legally allowed to drink, after all, so why shouldn't I take advantage of that? Drinking underage is the least of my law-breaking problems.

"Where's Cain?" I ask as Ben settles in next to Nate.

"He left." A tiny smirk touches Ben's nice lips. "I think he had something to take care of. Something about a five-knuckle shuffle."

"Oh." Disappointment drowns out my hopes. He didn't even stay long enough to hire me. It's my fault. I didn't interact with the crowd, after all. Not like the dancer before me, who was doing *downward-facing dog* in a piece of floss, inches away from a guy's face. And certainly not like China, who appears ready to peel off her . . . *Yup, there goes her thong.* I didn't even take my shorts off and she's fully nude. I don't know how a person does that. Maybe she's a better actress than I am.

A sharp twinge of pain strikes in my chest again, deepening the relentless throb that has only been growing these last few weeks. I'd like to think it's a bad case of heartburn, but I'm pretty sure it's not. What am I going to do if I don't get this job? As much as I hated being up there, as icky as I *still* feel, I *need* a new identity like the one that Sam arranged for me—the kind that lets you start completely over, legitimately.

Without that, I'll be forced to look for under-the-table work. I won't be able to drive legally, or open a bank account, or rent an apartment, or register for college. Or travel. Without a legitimate card with a name and my face on it, I won't be able to start fresh and lead a good, normal life. People don't realize how vital something like a piece of ID is.

If Cain doesn't hire me, I guess I'll have to go back to Sin City with my tail between my legs. Just the memory of that hairy, sweaty guy with his pants around his thighs makes my legs clamp shut.

"Here you go, my darling!" Ginger croons, handing me a glass of something. I drain it in one large gulp. "You did great out there!"

"I'm not so sure," I mutter, pleading with her pretty eyes—heavily lined with smoky blue kohl tonight—to convince me otherwise. "China didn't seem to think so."

Ginger's face scrunches up. "Ignore her. She's just giving you the gears. She's a bitch and she doesn't like new competition."

I heave a reluctant sigh. *Okay, hearing that helps a bit.* Ginger's always doing and saying things to try and make me feel better. I wonder if that means she's a real friend. I don't really know. I've only ever had superficial friends and casual acquaintances. The ones where people talked to me because I'm pretty and rich. I've never had a best friend before, one I could truly talk to about anything. Sam preferred it that way. I guess it all worked out for the best, as there was no one to miss me when I left Long Island. "Do you think Cain will give me the job?"

She shrugs. "I don't see why not." Leaning in, she strikes Nate in his rib cage. "Where's boss man?"

"Out."

She rolls her eyes. "For . . ."

"For the night."

"Thanks for elaborating, Nate." With an exasperated sigh, she offers me a comforting pat on the shoulder. "Don't worry. We'll get an answer tomorrow and I'm sure it will be a positive one." With a wink, she adds, "You'll be working the bar with me."

"Hey." Ben squeezes in between us, throwing a heavy, muscular arm over each of our shoulders. "You bring her in, Ginger?"

She looks at him warily. "Yeah. Why?"

A curious smile passes over his face. "How do you two know each other?"

He buckles when Ginger's fist rams into his side. "We're *friends*, Ben," she snarls as she stalks back toward the bar. Ben's mischievous grin follows her, not disguising his brief appreciation of her ass, quite visible in a tight red dress.

Turning that broad smile back to peer down at me, his arm still around my shoulders, Ben murmurs, "So, Charlie . . ."

This guy is piece of work. He doesn't hide the fact that he's a player, but that easygoing boyish charm of his somehow makes it kind of cute. And dimples. Deep dimples that pull a temporary shroud over my worry and make me feel like all is right in the world. I wonder if he's always this flirtatious.

I'm not overly experienced in the flirting department. As abnormal as my life is, my relationship experience probably matches that of the average high school girl. Except where other high school girls were busy crying over unanswered texts and catfighting with empty threats, I just moved on, more focused on theater.

So maybe I'm not average in any regard.

Given my naturally reserved demeanor and how I was raised, I'm usually the one to listen rather than speak. I've never pursued a guy. I had a couple of boyfriends in high school. We went out in groups a lot. The times that I was alone with a guy, there wasn't much need for flirting—or talking, in general.

I lost my virginity to Ryan Fleming—the lead in the high school play—during my junior year. We weren't even dating when it happened, but we had known each other for months and I knew he liked me. A lot of guys in high school seemed to like me. Ryan said it was because I was "mysterious" and "not annoying." A lot of girls in high school hated me and I think it's because of the attention I got from boys. And because I was marked a "snob" on account of my reserve.

Ryan was the first and only guy that I felt anything for. He was sweet and understanding. Very well-mannered. I knew he was a future Ivy Leaguer. We had been dating for two months when he asked me to his senior prom. I happily accepted, already mapping out in my mind how we might make a long-distance relationship work the following year.

Ryan never came to pick me up that night, though. He didn't answer his phone or my texts to him, either. When I called his house, his mother seemed surprised that I was expecting him. She stammered a little, confused, finally admitting that she thought we had broken up.

I sat on that spiral staircase of our foyer for hours, my shoulders hunched, my mind confused, my heart in dejected pieces.

When Sam arrived home, his face was a mask of calm. He gave nothing away—certainly no worry, no sympathy. Taking a seat next to me, he explained how this was for the best, how I was young and I shouldn't be tying myself down. I said nothing, simply looking up at him. And then he trained narrowed gray eyes on me as he said, in an even tone, that he wasn't pleased with the idea of me getting serious with *anyone.* That he kept his end of the deal by giving me everything I could ever want, by protecting me, by not leaving me alone in this world.

I've always had a visceral need to please Sam.

I heard through the grapevine that Ryan did end up at his prom, arriving solo, and leaving with my childhood nemesis, Becky Taylor. When I saw him in the hallway on Monday, he walked past me as if he didn't even know me, but I couldn't help notice that his back was rigid, his pace was quick, and his face was a shade of pale I wasn't used to seeing on him. As if he were terrified by the sight of me.

There was a flicker of a thought back then—that *Sam* could be involved with this strange twist in Ryan's behavior—but I quickly dismissed it. I mean, Sam would never allow me to be hurt so much.

Now, though, I can't help but wonder if Sam was the reason I sat on those steps in a violet dress until midnight, my phone in my hands, miserable.

It took me a while to get over Ryan, but I did, and there were other boys. All short-lived, all fumbling-in-the-dark notches in my senior-year belt. All guys that I dumped the second I felt any hint of emotion. And after what happened with Sal, I haven't had much interest in anyone.

Now this attractive blond man is ogling me like he wants to teach me all that a teenage boy can't, and then some.

"Ben! Back off." Nate's booming voice pulls Ben's attention away from my face with a small scowl.

"Yeah, yeah," Ben mutters, sliding his arm off me. But he shoots a wink at me immediately after. Nate doesn't seem to notice. He's busy listening to something in his earpiece. Something funny, apparently, because a broad smile splits that intimidating face in two. "Hey, Ginger! Your 'client' is here."

I look back in time to see Ginger's face twist with displeasure. She slams back a shot of something and then slaps a rag down onto the counter as she comes out from behind the bar. Marching past Ben, who's doubled over with laughter, she points her fingers at the two amused bouncers and says, "You just remember this sacrifice when you're sucking back a cold Heineken later tonight." With a pause and a wink, she adds, "Maybe next time you guys can take one for the team."

That cuts Ben's laughter off cold. "Oh, no," he says, shaking his head fervently. "I only play for one team, and King Kong and that fucking third leg of his are not allowed to join in my game."

"Feeling inadequate?" Nate responds with a grin and a slap over Ben's shoulder before his tone once again turns serious. "You better follow her back there for this."

Casting a lazy salute in my direction, Ben trails Ginger as she grabs her brown-haired dancer friend by the elbow and heads toward the V.I.P. rooms.

There's no need for me to get comfortable here, not knowing if I'll be allowed back, so I decide to go home. I prefer being alone, anyway. I take a long, scalding-hot shower so that perhaps I can rid myself of this vile feeling before I get up on that stage and strip again tomorrow.

And the next night.

And the next night.

I hope.

chapter seven

∎ ∎ ∎

CAIN

I grip my steering wheel with white-knuckled force. If I don't slow down, I'm going to get pulled over or wrap my truck around the guardrail. Acknowledging this, my foot still doesn't ease off the gas pedal.

She dances just like Penny did.

The style, the grace, the class.

With a mournful smile and her eyes closed. Like she has a secret. Like her mind has disappeared off somewhere, like she's imagining herself anywhere but on that stage.

It's a thing of rare beauty, the way her body smoothly swung and dipped and contorted, teasing the men without the need to lie spread-eagled or with her ass in the air like an everyday stripper.

I was hard the second she stepped onto the stage. I was thinking of ways to get her in a private room when her top finally came off.

I'm no better than Rick Cassidy or any of those other vultures.

Finally releasing the breath I'm holding, I lift my foot off the gas pedal, slowing my Navigator to the legal limit. Deep down, I know that's not true. I don't condone the girls getting high to loosen themselves up for lap dances and private shows. I don't take the girls for a test drive when I hire them, and I sure as hell don't demand late-afternoon blow jobs. The dancers don't even turn me on anymore. All I see are girls who need a second chance. Girls who need someone to protect them because no one ever has.

The way I should have protected my sister.

And Penny.

But here's a woman who I *want*. The second Ben started joking about how her breasts were too flawless to be natural and how he'd be finding out for himself later tonight, I told him he was fired, and I wasn't kidding. He and Nate exchanged a what-the-fuck-is-wrong-with-him look and then I guess Ben clued in, because he asked what was going on between Charlie and me. I decided that I needed to leave before I made more of an ass of myself.

So I bolted.

I don't know if I can handle knowing she's doing that in my club daily. A temptation that I might not be able to ignore indefinitely because, dammit, this feeling is as addictive as a heroin high.

Hiring her would be a bad idea.

I acknowledge this even as I glance at the stack of papers sitting on my passenger seat. Charlie's application, her identification, everything I need to forward to my investigator. Just looking at it, at the photocopy of her face, reminds me of my present discomfort. I adjust myself. It's a little after eleven o'clock. Even with my normal four hours of sleep and a two-hour workout, tonight will be a fucking long night.

I hit the dial button located on my steering wheel.

■ ■ ■

"It's been a while," Rebecka purrs, sauntering through my front door. The woman's voice has a crispness to it that borders on snotty. Until she's screaming, anyway.

"I've been busy," I manage to get out around a mouthful of cognac.

"I'm glad you called." Flipping her hands through her jet-black hair, she adds, "Even though it's late."

"I'm glad you came."

"And you will too, soon." Blood rushes to my cock with her promise. Sharp blue eyes roam my cabinetry as she steps into the kitchen. "Property value has gone up. I could make you a ton of money if you sold now." It was her real estate agency that sold this condo to me in the first place. Sometimes I think she keeps coming back as much for the business opportunity as the sex. I think she might just be that kind of woman.

"I'll keep that in mind," I assure her in a dry tone as I watch her turn and stalk toward me slowly, a teasing smile on those red-painted lips of hers.

Her fingers go right for my pants, deftly undoing the button and zipper. "You do that."

That will be the extent of our conversation for the night.

In seconds, Rebecka is on her knees with those lips wrapped around me, taking my entire length in. With a groan, I set my glass down. Grabbing the back of her head with a hand, I pull her against me. Normally I would never do that to a woman, but Rebecka likes it.

She asks me to do a lot of things other women might not like.

Things that should give me a few hours of distraction before I have to decide what to do about Charlie.

chapter eight

. . .

CHARLIE

"Charlie Rourke. Twenty-two . . ." Insipid brown eyes slide down my body as he does a slow circle around me. I'm down to nothing but my white thong underwear. He made me undress before any conversation began.

Now, it's all I can do to pace my breathing and not coil my arms around myself.

With that swollen belly protruding beneath an ill-fitted green-and-white striped golf tee, Rick Cassidy looks like he could be suffering from the impossible: male pregnancy. But it's not his belly that makes him so unappealing. It's not even the tuft of hair climbing out the back of his shirt, or his disproportionately skinny legs, or the comb-over, or his misshapen nose, or his porn-star mustache.

It's that phony smile—empty of authenticity, full of bad intentions—that makes my skin want to crawl into my bones. He's everything I pictured a strip club owner would be. "You're what . . ." Coming back around to face me, he reaches up to cup my left breast, giving it a rough squeeze. His breath reeks of stale coffee and cigarettes. "A C-cup?"

I swallow my revulsion. Outside of female retail specialists at Victoria's Secret, I've never had to answer that question. And they *certainly never groped me while they asked. So long as he focuses his grabby attention above my waist, I can stomach it.* "Yes, that's right."

"*And,*" *he says as his hand slides down to graze my abdomen with his knuckles,* "*I'd say maybe a twenty-two-inch waist.*" *He snorts.* "*Like your age.*"

Fighting the urge to shrink back from him, I distract myself by scanning the cramped office. There's a small desk off in one corner, covered in folded newspapers and cans of Diet Coke. Most of the space is taken up by a worn brown sectional leather couch. One that looks well used. There's no way I'm ever sitting on that. In the opposite corner, I find a camera pointing toward us, the flashing red light telling me that it's recording this "*interview.*"

Ugh.

"*Here,*" *I say, steadying my hand as I hold out a copy of my résumé. It seems ridiculous, offering him my information* now, *but I may as well since I've gone to all the trouble of making it up.* "*I worked in Vegas, at—*"

"*Don't care,*" *Rick dismisses with a wave of his hand as he saunters over to the couch.* "*As long as you can give a good lap dance, you're hired.*" *When he turns to face me—revealing a wide grin and a set of crooked front teeth—his fat fingers already have his belt undone and his zipper down.*

It only takes another second for those department store khakis to slide down to his knees. His black boxers follow next with the help of his hands, and my wide eyes automatically drop to see the veiny repulsion sticking out. Now I do wince. I can't help it. Letting himself fall back into the couch with a smile of anticipation, he says, "*Come show me how much you want a job at Sin City . . . and lose the panties.*"

It's still dark when I bolt upright in bed, drenched in sweat, struggling for air, shaking with disgust. That's the second time I've had that nightmare.

No, not nightmare. *Memory.* Because it happened.

Exactly. Like. That.

Thank God it had ended with me throwing on my dress—

skipping the bra—and running out the door. But, if Cain doesn't hire me for this job, the nightmare may very well have a new ending soon. I *need this* job. It *has* to be Penny's.

■ ■ ■

"You're a skeevy bastard!"

At least I have some entertainment from my neighbors.

If I can piece together the last five days at this place, it sounds like the guy has issues keeping his pants on with any and all willing females and the couple is trying to work their marital problems out with verbal abuse and flying objects. They usually make up by noon. Then I get to listen to them have wild monkey makeup sex. Today sounds more hostile, though, so I think she caught him in another compromising position last night.

I moved to this small studio apartment two weeks ago. With its sunny-colored stucco walls and red tile roof, the building looked approachable. Cozy, even. It was the low rent that won me over, though. The extended-stay hotel was costing thousands per month and, though Sam ensured I had more than enough to cover it, I decided that the whole I-need-enough-money-to-disappear-off-the-face-of-the-earth plan required extreme changes to my lifestyle. So, I quietly moved here. As far as Sam knows, I'm still at the extended stay.

Right now, I really wish I were.

Maybe I went a little *too* extreme.

Something loud hits the wall next to my bed. I'm picturing a skillet. I'm hoping it's not a head. I'd call the cops and report it, but I don't need them on my doorstep asking me any questions or taking my name. So I wait, crossing my fingers that someone else makes the call.

As I do, I check for any responses to my many chat-room inquiries. I know that I need a new identity. I just don't know the first thing about getting one. The internet seems like the best place to start my research. Unfortunately, I've gotten absolutely nowhere. Not even a little nudge in the right direction. Aside from one guy telling me that my problems can't be that bad and another one offering to send me pictures of his penis, I've had no response.

And today . . . nothing.

But I have time to figure things out, I tell myself. It's not as if I have the money right now, anyway.

Dragging myself out of bed to the tune of "you and your filthy dick can go straight to hell!" I stagger to the fridge to pour myself a glass of orange juice, keeping an eye on the liquid as it pours. I learned the hard way that roaches are common in low-rental apartment buildings, that they *can* get into a poorly maintained fridge, and that you should stick to screw-top jugs versus cartons or you may find brown corpses floating inside.

The day I learned that hard lesson, I also had a mini-meltdown before coming to terms with my situation. I'd rather deal with roaches here than roaches in a federal penitentiary for the next twenty-five to life.

This is a means to an end.

I'm savoring the cold liquid, rejoicing in the small miracle that I feel less vile about last night after some sleep, when a sudden hard rapping sounds against my door. It startles me and I freeze, my mouth full of juice.

No one visits me. No one knows where I live. This must be a mistake.

But what if it isn't? What if Sam found out that I moved? I don't think he'll be happy. He's always saying how important it is for us to tell each other the truth. Ironic, given that we speak in code and never truly admit to anything. What will Sam do when he finds out? The prospect makes my heart begin racing. On tiptoes, I scurry to the door and peer through the tiny peephole to find a dark-haired man with sunglasses on.

Holy shit.

It's Cain.

What is he doing here? Crap . . . my application. I gave him this address. I didn't think he'd use it.

I jump back as his fist rattles the door with another knock, followed quickly by, "Hi, Charlie." There's no inflection at the end, so he knows I'm standing on the other side of the door. He must have seen me move past the peephole.

"Uh . . . just a minute!" I call out, my eyes frantically scouring the apartment, my heart—already racing—ready to explode. I catch my reflection in the closet-door mirror.

"Shit!"

I don't have a stitch of makeup on and my hair is a straight, matted mess after my shower last night. He'll see exactly what I look like, with the added bonus of dark circles under my eyes. I don't want him to see the real me. He needs to see Charlie. Confident, well-put-together twenty-two-year-old pole-dancing diva Charlie Rourke from Indianapolis. But I also can't leave him standing out there for half an hour while I hide myself behind a mask of smooth curls and heavy kohl liner.

I can at least get dressed, I note, taking in my thong and tiny white tank top. *Not that he hasn't seen me in less.* Throwing on a pair of gym shorts and a more presentable tank top, I take a second to hide the assortment of wigs I use for drops under my sheets. With one last cringe at the state of my apartment, I finally open the door.

Damn. Cain looks different. Not that he didn't look good before, but he looks younger today—more relaxed—dressed in dark blue tailored jeans and a white golf shirt, untucked, made of that thin material that hangs so nicely off curves and muscles. And Cain has *a lot* of nice curves and muscles. His hair is combed back but a little messier, with wispy ends circling out around his neck.

I can't peg his age. He's one of those guys who could be twenty-five . . . or thirty-five. There's a hardness in his jaw and sharpness in his gaze that you don't get with youth. Plus, he's a successful businessman who runs a popular strip club. He has to be in his mid-thirties.

Whatever age he is, Cain is hot.

Sam was twenty-five years older than my mom when she married him. He didn't look anything like Cain does, but she certainly found something extremely appealing in him. Hopefully something aside from his money. I have only faint memories of my mother, but I do remember her smiling a lot after Sam came into our lives. I wonder if she'd still be smiling. I wonder if I'd even be in this situation, had she not died.

I've never been attracted to an older man before, but I think Cain is the kind of "older guy" I could be with. Dating Cain is not on the table, though. Right now, I don't know if having Cain as my boss is even on the table.

I am certainly not on the table, given my need to stay under the radar until I can vanish in a few months.

I need to stop thinking about Cain and tables.

I can feel his stare at me from behind those sunglasses. I can only imagine what he's thinking right now. I know I look *completely* different. Younger. I hope he doesn't start questioning my identity . . .

Shit!

My eyes. I forgot to put in my contacts.

I exhale ever so slowly. It's too late to do anything about it now. Maybe he won't notice. He is a guy, after all.

Cain slides his sunglasses off and settles those coffee-colored eyes on me, offering a warm smile. The first one I've seen from him. "I hope you don't mind me swinging by." Lifting the Starbucks tray he's carrying, he adds, "Cold and hot options. Ginger said you were a caffeine junkie?"

He's certainly much less intense than he was the first night I met him. His voice is softer, too. And it's sweet of him to ask Ginger about my preferences. I can't help but be suspicious that this coffee buffet is his way of lessening the blow that I suck as a stripper and don't have a job. That I'll be heading back to Sin City or some other seedy club to perform lewd acts for management. Ginger confirmed that Rick's not the exception in the sex trade industry. Maybe Cain would still let me bartend, at the least.

Regardless, I can't keep him standing here while I play mute. My tongue—temporarily frozen—starts working again. "Yes. I am. Please," I clear my throat and step back. "Come in."

He edges past me through the door and I catch that fresh woodsy scent that I first inhaled in his office. It's pleasant. More pleasant than mine, probably, given that I just spent the night in bed, perspiring. "I'm sorry. The air-conditioning unit broke down and the landlord hasn't fixed it yet. It's kind of hot in here." "Kind of hot" isn't the right description. It's stifling.

Cain's eyes roam over my space as if taking inventory. There's not much to catalogue. I rented it furnished, which entails a simple two-person folding table, a puke-orange love seat made of a weird vinyl-like material, and a bed that's called a double but is more like a twin. I'm not the neatest person in the world but, aside from a few shirts strewn over a chair and a hamper of washed but unfolded laundry, everything's put away. My kitchen is spotless. Not a crumb. That's more a necessity of survival than tidy habits. It's me against the roaches, and one open bag of bread will secure their victory. I've even strategically placed a can of Raid on my counter as a warning to them.

It's not really working.

Cain's focus settles on my hastily made bed for a moment and a thought hits me. Is this where he gives me the "if you want the job . . ." ultimatum that the dirtbag from Sin City did? Maybe that's his M.O.—in the privacy of my own apartment instead of his place of business? Maybe he lives by that "don't shit where you eat" philosophy.

Could I do it?

Unable to help myself, my eyes roll over the defined ridges

of Cain's back, visible through the clingy shirt. I don't think it's simply his physical appearance that catches women's attention. The way his body moves radiates a strength and control that many women would find sexy. I imagine he's quite demanding, maybe a touch aggressive. The type to take a woman up against the wall because that's what *he* felt like. I doubt much emotion ever plays into Cain's motives.

Still . . . I have to admit, sleeping with Cain for this job wouldn't exactly be comparable to, say, a public flaying. It would be sordid and completely physical, but just thinking about this man on top of me on my bed right now stirs a need in my belly, one I haven't felt for months.

But . . . *no!*

What the hell am I going to say if that's what he intends? Fresh beads of sweat are rolling down my back. And my superior improv skills? It's as if they never existed. Confident, witty Charlie Rourke has left the roach-infested building, leaving a wooden pawn in her place. I need to pull myself together. If I can do it for drug dealers, then I can certainly do it for a strip club owner.

Cain turns to regard me again and I fight the urge to fidget. His mouth opens and closes a few times before he says, "A girl like you shouldn't be living in this area."

By his authoritative tone, I can't help but feel like Cain is scolding me, and my cheeks heat slightly with embarrassment. I give a one-sided shrug. "It's not so bad."

That might have been convincing if not for the sudden screams of "skank bitch!" and "festering dick!" through the wall.

Silence hangs in the air as Cain regards me with an even stare, likely waiting for my response to that. There isn't much that I can say, short of trying to make light of it. I give him a sheepish grin. "Ike and Tina are getting awfully creative with their pet names."

He doesn't return the smile. Clearly, he didn't find that funny.

I wonder if he finds much funny. I can only imagine the kind of place Cain lives. He's so well put together, from his wavy dark hair down to his stylish but masculine shoes. If he only saw the kind of house I grew up in, maybe he wouldn't be looking at me with such pity now. Or maybe it would be ten times worse, because he'd be wondering how I fell so far from my privileged life.

"Here." He holds the tray of drinks toward me, his eyes locked on my face. "There's an iced latte, a Frappuccino, and a regular coffee—cream and sugar on the side."

"A caffeine overdose. Exactly what I need right now," I muse, tucking my hair back behind my ear.

Finally, that one earns an amused upper lip curl. "I'm sorry I left before you finished last night. I had to . . . ," he sighs, his eyes hooded for just a flash before returning to normal, ". . . to go."

Busying myself with the lid of the iced latte, I wordlessly await the ruling. Will it be pole-dancing topless and bartending at the best strip club in town or . . . worse? Much, much worse.

His low voice breaks the silence. "So, how many nights could you work?"

I stop fumbling with my cup and look up to find that unnerving gaze still on me. "Do you mean . . . do I have a job?"

Cain's head bows once, as if in assent. I catch a hint of something like conflict flash through his eyes, but when he's facing me dead-on again, the look is gone, replaced with a completely unreadable expression. "You can dance on the stage and bartend with Ginger. Working the floor will have to wait."

A burst of relief floods my chest as my escape moves one step toward reality. Shocking myself with a rare, uncontrolled reaction, I leap forward and throw my arms around him. "Thank you so much! I mean, I didn't think you would hire me! I thought I wasn't good enough. I . . ." The overwhelming relief has taken over all instincts and suddenly I'm babbling like an idiot. All the while my arms are wrapped around my new boss's neck and his body has gone rigid under my touch.

Oh God. Did I just break the record for quickest firing after hiring?

I rush to pull away, smoothing my shirt down. "I'm sorry. That was inappropriate. I'm . . ."

To my surprise, Cain begins to chuckle. It's such a lovely sound. "It's fine." I'm still probably standing too close to him but he's not moving away. I notice for the first time the golden flecks within his dark brown eyes and a scar above his left eyebrow.

I also notice that the tattoo on his neck, behind his ear reads "Penny." My heart throbs. She was obviously someone very important to him. He must have loved her. Where is she now?

Clearing his throat, he adds with an easy smile, "I'm used to *a lot* worse than a hug, Charlie. A hug is fine."

Okay. Maybe Cain isn't so intimidating *all* the time. I reach for my iced latte, which I can now enjoy with ease. Except . . .

"So, I guess my boss at The Playhouse had good things to say about me?" I try to sound as casual as possible.

"Still validating your references, but I'll give you the benefit of the doubt and let you start tonight," Cain confirms quietly.

"Awesome." So, I could still get fired. Or maybe I can impress him enough before then that he'll let it slide. "How many nights can I work?"

"As many as you want."

"Really? And everything I did was fine? I mean, the outfit and—"

"It was fine."

"Are you sure?" I swallow, not wanting to offer what I'm about to offer. "I could probably lose the shorts if you want me—"

"I don't," he cuts me off, his tone suddenly cutting.

"Okay," I force out between pursed lips. And we're back to stern Cain. If the dress incident and this reaction tell me anything, he has issues with the dancers doing things for him. Or maybe just *me* doing things for him. That's fine. *The shorts are staying on!*

Taking another glance around my apartment, his jaw muscles visibly tightening, Cain mutters, "I know of a better apartment building to live in. I could make a call—"

"It's fine, really. You've done enough for me already." The last thing I want to be is a charity case for Cain.

With a reluctant twist of his mouth, he inhales deeply through his nostrils. "Okay, well, I guess . . . I should go." I'm sensing that he's not pleased. His hand slides over his neck, over that tattoo. He does that a lot. I wonder if he even knows that he's doing it.

Lifting the giant latte up in the air in a sign of cheers, I offer him a smile and begin to thank him for the coffee and the job, only the shriek of, "Get out! Get out of my life and never come back!" cuts me off, followed by a piercing scream, a loud bang, and the sound of crashing glass inside my apartment.

Before I can figure out what just happened, Cain's strong body plows into me, pulling me to the ground, sending my drink out of my hand to splash all over the wall nearest us. His arms wrap around my body protectively, his palm cradles my head, and I can feel his breath against my cheek, he's that close to me.

"Are you okay? Are you hurt?"

When I don't say anything, one hand lifts to my chin. He gently turns my face so we're head-on, and he's a mere inch away. "Charlie. Are you okay?"

All I can manage is a nod and a swallow. I should be focusing on figuring out what the hell just happened in my apartment but instead, I'm inhaling that delicious mixture of soap and cologne, hyperaware of my body being pressed against his and each beat of his heart, its rhythm faster and harder than my own. Being this close to Cain is paralyzing. He could easily keep me like this all day long.

Unfortunately, that's not happening. "Okay. Stay down," he growls before leaping up and tearing out my front door, his shoes crunching over something as he passes. It takes me a moment to process that my mirror is shattered. A glance to the opposite wall shows me the small hole.

Those lunatics have a gun.

And, by the shouts I'm hearing, Cain just charged in there, unarmed.

chapter nine

. . .

CAIN

Charlie almost got shot.

Right in front of me, as I lingered there like a horny teenager—looking for an excuse to talk to her for a little bit longer, maybe persuade her to move—Charlie almost got shot.

And I just stood there, only seconds away from being shot myself.

The first thing I see when I step through the already open door of this shitty apartment in this shitty building in this shitty neighborhood is a scrawny white guy in a stained tank top and ripped cargo pants, with a trickle of blood running down the side of his face. His red, glossy eyes alternate between me and his hands, which are fumbling with a handgun. It's jammed, clearly, or I'm sure the strung-out ass would be firing bullets like Yosemite Sam right about now.

This fucker could have *killed* Charlie.

I can feel my nostrils flaring as I stand in the doorway, like a bull about to attack. My hands automatically tense—a natural tendency, dating back to my fighting days.

I need to get that gun out of his hands.

And then I'm going to beat the scumbag to within an inch of his life.

I'm halfway to him when I suddenly hear a scream and feel a weight land on my back. Someone starts thumping my shoulders like a chimp gone rabid. It's got to be his woman.

I don't have patience for women who defend men trying to kill them. I twist and spin, reaching up to dislodge and throw her a few feet away. She lands on her skinny ass beside the couch, without injury. Any additional injury, that is. Based on the nasty gash across her forehead, it looks like she's already been hit once.

In my peripheral vision, I catch Charlie standing in the doorway. I'm about to yell at her to get away when I hear a click, followed by a bang and a howl of pain. I turn to find the guy crumpled to the floor, his hands wrapped around his left foot. Blood is already beginning to trickle out.

The idiot just shot himself.

I'd laugh if there weren't a loaded gun lying on the floor beside his writhing body. I need to deal with that first. My rage has all but defused now—he got exactly what he deserved. Instead of punishing him further, I simply march over and kick the weapon under the couch.

And then I breathe a sigh of relief, thinking the situation under control.

"Cain!" Charlie screams a second before something heavy cracks me across the back of my skull. It's not enough to knock me out, but fuck if it doesn't hurt. Wincing and ducking, with my arm in the air to avoid further attack, I spin on my heels to find the crazy bitch back on two feet and the brass vase that she launched at me lying near my feet. She's frozen, those hateful eyes—red and glassy like her husband's—shifting between me and the gun pointing at her head.

Charlie's gun.

"Calm down or I will shoot you. Do you understand?" Charlie

says with an impressive degree of composure, slowly stepping into the apartment. Her hands aren't even shaking.

The woman has enough sense to realize that Charlie isn't bluffing. She edges back and around me—giving me a wide berth—until she reaches the moaning, writhing idiot on the floor. Dropping to her knees next to him, she starts sobbing as she presses her lips to his head, her arms loosely around his body. "I'm so sorry, babe! Are you going to be okay? I love you! I'm so sorry!"

Sirens sound in the distance. Someone has called the cops. "Charlie." My eyes land on the gun in her hand. "You should go back to your apartment. I'll take care of it from here."

I don't have to ask her twice. She tucks the piece under her shirt before she steps out, hiding it from any curious witnesses.

■ ■ ■

A few hours and a barrage of questions from the cops later, I'm facing a very quiet Charlie in her sweltering apartment once again.

"Here, take this." She holds out a bag of ice for me. But I don't take it. All I do is reach out and touch her delicate hand, attached to her delicate arm, attached to her delicate body, which would have crumpled to the ground had that bullet sailed only a few inches to the left.

She shifts from my touch, gingerly lifting the bag to my head while on tiptoes. I wince as it touches the bump. "Sorry, but you need to ice it. Come and sit. You're too tall for me." She wraps her fingers around my bicep and guides me toward the red folding chair next to her dining table. It's a foreign feeling, having some-one leading me. Ordering me.

Caring for me.

I go willingly, finding myself intrigued by this role-reversal.

Pulling up the other chair, she rests on it with one knee and continues her silent tending to my lump. Luckily, that was it. I don't want to deal with stitches. Charlie's mouth works as if she wants to say something but is hesitant. And so she says nothing, content to half stand, half lean while I simply stare up at that perfectly proportioned face. Because I can't help myself.

Charlie's eyes aren't brown. They're a deep, mesmerizing bluish-purple. I've never met anyone with violet irises. I've heard they do exist, but they're rare. Elizabeth Taylor apparently had violet eyes. If they looked anything like Charlie's, then it's not a wonder she kept landing husbands. Why the hell Charlie would want to hide those gorgeous things is beyond me.

Everything about Charlie looks different from the woman who showed up in my office two days ago. I knew those big, springy curls probably weren't natural, but they actually change the shape of her face, making it appear rounder than it really is. And why the fuck does she wear all that makeup? She's stunning without it. I've never seen natural lashes that long before. And her skin is porcelain smooth, like one of those dolls. That's what Charlie looks like. A perfect little doll. Except with that ultra-wide, sexy mouth.

A *young*, perfect little doll.

I'm not sure that she's twenty-two. It's so hard to tell with women these days. I've seen fourteen-year-olds look legal. It could be that Charlie's license is fake and she's a minor. I've already sent her paperwork off to my private eye and I'm expecting a call from him any minute. Short of robbing her previous employer blind or attacking other dancers, I don't care too much about her past experience at the Vegas club. But I am a little worried about her age . . . *fuck*.

What if I just put a fourteen-year-old on my stage?

I push that thought out of my head with force. Now I'm just looking for excuses, reasons for why hiring her is a fucking bad idea. Reasons besides my own selfish ones.

Short of being underage or being a criminal, she can have a job at Penny's for as long as she needs it. That, I know for sure. After distancing myself—with Rebecka's help—I was able to see that I was overreacting. I thought about telling her she can only bartend but decided against it. The stage means a difference of a couple hundred dollars a night. It'll be fine. I'll just have to get used to seeing Charlie topless every day. I'm not going to send her off to suck Rick's cock—or worse—because I want to avoid a case of blue balls.

So now here I am, with this angelic-looking violet-eyed young woman playing nursemaid to me. And all I want to do is touch her.

Fuck.

She clears her throat and then, with a slight chuckle, says, "Can you believe he shot himself in the foot?" The sound of her voice and the way her face softened are so contradictory given the words she just spoke, and what we just went through. Most women—and men, frankly—would be rattled after a bullet barely missed them in their own home. Penny would have cried. Ginger would be throwing a proper fit. Kacey, my former bartender, would have murdered the man with her bare hands. But Charlie continues to be surprisingly calm and unperturbed by the entire experience.

Is this the way she has always been? Or did something, or someone, make her like this?

"Drug addicts," I mutter, causing her giggle to die off abruptly. *Ah, Cain. If only you had a sense of humor, like Ben, she'd still be laughing.*

And probably on her back in that bed.

But none of what happened today is remotely funny. "Charlie, I really don't like the idea of you staying in an apartment next to gun-wielding neighbors. You could have been shot."

Her unreadable eyes flash to me. "And *you* could have been shot."

I sigh, not sure what else to say. I'm trying my best not to come off like the control freak that I can be. These girls don't need a dominating boss and I don't own their lives. They need to feel like they're making their own decisions, even if it's with my help. But, seriously . . . a bullet just flew past her head and she still doesn't want to move? Does she not have any common sense?

A cool finger suddenly grazes my skin behind my ear, where my tattoo is. "She must have been someone very important to you," Charlie murmurs, tracing the letters softly.

I don't answer, the feel of her skin against mine—despite the reminder of my past—igniting something deep inside. I need her to *not* be touching me like that right now. The intensity of the day is finally merging with my testosterone, creating a pent-up ball of stress inside. She's not wearing a bra and that shirt is cut way too low. When she hugged me earlier, I could feel her nipples through the thin fabric. I was so relieved when she pulled away, before she had a chance to feel the response in my jeans. But now she's basically shoving them in my face, the way she has positioned herself. I wonder if that's intentional.

"You have blood on your shirt," she murmurs suddenly, her finger moving from my neck to tap my shoulder.

My skin begins to tingle as I turn to indeed see the dark brownish-red stain. "Fuck. That woman must have bled all over me when she was on my back. I've got something in my car," I mutter, starting to rise as the first beads of sweat begin to form. I don't have many weaknesses. Other people's blood on me is a distracting weakness. I've had plenty of experience with that, but it never bothered me until the night Penny died, when I couldn't get her blood off my hands, no matter how hard I scrubbed.

Charlie's hand pushes down against my collarbone, instantly freezing me.

"Stay. I'll get it. You need to sit for a while." Removing her hand from my body, she holds it out, her brow arched expectantly.

Normally, I'd dismiss her assertiveness with a gentle shake of my head and smile. Normally, I wouldn't be in her apartment—ten feet away from her bed—in the first place. But I'm too agitated to focus. Besides, nothing seems to be normal today.

Charlie's eyes watch my hand as I slide it into my pocket to pull out my keys. I hope she doesn't notice the other bulge in my pants. "Black Navigator. Golf bag on the backseat."

I'm on my feet and yanking the soiled shirt off without a second's consideration, tossing it on the ground. It's garbage now. I won't even bother to wash it. Adjusting myself as my eyes roam the space, I wonder where she hid that gun. Or more important, why she has it in the first place. Protection, likely. She's a single woman in Miami and she lives *here*. I'd bet good money that the serial number is scratched off and she doesn't have a license to carry. But she seemed to know how to use it, as steady as her hands were.

Atheist or not, I need to say a small prayer that her neighbors didn't mention Charlie having a gun when the cops showed up. I doubt that even Storm's fiancé, Detective Dan Ryder, would have enough pull to bury that legal issue.

My eyes land on the rumpled bed again, on the silky white sheets that Charlie sleeps in. Without thinking, I stroll over to it, picking up the edge and sliding the material through my fingers. These are expensive. People who live in the Miami ghetto don't spend money on expensive bedding unless it's a luxury they've become accustomed to, a luxury they don't think twice about. And yet, this is not a place that someone accustomed to luxury would allow herself to be buried in. I mean . . . she knows that it's infested. The counter is lined with Tupperware containers and there's a fucking can of Raid next to her toaster, for Christ's sake. And to top the contradiction off nicely, a pair of fancy heels— identical to Vicki's—lie next to her bed. I'm a betting man and I'm betting that these aren't knockoffs. And if Vicki's wearing them, then they're by one of those high-end designers.

Maybe Charlie's a thief.

Perfect. I've hired an underage thief.

I pull my phone out of my pocket to check the screen for any missed calls from my private eye. Nothing. I let the phone drop back into my jeans and instinctively move to adjust myself again, silently cursing my dick for not focusing on the more pressing matter at hand.

The crunching sound of a piece of mirror glass missed in the cleanup is the only thing that warns me of Charlie's presence. I turn to find her standing in the doorway, her eyes wide with panic as she stares at me, standing over her bed with one hand on her sheets and my other one on myself. I let go of both, but it's not soon enough.

In seconds, the panic on her face smooths over. "What are you doing?" Her gaze shifts between my face and her bed. And my upper body, which is now bare.

And my groin.

For the first time in I don't know how long, I feel heat burn my ears. "Nothing weird." I think I may have just topped Rick Cassidy in terms of sleaze. *Bravo, Cain.* "Maybe a little weird," I correct, having nothing better to say to offset the awkwardness.

She slowly walks over to me, stealing furtive glances at my chest. I'm used to catching women's eyes on my body. I put several hours in at the gym each morning, so I know I'm in damn good shape—even better shape than when I was eighteen and fighting. But having Charlie's gaze on me makes my nerve endings spark like electric circuits gone haywire. It makes me unable to think straight.

She ducks her head, but I catch the adorable smile curling her lips when she looks up again, and my shoulders sag with relief that I haven't completely freaked her out. Holding up the black shirt that I had tucked into a bag for the rare morning of golf, she asks, "Is this good?"

"Perfect. Thanks." Our fingertips graze when she hands it to me, stirring my blood more. I watch as she turns to walk to the kitchen, her perfect round ass swaying in those little shorts. I need to get out of here before I explode in my pants.

She bends over to pull a small bottle of bleach from under the sink. Forcing my eyes away, I slide my arms through the sleeves and yank the shirt over my head.

Charlie lets out a shriek and jumps back from the sink area, tossing a small cleaning brush away, together with the bleach.

"They like dark, damp spots," I say softly, putting two-and-two together.

She nods and bites her bottom lip, a mixture of disgust and anger marring her beautiful face as she allows her body to shudder once. I grit my teeth against the tiny smile that threatens. Not because her situation is amusing, but because she finally reacted the way I'd expect her to. Because I finally see an expression on her face that seems unguarded and uncontrolled.

Persuasive Cain is gone. "You're not staying in this apartment, Charlie. Not for one more night." I slide my phone out of my pocket. "Pack your things. Now." I can't help the severity in my tone; it tends to escape in situations where I have to take control.

Charlie turns to regard me with a hard glare. I wonder how she'll react to my more unpleasant side. I don't give her a chance to argue. "This is nonnegotiable. If you want to work for me, you're not living next door to a bunch of crackheads. I don't want you anywhere near that shit." I hit "call" on my phone, adding, "I know of a good place."

Turning my back to her, I wait. Maybe she'll launch something at my head. It wouldn't be the first time . . .

The familiar, gruff voice answers on the third ring. "Tanner here."

chapter ten

. . .

CHARLIE

"You drive a brand-new Sorento and you live in the slums?" Ginger's pretty face twists up in bewilderment from my passenger side. She climbed in the second I pulled into the apartment complex parking lot, behind Cain. Her hair is styled poker-straight and smooth today, reaching all the way to her chin in multicolored stripes.

"I inherited it." The lie slides off my tongue so easily. It's the same lie I gave to Cain when he helped load my belongings into the back. I could tell by the blank stare that he might not buy it, but he didn't call me out.

Thank God Sam didn't send me here with another Volvo—this whole charade would be that much harder to sell. Then again, I imagine a Volvo wouldn't have lasted one night in the other apartment building's parking lot. The truth is I almost sold my SUV to bank the money. But that could get back to Sam through Jimmy, and it would raise questions. I figure I can get about twenty grand on its sale the second I'm ready to leave.

My eyes roll over the white-stucco apartment building in front of us. Despite the bars on the bottom-floor windows, it looks nice enough and well maintained. Nothing fancy, but hopefully not a place where I have to worry about getting shot, standing in the middle of my studio.

I think I did a pretty good job of hiding my emotions from Cain today. But, considering I carry a constant feeling of threat on my shoulders nowadays, I don't think this was as shocking for me as it would be for someone else. Either way, I didn't want to appear vulnerable in front of my new boss, so I did my best to focus on making light of the situation while I iced the bump on his head.

"So, you live here?"

"A bunch of us do. Me, Mercy, Hannah, China."

"China?" I repeat, tossing a sidelong glance at Ginger. "*The* China?" The viper who almost made me cry last night?

She snorts. "Yeah, the one and only. Bad news is she's a bitch. Good news is she's fine if you get on her good side." That's Ginger. She's blunt and snarky, but she always tries to keep things positive.

"Does Cain live here, too?"

"Cain? No way. He lives somewhere downtown. But he owns the building. Bought it two years ago."

"He owns this building," I repeat, my tone flat. "And four of his strip club employees live here."

"Five, now," Ginger corrects with a grin.

"You're kidding me, right?" I'll be stripping for him *and* living under his "roof"? If I don't get fired for providing false references, that is. What the hell? In my haste to get away from my domineering drug-dealing stepfather, have I allowed myself to be acquired by a pimp?

Ginger seems oblivious. "I know it's a little strange. Cain is a little strange. But you'll be my neighbor now!" She lets out an excited squeal. "We can have coffees in the mornings with Mercy and go to the gym together. You can be my guinea pig for testing recipes." Ginger is taking culinary classes but refuses to eat anything she makes, for fear of turning into a portly chef, she says.

"We can drive to work together, too! I hear you'll be working with me every night." With a raised brow, she adds, "That's a lot of Ginger time for you. I hope you realize how lucky you are."

Oh, man. Laying low is hard to do when you have people watching your every move . . . *Shit* . . . I can't have anyone seeing me heading to a drop, in disguise. That's how questions begin. I can't have people asking questions.

None of them can *ever* know what I'm into.

I should have kept my roach-infested apartment, but Cain made it clear that wasn't an option. He walked me to the superintendent and, after watching them have a heated conversation about bullet holes and appalling conditions, followed by threats about having the place condemned—I don't know if Cain can make that happen, but he sure as hell sounded convincing—I handed in my keys and the landlord handed me back my security deposit.

I watch as Cain's lean body slides out of his driver's seat, with his phone to his ear. I don't know whether to be thankful or angry with the way things played out today.

Or worried.

Sure, the fact that I might get a night's sleep without having to leave the lights on is more than enticing. But . . . why is he doing all this? I now have a job and what I assume will be a better place to live. What will he want in return? Everyone wants something.

Sam sure does.

And Cain is doing it all despite not knowing anything about me. Except that I have a gun, which he didn't even say a word about.

"He sure likes to get involved with his employees' lives," I say out loud.

Ginger's gaze locks on her boss. Now, *our* boss. "Yeah, he tends to." She pauses. "But not in a bad way. He's a good guy," she assures me. "A little different, sometimes. Reclusive. Charming, occasionally. And he can be moody, but who wouldn't, with all the shit he deals with."

I have to agree with her. I caught rare glimpses of a joking, playful Cain earlier today, with his soft chuckles. They were few and far between but when he loosened up, I couldn't deny there was a magnetic pull. Most of the time, though, he seems stressed—his back rigid, his keen eyes boring into me as if scouring for answers.

I watch him now as he begins to pace, one hand deftly adjusting the collar of his new shirt while he talks. By the deep wrinkles in his forehead, he doesn't look impressed with the conversation. Maybe it's my background check.

Not good.

When I came back from grabbing that shirt from his Navigator—a spotless, well-maintained vehicle that smelled fresh and clean, like him—I found him standing next to my bed and I immediately panicked. I thought he had discovered the wigs I'd hidden. But then I was distracted by the fact that my sheets were in his hand. The 1200-thread-count Egyptian cotton sheets that I had to buy because cheap sheets make my skin itch and keep me up half the night, paranoid that bugs are scurrying all over me.

And he was shirtless.

And his other hand was on his groin.

That was a super-awkward moment.

Awkward because I didn't know what he was doing, and awkward because I instantly wanted him to offer me the same ultimatum that Rick had. At that very moment, I would have submitted.

"And he's intense," Ginger says, cutting into my thoughts. She pauses. "And principled. Cain marches to a different beat. I mean, I've heard the kinds of things that some of these girls try on him, and he never takes the bait."

"Never?" I feel my face tightening with doubt as I gaze out at the tall, dark form again, still on the phone. "Bullshit." I don't believe it. It doesn't matter, because he can do whatever—or who-ever—he wants.

"No . . ." Ginger's soft chuckle fills my truck. "Ben jokes that Cain must have a malformed, Hobbit-sized penis, because there's no way any man can own a strip club and have the pick of the litter—Ben's words, not mine—and not take advantage."

"That'd be unfortunate," I mumble. The very idea of Cain with a malformed, Hobbit-sized penis leaves my insides heavy with disappointment. I feel Ginger's curious green eyes on me as I ask, "Has anyone ever seen him with a woman?"

"Nope. Well, maybe Nate, but good luck getting any dirt out of *him*. That guy is like Cain's own private Chinese wall."

I could see Cain preferring a sophisticated, suit-wearing woman with a pinched nose and a snotty attitude, who only ever has sex in a bed with the lights off. Who he would *never* bring around to a strip club. But, then, why would he own one in the first place? And why would she be okay with him owning it? Unless she doesn't know that he owns a club.

And may or may not be a pimp.

All these conflicting thoughts swirl around my head, none of them fitting the man I see before me. Unless . . . An even more disheartening thought pops into my head. "Do you think Cain's gay?"

Ginger's derisive snort and confident head shake tells me she doesn't think so, and a sigh of relief escapes me before I can help myself. "He may not ever touch the girls, but that doesn't mean I haven't caught him adjusting himself when one of them walks by and *accidentally*," she uses air quotes, "brushes her ass into his groin." She pauses. "He doesn't fire them for it, though some of them deserve to be tossed out. I've actually never seen him fire a dancer, not once. Oh," she scowls. "I lied. There was one. But that girl was dealing drugs out of Penny's. Cain has a *huge* issue with drugs. I think it's one of the reasons he hates Rick Cassidy so much. We don't know if Rick's the one supplying the girls with drugs or if he's got some slimeball dealer working with him, but all the girls that go in to Sin City seem to come out addicts."

Heat crawls up my neck and ears and I feel a light sheen form on my forehead.

Ginger continues, though, unaware of my rising discomfort. "There was this girl—Mindy—who worked at Penny's a few years back. She was super nice, and she worked hard. But then she started dating this local pot dealer. Complete douchebag. Cain wouldn't even let him in the parking lot to pick her up. Sure as hell wasn't allowed inside Penny's. For weeks, Cain and Nate were driving Mindy home at night because she didn't have her license and Cain didn't like the idea of her riding the bus at that hour."

There's a long pause, during which Ginger says nothing while studying her green fingernail polish, and I finally have to prod her. "So what happened?"

I get a dismissive flip of her hand. "Oh, Cain finally got through to her and she dumped the guy. It was around the same time that he ended up busted by the cops." She grins. "All those dirtbags tend to get what's coming to them when Cain is involved." Ginger's perfectly shaped eyebrows pull together. "My point is, don't worry. Short of breaking the law, your job is safe."

Oh, Ginger . . . if you only knew. Would Cain spend weeks trying to talk me out of my crooked life? Doubtful. Would he fire my ass in a second? Likely. Would he go as far as to make sure that I end up behind bars, where I belong?

Being around someone like Cain is sounding more dangerous to my future by the second.

"Anyways, Penny's is his life. He practically lives there. He makes a point of *not* watching the dancers perform and he doesn't sleep with the staff. He stays in his office when the club is open. He's a quiet, private guy who doesn't say a lot, but you can tell he has a lot to say." Her little nose scrunches up. "You know what I mean?"

I nod slowly. "Yeah, I know." I could tell by the way his eyes stayed glued to my face that those wheels were constantly turn-ing. Even now, as Cain seems to be engrossed in conversation, his hand continues rubbing his neck, over that tattoo. "Who's Penny?"

"Oh . . ." Ginger's face falls. "A dancer who worked for him. She was killed by her fiancé in his first club."

"Jeez," I mutter. I knew there was a story behind that. A man doesn't name a bar after a woman and tattoo her name on his neck for no reason. "Did Cain have a thing with her?"

"No one really knows what happened." I can feel Ginger's eyes drilling into the side of my face as I continue to watch Cain. "Look at me, Charlie." I do, and I find that she's turned in her seat to face me square-on. Her mouth opens to say something, but she frowns suddenly. "You're impossible to read, do you know that?" There's a mixture of awe and annoyance in her tone that makes me smile. I know I am. I like that I am. Sam has always said that I have an incredible poker face. Now, I merely give Ginger a "can't help it" shrug.

Rolling her eyes, she switches back to the topic at hand. "Lis-ten, I know Cain is very appealing and the attention he gives you can make you feel *really* good about yourself. And confused about him and his intentions. I've seen a lot of women come through Penny's and start thinking that there's something there. They start *hoping* that there's something there." Ginger's voice takes on this calm, authoritative tone. "There isn't, Charlie. He's just a really kind man who goes out of his way to help his employees. It's that simple."

"Don't worry. I'm not about to throw myself at him." I'm leaving in a few months anyway. There's no point complicating my life with a guy that I'll have to lie to daily and walk away from eventually. Still, as strange as he is, and as wary as I am of his intentions, there's an unexpected blip of disappointment in my belly at her warning.

"Good girl." Ginger snorts, as if remembering something.

"And ignore whatever you hear around Penny's. Those girls talk shit all the time. They're worse than guys, I swear. Apparently I get to make the schedule because I give Cain blow jobs every night before my shift." She rolls her eyes but then laughs.

"And . . ."

Her cat eyes narrow. "And what?"

"And *you've* never wanted anything to happen with him?"

"He's not my type." Her brow furrows and she looks at me oddly, hesitating for a moment before adding, "A little bit too much penis for me."

Of all the answers I had expected from Ginger, I hadn't expected that one. But it makes complete sense. I feel my mouth shift into an "O" shape as I search for a response. She has *never* mentioned her preferences. Not at the gym, not at lunch, not out shopping, when I swapped clothes in front of her . . . *Uh-oh. Was she checking me out?*

I don't know what to say now. It doesn't matter to me—I just don't know how to respond. Finally, all I can come up with is, "I've never had a gay friend before."

By the way her face splits into a wide grin, she's okay with that reaction. "And now, when you feel the need to defend your pro–gay rights stance with some lame statement like, 'I have a gay friend,' you won't be lying anymore." She winks as she swings the car door open and slides out. "And, by the way, I was never checking you out in the change room . . ." She rolls her eyes. "All you straight chicks think the same thing."

I chuckle as I climb out of my car.

In the back of my truck are two suitcases, a box with canned food, and a garbage bag with my nice towels and 1200-thread-count sheets. That's all I have in Miami. I made Cain leave my apartment to get me a fresh coffee while I quickly packed everything up. I didn't want him seeing all those stupid wigs. They're hard to explain.

"Let me take that." Cain sneaks up on me from behind, one

hand resting over my shoulder as he reaches in to pull the box out. It's a platonic gesture, and I'm still in knots with confusion over my new boss, but I feel the chill course through me. He carries it toward the gated entrance as I trail behind, studying his arms as they strain beautifully against the weight.

Ginger opens the gate and leads us through, where a middle-aged balding man in plaid shorts and a faded T-shirt that stretches over a protruding belly meets us. Cain steps in and places the box on the ground so he can clasp hands with the man.

"Well, well." The man's face shifts from Cain to me and back to Cain. "Good seeing you again."

Cain's lips curl up into a charming smile. "You as well, Tanner."

"Yeah . . ." Tanner pauses for only a second before saying, "And who do we have here?" He settles his lopsided eyes on me. "You're the one looking for a place?"

A quick flash to Cain tells me he's watching me keenly. "I suppose I am."

"Well." Tanner's feet start shuffling along the concrete path. I guess that's our cue to follow him as he passes the hibachi, the smell of cooking meat reminding me that it's early afternoon and I haven't eaten yet. "It's a good thing Cain called when he did," Tanner says over his shoulder. "I was just about to offer this place to someone else."

"Looks good out here, Tanner," Cain calls out, his eyes drifting over the small courtyard where it's clear someone has been working hard to maintain some semblance of a garden, despite the oppressive heat and drought.

Tanner stops for a moment, his hand lifting to scratch his belly absently as he takes the space in. "Yeah, Livie comes here once a week to kick my butt into gear," he grumbles, but it's followed by a crooked smile, so I know he's not really annoyed by this Livie person. "I don't know what'll happen when she leaves for college at the end of summer."

"She's hired me as the replacement butt-kicker," a sweet female voice calls out. We all turn to see a pretty blond woman in a white eyelet sundress slowly taking a set of steps from the second floor, one hand on the railing, the other resting on the small bump on her belly. It's hardly noticeable but, by the way she's cradling it, I'm guessing she's pregnant.

Cain doesn't hesitate, walking swiftly to the bottom of the steps to meet her, his arms held wide. She throws her arms around his neck and practically leaps into a hug. It's obvious they're close. How close, I have to wonder.

I don't have to wonder whether this woman danced at Penny's. Based on her ridiculously huge fake breasts, it's a safe bet to assume she did.

I also don't have to wonder if Cain and I will ever be this close, because I know that I won't be here long enough to develop that kind of friendship.

"That's Storm," Ginger confirms. "She used to live here. We tended bar together a lot." She steps forward to give the woman a hug. When she peels back, Ginger's hands instantly move to the woman's belly. "You're starting to show!"

Storm's ponytail wags as she dips her head in a giggle. "I know! Much earlier than I did with Mia. I'm going to be a whale by my third trimester."

"You look as beautiful as always, sweetheart," Cain says. The beaming grin hasn't left his face. "What are you doing here?"

The happy smile is transformed into one of sadness as sorrow enters her tone. "Dropping off some soup for Mrs. Potterage." Storm sighs. "She's not doing well. The cancer has spread. I just figured that I'd help however I can, after how much she helped me with Mia." There's a pause and then Storm sticks her hand out in my direction, introducing herself formally. "Hi, I'm Nora. But everyone still calls me Storm."

I accept it with a polite nod. "Charlie."

"Charlie," she repeats, her bright blue eyes twinkling. Really, there's nothing *not* beautiful about this woman. From her perfectly straight white teeth, to her glowing skin, to her wide, heartwarming smile, to the fact that she's delivering soup to a dying woman.

"Looks like you're moving in here?" She eyes my things, still sitting by the gate. Aside from the clothes I desperately need to dry-clean—pricey designer dresses that Sam bought for me as going-away gifts—everything is running through a scalding laundry cycle before a single thread enters my new apartment.

"Into 1-D," Tanner answers for me.

Storm's eyes widen with excitement as she looks at the super. "Trent's old place!"

"Yes, but vastly improved since that joker lived there," Tanner teases.

She shakes her head and laughs. "Wait till I tell him." By their easy banter, I can tell he must have liked having her as a tenant. That doesn't surprise me. I'm sure Tanner doesn't complain much about having a bunch of hot strippers living in his building.

Reaching up to squeeze Cain's elbow, Storm murmurs, "Make sure you swing by. Soon. Everyone would love to see you."

"I'll be there for the wedding," Cain confirms.

Storm's shaking head tells me she disapproves. "Not soon enough."

Cain's head dips as he chuckles at her. It's such a boyish gesture and so odd on him. I like seeing it. Storm must too, because she starts to giggle and squeezes his arm. Again. They touch each other an awful lot.

"Will you be working at Penny's, Charlie?" Storm asks.

I nod.

"Well..." Her hand—again—slides up and down Cain's arm. "I can say that you've lucked out. Cain's a dream boss."

I feel the heat crawl up my cheeks. I'd gladly replace my nightmares with dreams of Cain. But the words *dream* and *Cain* in one sentence stir nervousness in my stomach to the point where I'm afraid anything that comes out of my mouth will sound inappropriate. So I simply press my lips together and offer her a smile.

"All right already." Cain shakes his head, with a look of sheepishness that just doesn't fit his typical facade.

With a wink, Storm announces, "Well, I need to pick Mia up from her play date and start dinner. Enjoy the new place, Charlie."

"I'm sure I will." I watch her dress and her hair swish in tandem as she strolls away, humming softly, thinking how nice she really is. That could be me, in a few years. In my new life.

With that, Tanner leads us into 1-D, jingling a large set of keys to get the door open. As I step in, I'm immediately hit with a blast of cool air and I can't help but tip my head back and close my eyes, sighing.

Cain chuckles next to me. "A new owner bought the building two years ago and spent some money improving things, including retrofitting for central air."

I feel myself frown without meaning to. *A new owner?* "I thought you own this complex?"

A sharp glare thrown Ginger's way tells me that maybe she wasn't supposed to mention that to me. *Hmm . . . interesting.* Another layer of mystery to the already puzzling Cain.

"The place was just remodeled," Tanner cuts in, opening the oven and peering in as if expecting something inside. The apartment is pristine from what I can see—the energy-efficient labels are still on the appliances and the air smells of fresh paint and carpet fiber. I highly doubt any residents of the six-legged variety are allowed to stay.

"Jeez, when is *my* place being renovated?" Ginger chirps, poking her head into what looks like the bathroom, based on the tile wall beyond the door. "I think I need to swap with Charlie. You know, seniority rules."

This place may as well be the Ritz-Carlton, compared to the dive I relegated myself to for the past month. The very idea that I don't have to imagine a line of roaches doing the conga along my kitchen counter while I sleep lets the tension in my back slide out. But . . . "I think this place is a bit out of my price range." A self-induced below-poverty-level one; but one, all the same.

Cain settles a sharp gaze on me. "How much was your last place?"

I hesitate. "Six fifty."

"Huh, what a coincidence. Same here. Right, Tanner?" I almost laugh at the deadpan manner in which he says that.

"Yes, sir," Tanner confirms too quickly, averting his attention to the light-switch panel on the wall.

That's a load of bullshit, if I've ever heard one. Dear God . . . I've managed to get myself a pimp. Of course. I knew Ginger's ravings about this guy were too good to be true.

Tanner holds up a key on a ring. "The place comes furnished. There's a bed, couch, and kitchen table arriving shortly. All new. Part of the renovation." *Sure it is.*

"Thanks, Tanner. This is . . . perfect," I finally offer with a gritted-tooth smile. It's not Tanner's fault. He works for a pimp, too.

He grunts in response and then proceeds toward the door. "Gotta get back to my burgers." It's a valid excuse to leave, and yet I'm getting the impression that the awkward man is more anxious for solitary time than he is about his food.

Cain turns to look at me, a pained expression on his face. "I'm sorry about earlier. I just couldn't in good conscience leave you there. This place is cleaner. Safer."

I bite my lip to stay quiet.

Cleaner and safer for whom? My future clientele? Could Ginger be flat-out lying to me? She doesn't strip, but that doesn't mean she doesn't secretly sell herself. Look what *I* do, secretly! At 650 bucks a month in rent, Cain's going to want compensation somehow, and apparently it won't be by having sex with *him*. Ginger could be lying about that too, though. Or just oblivious?

Something doesn't add up. I guess I'll have to take this day-by-day. I have a job at Penny's and a decent apartment. For now.

I'm going to make a lot of money, fast. I'll stay, but when the first customer shows up at my door, I'm out. Until then, I have to stick to my plan.

■ ■ ■

"How about over here?" Ginger says, her hands gesturing to the long wall in my apartment. The living room is small and yet she's managed to make the movers lift, drag, and drop the soft, gray microfiber couch to five different spots. All it has taken her are a few winks, "my-what-big-arms-you-have" touches, and a slice of her homemade peach cream pie. If I didn't know better, I'd think she is seconds away from asking the blond guy back to her apartment to "move" her bed. I'm certain, by the way he's dogging her around, that he's hoping for the same thing. The woman is almost as deceptive as I am.

Ginger hasn't left my side all afternoon. She insisted on going grocery shopping with me, doing laundry with me, waiting on furniture with me, unpacking with me. Either she's lying and she really *is* hoping I swing her way or that whisper I caught from Cain to her earlier was a directive to not let me out of her sight.

I follow the movers, begrudgingly handing them a thirty-dollar tip on account of Ginger's demands, and stay a few minutes to look out over what she told me is called the commons. Beads of sweat instantly form on my skin from this crazy Miami summer heat, and I remind myself to be thankful for the air conditioner in my apartment. It's almost six and Tanner is out there—his plaid shorts showing off those knobby knees—spraying a flaming hibachi with a two-handed children's water gun. He looks absolutely outrageous but quite content. The air smells of burgers again. I'm guessing Tanner is one of those bachelors with a very uncreative meal plan comprised of grilled meat.

I'm still watching him when an apartment door across the way opens and a dark-haired man strolls out.

My breath hitches.

Cain.

He doesn't look my way, so he doesn't see me as he strides quickly past Tanner with a half-salute, seemingly in a rush to get out of there. When I glance back to the apartment he left, I find China leaning in her doorway, in the tiniest, tightest pair of short shorts and tank top, watching his retreating back, her hair tousled, a secretive smile softening her features.

She turns to go back into her apartment but stops, her stony eyes locking on mine. A wide smirk of satisfaction spans her face and I assume she has figured out that I saw Cain leave her apartment. Stretching her arms over her head, she slowly turns and saunters back inside. I'm instantly hit with an image of a cat, gratified after devouring a can of salmon and ready to mosey over to bathe in a patch of sun.

"Never, my ass, Ginger," I mutter. I'm pretty sure Cain was her can of salmon.

China may be unfriendly and arrogant, but she's probably *very* talented. I'm not surprised and yet I can't ignore the heaviness of disappointment, knowing that Cain would be interested in someone like her.

"Hey! Why do you have all these wigs?" I hear Ginger call out. I deny my panic from surfacing as I spin around and stalk back in, finding her prancing around with my long black wig on her head.

Bloody hell! At least she hasn't found my gun yet. "I'm in theater. Those are props," I answer simply.

"Huh . . . theater. You know, I have a thing for dark-haired women," she says with an exaggerated wink.

I sigh.

chapter eleven

■ ■ ■

CAIN

Charlie doesn't trust me.

Though she kept her face carefully controlled, she couldn't hide the hard look in those eyes as we stood in her new apartment.

I should have warned Ginger against telling her that I owned the building. *Fuck*, I wish no one had ever found out to begin with! I know what I look like, having several of my dancers live there. And now Charlie, too.

Still, I'm relieved that she's questioning my motives. That tells me she's smart and less likely to get taken advantage of. I thought about swinging by her apartment after finishing up with China but decided against it. Ginger's there, anyway. I asked her to stay—to help Charlie get settled in but, more importantly, to make sure she's really okay after what happened earlier today.

I'll get to see her again tonight, anyway.

I grit my teeth against the unwanted excitement that goes along with that thought.

chapter twelve

■ ■ ■

CHARLIE

"One minute, Charlie," Terry mouths, just like he did last night. I stand within the shadows, just like I did the first night, waiting for the first chords of my song to blast through the speakers— "Supermassive Black Hole" by Muse this time. Only tonight, I'm no longer on trial. I have the job. Despite my relatively modest outfit, my lack of crowd interaction, and my strange song selection, Cain hired me. I should be happy. I should be less nervous.

So, why am I seconds away from having pee run down my leg?

I instinctively curl my arms over my chest.

I've been at the bar for several hours now. Given that I have absolutely no experience behind a bar and, some would argue no business being anywhere near a bar, I stuck to cleaning, stocking, and cashing out. It was a good distraction.

But now I'm here, cowering. I'm about to get on that scary-ass roller coaster for the second time, even though I know just how scary-ass it is. Maybe it won't be so crowded tonight. Maybe . . . Holding my breath, I peek out around the divider and see a sea of heads. They may have multiplied in the last ten minutes.

This is ridiculous. I'm playing a part. Charlie Rourke is a confident pole-dancing diva. That's all this is. An acting role. Actors do uncomfortable scenes all the time. I am an actor and this is merely an uncomfortable scene.

That I will play over and over again.

Six nights a week.

For months.

Oh, God. I'm going to be sick.

I take a deep, calming breath and remind myself with a mutter, "You deserve this, you drug-trafficking wench."

"How's your stage-fright thing?" a husky voice calls out behind me.

"Ginger!" I shriek—partly in happiness, mostly in panic that she may have heard my little pep talk. By the smile on her face, I know she didn't. I throw my arms around her neck, as I did the previous night. "I hate doing this," I admit in a rare burst of weakness.

"Wow, you really do have bad nerves." She chuckles as I peel myself off her. "You'll do fine. You're incredible up there." Waggling her eyebrows, she adds, "I should know." There's a pause and then a tiny smirk curls her lips. "Cain's watching."

"What?" I feel my eyes widen as I spin and peer out again. Sure enough, I spot his lean frame hanging over the railing next to Nate, his gorgeous dark eyes on the stage. Quietly waiting. My heart starts pounding against my chest wall. "You said he never comes out to the club!" He wasn't out there when I left the bar area to get changed.

And I know because I was watching for him.

She shrugs in an I-don't-know-what-to-tell-you way. "He doesn't. He *never* watches the dancers, Charlie."

"Yeah, he also never *sleeps* with the dancers, right?" I mutter derisively, earning her questioning frown. With a sigh, I explain, "I saw him leave China's tonight. It was pretty clear what our pimp daddy was doing over there."

"Oh." Ginger's face scrunches up tightly as she waves me

off. "He was helping her study for her GED. The girl is majorly dyslexic. She couldn't string five words together when he hired her and now she wants a high school diploma. That's all that was. Trust me."

I look out at the suave strip club owner. Helping her *study*? Really? "She sure didn't make it look like that," I say and my doubt is obvious in my tone, though I feel a wave of relief course through my body.

"Of course she didn't. China's been in love with Cain for years. Any chance she gets to claim her fictional territory over him, she'll take it. And, word of warning," she adds, "don't *ever* let Cain hear you calling him a pimp. That's a sensitive spot for him. Your favorite, Rick Cassidy, called him that once, to his face. Cain beat his ass good. Nate pulled him off before he could kill the guy."

I try to picture that reserved man out there pounding the crap out of someone. It's hard. Even today, when he was dealing with my crazy neighbors, he was unusually calm. The only signal that he was ready to deliver a beating was the tensed hands at his sides.

"Why is he out there, Ginger?" The last thing I want to do is make Cain regret hiring me.

"Well, according to Ben, Cain *really* enjoyed your show last night."

"Enjoyed as in . . ."

I look over to find a lascivious grin. "As in *enjoyed*." How the hell would Ben know? Were they talking about me? A new and more powerful rash of nervous flutters hits me. I tense as her cool hand rubs over my shoulder. "So you should go out there and tease him."

"What?" I shriek. Cain does not seem like the kind of guy who would appreciate teasing.

Her slender, bare shoulders shake as she giggles. "Look, if I had to go out there and strip for a bar full of men, I'd pick one and pretend no one else is out there. One who I'd actually *want* to strip for in a room, alone. You know . . . if I weren't a lesbian."

"You're nuts." A knock against the glass above me tells me Terry's about to hit play and my stomach constricts.

"I am, but that's beside the point. Hannah hates getting up on the stage and so that's what she does. It works for her."

"Why Cain?"

She snorts. "Because I know you think he's gorgeous. And I can tell you for a fact that he *is* an incredible man. And because every single one of the dancers here would die to have Cain's attention on her. So take advantage of it. He's sexy and he's *safe*."

Music starts pulsing through the speakers.

Strip for Cain. "I don't know if doing that is going to help with my nerves, Ginger."

She shrugs. "Worth a shot. You said you were into acting, right?"

"Yeah."

"Well, go and *act* like you're trying to seduce your sexy, gorgeous, rich, untouchable boss. He can be a prop, like your wig." She snorts. "Could be fun."

■ ■ ■

There's a chance I just got myself fired.

I don't know why I listened to Ginger. Probably because I was desperate. And stripping for Cain *would* be enjoyable. Ideally, not with a hundred other men watching. And, truth be told, it did make being on that stage a little easier.

The fact that Cain apparently "enjoyed" watching me last night spurred a need in me to please him again. But the fact that he has already asked me not to take my clothes off for him should have stopped me.

Maybe he didn't notice what I was doing? By the cool, hard expression on his face, and the way his body shifted until he was standing stiffly, I'm seriously doubting that.

When he approaches me tonight, I'll deny it, of course.

But he doesn't approach me after the show. He leaves immediately after I get off the stage and no one sees him out there again.

And so I finish my shift, pushing the reality of stripping into a tiny, neat box. I tuck it away into the recesses of my mind, as just something I have to do, for now. Just like what I do for Sam.

It won't be forever.

chapter thirteen

■ ■ ■

CAIN

Show Number Three

I thought it was my imagination yesterday. Just my dick's wishful thinking.

I came out to watch Charlie perform. Call it a gut instinct. More like a groin instinct, if I'm being completely honest. Either way, I came out to see if her second night would be as good as the first.

It wasn't.

It was better.

Because her eyes were on me the second she stalked out. And they kept stealing passes on her way around, sliding over mine intimately, as if sharing a secret.

And each article of clothing that came off was done facing me, so I got the full impact of the reveal, her breasts springing out to greet me.

So did every other guy in my vicinity, but fuck them.

My dick told me that was *all* for me.

So of course I needed to come out here tonight, just to see if my dick was playing tricks on me before.

I think Charlie just winked at me.

I shouldn't be enjoying this but I can't help myself. I am. Too much.

I need to stop coming out here when Charlie dances.

chapter fourteen

...

CHARLIE

Show Number Seven

I'm playing the role of a stripper who's taunting her stoic boss. That's all this is.

And I must be doing it very well, because there's no doubt in my mind that Cain is enjoying it. I can tell by the way he leans forward, the way his mouth parts, the way his hands grasp the railing so tightly that the tension ripples up through those arms . . . By the very fact that he's out there, watching. Night after night.

I take a deep breath and roll my hips with the slow guitar twang of Head of the Herd's "By This Time Tomorrow" as I reach up to loop my finger through the tie of my bikini top. Baring my breasts like this still feels like a punch to my stomach. The only thing that makes it easier is ensuring that I'm facing Cain when I feel the cool air hit my skin and I toss the small scrap of sequined material down. I don't mind Cain looking at me like that, and it helps block out the random catcalls and hoots of appreciation from the *real* customers.

I do that again now, as I have every night since my second

show, slowing my hips and locking eyes with his as I toss my top in his direction. Normally I'll catch his eyes drop to my body for a second before lifting to my face again.

Tonight, though . . . Cain's hand slides off the railing to reach down and adjust himself. I'm not sure if he meant for me to see it. It would be the first time he's done something so visibly sexual. I can't help my jaw from dropping for a split second. When my eyes snap back up to his face, I see his usual indecipherable mask and I assume he doesn't realize that he did it.

Until he winks.

The simple act sends a jolt through my body, right down to my thighs. Taking a deep breath, I'm unable to suppress my smile as I dive into an invert.

It appears that I'm not the only player in this little game anymore.

■ ■ ■

"Oh, come on. Like you weren't *trying* to make those drinks unpalatable," Ginger mutters, pouring a round of Guinness as her hips bop to the music. Ginger doesn't stand still. Ever. "Who doesn't know how to mix a Harvey Wallbanger?"

My third night here, Ginger decided it would be a good idea to move me on from pouring straight shots and pints of beer to mixing cocktails. Without instruction. The customers didn't seem to mind, especially when she announced my "de-virging" was on her.

After my first creation twisted a customer's face so sickly that DeeDee ran for a bucket, it quickly became a game. Ginger makes me do at least one foreign-to-me drink per night, awarding my concoction with a new name based on her mood and what that brave customer's face looks like the instant his taste buds get assaulted.

The names usually make my jaw drop.

Ginger has a surprisingly foul imagination.

I raise one hand to cheek level. "Clearly, me."

"Oh, still so much to learn," she murmurs, winking at me as she slides the drinks over the counter. "I swear I'd think you never partied a day in your life before Penny's."

Do high school house parties with cases of beer and Smirnoff coolers count? Sam was strict about only a few things, and drinking was one of them. He said it was dangerous, that you end up saying things you shouldn't say and getting yourself into a lot of trouble. Well, I sure didn't want to slip about anything I was doing, so I avoided alcohol for the most part, nursing a drink all night just so I wouldn't be empty-handed. So I'd fit in.

I've been working at Penny's for over a week and, as shocking as it is to admit, I don't know that I've ever had more fun in my life. Hanging out with Ginger and DeeDee on the bar all night is entertaining, the nights go by quickly, and I'm making good money. Not as good as what I'd be making in the V.I.P. rooms, but Cain hasn't allowed it yet. I'd be lying if I said I wasn't relieved about that. And dreading the day he gives his okay.

Because then I'll have no valid excuse.

Stripping onstage is still a horrendous, nerve-wracking four minutes, at best, but my mind no longer has to wander off to the mountains and the beach and all those other places I imagine myself going when I'm finished being Charlie Rourke. It keeps getting stuck in a dimly lit room, alone with Cain.

In his office.

In a V.I.P. room.

In the walk-in beer cooler.

Really . . . anywhere.

Ginger has created a monster.

And what feeds these illicit thoughts is the fact that Cain keeps coming out to watch. There haven't been any more cock-adjusting, winking moments. He's made no effort to speak to me since hiring me. The few times I've crossed paths with him in the back hallways, I've gotten nothing more than a nod.

But while I'm on that stage, I feel those dark eyes on me, like those of a predator stalking his prey, while the music vibrates through my body, and my limbs coil around the cool brass, and my hips swirl and curl and dip and bend.

I really am a fantastic actress.

And Cain is an even more fantastic distraction.

■ ■ ■

Show Number Thirteen

I've become bold. I've switched up my short shorts because, despite what he said, I don't want Cain getting bored. So I've adopted this little short-skirt–bikini-bottom combo that is more revealing but not completely. Like a skimpy bathing suit, I tell myself.

And I don't bother to hide what I'm doing anymore. I face him head-on as my fingers curl around the fabric of my top and peel it off. As I offer him a wink I see his lips part slightly and his ghost of a smile as his eyes rake over my body, shamelessly. Even from here, I see the fire in them.

I love the feel of his eyes on me.

Although the possibility of him being my pimp has faded, I still don't know what the hell to think about Cain. At night, when I'm lying in bed, relieving myself of this pent-up frustration so I can actually fall asleep, I'm still picturing him as an unemotional, demanding man.

Only now, it's in a very appealing way.

I'm not sure how accurate Ginger was when she called him "safe."

This is my boss.

But, while I silently wait to escape my life, this is also one hell of an intoxicating game.

chapter fifteen

...

CAIN

"Cain!"

"Two and a half weeks for a simple background check! What the fuck am I paying you for, John?" I'm glad I had the good sense to install a sound barrier in the walls of my office. It doesn't completely drown out the throbbing music in the club, but I can at least have a phone conversation without shouting.

A horn blasts in the background and I picture my P.I.'s round belly pressed up against the steering wheel of his nondescript black sedan, tailing someone's cheating spouse or a fraudulent insurance claim through the streets of L.A. He spends most of his days doing just that. And they're long-ass days from what he tells me. John works more than I do. After his third wife left him, he figured out that marriage and his career don't mix.

I met John ten years ago, when he was still a cop. He's well connected, fast, trustworthy, and—most important—he's as discreet as they come. He's also expensive, but it's worth it. I use him for all of my employee history checks. He finds things that no typical background check would ever uncover, and I can usually get answers from him within a few days.

"Yeah, well, this isn't Backgrounds R Us," he grumbles

wryly—the usual dig at the kinds of places normal employers use. "This one took a little bit more work . . ."

My stomach tightens as I silently await his verdict, wondering what he uncovered. I've been dreading this moment.

"You've got yourself a runaway there, Cain. Charlie Rourke was last seen four years ago in Indianapolis. She took off on her eighteenth birthday and no one's seen her since. No police record to speak of. She's been a ghost until she opened a bank account and booked a flight from New York to Miami in May."

"Huh." I shouldn't be surprised, and yet I am. I've had other runaways here before. Kacey, an exceptionally bright redheaded bartender and Storm's best friend, was one. It hadn't taken John long to gather the basics that explained the unapproachable fiery-haired woman—the accident that killed her parents, her serious injuries, the long physical recovery, the nonexistent mental recovery.

The self-destructive aftereffects.

But it wasn't hard to figure out what Kacey was trying to escape. "What's Charlie running from?"

"My guess is her drunk, abusive father. Beat the shit out of her mother, who finally bit the bullet three years ago. Daddy-O's in Pendleton for life for that one."

"Shit . . ." I run a hand back through my hair. If she's been on the run for four years, I wonder if she even knows that her mother is dead. "Any other family?"

"Useless uncle. Father's brother. Otherwise, no one."

"So she's legit. I mean, her age, everything else checks out?" I hold my breath. There's nothing about the woman teasing me on that stage that says "child."

"Yeah, looks like it."

I sink back into my chair, weeks of tension pouring out of me.

"Driver's license that came up is the same as the one you sent me. No previous one on file. I also found an older picture of her. They look like the same girl. Hard to tell with those, though, especially when your girl's all done up like she is."

That doesn't surprise me. I've seen Charlie under all that makeup. She looks like a completely different person. "Her eye color?"

"Blue, I think. Wait . . ." There's a rustling sound. "Yup . . . blue."

Violet could be mistaken for blue. Unless the photo is a good-quality close-up, no one would be able to tell. "And I wasn't able to confirm her working at that club in Vegas, but my sources tell me the owner's been known to do under-the-table hires, so it's quite possible she's telling the truth."

"Huh." I don't doubt that she worked there. The way she dances, she knows what she's doing. "Okay, good."

"Why . . . you tapping that?"

"John . . ."

"Yeah, yeah. I've heard it all before." His disbelief annoys me. "I'm gonna be in Miami in a few months, I think. I'll swing by. Enjoy a show or two."

"You do that. Ask for Mercy. Your fat old ass will have a heart attack."

The responding roar of laughter makes me shake my head and smile. John is in his early fifties and, if he's as I remember him, he's still living off black coffee and greasy burgers. "It'd be good to see you again, my friend."

Hanging up the phone, I flip through the stack of papers with Charlie's scrawled handwriting. So, she's been off the grid for four years. She would have been crashing at friends' places. Guys' places. Taking jobs under the table to make ends meet. I guess that's why there's no record of her. No gas bills, no credit cards. Nothing.

Maybe she was afraid of being found and that's why she laid low. Or maybe she found out that her dad is in jail for life and figures she's safe, so she's come out of hiding.

Speculation. That's all I've got.

That she refused Rick Cassidy's demands tells me she probably wasn't making ends meet in alleyways. I find myself breathing easier over that knowledge. But she's got the designer shoes and clothes. And the brand-new car that she got from a supposed inheritance. I find that detail hard to believe, especially now.

I rub my chin slowly as I ponder this riddle. There's an excellent possibility that Charlie was getting paid for sex, but if so, with a very wealthy clientele. A sugar daddy, even. But then, where's all the money? Where did it go? Why no bank account until a few months ago?

It doesn't matter, I decide, with steely resolve. If she's here, she must be trying to start over. And it's time that I stop avoiding her because, just maybe, I can help.

If she'll trust me.

And if I can control myself around her.

• • •

Blasts of music hit me as I stroll out to the floor. Ben's face splits into a wide smile when he sees me, and his mouth starts moving as he says something into his earpiece to all the bouncers. I have a good idea what it is, because Nate filled me in on the rising chatter. I just shoot him a severe look and keep walking. For years, I made a few laps around the club each night. But the customers started getting on my nerves, and watching my employees flaunt their bodies has never been my thing. So I stopped coming out about two years ago, unless there was an issue that security couldn't handle.

And yet, every night for the past two weeks, when the hands on my wall clock approach eleven, I find myself wandering out with a glass of cognac in hand to lean against the rail.

Like Pavlov's dog.

Only there's no juicy bone at the end of the road. Just a gorgeous dancer and mounting frustration.

I've become a masochist. The affliction seems to have developed overnight. The night that Charlie started working here, to be precise. And each night after that, as I came out to watch her strip.

For me.

It's very clearly, very obviously, for me.

The tension between the two of us is palpable and growing at an alarming rate into a heady, and highly risky, intimate connection. I'm addicted. There's no way in hell that I can sit still in my office while Charlie's up here on my stage anymore. Worse . . . I've started coming out to the bar later in the night. I have enough common sense to stay away from her, killing the time by having conversations with Nate, some of the other dancers, and the few regular customers whom I don't want to choke.

But the electric charge between us keeps intensifying.

I find Nate standing in his stationary spot—with the best view of the floor—and slap him over the shoulder. He knows better than to comment about my timed appearance. "How's it going? Crammed again, I see."

With a grunt, he reports, "Tossed two guys out, but it's been pretty tame so far."

"Good." My eyes drift over the floor, mentally calculating how much an average girl will take home tonight with this big a crowd. A solid amount, thankfully. A glance at the stage shows me that Cherry is nearing the tail end of her show.

She's up next.

Nate's attention shifts to his earpiece for a moment. With a scowl, I hear him announce, "Kinsley and China are at it again. Ben's heading into the dressing room now to break it up."

"Shit," I mutter. "What am I going to do? One of them is gonna have to go if this keeps up." It will have to be Kinsley. The girl is putting herself through college with this job, but I'm not as worried about her making the kind of stupid, desperate decisions that China might make. She'd end up back somewhere like Sin City if I fired her.

"Maybe you should go and talk to them," Nate suggests.

"Maybe *you* should," I throw back. The last time I went into a dressing room to break up a catfight, it ended in tears and two sobbing, naked women rubbing themselves up against my sides and pleading with me to forgive them.

"Hell, no. I take care of security. Find a manager to deal with that shit."

"Sure thing! Just introduce me to someone who won't rob me or treat my employees like whores." Twice in the past, I hired managers because I knew that I needed help running a club this size. I caught the first one skimming from the late-night deposits, while trying to pin it on the bartenders. I caught the second one in a private room, demanding lap dances in exchange for better time slots onstage. The idiot didn't even have the sense to turn the cameras off. When I played it for him, his only response was a shrug and, "I thought you were kidding about that."

I shake my head. "I need a female manager to handle this shit." Ginger already takes care of most of the female staff shift scheduling. She offered to take that on years ago, after one of the dancers handed me a sheet of paper with her menstrual cycle dates to plan around. I'm good at lining up apartments and chasing off deadbeat boyfriends. I'm not the guy who keeps track of hormonal schedules.

"And an onsite shrink," Nate pipes in, earning my grunt of agreement.

Terry's voice booms over the sound system as Ben sidles up next to me. "All sorted out. For now."

"How?"

Ben runs his hands up and down his chest. "I told them they don't have to fight over me. I'll gladly take both of them out after work tonight."

"So you threatened them . . ."

Ben chuckles softly. After a moment's pause, he casually asks, "What are you doing out here, boss? Oh, wait." Glancing at his nonexistent watch with a mock frown, he announces, "Is it eleven *already*?"

"You can wipe that shit-eating grin off your face anytime now, Morris."

It only gets wider.

"When do those bar results come back?" I keep my voice flat as I turn back to watch the stage.

"Why?"

"So I can fire your ass for real."

"September." He smirks, not in the least bit worried. "So . . . she's still single, from the sounds of it," Ben remarks as the first chords of a hard song come on. Every one of Charlie's picks is different from the usual pop dance tunes. The songs are fast-paced and energetic, but with an edge, much like her on that stage. It's as if she transforms into another person.

By the twinkle in Ben's eyes, I know he's egging me on. "No idea." That's a lie. I do have an idea. I'm pretty sure she's single. Tanner hasn't seen anyone coming in or out of her place, from what he's told me.

And of course, I've asked him to keep an eye out.

"She's something else," Ben murmurs, standing straight as the curvy figure stalks out in a new outfit—a short, pleated skirt and torn-up tee—and dives right into a fancy, spinning move as her eyes graze over mine. "Shit, did you see that look she just gave me?"

"That wasn't for—" I bite back the rest of my response. *Fuck*, I took the bait and Ben knows it, but he doesn't call me on it. He only continues being an ass.

"Quiet and calm. Focused. Not annoying and whiny. Just so . . . mysterious. I could see myself with her." I feel my teeth grinding together as Ben leans in toward me. "You've got a little while longer to grow a pair, but when I leave here . . . I make no promises. Except one." His brow arches. "She won't turn me down."

"Get to work, Morris." I'm ready to knock a few of his pretty-boy white teeth out of that arrogant mouth. But mostly, I want him to go away so I can focus all my attention on my girl.

Shit, not *my* girl.

Ben leaves with a triumphant grin on his face. I don't know if he's just goading me or if he's not kidding about going after her. With Ben, you never really know. But what if the cocky bastard's right and she doesn't turn him down?

Ah, fuck.

I turn back to watch Charlie's hips roll in a provocative twist, the tiny bikini bottoms beneath her skirt revealing enough ass to stir the all-too-familiar throb between my legs. She doesn't even have to be naked for that to happen. She's drop-dead beautiful, fully clothed. I'm kind of glad that she does herself up the way she does onstage, with the curls and the heavy makeup and the contacts. It means the crowd doesn't get to see her as she is. The real her. What I got to see.

And maybe that's what she's hiding.

"She's as good as Penny was." Those words feels like a punch to my gut. Nate never brings Penny up. In fact, he hardly ever refers to this place by its name. It's always just *the bar*, or *the club*.

"She is." Maybe even better. The crowd loved Penny. She was beautiful and sweet and, despite working the V.I.P. rooms, she still somehow maintained that air of innocence. I think she was just looking for someone to love her. Using her body as enticement was the only way she thought they might.

"Is that what all this is about?" Nate prods. "She reminds you of Penny?"

I run my tongue over my teeth, deciding what I want to say. Nate's not a guy I brush off. Not after everything we've been through together. Not when he brings up Penny. "No. I mean, she looks like her and dances like her, but . . ." Charlie doesn't seem so innocent. And where Penny was bubbly and sweet and transparent, Charlie is reserved and impossible to decipher. I don't think she's devoid of emotion; I think she just internalizes it more than most. But why?

"She seems to have her head on straight, from what I'm hearing. And she can't keep her eyes off you."

Here we go. This is what I've been putting up with from Ben and Ginger. Apparently, now I'm going to get it from Nate. "I don't know when this place turned into a fucking high school cafeteria at lunchtime, Nate."

He ignores me. "You know, everyone here would be happy if you'd make a move."

I peel my focus off Charlie's muscular legs looping around the pole to look my giant confidante straight in the eye now. "Oh, yeah. They'd be really happy to watch the boss exploit the fresh twenty-two-year-old stripper," I mutter, my voice full of sarcasm.

Nate's voice turns rough as he crosses his arms. "Yeah, they would, Cain. Well," he adds, "maybe not China, but she'd get over it."

My eyes roll. China's had a thing for me for years now. While she's respected my insistence that we keep our relationship platonic, I'm no idiot. I know her interests have lingered.

"My point is that you've proven *your* point. You're not in this for the ass or the money or a power trip. You're not a fucking criminal." He levels me with one of his more ominous Nate stares. "You're *not* your parents."

I match his stare and lower my voice. "Charlie doesn't need to be tied to someone like me. I can't do that to her." He knows what I'm talking about. He carries my guilty secrets with him as if they were his own.

A loud round of cheers erupts and I turn back to the stage in time to see Charlie's top fly off, a coy smile curving that wide mouth of hers as she watches me take in her black lace bra. Beneath that . . . My breath hitches. *Damn. I'm pretty sure I could have that. Tonight, if I wanted. If I were a complete asshole.*

Thank God my office came equipped with a private shower. I'll have that dial cranked to ball-shrinking cold tonight. Just like every other night since she started this whole game of hers.

I never expected this from her.

And I never expected to enjoy it so much.

"Why haven't you let her work the rooms yet, then?" Nate asks.

I take a sip of my drink. My fourth of the night. "I don't think she's ever worked a V.I.P. room before."

"So what? Neither had Mercy. Or Hannah. Or Levi . . ."

I know exactly what Nate's getting at. I've never stopped any of the girls from doing what they want to make money, as long as they're safe and it's legal, because I'm smart enough to know that if they've wrapped their heads around the idea of doing it, then me telling them no isn't going to stop it from happening. They'll just end up at some sleazy place like Sin City or Teasers. Or worse . . . in a back alley. Somewhere no one's looking out for them. "You know, for a man with a daily word maximum of ten, you've gone *way* over today."

The only response I get is a snort. And that lethal stare.

"Fine. I don't want Charlie doing that shit with anyone." I don't judge these girls for what they do and I won't treat them with less respect because of it. Hell, I'm enabling them. But I remember the knots in my stomach every time I saw Penny go back into a V.I.P. room. I hated her going back in there. I hated the idea of her on those guys' laps.

But I let it happen.

And every time I tried to picture myself with Penny, the knowledge that I allowed her to sell herself like that crept into the image, like dirty fingerprints on an otherwise beautiful canvas. When I clued in that Charlie likely hasn't worked the V.I.P. room before . . . I'm not going to lie, excitement coursed through me.

She's not tainted by those dirty fingerprints.

Yet.

And I selfishly don't want to let it happen.

"With anyone except you, you mean," Nate cuts into my thoughts with that knowing tone of his.

"I haven't laid a—"

"But you want to. Admit it."

I say nothing.

"She's the first person I've seen you look at twice since Penny was around. And you never used to come out and watch Penny onstage like this. Charlie's gotten under your skin. That's gotta mean something, Cain."

"It means I must be really hard up." That's the understatement of the fucking century. The night I moved Charlie into her new place, Grace—a twenty-eight-year-old heiress to a prominent Sonoma Valley vineyard—was in town and paid me a late-night visit. I couldn't keep Charlie's violet eyes and doll face out of my head. That would have been fine, had I not called her name out as I was coming.

After that night, I've avoided calling Vicki or Rebecka or any of the others on my speed dial, figuring I'd get my infatuation with the girl under control before I risked insulting another woman like that. Two weeks later, my balls are ready to burst. I don't know how the monks survive. Probably by not watching live strip shows daily.

I inhale sharply as Charlie unclasps the black lace bra, wincing with a spasm of pain in my groin as two candy-pink nipples appear. Ben is right. They *should* be fake, they're so perfectly round and . . . perfect. I both love and hate that she's up there on the stage. Love because it's the only way I'll get to see her like this and it feeds the sick fantasies constantly swirling around in my head. Hate because everyone else is seeing her like this and having those same fucking dirty thoughts.

Looking at those strong yet delicate limbs, I can't help but wonder if her abusive father had dirty thoughts of her. My teeth instantly clench at that question, taking my desire down a few notches. How many times were those beautiful body parts bruised and broken by that jerk-off? Thank God he's in jail or I'd hunt him down and make him really suffer.

"John got back to me, Nate. Charlie's got a past, full of ass-holes. She doesn't need another one to add to her collection."

Nate heaves a sigh, shaking his head. "Shit," I hear him mut-ter under his breath. If there's one guy whose soft spot for these girls is as sensitive as mine, it's Nate.

"She's here to make money, not deal with her boss hitting on her." *Even though she seems intent on torturing me.* "And I have enough to deal with. I don't need to add an affair with an em-ployee to my own plate. I'm doing the right thing by staying away from her." I can hear the tone in my voice. It's solid and convinc-ing. I'm not really trying to convince Nate, though.

It's *me* who needs the convincing, as I watch her, imagining what her sweat tastes like.

"Maybe you shouldn't be standing out here like a starving kid waiting for a piece of fresh bread, then," he scolds in a dry tone. "You're tormenting yourself, you dumbass."

"Fuck off," I throw back. A heavyset guy on the side of the stage catches my eye. He's hollering something at Charlie. I can't hear him but I can read his lips, the vile words forming in his mouth. The way he's gesturing crudely at his lap.

"And get that fucker in the yellow shirt out of my club, right now," I bark. Normally, I don't kick patrons out for yelling things and gesturing. It's an adult entertainment club where women grind on guys' laps until they explode in their pants, for God's sake. And yet I've been booting out customers every night for two weeks when Charlie comes on.

Nate doesn't say a word. He simply strolls over and, with a heavy hand on the man's shoulder and what I imagine is a forceful instruction in his ear, he escorts the guy out without argument. No one ever argues with Nate.

From where Ben is standing, I catch him shaking his head at me.

Yeah, I probably deserve that.

chapter sixteen

. . .

CHARLIE

"Did you see how Cain kicked out yet *another* customer?" a girl with bright pink hair says as she leans in her chair to fasten the straps of her absurdly high-heeled shoes, to match her absurdly revealing silver-and-black polka-dot bikini.

"He sure is wound up about something," Ginger's friend, a sweet brown-haired girl named Hannah, says. After a pause, she observes, "Can't be about money. It's coming in by the truckload."

I change quietly, listening to the group of them chatter, not sure what I can possibly add to the conversation. I'm kind of hoping they don't notice that I'm here.

"He just needs a good fuck," Kendra, a dark-skinned dancer with shiny black hair, jokes as she peels her lime-green skin-tight dress off in exchange for a concoction of feathers and bows—her stage outfit. "Levi, why don't you let him come all over those tits again."

The gorgeous blonde with very large, very fake breasts winks devilishly and the group of five women break out in titters.

They're on a roll with the sexual tales at Cain's expense tonight. I'm wondering if this really is all just harmless banter or if there's an ounce of truth to it, when Kendra murmurs, "Someone must be teasing that dreamy cock of his to no end . . ." Five sets of heavily kohl-lined eyes turn to stare at me.

Ah, yes. The rumors.

"I'm just doing my job," I manage to get out around a swallow, ducking my head to hide my heated cheeks.

The cackles of laughter in the dressing room don't settle down, even as the door bangs open and China strolls in, carrying her stage outfit and wearing a bikini made for an eight-year-old. I'm surprised she bothered putting anything back on after her show. That woman is missing all modicum of modesty.

"What's so funny?"

"Oh, New Girl was just telling us how she plans on polishing the boss's knob in his office tonight."

I feel my face burst with heat as I shake my head. These women are not only crass; they're relentless.

"Of course." China's mirthless chuckle follows her as she takes a seat by a locker. "Though I'm sure New Girl already knows she doesn't have what it takes to interest a guy like Cain." Her sharp eyes roll up and down my frame with a pointed smirk.

There's an edge to her tone—a warning, almost—that I catch immediately. And it annoys the hell out of me. Instead of being decent, this woman made me want to cry coming off the stage that first night. Since then, she's done nothing but shoot me vicious glares. I'm pretty sure she started the rumor that I'm a terrible lay. And that I have crabs. Now, she's trying to put me in my place, and that place is clearly beneath her and away from Cain.

I'm no idiot. I dealt with jealous girls all through high school. But I should probably be careful around her. Sam taught me to always keep my thoughts to myself. "Guard your words," he'd say. "Only reveal what is absolutely necessary." The way I was raised, the real me avoided confrontation and argument. I was complacent to let others lead, to go with the flow.

But Charlie Rourke is not putting up with this bitch. She has enough to put up with. "I'm sure if the new girl were interested, she'd have his cock in her hands in under two seconds," I answer sweetly, as I pull my shirt over my head. I silently thank my sophomore drama teacher for casting me as Regina George in our school's modified rendition of *Mean Girls*.

Of course, there was no cock talk in that performance.

But Charlie Rourke can adapt to any situation.

A loud eruption of whistles and catcalls fills the room, followed by slaps on my legs. I guess that means I've officially joined the inner stripper club. Unfortunately, the raven-haired viper staring at me with an icy gaze right now isn't rolling out a welcome mat.

■ ■ ■

I watch Ginger with interest as she accepts a twenty and throws a suggestive wink at a customer. It's fascinating—the way she flirts with these men. I'd never in a million years guess that she's not interested in anything but their tips. And, by the beaming grin that explodes on the man's face, neither would he.

"Hey," Ginger says as she adjusts one of her messy spikes that has lost its height and is now falling over her eye. "When's your birthday?" It's late and the bar has finally slowed down, allowing us a chance to chatter.

"February fourteenth," I automatically answer as I dump the limes and ice out of the dirty cups.

"Valentine's Day?" she exclaims, excited.

I freeze. That's not Charlie's birthday. That's my real birthday. *Dammit!* I grit my teeth, angry with myself for the slip-up. I'm normally so good at keeping my stories straight. Ginger has a way of relaxing me, though, of making me forget why I'm here in the first place. Charlie's birthday is September twenty-third, but it's too late to correct it now. As long as she never sees my ID, I should be fine. "Why?"

She shrugs. "Just thought I should know. I see you every single day, after all. Wouldn't want to be sitting around, talking about . . . I don't know . . ." She pauses, searching for something no doubt appalling. "Brazilian waxes and toe fungus, when I should have baked you a cake."

I wrinkle my nose in feigned disgust, while inside my head, I'm doing the math. I should be gone by next February, so I won't have to worry about it. I'll be completely alone in the world to celebrate the day. The thought brings a pang of sadness to my chest. Given our proximity at home and work and Ginger's forceful nature, we've become close friends in a short period of time.

I'll miss her.

"Well, mine's December twenty-fifth, by the way. So we both have easy birthdays to remember. Start thinking about an awesome gift for me now."

"Huh. You're like baby Jesus." I mentally make a promise to send Ginger a card every year, no matter where I am.

"Didn't you know? I'm the second coming. Commence bowing now."

I launch a straw at her head instead, earning a wink.

"Or maybe I should be bowing down to you." She begins scrubbing the counter, avoiding my questioning look. "Cain should be out shortly." She shoots those cat eyes at me with a pointed glare, adding in dry tone, "Again."

Of course.

"Something you want to admit, Charlie?"

Passing through the entry of the bar and rounding the corner to wipe a spill over the counter, I can't help the grin from stretching across my face as a thrill courses through my body. It makes the denial that's about to come from my mouth sound completely dishonest.

"Oh, just forget it!" Ginger snaps, her hand waving me away.

I'm giggling when I hear, "Hey, beautiful." A tall, lanky, middle-aged guy leans into the bar next to me. I've seen him here before. He's a regular on weekends. He's careful not to rub up against me, for which I'm thankful. "Weren't you up on that stage earlier?" His eyes drift down to my chest and my mind automatically converts his question to, *Weren't those breasts up on that stage earlier?*

I'm getting used to this. It happens every night. The fact that I'm not available for private dances seems to make me that much more appealing. I offer him a tight-lipped smile—the same one I offer to all the guys who approach me at the bar, while I wait for a bouncer to chase them off—and shrug. "Maybe."

By the crooked curl of his lips, he must think I'm playing coy. "Well, *maybe* you could give me a one-on-one reenactment. I know the going rate's six for an hour, but seeing as I heard you don't do private shows," he says as he starts to pull his wallet out, "I thought a grand might change your mind."

I fight to keep my eyes from bugging out. I could make *a thousand dollars for an hour* tonight if I could just do what I do onstage, in a private room? Well, there'd be more to it than that. Ginger explained exactly what's involved with a "full-friction" dance. My eyes drift to the row of five tequila shots that DeeDee's pouring. Maybe if I down all of them *right now . . .*

A protective hand lands on my shoulder. "I think Mercy—the blond in the red dress over there—is available to give you that dance," Ben announces, wedging himself between me and the guy, squashing the proposition like a bug. The lanky guy quickly vacates the bar area with a nod and a sheepish smile.

"Thanks, Ben," I offer. Ben is usually the one rescuing me.

He flashes those dimples. "Beating guys off you is my job."

"And beating off is your hobby. Hey! Ho! . . ." Ginger sings, following it up with a silly arm-waving dance, earning chuckles from the patrons around us.

I roll my eyes but laugh. "Well, either way. Can you believe he offered me a grand?" I peer up at Ben's pleasing face with incredulity. We've ended up chatting a bit over the last couple of weeks, enough that I might call him a friend. An attractive, funny, sometimes offensive friend who would have his pants undone in under two seconds if I invited it.

But still a friend.

"I'm not surprised in the least." His eyes slide down for a split second and I know he just stole a glance at my cleavage. Ben's a boob guy. And a leg guy. And an ass guy. "But I'm glad you're not taking it."

"Yeah." I shift my body slightly to wipe up the rest of the beer with my cloth. *Why is that, again?*

"How's everything out here tonight?" the familiar smooth male voice behind me asks, and a blip of nerves spikes in my stomach. Turning, I find Cain flanking my other side, one hand resting on the bar, the other sitting in his pocket.

Oh, that's right. Because my sexy boss—who allows everyone else to—won't allow me. Ginger said his reasoning doesn't make sense. It's busy enough that, if I were to do one or two private dances a night, none of the other dancers would get her feathers in a bunch over it. Except for China, of course, but she's pissed with me no matter what.

"All handled," Ben mutters, taking a step back, a mixture of annoyance and amusement on his face. "Just another guy who finally grew a set and approached Charlie. Probably comes here *every* night to watch her dance."

A rare flash of anger sparks in Cain's eyes, but it quickly vanishes at the sound of Ginger's voice. "Cain! What a surprise!" The playfulness in her tone is impossible to miss.

Those two have no shame when it comes to teasing their boss. Then again, apparently neither do I. Only, I'm doing it in a very different way.

Cain ignores them, turning his focus on me. "How are things going for you, Charlie?"

My mouth opens but I falter for a second. "Uh, good . . . Good." He's talking to me. It's been weeks and he's actually talking to me. Peering up into that gorgeous face as his eyes settle on me, I feel heat instantly rush up my thighs. Thanks to the unconventional and completely unfulfilling foreplay between us, I'm feeling all kinds of awkward right now.

His gaze drifts down to my chest and then snaps back up. I let a satisfactory smile touch my lips so that he knows I caught him. Could Cain *actually* be attracted enough to me to do something about it? It's impossible to tell. I've spent time studying him: his face is usually without expression, regardless of the situation. Like mine. I wonder if he comes by it naturally—like me—or if he has consciously trained himself to be so unreadable. His hands remain still when he talks, and when he's listening to others speak—which is often, because Cain seems to prefer listening—he'll absently trace the rim of his glass with his fingertip.

He has no issues with eye contact, though. Those dark brown eyes drill right into you. You get the feeling that he's mentally trapping your words for future reference.

He has only a few habitual moves. The most common is when his hand absently rubs the side of his neck, behind his left ear. Where that tattoo is. And, occasionally, when he catches me studying him, his top lip will curl up on one side in a crooked smile.

And he's caught me staring at him. A lot.

"Things are fine, Cain," I offer, adding, "Though it's hot. Miami's hot." The weather. Boring, but safe.

He shifts his body to face out, his elbows resting on the bar, stretching the material of his shirt over his taut chest. In the club, Cain always wears a fitted button-down shirt and dress pants that highlight his ass nicely. With the air cranked to the max, he can easily get away with it.

And dammit if it doesn't make him even more attractive.

My nose catches a hint of his delicious woodsy cologne and I inhale deeply.

"That's right, you're not from here originally. Where are you from?"

"Indianapolis."

He nods slowly. "Did you live there long?"

"All my life." The trick to keeping the lies straight is to make them simple to remember. Charlie Rourke is from Indianapolis. Period.

I watch as Cain lifts his glass to his lips to take a small sip, holding a bit of the liquor in his mouth for a moment before the muscles in his throat tense to swallow. Hell, even his swallows are sexy. "And your parents? Are they still there?"

My gut tells me this is a fishing expedition, and that makes me nervous to say anything at all. "Yup."

His gaze rolls over the crowd again, never stopping on the stage as the dancer named Delyla peels off another layer. "Do they know about you dancing?"

I frown and shake my head. That sounds like the right answer. What parents would want to know their kid is doing this? Sam actually did know about my pole-dancing lessons. He didn't seem to care about it. It worked well as a cover. I'd hand a small bag to one of the managers there once a week before class.

"Money is good, right?"

"Yeah, money's good." The money is really good. Between the bar and the stage, I'm bringing in several thousand a week. "Could be better, though. A guy just offered a grand for an hour. Isn't that crazy?"

I catch the almost imperceptible tensing in Cain's jaw. "Not surprising." There's a pause. "Are you upset with me for not putting you in there?"

I should say that I am, but my head is shaking before I can get the lie out. When his shoulders seem to sag in relief, I'm glad I told the truth.

"You've never worked a private room before, right?" He asks it so gently, and yet panic suddenly courses through me. Has he figured out that I lied about stripping in Vegas? Is he going to fire me? Is that why he's out here, talking to me now? Ginger said it's next to impossible to get fired from Penny's, but she also said not to lie to him.

And all I've told him is lies.

Biting the inside of my mouth to keep my alarm from showing, I look out over the crowd as I decide how to answer. If he told me right now that I could work those rooms, *could* I?

I was alone in a room with Sal when *it* happened. He said it was standard to remove your pants for a search. Hiding my panic, I laughed in his face and told him I wasn't new to this. Then I asked him if he demanded that of all the men who came to visit him, too. Sal flashed a wicked grin—complete with crooked, stained teeth—before gripping the back of my neck and slamming my body over the table, asking me if I wanted to go about this the easy way or the hard way.

I'm still not sure which way he went about it.

I remember holding my breath and watching the door, waiting for the other guy—the one I normally dealt with—to come back. He'd always been respectful to me, as far as drug dealers go. He wouldn't allow this.

Sal didn't rape me in the traditional sense, as surprising as that is, given everything else he did to me. Sometimes I still get flashes of his rough, callused hands as they delved into my body. When I didn't react—not a sound, not a tear, even when I should have cried out from the pain—I guess he got bored. Like a cat batting around a mouse that doesn't run. He called me a cold bitch and turned his back on me to check the delivery, giving me time to pull my pants back up. At the time, I was relieved that he let me go without taking full advantage. Most men would have.

It wasn't until after I ran to my car, after I drove to the drop site, after I burst into tears in front of Sam, that the shock wore off and the worst part of it all hit. The part where I emptied my stomach of the vileness but didn't feel purged. Where I stood under the scalding-hot water until my skin was raw but still could not feel clean. Where I put fresh clothing on and still felt naked. Where I curled up into a ball until the sleeping pills kicked in, only to wake up squeezing my thighs together, feeling like his dirty fingers had *just* been *there*.

The actual event with Sal, while horrendous and humiliating, lasted no more than thirty seconds. But the feeling of complete and utter filth lingered for weeks. "Charlie?" Cain's voice breaks into my thoughts.

"I just can't do it." The truth slips out of me before I can control it, and I feel Cain's eyes bore into the side of my face.

I'm surprised when a warm hand curls around my arm, the pad of his thumb running up and down my bicep affectionately. Turning, I find Cain's normally expressionless face pinched with worry. "If you ever feel like you *can* do it, promise me you'll come talk to me?"

I nod in response. I know without a doubt that Cain would certainly not make me feel vile. Cain would make me feel *really, really* good.

And now I'm pretty sure I know why Cain didn't allow me to work the floors. Ginger was right. It isn't about being overstaffed. He knows I haven't worked one of those rooms and he's doing his best to keep me away. To keep me *safe*.

I'm living a life where safety is a luxury, where the only family I have risks my well-being without thinking twice. Yet it took this man—a stranger—mere seconds to decide that he would protect me.

Beyond my frustrated physical feelings for Cain, I feel a pang of something new. Something unwanted. Something that Sam would never approve of.

It's only amplified by Cain's next words. "You know that you can come to me for anything at all, right, Charlie? I will help you however I can."

Pursing my lips together, I nod as I struggle to wrap my mind around this version of Cain. This interaction is so different from any other that we've had. I'm forced to come to the conclusion that Cain just may be a truly *good* man.

A man who deserves a *good* woman.

The tightness in my chest tells me that woman is not me.

But whether I deserve his attention or not, the devil in me wants it. "How are you enjoying the show?" I ask, keeping my tone casual.

I catch the flash of surprise before he dips his head and chuckles, his hand sliding over that tattoo. His mouth opens and closes several times before glancing back up at me with a dangerous look, his tone having suddenly dropped by a few octaves. "It's quite the game you're playing, Charlie."

I shouldn't ask. I shouldn't. Don't ask. Don't . . .

"And do you like playing it?" I'm surprised he even heard me, what with my voice as low as it is.

But he must have—that or he read my lips, where his focus is locked right now—because he steps in closer, until our chests are almost touching but aren't. I hold the air in my lungs as he leans in toward my ear, his warm breath skating along my neck. "Yes, I do. Too much."

I watch his retreating back as he turns around, unable to breathe for several long seconds as the butterflies thrash about in my stomach.

And I wonder if maybe there is also another side—a darker, less controlled, not so *good* side—to Cain, after all.

chapter seventeen

■ ■ ■

CAIN

"I thought you said you were staying away from her."

I look up from my desk to see Nate's dark form looming over me, his arms crossed over his chest.

Of all the ways I should have answered her question . . .

"I don't know what you're talking about, Charlie."

"It's inappropriate."

"Maybe you should interact more with the customers so you can make more money."

But, no. I just kicked the door wide open and invited a mountain of trouble in because Charlie Rourke has swung a wrecking ball into my willpower.

Picking up a pen and tossing it, I groan. "She's driving me fucking crazy! And yes!" I throw my hands up in the air. "I'm well aware that I keep going out there to let her do it."

"Cain, you are a damn stubborn fool." In front of others, Nate bites his tongue. But the club is closed and empty, and he won't hold back now. It's both annoying and refreshing.

With a snort, I mutter, "Tell me something I don't know."

"I think you need to get out of this business."

"Yeah . . ." My focus shifts to the stack of supply order forms on my desk, quickly dismissing him. I've heard it before. "Maybe I could get her off the stage and doing management. I'll pay her well. It'll be less distracting for me."

There's a pause, and then Nate's hand finds its way to the bridge of his nose to squeeze it, as if he has a sudden headache coming on. "Management, Cain? Those dancers will eat her alive."

I shrug. "She's quiet, but she's not shy." She sure as hell wasn't tonight. He's right, though. You need to have Ginger's personality—loud, pushy, borderline insensitive—to not get walked all over around here. "Maybe I can get China to back her up. People defer to her," I toss out without thinking.

Nate barks with laughter. "China's going to help the woman you're nailing?"

"I'm not—"

"Doesn't matter. Everyone in this place thinks you are."

I sigh. "Maybe taking Charlie off the stage will kill all that."

"That won't *stop* the rumors! It'll only add fuel to the fire." He shakes his head at me.

"Whatever." I wave a dismissive hand. "I don't give a fuck about gossip anymore. It's been going on for years." Only this gossip might become fact, the way things are going.

Nate makes his way toward the door. I don't blame him for wanting to head home; it's almost four a.m. But he suddenly stops. "Man, I've been through hell and back with you, Cain. I owe you everything. But I'm tired of watching you chase ghosts and punish yourself for shit you can't change—shit that happened years ago and wasn't your fault.

"Do you remember the night we opened this place? You sat in *that* chair, pissed out of your skull, watching an old surveillance video of Penny onstage, promising that if you ever met another girl like her, you'd do things differently. You wouldn't sit back and make excuses. Hell, you said you'd walk away from this business in a heartbeat if you could just have another chance."

I think back to that night. I remember wanting to shoot myself in the head the next morning after downing half a bottle of cognac. Then I remember seeing the frozen screen shot of Penny's face on the monitor and wanting to down the other half of the bottle. But I sure as hell don't remember saying any of that.

Nate doesn't wait for my denial. "And here you are, doing the exact same thing with Charlie."

"This is nothing like—"

"It's the *exact* same thing!" Nate rarely raises his voice but, when he does, it reminds me that he's not the scrawny little kid I knew back in South Central. "You knew you wanted Penny and you waited, giving excuse after excuse as to why you weren't good enough, why she deserved better, why you'd be taking advantage of her. Playing a fucking martyr. And then you *finally* made a move, when she was on her way to the altar!" His voice suddenly quiets because he knows his words have already pummeled me and his next ones will kick me while I'm down. "And it was too late."

The air hangs silent and heavy in the room. Nate has hit old wounds that closed over but never truly healed. I should have swept Penny off her feet the second she walked through my door. But I did what I thought was the "right thing" by staying back. I figured I'd wait. Wait until she got out of this business, until she was no longer working for me, and then *maybe* I'd tell her how I felt.

But a plumber named Roger beat me to it. He came along, showering her with flowers and romantic dinners, making her feel as special as I wanted to. As I should have. He proposed to her within four months. It was fast and unexpected and it hit me like a freight train but still, I held my resolve, convincing myself that he could give her a life I couldn't. She deserved a white picket fence and a respectable father for her babies. I was a fucking strip club owner with a cargo plane's worth of skeletons.

The night she came to me to tell me they had decided to elope the coming weekend and she wouldn't be coming back to Penny's, I panicked. I couldn't deny it any longer—I was in love with her and I selfishly wanted her for myself.

So I spilled my guts. I dropped to my knees, my hands wrapped around her legs, begging her not to marry him, to stay with me, to give me a chance. I told her everything about me. *Everything!* It all just tumbled out.

She yelled at me for not telling her how I felt sooner, cried that she couldn't do that to Roger, that he was good to her and it would kill him. And then she completely broke down, spilling into my arms. We made love that night in my office, for the first and last time. She left with a "sorry."

No one but Roger will ever know exactly what happened the next night. The video surveillance showed her working her last shift with a sad smile. Everyone assumed it was because she would miss the friends she had made. I couldn't face her, and so I hid in my office like a coward, burying myself in paperwork.

Around midnight, the last cameras caught Penny and Roger in a whispered conversation. By the tears in her eyes and the repeated "I'm sorry" forming on her lips while she fumbled with her ring, as if trying to take it off, I have a good idea what they were talking about.

Why she decided to do it then, at the bar, I'll never know.

I wish I had been out there. I wish Nate had been closer. I wish I had swept her off her feet in the first four seconds that she walked into my life. I wish a lot of things . . .

I wish I'd known that Roger had one hell of a temper.

"You're scared, man," Nate proclaims now with that penetrating stare fixed on me. "Make all the excuses you want—you're plain scared of getting hurt again. That's why you're letting Charlie play this little game of hers, enjoying the view while not taking the leap. You think avoiding the conversation will somehow keep you safe. I've got news for you, Cain. You're already hung up on that girl. You can't focus on anything else when she's in the building. It took me a whole ten seconds to grab your attention tonight and you were standing right *beside* me!"

I rub my hands over my face. I was watching Charlie and

Ginger react to something Ben had said. I had never seen Charlie burst out laughing before, but tonight she did. I was desperate to know what was so funny, and bitter that it was Ben making her laugh like that and not me.

"But what if she doesn't want anything to do with me?" Penny may have given herself to me that night and she may have been breaking off her engagement *for me*, but I saw the fear in her eyes when I laid out my past. The disgust. I wasn't the kind of guy she was looking for. And I also saw the confusion because, despite her upcoming wedding, despite me not being the model citizen, she *did* feel something for me. Whether she wanted to or not. "Doesn't Charlie deserve someone normal?"

"You mean like a nice, quiet plumber who will bash her brains into the ground?" His words stab me in the chest as he turns and slowly walks toward the door again. "Make it easier on everyone, including yourself, Cain. Tell Charlie whatever you feel you need to about yourself. Or don't tell her anything about your past, because it's the past and I don't think it matters as much as you think it does. Either way, make a damn move. Make it now."

chapter eighteen

. . .

CHARLIE

"Charlie!" I hear Ginger's voice yell out over my hair dryer.

"Yeah?" I yell back, turning to see her holding a phone out.

The new burner phone I picked up from the extended-stay hotel this morning.

Switching off my hair dryer, I smooth my expression as I take it from her. By the lit-up screen displaying "unknown caller," someone has called and Ginger has answered.

I feel the blood drain from my face.

Oh no . . .

"It was ringing, so I got it," Ginger explains, though by her drawn brow and hesitant tone, I think she's wondering if maybe that was a mistake.

I'd love to tell her that she sure as hell shouldn't have gone into my purse to answer it, but now is not the time. Swallowing the rising bubble of panic, I say, "Thanks. I'll be out in a second."

She opens her mouth but then pauses as if in thought. She must have decided it's better left unsaid. Spinning on her heels, she walks back over to my couch and dives into it.

I take a deep breath as I pull the door almost shut but not quite—to ensure Ginger doesn't scurry back over to press her ear up and eavesdrop. She'd be the type to do that. Holding the phone up to my ear, I say with a slight wobble in my voice, "Hello."

"Hello, Little Mouse." It's the standard greeting, only there's the tightness in Sam's voice that I hear when he's displeased with me. "Who is Ginger?"

Shit.

He knows her name.

That means they talked.

What did he say to her? What did she tell him? Does he know I have a job? That I'm working at a strip club? That I moved? My hand finds its way to clutch my throat and I can feel my racing pulse beneath my fingertips as I swallow once, twice, three times. *Dammit, Ginger!* In only minutes, she may have just unraveled my life, my plan!

Swallowing the crippling lump in my throat, I explain, "A friend."

"A friend who answers *this* phone?"

"I was in the bathroom and she heard the ring."

There's an unnaturally long pause. That's how Sam typically shows his irritation. Silence. I think he believes the mounting anxiety is more effective than yelling.

I think he's right.

"Is your *friend* Ginger going to be answering your phone from now on?"

"No. Definitely not."

There's another long pause. "I told you to lay low down there. Making friends is not laying low."

Okay, deep breaths. It doesn't sound like she's told him anything. "I'm sorry. It's really nothing . . . she's just a neighbor who comes over for coffee sometimes."

"A neighbor who you let answer *that* phone?" My stomach muscles spasm as I peek out at Ginger, still stretched out on my couch, flipping through a magazine. "Do I need to come down there to check on you?"

I bite back the scream, keeping my teeth gritted until I can manage to get out in a relatively calm tone, "No. It's all good." He hasn't been keeping tabs on me so far, from the sounds of it, and I sure as hell don't want him to start now. The very idea of Sam infiltrating my little make-believe life causes me chest pains. I don't need him coming down here. Finding out that I've moved.

Finding out that I've been lying to him.

Finding Ginger.

God knows what he'd do to her then.

"This isn't a game. Get rid of her and check your email right away," Sam demands in a clipped tone.

"Okay." I don't hesitate, not for a split second. Even though I wasn't expecting a call for another week or two and I really don't want to do a drop today. But I guess business is good for Sam.

For *us*.

The phone goes dead and I shut the bathroom door before taking a seat on the toilet, clutching my nauseous stomach with my arms. *Stupid, stupid Charlie!* What was I thinking? I need to be smarter about this. This is all pretend. A pretend life, pretend friends, pretend laughter.

Pretend feelings.

I'm getting comfortable here, and that's a bad move. It's too risky. I can slip up too easily. One simple phone call just proved that if I'm not careful, Sam will become suspicious.

And having Sam suspicious can't possibly end well.

Pulling out my other phone—of course, I remembered to keep that one close to me!—I quickly find his instructions. Bob and Eddie again. Today at three p.m. I sigh. Today is Monday, our day off. Ginger and I were going shopping this afternoon. I was actually looking forward to it. I needed another outfit for the stage.

I guess I'll have to ditch her.

Bitterness swells inside my chest over the prospect. He's a thousand miles away, but Sam continues to keep me firmly pressed under his thumb. What kind of father wouldn't want his child to have a friend? Just one!

Checking my face in the mirror, I see that my complexion is still sickly pale. That should help my cause.

Ginger is on me the second I get out. "Why do you have two phones?"

I open my mouth to answer but falter. My prepared response has always been simple. *Work.* Only I can't use that excuse now.

Ginger has her own ideas, though. "Are you an undercover cop?"

The very suggestion has me bursting out with laughter. *If you only knew how far off you really are!* Thankfully, the laugh is what I needed to jog my mind into what I hope is a plausible answer. "That carrier has a better long-distance plan on it, so I use it to call my parents."

"Oh . . ." Her lips twist. "That was your dad?"

I nod.

Making a point of flipping her magazine closed and tossing it on the coffee table, Ginger announces, "Well, sorry to say, but your dad's not very nice."

"What'd he say to you?"

"Besides the interrogation? Not much."

I fight to keep calm as another bubble of panic bursts inside my throat and the blood drains from my face once again. *Oh no . . .* "What did you tell him, Ginger?"

"Nothing, other than my name. He wouldn't tell me who he was, so I wasn't offering him any more info. He probably told you I was a bitch."

The sigh of relief escapes my lips before I can control myself. I know I shouldn't say it. I know it will only raise suspicion, but I can't risk the alternative. "Ginger, please don't *ever* answer my phone again."

She sits up straight, her frown back, only deeper. "I was only trying to help."

"I know." Ginger is generally easygoing, but I've seen her get bent out of shape when criticized for doing something she thinks is helpful. "Just . . . next time, bring the phone to me, rather than answer it."

Flopping back onto my couch, she mutters, "Fine. Whatever." There's a pause as she stares at me. "Are you okay? You're looking a little pale."

That played out nicely . . . "Actually, I'm not feeling great, Ginger. I think that yogurt I ate may have been bad. My stomach's acting up."

Ginger's pretty face falls, her irritation vanishing in a second. "Oh, I'm sorry. Don't worry about shopping today, then. Go rest." She gets up and walks over to rub my shoulders. "Let me know if you need anything."

I grit my teeth against my rising guilt for lying to my friend.

. . .

Ginger is supposed to be at the beach but she's not. I can see through my window that she's stretched out on a lounge chair in the common area, suntanning. To make matters worse, Tanner is out there too, doing his best to avoid looking in her general direction while he grills and she chatters at him.

And now I'm stuck in my apartment with a pair of yoga shorts, a tank top, and a wig in a gym bag, with less than an hour until my drop time, wondering how the hell I'm going to get past them. I've already tested the bars on the windows to see if I could sneak out the back way. I can't. As luck would have it, they're not just for decoration.

Why did I use the sick excuse? Why didn't I just say I had an appointment that I forgot about? *Dammit!* Now there's no way I can get out there without being caught in my lie.

I wait another twenty minutes with my fingers crossed that they'll leave, but they don't. Finally, I can't wait any longer. With a deep breath, and an excuse that I hope will work, I quietly open my door. There's a small—stupid—part of me that thinks they won't notice me sneak out if I'm quiet.

"Charlie!" Ginger's long, sculpted body is out of her chair in a second. She really could be a stripper, with those curves. Tanner turns to acknowledge me, catches Ginger in her bikini, and quickly diverts his attention back to his chicken wings with a slight flush to his cheeks.

"Are you feeling better? Do you need something?" Her worry is genuine and sweet.

And feeding my guilt.

"I'm just running to the store for some medicine."

"Oh, you stay home. I'll get it for you," Ginger quickly insists, her hands on my shoulders to stop me. I feel her strength as she attempts to turn me around and push me back into my apartment. "I stuck around in case you needed anything."

Shit. Ginger isn't making this easy. Think fast! "It's okay, Ginger. I need to see all of the packaging. There's only one type of pill that doesn't make me sick and I can't remember the name of it."

Her furrowed brow tells me she's not accepting this answer. "Well, I'll take pictures of all the packages and send them to you."

I'm already shaking my head and backing away toward the gate. I can't come up with anything more than, "No, no . . ."

Ginger pauses as if thinking this over. "Well, then wait up! Let me throw some clothes on. I'll come with you."

"No!" I don't mean it to come out in a yell but it does. *Dammit!* Why does Ginger have to be so pushy and . . . such a good friend. I just need to leave. I need to run out of here and not have to explain myself or my actions. I knew this would happen. I knew living so close to friends would cause problems. I was better off in the roach-infested place. No one asked questions there. No one cared.

She bites her lip, and her eyes finally flicker to the straps around my shoulder. I intentionally have my gym bag tucked behind me, trying to hide it. A grimace forms on her face as she ponders something. "You're not really sick, are you? You're trying to ditch me."

"I *am* sick, Ginger! Good grief. You're paranoid." *I'm such a shitty friend.*

Tanner clears his throat several times, as if to remind us that he's standing right there, able to hear the conversation.

Ginger ignores him. "Are you going to the gym without me?"

"No, Ginger. I swear I'm not."

With her hands landing on her hips, she heaves a sigh. "You're pretending to be sick so you can ditch me for a guy. That's what this is." I can't tell whether she's annoyed or hurt or curious, or maybe a combination of all three. "Is this about Cain?"

Another throat clearing from Tanner. "No, Ginger. I'm not going to see a guy."

Folding arms across her chest, her head tilting, she says, "Then it's about the guy on the phone. He isn't really your father, is he?"

As if on cue, the burner phone in my purse begins ringing again. I should already be at the café to meet Jimmy. I have no more time for this. "I'll talk to you later, Ginger," I say as I walk briskly away. Except I don't know that she'll talk to *me*. I may have just lost my first real friend.

■ ■ ■

"This isn't a fucking hair appointment and we're not girlfriends," Bob snaps the second the door to the hotel bedroom is shut.

"I'm sorry. There was construction," I mutter. I've already gotten an earful from Jimmy, and I'm sure I'll get Sam's silent treatment when I talk to him afterward.

"Let's just get this over with," Eddie mutters, sitting in his usual spot, watching the television screen and appearing indifferent.

Bob is a different story. "I don't fucking care if a road blew up. This is the big leagues. You get here on time and everything goes smoothly. It's called respect. You show up late and I get pissed off. You don't want me pissed off."

I give a curt nod, wondering if I've misread Bob's role here. I thought he was just the muscle. Right now, as his meaty paws begin their rough and invasive search of my body, he's acting like he runs the whole show and me being fifteen minutes late is a personal attack upon him.

When his hands reach my inner thighs and I involuntarily stiffen, he stands to meet my eyes, a flicker of amusement touching his otherwise cheerless face. "Don't think because you're late that we're going to skip a wire search." He makes a point of holding my eyes as his hands reach around to prod my ass, as if silently telling me that he can get away with just about anything right now. I say nothing, keeping my face calm, unperturbed. I can't keep the sweat from beginning to trickle, though. I'm not *that* controlled.

Grabbing my hips and spinning me around to face the wall, Bob doesn't warn me before he yanks my shirt up, stretching the bottom over my shoulders. I feel his fingers curl around the back of my sports bra as he begins tugging at the clasps.

What the fuck? This is new. This didn't happen last time . . .

"It's easy to hide wires in these things," he explains, though I can't help but hear the wicked smile in his voice. *Bullshit.* This is Bob trying to assert authority over me. I bite my tongue to keep the complaints at bay.

This will be over soon.

When Bob is still struggling with the clasps after ten seconds, a chuckle slips out of my lips, unbidden. "Not a lot of experience with those, Bob?"

Eddie's bark of laughter sounds a second before my body jerks from a violent tug. I hear the tear of fabric as the feeling of support disappears, and I know that Bob has ruined a very good sports bra. He begins stretching, pulling, and twisting the material as he mutters, "Keep it up, *Jane*. I've done strip searches before. Never can be too cautious of a rat."

My stomach flips with his words and I grit my teeth before anything else rash and stupid slips out of my mouth. I know that I was lucky Sal never raped me. I know that I won't be so lucky a second time. But I can't let Bob see that I'm afraid, and I sure as hell can't let him talk to me like this or I'll never have a solid footing in these drops again. From somewhere deep inside, I manage to pull out an icy tone to retort, "Maybe I should give details about these romantic little sessions of ours when I speak to Big Sam on the phone."

Eddie's snort sounds in the background. "We're going to be doing business together for a while. How about you two lovebirds start getting along."

Bob's invasive hands reach around to slide over my breasts. He says nothing, but I hear his sharp exhale as he cups each of them for a tad too long.

"All right . . ." Eddie growls.

Bob's hands finally fall away and he announces, "All clear."

I yank my shirt down and turn around, fighting the urge to wrap my arms around my chest as we complete the rest of the transaction. It takes mere minutes and then I'm out.

Another successful drug drop to add to my résumé.

Another horrid memory to bury with my sordid past when I get away.

I have to focus on taking deliberate steps to keep myself from running down the hall, out of the elevator, and away from that hotel. And for some reason, I can't shake the image of a beautiful dark-haired man from my mind, only it's marred by a look of disgust. The same look Cain had on his face the day he moved me out of my apartment.

The look isn't meant for my drug addict neighbors, though.

It's meant for me.

Despite the oppressive late afternoon heat, I feel a chill course through my body.

. . .

Something has shifted in the air since our conversation two nights ago. I can't quite peg it. It's not the music, though the song I've chosen—"Sail," by Awolnation—is decidedly slower. It's not my routine, though I need to temper some of the moves to flow with the music. It's certainly not Cain's attention. He's still standing in his customary location, still watching with that intense gaze as I peel articles of clothing off. It's not the lighting or the location or the crowd—it's as congested as always.

And yet there is suddenly *more*. Something much deeper and more substantial lingering in the air.

A magnetic pull.

An ache in my chest.

Is it what was said the other night? His confession, however brief?

I can't place what has changed but I still feel it after I leave the stage, and it's both enticing and troublesome.

I'm so distracted as I trot down the steps, on my way to the dressing room, that I don't see the man until I run smack into him.

"Excuse me," I begin to mutter until I look up and into cold blue eyes.

And gasp.

If there was any question in his mind, any doubt as to whether I was the same girl that delivered heroin to him yesterday, my reaction confirms it.

Bob's mouth stretches into a wide, wicked grin. "Well, well. Came in for a show. Didn't expect a shock."

This is bad. So very bad. If only I weren't so fixated on Cain, I would have seen Bob coming. I would have spotted him in the crowd and hidden my face from him. *Fuck!* Of all the clubs he could be in, he has to be in *this* one? Is this a fluke? Or did he tail me here?

Based on the look on his face, I don't think so. I think he's telling me the truth and he's as surprised to find me here as I am to see him.

"I guess you'll be stripping for us from now on, seeing as you're a professional. Isn't that right, *Charlie*?" A slight slur in his words tells me he's far from sober.

Even better. I don't know what kind of drunk he is and whether I can trust him to keep his mouth shut. But the fact that he approached me so openly tells me I can't. With hesitation, my eyes flash over to Cain. I breathe a small sigh of relief. He's still there, talking to Nate, his eyes trained on something else. It doesn't look like he has noticed me with Bob yet.

If I stand here any longer, he surely will. Or Nate will. Or Ben. I can't have any of them talking to my drunk, drug-trafficking partner.

I need to deal with this potentially explosive situation and fast.

Swallowing my revulsion, I offer Bob a fake friendly smile as I loop my arm through his and lead him to the one place I will have privacy until I convince him to turn around and leave. I approach the two no-neck bouncers guarding the V.I.P. room entrance, readying my lie that Cain has given me the go-ahead.

And I pray that Cain isn't watching my back right now.

The two guys—seemingly as wide as they are tall—look at me, then at Bob, and give me a single nod. I don't waste another second, leading Bob into the first available room. Ginger gave me a tour weeks ago, so I know the rooms are all the same—clean, dimly lit, and simply furnished. Since then, I've visited these rooms only in my dreams, both on the stage and at night. Cain has always been the one waiting for me inside.

Being in here with Bob has turned the setting into a nightmare.

"What would Mom and Pop say about their little *Charlie* showing her tits onstage and traffic—"

"Shut up!" I snap, whirling around to face him. He must be drunker than I first believed. "For someone in the *big leagues*," I air quote that, mocking him for his earlier scolding, "you sure shoot your mouth off." I tilt my head toward the camera in the corner of the room, my brow intentionally arched.

Bob catches my move and dismisses it with a snort and a lazy wave. "Those are for show. None of these owners actually want proof of what happens in here."

"*This* owner does," I warn slowly, though I silently pray that he's right. I also pray that the sound doesn't work on the recording. I'm hoping the music pumping out over the speakers will muffle our words, in any case.

Rubbing his chin, a pondering look suddenly touching his face, Bob murmurs, "You know, Eddie's been trying to connect with this guy for years. Seeing as you work here—"

"Not happening. Cain will have you thrown in jail before you get the proposal out of your mouth. He wants nothing to do with that world. You need to leave, right now."

Bob's face twists with displeasure. I gather he doesn't like being told what to do. Just as quickly, though, it smooths over. "Sure thing, *Charlie*."

Suppressing an eye roll, I turn toward the door, intent on leaving the room. A vise-like grip over my wrist stops me. "Don't turn your back on me."

I take a deep breath, trying to calm my nerves as I quickly assess the situation I've put myself in. Bob is semi-respectable when he's sober. But he's not sober now and, clearly, not at all respectable. He's also a big, muscular drug dealer who may not have hurt me yet but could easily do so tonight, And for some reason, he now thinks he has the upper hand on me because he's invaded my "real" life.

In a way, he does.

And my gut says he's going to use it to his full advantage.

Swallowing, I explain calmly, "I have to finish my shift behind the bar. And you should go. I happen to know the bouncers here aren't very friendly to patrons who lay hands on the girls."

"Then it's a good thing that no one's gonna tell them, right?" He gives my arm a painful squeeze in warning. "As soon as I get a private show, you can do whatever the fuck you want. On the house, of course."

He's drunk, I remind myself. His reflexes will be slower . . . "Okay, sure. One song. Sit down in the chair," I agree calmly, trying to placate him.

The second his fingers release me, I run for the door.

Drunk or not, Bob's not as dumb or as slow as I had hoped, and he was expecting my dodge. Pain shoots through my scalp as he grabs a fistful of my hair and yanks me into him, until my back is against his chest. He coils his fingers around my hair, pulling my head back until my entire body twists in an awkward angle as I look up at his face.

And then he slaps me across the cheek.

It's open-handed but it's with the back of his hand, and it's hard enough that the sting brings tears to my eyes. I'm sure there will be a mark.

"You're not afraid of me. You should be." He jerks my head, earning another wince. "You think you're protected? You think you're safe?" A wicked chuckle escapes his lips. "I kind of like you, Jane . . . Charlie . . . whatever the fuck your name is. You've got balls. Well . . ." His eyes drift downward as his free hand finds its way under my skirt, looping around the back of my tiny bikini bottoms, making as if to pull them off.

Breathe in, breathe out.

He leaves them on. "Metaphorical ones, anyway. But I don't like that you think you can just dismiss me. I don't like that at all." He launches me toward the pole. I manage to grab hold of it before I lose my balance and tumble to the ground. Crossing his arms over his broad chest and planting his feet solidly on the ground—clearly poised to block any more of my attempts to flee—he snaps, "Any time now."

My eyes dart to the door. It's only five feet away.

That earns Bob's toothy grin. "Take your pick—it's here or the next time I see you."

I'm no idiot. If I give in now, he'll still try to make me do it at the drop and there are no bouncers there to save me. "Eddie wouldn't allow that," I answer, forcing certainty into my voice. I have no idea what Eddie might allow but he hasn't had patience for Bob's leisurely search tactics so far, so I can only hope I'm right.

By the narrowing of Bob's eyes and the sudden flushing of his cheeks, that was the wrong thing to say. He's on me in a flash, kicking my feet out from under me and pushing me down onto the ground. I land with a hard thud, knocking the wind out of my lungs. "You think what Eddie says goes?" He reaches down to grab and lift me up by the face, his strong fingers squeezing my jaw until tears spring to my eyes. "Eddie doesn't own me. I do what I want!"

Bob's muscular arm pulls back and I see him make a fist. I close my eyes and wince, bracing myself against the impact that's about to come, knowing it's going to cause severe damage.

It never comes, though.

The sound of the door being thrown open and a shout comes a split second before Bob's painful grip vanishes and I drop to the ground again, spending a few seconds working the ache out of my face by wriggling my jaw. When I manage to pick myself up, I find Nate and Ben flanking Cain, who has Bob on his knees with a white-knuckled grip of his shirt collar. Bob has at least thirty pounds on Cain but right now, with the blazing rage in my boss's dark eyes and the way his muscles cord along his neck and arms, I don't doubt that Cain could bury Bob in seconds.

And that he very well might.

"Who the fuck are you?" Cain growls, all semblance of his

reserved, professional nature gone. When Bob doesn't answer, his eyes panning back and forth between Nate, Ben, and the door, Cain's nostrils begin to flare. "You've got about four seconds to start talking."

"Easy to threaten when you're three on one, isn't it?" Bob tosses back with a sneer, trying to stand his ground, even while on his knees.

That makes Cain's lips curl into a smile. Not the smile I love. A wicked smile that doesn't touch his eyes. As if he was waiting for an invitation. "Nate, Ben . . . take Charlie and step outside." His icy tone sends a shiver through my insides.

Ben and Nate share a look but don't move.

"Outside. Now!" Cain's bark makes me jump.

Ben moves as if to comply, reaching out to me with a hand. Nate doesn't budge, though. "You know I can't do that, boss."

"And why is that?" Cain taunts, never leaving Bob's eyes. It's as if he knows the answer but wants Nate to say it out loud, to have Bob hear it.

"Because this fool will not walk out of here if I leave you alone with him," Nate answers, just as calmly. "So why don't you let me take care of him." Adding a little more softly, "Let it go, Cain."

I haven't taken a single breath since they stormed in. I have to take one now. It's small and shaky and, as I study Cain's face—a mask of cold, detached hatred—I realize that I've now gone from one dangerous situation to another.

I need Bob gone. Immediately.

"I'm fine, Cain. He's just some guy who thought I was someone else," I explain, taking a step forward.

Cain's severe gaze finally settles on me. There is a turmoil within his eyes that can't be missed—fear? Panic? Anger? Shock? With tentative steps, I close the distance and place a gentle hand on his forearm, which is taut with tension. His eyes haven't left mine. "Cain, please. Just let Nate take him out." I hate the pleading in my tone but at this point, I'm desperate. I can't have Bob saying a word and I definitely can't have Cain beating the hell out of him. That will just end badly for me down the road. As it is, I don't know what this is going to mean at my next drop. I can't think about it right now.

Right now I have to defuse this situation.

I slowly rub my hand back and forth over Cain's arm, each muscle ripped, as tightly wound as he is.

After another long pause, he finally releases Bob from his death grip and steps in front of me, shielding my body behind him protectively.

As Bob struggles to get up, his eyes flash to me. I see the promise in them.

The promise of retribution.

I fight the tremble that skates along my spine.

"Your type isn't welcome in this club," Cain warns. "Stay the fuck out."

Bob snorts, trailing beside Nate, who's got one mammoth hand resting on his shoulder to steer him in the right direction as quickly and quietly as possible. Bob throws back, "Maybe you should look more closely at the type of whores you hire in here."

Nate and Ben—obviously knowing their boss too well—anticipated his reaction because they move fast, Nate shoving Bob out of the room while Ben blocks Cain from chasing after him. "Don't worry. We'll take care of him," Ben says, stepping backward slowly, "and you take care of Charlie."

My hands find my stomach, pressing against the growing tangle of nerves inside. Why couldn't I just keep these lives separate for a while longer? It's as if the universe is conspiring against me, reminding me that I don't have an indefinite amount of time. That everything will come crashing down. With just one phone call, just one visit . . .

Ginger already suspects something. She's still talking to me, but she's moody.

Now Bob knows how to find me. What if that had been Jimmy coming in here? Hell, tomorrow it *could* be Jimmy out there, watching me strip. My insides coil tighter at the thought.

And Cain . . .

At some point he made his way back into the V.I.P. room. He's studying me with those hawkish eyes. Can he see my inner turmoil? My guilt? My duplicity? If he does, he doesn't let on. He just stands there, studying me in silence until I'm ready to scream.

"Say something," I finally demand in a hoarse whisper. I wait for him to growl at me as he did at Bob. To fire me for being in the V.I.P. room with a customer, though clearly I wasn't doing any entertaining. I wait for him to look at me with hateful, disgusted eyes. To interrogate me, hammering me with questions, accusations, theories.

But he does none of that. He calmly pushes the door shut. Then, so fluidly that I miss his movement, I feel my body tugged toward him by the wrist, into his firm chest as his arms wrap around my frame, pulling me close, until I can almost feel the mess of emotions radiating from him—that same worry and pain and fear that I saw in his eyes.

And the last thing I expect him to do at this moment is the first thing he does.

With one hand lifting to curl around the back of my neck, Cain's head dips to seal his mouth over mine. There's no hesitation, there's no doubt. There's certainly no shyness, his tongue coaxing my lips apart and then diving in to claim my mouth as if it belongs to him already, skillfully stroking in a way that makes my knees weak and a low moan rumble in my throat.

It takes a few seconds for my shocked brain to fully grasp what's happening but my willingness is immediate when I do, falling into him, my hands crawling up his stomach and chest— relishing every hard ridge that I've envisioned touching for weeks. He deepens the kiss, his arms pulling me tight to his body, trapping my hand over the spot on his chest where his heart rests. I feel it beating more wildly than my own and I marvel that I may be doing that to him.

His lips steal my breath completely, kissing me with demanding thirst, as if he's been waiting forever to do this and he'll be waiting forever to do it again. But I can't ignore the tremble in his body, this close to him.

Cain is shaking.

This game we've been playing doesn't feel like a game anymore and I'm not sure how I feel about that.

Just as suddenly, he breaks free of me.

chapter nineteen

...

CAIN

"Cain!" Nate's fist pounds on the steel door of my office so hard that the picture frame hanging on the inside crashes to the ground. Normally I have a hard time hearing anything because the walls aren't sound-proofed and the music from the club resonates loudly. But I hear the unnatural shrillness to his natural boom and it sets off alarms.

Sprinting to unlock the door—I always lock it when the safe is open—I meet Nate's ashen face, his eyes wide as he stares down at the ground, mumbling, "I tried to get here. It all just happened so fast."

I follow his gaze.

And I stop breathing.

Penny's crumpled, frail body sits in a heap, facedown. I can see the gaping gash along the back of her head, the blood flow darkening her blond hair.

The crimson trail starting five feet down the hall tells me that she managed to pull herself a fair distance. And the way her hand lays, stretched out toward my door . . . I see the streak of blood along the bottom half of the steel.

Finger smears.

Reaching.

The smudges of blood around the door's handle.

■ ■ ■

I can't keep my hands off of her.

The second I saw Charlie's face—her eyes shut tightly against the coming blow from her attacker—my fear exploded.

It could have happened. Again.

"Cain, are you all right?" Charlie's voice brings me back to reality, a sweet song to remind me that she is not Penny. She is not dead. She is right here, in front of me, my forehead pressed against hers as I grip her arms, as I struggle to calm my ragged breath.

I just kissed her.

I *needed* to do it. I *needed* to be close to her, to feel her heat, her life, against me. And now, as I focus on that beautiful face so close to mine, her soft pants caressing my skin, her ever-perceptive eyes watching me with unguarded apprehension, I'm fighting myself to keep from doing it again.

No. Not in a fucking V.I.P. room, where hundreds of guys have gotten off for a nominal fee, after she's just been attacked, you asshole!

I grit my teeth against the consuming urge but I know that if I remain this close, my self-control will lose. So I pull away. Just far enough that I can get a good look at her face, my hands cupping her chin in a gentle grasp. "Where are you hurt?"

"Just my cheek." A tiny scowl flashes over her face, as if re-membering the pain, "and my scalp, when he pulled my hair like a fucking little girl."

I slip my hand around to the back of her skull—through her silky hair that is *not* matted in blood because she's not Penny, I remind myself—and let my fingers rub gently. Soothingly.

She closes her eyes as her lips fall apart, clearly enjoying the attention, and I yet again fight the urge to bend down and kiss that wide mouth. I've been watching her on the stage for weeks, thinking about her nonstop, telling myself a thousand different ways that *this* can't happen.

It almost doesn't seem real.

"Better?"

"Hmm . . ." Her hand reaches up to steal mine from where it rests on the back of her head, pulling it down to sit laced within her fingers. I don't know that I've ever held a woman's hand like this. It's making my nerves short-circuit. I wonder if she feels it too, or if it's just me. Vibrant eyes open to skate over my features, settling on my mouth. "You're shaking."

She's right. I *am* shaking. I hadn't even noticed.

I exhale deeply, trying to regulate my pounding heart. We're standing so close that I wonder if she can sense it. "When I came in and saw that guy ready to hit you—" My voice cuts off with a crack. "It reminded me of someone. Of something that happened, years ago."

Charlie's cool fingers crawl over my neck, tracing the letters of my tattoo, as if showing her understanding without uttering a word.

Keeping my eyes locked on her I ask cautiously, "Who was he, Charlie?" I try to keep the bitterness from my voice but it's impossible. Even thinking about the bald fucker makes my fists clench. As happy as I am here with Charlie, a small part of me wants to run out to the parking lot to cripple him. I know Nate will likely rough him up a bit in warning, but it's not enough.

Her hand finds its way to my cheek, her delicate touch smoothing over my light stubble. I instinctively turn in toward it, letting her fingers graze over my mouth. "I told you, he thought I was someone else," she purrs, feigning disinterest. But by the sudden tensing in her body, I know it's all an act. She leans in to rest her cheek against my chest, snaking her arms around my waist, and I selfishly accept the affection, wrapping my arms tightly around her warm, strong body once again, while I let my chin rest on top of her head.

And I marvel at how fast things can change. Ten minutes ago, my cock was throbbing as I watched Charlie's perfect body torment me onstage, wondering what the hell I would say to her tonight. Wondering if there was anything more to this than an irrepressible physical attraction.

Three minutes ago, I watched someone try to break that same perfect body and the ground opened up beneath me, reminding me how easily I could lose my chance to find out.

And in just seconds, I'm sure that something more profound than strip shows and physical attraction is beginning to develop between us.

In seconds.

I shouldn't have waited this long. I should have swept her off her feet when she walked through my door. Every second since then, I've been losing precious time and possibilities, repeating the mistakes of my past. Nate is right. I can't change anything that's happened. I can only learn from it.

But what if this is nothing more than a game for Charlie? I know she's lying to me about that guy. The only reason I even found out she was in there was because Jeff—one of the bouncers—said something over the earpiece about her going in and Nate caught it.

I thought I was walking into a completely different scene when I barged through that door and yet I barged in anyway, like a jealous freak, ready to scream at her for toying with me the way she has. A part of me is relieved by what I found instead. Knowing that makes me nauseous.

So what the fuck should I do now? Pushing her to tell me who that guy really is won't get me anywhere. I sense that by the way she's acting. But I also can't have her under a spotlight, having more guys "mistake her" for someone else.

Maybe that's why the command slips out. "You're not going up on that stage again for a while." I hear the tone—the possessive, controlling one that I hate—creep into my words and I immediately recognize that command for what it *really* is: an excuse to stop her from stripping.

Her arms loosen their hold of my waist as she starts to pull away. "I need the money, Cain." Her refusal sounds half-hearted, as if she's saying it because she feels she has to.

I can't say I'm not fucking ecstatic about that. I want her to hate the stage and hate stripping.

For anyone but me, that is.

Pushing back a strand of hair that's fallen across her forehead, I don't hesitate to offer, "I've got some administrative stuff around here you can help me with. It's easy and I'll pay you the same. And you'll be with me."

Nodding slowly as if processing that possibility, she murmurs, "I guess that will work . . ." In her calculating eyes, I catch a flicker of softness. Relief? "For how long?"

"We'll see." *Yeah, we'll see, all right . . .* My gaze can't help from drifting down to the two firm mounds pressed up against my rib cage. If I have my way, this body will never see the stage again. I want these long, muscular limbs, and these perfect tits, and this soft, silky skin to be for my eyes only. I want all of her to myself . . .

A light gasp escapes her lips. Her big brown irises begin to sparkle as she looks up at me and I realize just how close she's standing to me. By the ghost of a smile touching her lips, she felt that movement.

Exhaling slowly and heavily, I move my hands to grip her waist and force myself to step away from her before this goes from zero to naked in sixty seconds. There's wasting time and then there's wasting the first time. Taking Charlie in one of my V.I.P. rooms right now would be just wrong. "Come." I loop my arm around her waist and pull her close to me. "Let's ice that cheek."

Charlie remains quiet as I lead her into my office. In fact, she hasn't said a word aside from thanking Ginger, who—after forcing details out of Ben—ran to us just outside the hall to the private rooms with a bag of ice.

Now she suddenly seems nervous. Or unsure of how to act around me.

That makes two of us.

I pull up a chair and motion for her to sit. Leaning back against my desk in front of her, I pull the chair forward until her bare legs—looking long and sexy in that tiny skirt—butt up against the side of my thigh. Practically, it will allow me to hold the ice against her cheek for her. Greedily, I need to touch her. The fact that she doesn't shift away tells me she's okay with that.

The angry red mark will likely be a bruise in a few days, but nothing to damage that gorgeous doll face of hers. Charlie is perfection. She has a face I could lose myself in. And I do right now, settling my gaze on her lush mouth. I can't help myself from dragging the pad of my thumb along her bottom lip. Her lips are so much softer than I had even imagined.

Glossy eyes look up at me, waiting expectantly. And I still my hand. I don't know where to go next. What's right? What do I allow to happen? Do I just let things happen? Do I unload my past on her as I did on Penny, so she knows the kind of man she's getting involved with, the kind of violence I've seen, the kind of company I've kept?

Or perhaps Nate is right. Should any of that matter? It matters to me, but will it matter to her? I know Charlie's coming with her own bag of secrets. But, frankly, as long as she's not willfully doing something immoral, I don't give a shit what she's done. I just want to help her get away from it.

She lifts her hand to press mine tightly against her mouth.

Are we really doing this?

"I don't know how to do this, Charlie," I say, barely above a whisper, hoping she understands me. "I've never done . . . *this*."

After a long pause, her lips tickle my skin as she whispers, "I think you're doing just fine."

I feel my lip curl up in a smile, her attempts to build my confidence charming. I'm learning quickly about Charlie and the more I learn, the more I like. She doesn't ask a lot of questions and yet she always seems to know what to say.

She drops my hand, allowing me to tend to her cheek with the ice again. "Are you sure you want me doing office stuff for you?" she asks. "I have no experience." She squeezes her eyes shut, adding in a rush, "With office stuff. I have lots of other experience." Then her cheeks explode with color.

It's such a rare sight to see Charlie flustered that I can't help but chuckle, which makes her cheeks burn brighter and a giggle escape her lips. And that giggle is music to my ears.

Parroting her earlier words, I tease, "I think you'll do just fine." *I, on the other hand, trying to keep my hands off of you while you're in my office, will not.* "How about you come in at four tomorrow afternoon?"

She smiles and dips her head in assent. "Charlie Rourke, administrative assistant, at your service."

Hmm . . . I like the sound of that. "You know I'm looking for a female manager, right?"

"To do what, exactly?"

I shrug. "To help me manage this place. It's a lot to do on my own."

She bobs her head slowly as if considering it.

"Think about it." Lifting the ice bag off her, I inspect her cheek. If I look hard enough, I can see where his knuckles made contact. *If I ever see that guy again . . .* My fists clench in anticipation. "Does it hurt?"

She waves her hand dismissively. "It's just a bruise. Nothing's broken. Trust me, I've had *plenty* of them."

"Your father?" *Fuck.* Did I just ask that out loud? I hold my breath, hoping Charlie missed it.

"No, from . . ." She pauses, her brow furrowing deeply. "My father?" She swallows. "What do you mean?"

Ah, crap. What is it about Charlie that makes me say stupid shit? I never say stupid shit! Quickly trying to cover my tracks, I clear my throat and say, "Nothing. I mean, a lot of girls working here have had abusive fathers and I just assumed—"

"Cain." The edge in her tone is unmistakable. It's sharp with equal parts wariness and panic. She adjusts her body so that her legs no longer touch mine and her back is rigid. "You're a terrible liar."

Charlie is too damn perceptive. No one but Storm and Nate knows about John and how I have him basically burglarize my employees' private lives. Now Charlie's going to know because, though I've never done this relationship thing before, I'm smart enough to realize that it won't work by lying to someone's face.

I sigh with regret and then begin to rattle off what John told me. "George Rourke, born May first, 1962. Truck driver with a drinking problem and a history of abusing your mother until her death." *Does Charlie even know that her mother died?* By the deer-caught-in-the-headlights look, I'm suspecting she might not have known. *Fuck!* My insides are twisting. This is just getting worse and worse. "You ran away on your eighteenth birthday and there's been no trace of you until you flew from New York to Miami two months ago. Look, I have fairly extensive background checks done on all of my employees. The private investigative type."

Clearing her throat, she barely manages to get out, "I need to take the rest of the night off." I reach for my keys to drive her but she's already shaking her head, a hand out to stop me, trembling slightly. "No, Cain. Just—" She swallows, her voice hoarse. "No."

I feel like a dump truck has just slammed into my chest. "Wait. Please tell me you knew about your mother. Please tell me you didn't just find out." If she didn't know, I think I'm going to lose my mind.

I see her hard swallow and then she manages to get out a tight, "Yes. I knew about my mother's death."

I reach for her hand but she pulls it away. "I know what it looks like, but you can trust me."

"You're wrong, Cain. I actually don't know anything about you at all." Spinning on her heels, she's gone.

Just like that. In seconds, any trust I may have gained . . . lost.

I last about three minutes. I can't let her leave like that. Despite her protests, I'm on my feet, keys in my hand, and heading toward the door to chase after her. Ginger's colorful head stops me.

"Is Charlie okay? Levi said she saw her storm out of here."

I'm already maneuvering my way around her. I don't have time for Ginger's antics right now. "No, she's not."

Her hand clamps over my arm to stop me. "Wait . . ."

"Not now, Gin—"

"Were you with Charlie yesterday afternoon?"

That slows my steps. Why would she ask that? "No." I turn to give her a questioning look.

She purses her lips together. "I wasn't going to say anything, but after what Ben told me happened tonight . . ." She groans. "I need to tell you about yesterday. Maybe you can make sense of it."

I glance toward the exit door and then back at Ginger, torn between what she might have to say and getting to Charlie.

"I talked to some guy on her phone yesterday. She said he was her father but I'm not so sure."

chapter twenty

• • •

CHARLIE

Who the fuck is George Rourke?

This was supposed to be a fake ID. Fake! But the way Cain just went on, talking about these people I supposedly know, makes me believe that Charlie has a real life involving real people . . .

Charlie is a *real person*.

Apparently, up until four years ago, a person who probably laughed and cried and partied with her friends. People called her Charlie and she responded. She looked in a mirror and saw a face that was not my face, the one that has assumed her identity.

And then she *disappeared* without a trace? People don't just disappear. I know, because I'm trying to. There's only one explanation that makes sense.

Oh, God.

I'm forced to pull off the road. I barely get my seat belt off and the door open before my stomach's contents spill out onto the pavement. Thank God it's late and I'm on a quiet side street with no witnesses aside from the stray cat across the way, inspecting a trash bin. When I have nothing left to expel, I climb back into the driver's seat. Tears begin to stream, but I wipe them away furiously.

I have to know.

With blood pounding through my ears like an incessant drum, I glance at the clock on the dashboard. It's just after midnight. Sam will still be up. Despite his age, he's a night owl *and* an early riser.

I know I shouldn't do this. I'm never supposed to contact him, but I need him to convince me that my suspicions are wrong. I punch in the number of the Long Island house from the burner phone, hoping it can't be traced if there's a wiretap on the home phone.

With trembling hands and ragged breaths, I wait, my heart feeling like it's going to give out soon if I don't find some relief for it. I don't even know if he'll be home. He's hardly ever home . . .

Sam answers on the third ring.

Forcing my fear aside with a hard swallow, I waste no time. "Who was Charlie?"

I hear nothing.

Nothing.

And then a click.

I force myself to breathe as I press the phone to my chest. Did he hear me? Did he think it was a prank call? Should I call back?

The ring that breaks into the silence makes me jump.

I hit "talk," and listen, pursing my lips.

"Why are you asking?" His tone is low and harsh. Sam can be demanding, but I've heard him use this voice only once before—with Dominic *that* night. I'll bet he switched phones. He's probably also in the unfinished cellar. The room is completely bare, making it difficult to hide any bugs within, should someone ever manage to get past Simba and Duke—two of the largest and most unfriendly Rottweilers I've ever seen.

I grit my teeth, searching for an excuse. In my frenzy, I didn't consider how this conversation would go. I was simply looking for an answer to calm me. I can't tell him what I know. I can't tell him anything about Cain or his investigative practices. *Stupid girl!*

What is happening to me? I'm always so vigilant. Now, when I most need to keep my head, I'm losing it!

But it's too late. Sam needs an answer. I swallow my fear. "Was she a real person?"

His low, menacing chuckle makes me cringe. "Well, of course she's real. She's you."

I shut my eyes as dread swirls. He's being evasive. "Was she someone else before she was me?"

There's a pause and then, to my surprise, Sam actually answers. "Yes."

Prickles run down my neck. "Where is she now?"

"So many questions, my little mouse . . . I have to wonder why." I hear the familiar pull of the chain affixed to the light in the cellar. *On . . . off . . . on . . . off . . .* and I think back to the day he handed me all of Charlie's identification. The day he collected all of mine. What was he going to do with it? Sell it to someone else so she can pretend to be me?

I press my lips together to keep from speaking. I've never questioned Sam. *Never.* And now he gets a phone call from me in the middle of the night, riddled with unspoken accusations. It's going to make him suspicious.

"Answer me!" he finally demands.

"I'm just wondering if she's . . ." I force down the bile rising again in my throat. "What happened to her?" *Did you kill her, Sam? Was it for me? Did you have this all planned out four years ago? Maybe earlier?*

Of course I don't expect Sam to admit to anything. He's never shared anything incriminating with me. If I ever went to the cops, I'd have nothing but accusations and circumstantial evidence that wouldn't hold up. Certainly no valuable information to barter for my exoneration. Aside from Dominic and now Jimmy, I've never met any of his associates. I rarely step foot inside his legitimate companies. I don't know how he gets the heroin; I would never ask. I know he's made trips to the Middle East over the last few years on "business." But I highly doubt his real estate firm, his roofing company, his franchise steakhouse, or any of the other dozen ventures he's involved in has anything to do with the Middle East.

I'm sure the DEA would question his trips as well, if they were watching. I've never felt their presence, though. Then again, I don't know what having the DEA's attention would feel like. For all I know, that guy sniffing around me last spring wasn't Sam's friend and was in fact the DEA. Either they're discreet or they haven't caught on to Sam yet. I guess when you're really good at what you do, it's harder to pin things on you.

I hear the hiss of air through Sam's teeth on the other end before he offers in a phony nonchalant tone, "Who knows? Maybe she betrayed someone who gave her everything. Maybe she wasn't a good little mouse."

My heart begins to race, pounding against my rib cage. He evaded the question but to me, it's clearly an answer.

And a warning.

"Is that what you wanted to know?"

Clearing my throat, I manage to get out, "Yes."

"I hope I don't have anything to worry about. Remember, we're in this *together*. There's no room to get sloppy. Yesterday, you were sloppy."

Sloppy. The same thing he accused Dominic of being.

"I know, S—" The coppery taste of blood taints my taste buds as I bite my tongue hard, to avoid saying his name. "It won't happen again."

"Good. Because we have a really good thing going. And it's going to get much better." There's a pause. "I see you're running low on money. I'll deposit another ten in your account tomorrow. Go buy yourself something nice."

"I will. Thank you." Money . . . It all comes down to money. How Sam values that over everything else and how he assumes everyone else does, too. The funny thing is, Sam could deposit ten times that much into my account without feeling it financially. But he never gives me too much. Just enough to keep me around, *needing* him.

I listen to the static on the phone for I don't know how long after Sam hangs up. Finally, I sink back into my seat.

Charlie Rourke *was* a real person.

And the real Charlie Rourke is dead.

I've been obliviously pretending to be a dead girl for months now. I've turned her into a stripper and a drug trafficker. I've looked forward to the day I can shred her ID up into little bits and pretend that she never existed.

But she did exist.

And Sam likely had a hand in her death.

Was she just some unfortunate girl who met the wrong person one night? Someone looking for a blond runaway who no one would miss? Or did Sam know the real Charlie Rourke? Was she running drugs for him? Did she do something to fall into his bad graces?

Am *I* about to fall into Sam's bad graces? With Ginger answering my burner phone, with the sudden questions, with whatever he may have yet to hear from Bob. What if Bob tells him about Cain?

Cain.

My chest throbs as his name touches my thoughts. I was too distracted, running from Penny's tonight, to think about all that had transpired. I don't know what that was back there, but I know I didn't want it to end. He seemed intent on keeping his hands on me and I was intent on letting him do so, all the way to his home and into his bed, if he invited me.

But now Cain is right in the thick of it. He's made an enemy out of Bob. He thinks he has my entire history. I can't be angry with him about hiring the investigator. I understand why he does it. It's to protect himself from people *exactly like me.*

But he's not protected. Sam's too smart for him. Sam's too smart for everyone.

This foolish plan I have? That's all it is . . . foolish. I'm never going to be able to buy an identity like the one Sam arranged for me because Sam probably *killed* for it. All I can do is take my money and run.

I have twenty-five grand in my account—a "secret" account, different from the joint one with Sam—saved. Add ten grand coming tomorrow and another twenty or so for my SUV, and I can make a clean break with a good chunk of money. Of course, I'll have to drain both accounts and, what . . . carry $55,000 in my gym bag? Because I can't open a bank account without any ID and I won't risk using Charlie's. I don't know if Sam could find a way to trace a bank account in her name, but I can't risk it. To be safe, I have to assume that if the second "Charlie Rourke" is entered into any computer, he can find me.

I'll just jump on a bus and go . . . where? I've always wanted to see the Deep South. Maybe somewhere in Louisiana or Alabama. Some low-key town where I might be able to work under the table and rent a small apartment without all the necessary background checks. Or I could cross the border into Mexico. But then I'll never get back in, because I'll never get a passport again. No . . . I have to stay in the country. Forever. I'll never get to go to Europe or the Caribbean. Not until Sam dies and I somehow assume my real identity again. When will that happen? In twenty years? Thirty years? After thirty years of anonymity?

Heaving a sigh, I take a look at my reflection in the rearview mirror. I'll cut my hair, for sure. Maybe dye it. Would I still wear colored contacts? Hide my violet eyes?

What name would I use? Not my real name and not Charlie. Something new.

A month ago, when I thought about this—leaving all of my past behind and starting completely fresh—a feeling of exhilaration coursed through me. Like locks releasing, chains tumbling, and being able to just run without ever looking back. Now, though, now that it's really happening—not as I had planned it but happening nonetheless—I somehow feel more trapped than before.

I will have *no one*.

I will have *nothing*.

"Why, Sam? Why would you do this to me?" For years, I felt nothing but gratitude and loyalty to Sam. But now, I feel nothing but bitter hurt.

I have no other choice.

I have to run.

Now.

Pressing my forehead to the steering wheel, I let the tears pour freely.

. . .

"Ginger?"

Her eyes flash open. "Yes?"

"Did you get locked out of your apartment?"

"No. Why?"

"Well . . ." I do a cursory glance around the commons to see that no one else is outside. "Because it's two a.m. and you're sitting outside my apartment door, asleep."

Making a point of stretching her arms over her head, Ginger lithely climbs to her feet and moves away. I unlock and open my door. Without invitation, she's trailing me in.

"Did Cain send you here to check up on me?" I toss my keys onto the end table and turn on the only lamp in the living room.

"Why would he do that?" she asks coyly, averting her eyes to a chipped nail. Ginger would lose her shirt in a game of poker.

With a sigh, I flop down onto my couch, my focus on the stippled ceiling. I'm drained. Emotionally and physically drained. "Because you should still be at Penny's and yet you left early to sit outside my apartment door." I can't ignore the twinge of disappointment in my stomach that it wasn't Cain waiting for me. I know I told him to leave me alone and it's for the best, but . . . still.

I feel Ginger's eyes on me, on my bloodshot eyes and the streaks of mascara I'm sure have gathered. Two hours of crying will do that. She finally settles on, "How's your cheek?"

"Fine." As long as I don't touch it or smile, or vomit on the side of the road, I barely notice it.

With the tiniest sigh, I hear her nimble steps as she strolls over to my fridge. The clanging sound of glass tells me she's pulled out two bottles of beer. "Here." Handing one to me, she grabs the remote and flicks on the television, quickly scanning the channels. I instantly know what she's searching for. We discovered early on that we share a love of *Seinfeld*. There doesn't seem to be an episode on at this time of night, though, and so she lands on the tail end of *Seven*. "Oh, I love this part! Gives me chills," she exclaims, exaggerating a shudder as she tucks her legs up under herself on the opposite corner of the couch. We settle into silence as we watch Brad Pitt open up a box to find Gwyneth Paltrow's head inside.

I can't say that being around Ginger is completely comfortable, with this cloud hanging over us. But I'm pretty sure she's not mad at me. If anything, I think she's worried.

I don't remember what it's like to have someone worried about me. Sam never worries, period. And my mom? Well, I remember her fussing over her fitted clothes in front of the mirror a lot. She was young and blond and beautiful. She wore a lot of makeup and a sweet-smelling perfume, and put a great deal of effort into her appearance. I remember her smoothing her clothes over and over again when we went out, even at gymnastics, while she talked to the fathers and I worked on my balance and my basic beginner moves. I remember her brow knitting tightly as she sat at the kitchen table, sorting through what I assumed were bills. I remember her worrying about not ever finding a good husband with all her "baggage."

But I don't ever remember her worrying over *me*.

Then, when Sam came along, I'm pretty sure all of her worries vanished.

Ginger finally breaks the silence. "Cain seemed pretty spooked tonight." Her gaze never leaves the television as she sips her beer.

"I don't know how to do this," he had said. Do what? Have a relationship? Is that what Cain thinks is going to happen between us? It can't! And yet when he said it, I can't pretend I didn't feel a burst of warmth in my chest, radiating outward to my limbs, my desire to curl into him overpowering.

"I've never done this." If that's true, then I can't help but wonder . . . what was Penny to him?

"Did you ever meet her?" I ask. "Penny?"

Ginger sighs. "Oh . . . yeah. I started working at The Bank about two months before she died."

"What was she like?"

"I didn't know her well. She was *gorgeous*. Blond, brown eyes, like you. So many customers came in just for her. She seemed nice. Not catty, like some of the other girls." With a chuckle, she admits, "She was a pole dancer as well. You remind me of her. Your style, I mean. You're classy and kind of artistic, if you can use the word *artistic* to describe that sort of thing."

"And her fiancé? You said he killed her?"

She takes a long sip of her drink as her head bobs up and down. "Yeah . . . their relationship was all a little bit fast and strange. I think Penny had really low self-esteem and was just looking for a nice guy who'd want her. She wasn't the kind of girl who ever took school seriously or had a lot of ambition. More the type to pop out a baseball team and bake pies for the rest of her life." A quick hand goes up. "No judgment here! That many babies is ambitious. And I plan on baking pies too. Only I'll be doing it for customers at my high-end wine country inn. But . . ." She pauses. "The guy was a customer. A quiet, balding man. Nothing special. But one private dance from her and he was sunk."

I wonder if that's why Cain won't let *me* do private dances.

Ginger nods slowly. "He came in to visit almost every night. Took her out to dinner and sent her flowers *a lot*. We weren't too surprised when she showed up at work with a rock on her hand after only a few months. He didn't want her dancing anymore, and I remember her saying that no one other than her husband could tell her what to do, so . . ." Ginger's shoulders lift and drop.

"What else do you remember about her?"

Ginger's mouth twists in thought. "She was a bit flighty. One week she was gushing over the beach wedding they were going to have, the next week it was going to be a big church wedding in her hometown. Then, all of a sudden, she was leaving the next day for Vegas."

"And Cain? How did he take it?"

Ginger's shoulders bob. "He shook the guy's hand, said congratulations. I don't know . . . Cain is Cain. If something was going on between them, they hid it well. He never came out to drool over her onstage every night . . ." I feel Ginger's sidelong glance at me, but I keep my eyes trained on the television. "I don't know that Penny was the type to hold a secret like sleeping with the boss, though."

"What happened after she died?"

Ginger puffs out her cheeks and releases a lung's worth of air. "It was messy. Roger was convicted and he went to jail. The Bank never reopened after that night. Cain sold it as soon as the cops were done with their investigation. Apparently he disappeared for a month to do God knows what. The only person he'd talk to was Nate, who lived with him at the time.

"And then suddenly he showed up at my apartment one day a few months later, telling me he was opening up a new club in Penny's name and asking me if I wanted a job."

We fall into silence then as I mull over her words. Is that why he has taken to me as he has? Because I remind him of someone he clearly cared deeply for? Possibly loved? Am I just a living memory?

I'll never get a chance to find out. I've accepted that I have to leave.

Tomorrow.

I can't risk going to another drop after what happened with Bob. And I've likely inspired some doubt on Sam's part now, with my questions. For all I know, Sam could be on a plane, heading down here to interrogate me.

But am I ready for this?

Can I just pick up and walk away from this little apartment I've unintentionally started thinking of as home? Can I say good night to Ginger tonight when really I mean goodbye?

Can I just walk away from Cain? Forget what might have been?

Into the quiet, dimmed apartment, I hear myself say, "Ginger, you're a really good friend."

There's a long pause, and I imagine she's wondering if there's something else I'm not saying. Finally she just sighs. "I know I am, Charlie."

. . .

I may be a tad paranoid.

Still, I hold my gun close to my thigh as I peer through the blinds at the unfamiliar man outside my window, a slight tremble to my grip. In his dark khaki pants and white golf shirt, with an electronic signature machine and a large white box in his hands, he definitely looks like a delivery guy. But what is he delivering? And how did he get in here? I didn't buzz him in.

I flip the safety switch off but then quickly flip it back on as memories of my old neighbor shooting himself in the foot flash through my mind. I shouldn't even be holding a gun right now, as tired as I am after tossing and turning all night, my stomach roiling, unable to shut my mind off as it tried to convince me to stay. At about six a.m. I finally gave up and crawled out of bed to pack.

The only thing I've been certain of since is that I have to watch my back. Be wary of strange things. Like deliverymen outside my door. For all I know, Sam knows exactly where I moved and is sending me another warning, because last night's warning wasn't quite clear enough.

Maybe it's a severed head.

With a shudder, I stay frozen behind the curtain, thankful that he can't see me, watching quietly as the stranger knocks again, louder this time. He waits another minute and then turns to leave, muttering under his breath something unintelligible.

I breathe a sigh of relief. Threat abandoned.

That is, until I see Tanner lumbering through the common area in his requisite plaid shorts and too-tight T-shirt. The guy quickly intercepts him, holding the package out. Tanner's hand reaches out for the electronic signature machine.

Shit.

What if Tanner is nosy? What if he takes the box inside his apartment and opens it up? There's no reasonable explanation for why a person would send me a human head.

I quickly set my gun on the floor and then dart out my apartment door and run toward them, just as the delivery guy is handing the box over to Tanner. "Hello!" I yell in a rush. "I think that's for me!" Both of them turn to stare at me.

I yank the box out of Tanner's hands before he has a chance to object. "Sorry, I just missed the door," I offer to the middle-aged delivery guy, whose jaw is hanging open. With a glance down, I realize that I'm still in the white tank top—sans bra—and thong that I slept in.

Stripper or not, I should be embarrassed to be caught like this outside of work, but I'm too on edge right now. With my heart pounding inside my chest, I turn and hustle back into my apartment—fully aware of the view the deliveryman and Tanner are getting—before I slam the door shut behind me and hug the box to my chest.

My skin prickles. The box is cold. Like it's been in refrigeration.

Severed heads need refrigeration.

"Damn Ginger and that fucking movie!" I know it's insane and highly improbable, and yet I can't dislodge the thought now, as I walk with a sinking stomach and wobbly knees toward my dining table to set the parcel down. With my fingers balled up into tight fists, I stare at the simple, tall white box, adorned with a purple ribbon but displaying no other identifiable markings.

A head would fit nicely in there.

Maybe the real Charlie Rourke's head?

Holding my breath, I rip open the top of the box and pull back the tissue paper.

And exhale noisily.

Flowers?

Someone sent me flowers?

My curiosity peaked and my heart saved from explosion, I reach inside and pull out a stunning bouquet in a plain glass vase. All kinds of flowers—at least a dozen different varieties. But they all have one thing in common: their color.

They're all violet.

The exact bluish-purple hue of my eyes.

Few people know about my natural eye color. Only one person in Miami knows. Flutters stir inside my chest as I pull out the small card tucked within. The words are simple, the request clear:

Your secrets are safe with me. Please give me a chance—Cain

I had wondered if Cain noticed that my eyes were not truly brown that day at my old apartment. It would be hard not to, but then again, he *is* a guy and most guys don't notice basic details like eye color. Cain obviously had, but he never uttered a word.

Please give me a chance . . . "I wish I could," I whisper, that painful lump forming in my throat again as I let my fingers rub the velvety petals.

■ ■ ■

If I wait any longer, Ginger will be at my door for coffee.

I have to leave now.

I shut the door of my apartment for the last time and drop the key in through the mailbox slot. Tanner will find it when they figure out that I'm gone. Quickly and quietly wheeling my suitcase down the path, I make my way out the gate and to my SUV, which I'll be selling at a dealership fifteen minutes away after I pull all my money from the bank.

With my hands gripping the steering wheel, I take a few minutes to stare at the white stucco of the building for the last time, recalling Cain's gorgeous form pacing around this very parking lot only three weeks ago. Glancing down at the flowers on my passenger side, which I can't bear to abandon, I feel the hot tears begin streaming down my cheeks.

I know leaving is the right decision. I do.

And yet each step is taking every ounce of willpower that I have.

chapter twenty-one

∎ ∎ ∎

CAIN

"Ronald Sullivan. Forty-two. No wife, no kids. Assault charge back in '95 that was dropped. Suspected of selling narcotics but hasn't been nailed with anything. I'll fax through his picture so you can validate it. I have his address too, if you want it. He lives in an apartment off Twenty-third."

Oh, Charlie. What did you get yourself into? "As always, you're invaluable, John."

"And you are single-handedly funding my retirement villa in Tahiti. Just don't tell the witches of Eastwick." I have to pull my phone from my ear as John's boisterous laugh blasts through.

"I have no reason to talk to your ex-wives, John. Unless it's about how big of a shmuck you are."

Another round of laughter sounds as my ribbing rolls off John's sturdy back. "Is this all about the girl?"

With a sigh, I mutter, "Everything is about the girl, these days." After Ginger filled me in on what happened on Monday—the call from a "father" on Charlie's second phone, who I *know* couldn't be her father because her father is in jail and only making collect calls these days—I sent her home early to check up on Charlie. Then I reviewed the surveillance video of V.I.P. room two.

There's no doubt in my mind that Charlie knew who that guy was. The way she strolled into the room, arm-in-arm with him, the covert way she warned him about the camera. Everything about the interaction screamed familiarity. When I watched his hand reach up under her skirt, my jaw cracked from the tension in my face. When I saw him backhand her, I had to pause and take a deep, calming breath.

As usual, I could count on Nate to handle the situation. After delivering a blow to the guy's gut in a quiet corner of the parking lot outside—I watched that surveillance tape too, with a big fucking grin on my face—Nate dragged him to the black Camry he pointed out as his and left him writhing in pain on the ground while he searched his wallet and car, taking down as much information as he could. Once Nate had confiscated the loaded gun that he found beneath the seat, he tossed the guy into the driver's side as if he were a chew toy. Next to Nate, everyone looks like a chew toy.

Nate made it clear that if anything ever happened to Charlie, that surveillance tape would go to the police along with all of Ronald's info, and then it would be a race to see who got to him first, me or the cops.

And Ronald would want it to be the cops.

As a parting gift, Nate dropped one last brutal punch to the douchebag's nose and left him there, cupping his face against the rush of blood. I imagine Ronald Sullivan spent the night in a lot of pain and possibly in the ER.

Nate and I know we'll have to watch our backs for a while. But if I see the guy here again, I won't hesitate to put him down.

"And her father's still locked up, right?"

"Yes, sir. He won't be getting out for a *long* time."

"Thanks for the quick turnaround, John," I offer before I hang up, looking at the clock as I take a long draw of my drink. It's four thirty. Charlie was supposed to be here at four for that administrative work and she's never late. I shouldn't be surprised that she hasn't shown up. After last night, I'll be surprised if she comes at all.

She hasn't answered my calls, though the florist confirmed that she received my flowers this morning. I've never sent a woman flowers. I hope it wasn't too much. I hope she didn't think it was tacky. I'm still at a loss for what to say, what to do, how much time and space I should give her.

What if she won't want me once she knows what I'm all about?

My hands find their way behind my neck, where they clasp tightly. How is this going to go? Will she see me as another Ronald Sullivan? Or someone as violent as her father? Or some other guy who's probably taken advantage of her in the past, who may still be doing so?

Maybe she will see me as any or all of them. Maybe I'll spill my guts to her and she'll run away from me and into the arms of a normal guy with normal parents and a normal career. Maybe that would be for the best.

· · ·

I'm sure my body visibly slackened the second I walked out into the club earlier tonight, to see Charlie behind the bar. I had convinced myself that she wasn't coming in, but she's here, mixing drinks, smiling at customers.

Avoiding me.

She immediately shifted to the opposite end of the bar when I approached her. I'm not going to lie—that felt like a punch to the heart. I fought the urge to throw her over my shoulder and demand we talk. I had to hide out in my office to calm myself.

But now I'm back, because I can't stay away from her. It's ten o'clock. I'm just waiting for her to attempt to get up on that stage again. I *will* throw her over my shoulder if she tries that.

"Cain!" a familiar voice calls out, a second before a hand smacks my shoulder. It's Storm's fiancé, Dan, and Ginger is lining shots up in front of him.

In my peripheral vision, I catch Charlie looking up at the sound of my name being called, but her eyes are already down when I try to make eye contact. With a sigh, I turn my attention back to Dan for the time being. "What are you doing here?" I *am* genuinely curious, given that he's not the type to frequent strip clubs. He hated Storm working here—rightfully so—and was only too happy the day she quit.

A guy behind him, who's obviously part of Dan's group, slaps his back and shouts, "Celebrating! You're looking at Special Agent Dan Ryder."

Dan just shakes his head, but he can't keep the wide grin from escaping.

And I can't help but match it, announcing, "Next round's on me!"

When John did the background check on Dan—of course I had Storm's guy investigated—he came back stamping Dan as the last true Boy Scout. And everything Dan has done since that day has only strengthened the claim. The guy inherited a shitload of money a few years back from his oil-tycoon grandma. Enough that he could be spending the rest of his life lying on a beach, fishing . . . doing anything, really. Instead, he kept chasing criminals, holding out hope to join the DEA. And he finally made it. He's about to be chasing dangerous lowlifes, making a big difference.

Dan's one of the few good guys. And being friends with him has helped me out greatly. For years, I'd routinely have cops at my door, looking for reasons to shut me down. I've been hauled into the station, questioned for hours, tailed around the city. I did get shut down once for a few days, until my lawyers worked their magic. Since Dan started dating Storm, though, I've had only a handful of issues. Everyone loves and respects the guy. Sure, I still get the odd threat, but all I need to do is give Dan a call and the threats seem to disappear on their own.

"What about a dance for the special agent?" one of Dan's friends shouts.

I'm already shaking my head, a laugh escaping. "Storm would have my balls in a sack if she heard that anyone touched him."

The friend—drunk and clearly not interested in spousal approval—waves his wallet toward China. "We've got a grand. She'll take that!"

Dan gives me an almost imperceptible head shake, his eyes widening as he takes in China's electric-blue dress. There's no need. With a wave, I catch Nate's attention and, pointing at Dan, I mouth, "No dances." It's not worth being murdered by a pregnant woman. Or more likely, her best friend and henchwoman, Kacey.

To Dan I ask, "So, does Storm know?"

"Yeah, Nora knows." Dan still refuses to acknowledge her by the name everyone else calls her, even though she doesn't mind it. "I just got the call at the end of my shift. The guys decided to bring me here to celebrate."

"When do you start?"

He takes a long sip of his drink. "Next week."

"New job, wedding, baby on the way . . . You're going to be busy."

"Yeah." Dan's head bobs up and down as he scratches the back of his neck, adding absently, "And it's about to get a lot busier from the shit we're hearing on the streets."

Another one of Dan's officer friends lifts his shot glass in the air, saluting, "To Special Agent Dan Ryder, newest member of the DEA!" A loud cheer explodes from around us.

Seconds later, I hear a squeal of panic. My attention flies to the bar to find Ginger hovering over where Charlie was just standing. Looking down.

chapter twenty-two

. . .

CHARLIE

"Charlie?"

I open my eyes to see a masculine furrowed brow and rows of shelves and boxes. I'm lying on the couch in Cain's office.

"Are you okay?" Cain is seated on the couch, his body hovering over me protectively. I feel the warmth of his hand as it cradles my neck, and the intimacy of his thumb as it gently rubs back and forth, catching the corner of my mouth—and my breath—with each pass.

What happened? Oh, right.

Cain is friends with a DEA agent.

Cain is a law-abiding citizen who hates anything to do with drugs and he's friends with a DEA agent.

And *I* am trafficking heroin.

"Charlie?"

"I'm fine," I croak out.

Ginger runs in with a glass of water and I immediately move to sit up. With a hand sliding beneath me to my shoulder blades, Cain helps me, his other hand smoothing the skirt of my short dress down to a respectable level. I shudder in response.

"You dropped like a bag of bricks. What happened?" Ginger frowns.

I shrug, trying to play it off. "Not sure. Just got dizzy for a minute. I'm fine now." I'm so not fine. My heart is racing.

I'm supposed to be gone. I should be on a bus, close to Louisiana or Alabama—wherever my coin toss lands me. I would have been, if the bank had released my money. They told me it would take twenty-four hours to withdraw such a large sum from my accounts. When I protested that it wasn't *that* large a sum, I learned that Sam had deposited 25,000 dollars instead of the ten he mentioned. I'm wondering if that's his way of apologizing. That's typically how Sam operates, after all.

It's funny . . . the second the teller informed me that I couldn't pull all that money out—that I couldn't leave today after all—a sudden lightness washed over me.

Relief.

Relief that I had a valid excuse to stay for one more night.

It was like fate intervening, pointing me *once again* toward Penny's.

I can have tonight with Cain. I'll take *one night* with him, with whatever he's willing to give me, to earn myself memories that I can hold on to.

Cain's concern hasn't disappeared. "Was it too hot? Too loud? What did you eat today?" There's a frantic tone to his voice that tells me the I-don't-know-what-happened brush-off isn't going to work and he's truly worried about me.

"Oh, crap." I roll my eyes rather dramatically so he doesn't miss it. "I haven't eaten since lunch. I *completely* forgot." That's partly true. I didn't eat, but I was well aware of it. I just didn't feel like it, my stomach twisting and churning into anxious knots.

Cain heaves a sigh. "Can you walk?" He stands and holds a hand out. I take it, and an electric current instantly dances along my limbs and through my core.

"Good." His eyes drift to my mouth. "I can't have you passing out behind my bar. You need to eat."

■ ■ ■

"This place is nice," I admit, peering out over the white railing to Biscayne Bay just below. We're seated at a small corner table on a patio with palm trees hovering behind and a band playing soft alt-country music in the opposite corner.

I was careful to watch for tails on my way to work, and again when I climbed into Cain's Nav. But now, we're far away from the noise of the club, the hustle of Miami's streets, and for the first time all day, I feel safe. Sheltered.

A rare, broad smile on Cain's face tells me that he's pleased. "It's one of my favorite restaurants. I live just over there." His index finger points out one of the tall luxury condominium buildings on the water. It doesn't surprise me. Cain has "downtown bachelor" written all over him. He adds as an afterthought, "I haven't been here in a while."

"What does that tell you?" I mutter dryly.

His head dips once in assent. "Yes, I know. I need a life. Storm and Nate keep reminding me." A light chuckle escapes his lips.

It acts as a sedative for me, warmth and relaxation creeping into my limbs. The waitress arrives with a bottle of wine and we say nothing, silently stealing glances at each other as she fills our glasses with cabernet, the soft buzz of conversation and music floating around us.

When the waitress leaves with our order, Cain finally speaks up, his voice calm. "You scared me tonight."

I feel my cheeks burning. Now that the shock has worn off, I'm more embarrassed than anything. "I don't do that often." I've actually never passed out before but I don't want Cain to know that, so I make sure my hand is steady as I take a sip of my wine. He watches me do so quietly, leaning back in his chair in a white dress shirt, unbuttoned at the top and looking casual yet tailored.

His dark hair, normally styled tidily, is slightly unkempt now, and there's the slightest five o'clock shadow across his jaw.

He's a kind of handsome I've never seen in real life. I can't believe I've been stripping for him nightly on a stage. And he's been watching me. And he kissed me last night with a kind of reckless abandon I didn't know possible. And now I'm sitting across from him at a table. And I'm desperate to go home with him tonight.

The Cain I've been using as a prop onstage all these weeks is an emotionless man who wants nothing more than sex. He's aggressive and demanding and walks away when he's gotten his fill. Aside from a lustful crush, it's difficult to picture myself forming an attachment to a man like that.

But the Cain I experienced last night is nothing like that prop. That Cain is passionate and gentle and, I'm afraid, has the ability to consume me.

That's a treacherous position to be in, for a girl who is running. Tomorrow.

"Charlie?" He leans forward to plead softly, "Am I forgiven?"

I don't blame him for investigating his employees. But still, not many people go to that level of trouble. "Why not just a simple background check?"

A hand slides up to his neck, to that tattoo, rubbing it slowly as his eyes drift over the crowd. "I know the kind of world I live in, in this industry. I do a lot of things to protect myself."

I hesitate. And then I remind myself that tonight is my only night with Cain. "*Why* do you do what you do? I mean the club . . . the apartment building . . ."

His face crinkles into a quick smile and then relaxes into a look of contemplation. As he takes a sip of his wine, I suspect he's collecting his thoughts. Deciding what he wants to admit to. "Over the years, I've had to arrange for a lot of apartments for the dancers. Abusive boyfriends . . . infested complexes . . . ," he gestures at me, "dangerous neighbors. It made sense to buy a building so I had a safe place to send them." His teeth visibly clench. "I didn't want anyone knowing that I owned it. But Tanner accidentally let it get out . . ."

"Why does it matter?"

He sighs. "I don't want the dancers feeling overwhelmed by me." There's a pause. "I don't know how to explain it. I just . . . I'm afraid they'll think I'm trying to own them. I want to help these women get away from this lifestyle. The last thing I'm trying to do is exploit them."

"But, you're . . ." I let my voice drift off as I see him frown.

"Yes, I'm exploiting them because I own and operate the strip club where they work." I hear the tightness in his voice and I'm sure I've offended him. "I know exactly what it looks like. I feel conflicted about it every day." His finger drags up the outside of his wineglass to catch a drop of wine. "I made most of my money before I ever opened a club. Penny's earns a lot, but I don't take the cuts other owners would. The dancers tip out the bartenders and bouncers, but I don't take anything. They keep everything else that they earn. I also spend a lot of time and money trying to help where I can. Counseling, tutoring, whatever they need." A dark, serious gaze settles on him. "If they're going to choose this life, I can't stop them. But I can give them a safe place while they're in it, until they can decide to get out of it."

"That's very . . ." My voice drifts as I search for the right word, ". . . noble."

"It's more like compensating," he says quietly, taking another small sip as he holds my gaze carefully, as if he can see me processing his vague words.

Compensating for things he has done in his past? So Cain isn't perfect. I wonder what he's done that's so bad. I wonder if it's as bad as what I've done. What if it's worse? Would I forgive him if I found out he was a rapist or a murderer? Is that worse than trafficking deadly drugs, ruining lives?

Is it the same?

Who decides?

Resting his elbows on the table and leaning in closer to me, he asks quietly, "Do you want to talk about what happened between us and what it means?"

I hadn't expected him to bring it up so abruptly and boldly. Stalling with a long, slow sip of my wine, I finally manage to get out, "Are you always so direct?"

That earns a sheepish smile. "I don't do small talk well." His finger trails around the rim of his glass. "It seems like a waste of time."

"It can be," I agree. In the case of Cain and me, this couldn't be more true. There is a clock ticking for us and it is going to stop.

Tomorrow.

Will it bother Cain when I leave? Will he be upset with me if I don't say goodbye? Should I tell him? Maybe I should let him know that I won't be around much longer, so he knows this can't turn into anything—

"Cain! What a pleasant surprise." The female voice next to our table catches me completely off guard and I let out an exhale, not realizing I had been holding my breath. I turn to find a tall redheaded woman with shiny pink lips and creamy skin standing next to us, her eyes locked on Cain.

His expression doesn't give anything away, but the four-second pause sure does. He's shocked to see this woman and, though I can't be sure, he may not be happy. "Larissa." Pushing his chair out, he stands to place a kiss on each cheek. "What are you doing in Miami?" He's completely polite, but I catch the slightest strain in his tone.

If I had to guess, I'd say the woman is in her early thirties. By her Manolos and her designer suit, she's got money. By the way she's smiling at Cain right now, she has good taste in men.

By the hardening in my stomach, I think she's had a taste of Cain.

She certainly doesn't look like a woman who has ever graced the stage of Penny's before.

Her manicured finger points toward a building across the water, on the other side of the bay. "My firm did the interior design for the new luxury hotel that opened this weekend. I needed to show my face. It was a big *thing* in the media."

Her firm. Yeah, she's got money, all right.

"I left you a voice message yesterday to let you know I'd be in town. Didn't you get it?" The way her head cocks to the side and her hand reaches out to graze his forearm, I no longer question whether she and Cain have had some sort of relationship. I know it.

And now I see the kind of woman that normally attracts Cain. Neither the real me nor the Charlie Rourke version of me plays in her league. It makes me wonder why I've gotten his attention at all. Is this still because I remind him of Penny?

Clearing his throat, Cain takes a step back from her and gestures to me. "Larissa, this is Charlie."

I have to consciously unclench my jaw as green eyes turn to dissect me, flittering over my hair, lingering on my dress and my shoes for too long. I, too, am wearing a pair of Manolos, along with a simple and sexy black strapless dress from a high-end New York designer—both gifts from Sam. There's nothing cheap about what I'm wearing.

And yet she sneers anyway.

"Charlie . . . cute." By the haughty look on her face, I know that "cute" means something entirely different and not at all pleasant. And by Cain's clenched jaw and the apology in his eyes, I can tell he sees it as well. "Is it short for anything?"

I wonder when he was with her last. I wonder when he'll be with her next. That thought fills my stomach with dread. But I won't show those thoughts.

"Nope. Just Charlie," I say, leaning back in my chair as if completely at ease, offering a smile of my own. A smug smile that says, "I'm having dinner with the man you want to be with and as far as you know, we're doing it like rabbits when we get home." And, if that's not clear enough, I turn to Cain and say sweetly, "I'm sorry, babe. I turned your phone off before bed last night. I didn't want us to be disturbed."

I'm not sure how he's going to take that, but the devil inside me doesn't care.

Cain clears his throat for a second time and sits down. He winks at me before taking a sip of his wine, that smile hiding behind it again.

But this woman either hasn't taken the hint or is too full of herself to accept it. "So how do you know each other?"

Cain's tongue darts over his top lip—a sign that he's annoyed. He's annoyed by her questioning. Or her, in general. Or both. "Charlie works for me."

Awesome. Now "Design Firm" Larissa can properly gaze down her nose at me.

"Really? You don't seem like the type to be in investment banking."

Her eyes are on Cain, so she can't see that my mouth drops open momentarily. *Investment banking? Is that what she thinks he does?* Apparently, I'm not the only one who leads an alternate life.

Cain is watching me like a hawk now. He must be wondering if I'll play along. "I guess looks can be deceiving. And I assist Cain with the office work."

"Assist?" An amused smirk touches her lips, her eyes drifting over my frame again but in a different way now. An inquisitive way.

In my peripheral vision, I see Cain's lips curl in as he inhales sharply and I wonder what that's about. Thankfully, the server comes with our meal, breaking up the awkwardness. "I'm here until Monday, Cain, so if you'd like to give me a call we can catch up. *My* assistant's in town, as well. I'm sure she'd *love* to see you." That's an inside joke with sexual undertones if I've ever heard one.

Forget Cain being annoyed. I'm damned annoyed now. She's taking up my precious time with him. Without even thinking,

I reach forward to clasp Cain's hand and lock eyes with him. To my pleasant surprise, Cain doesn't waste a moment, rolling my hand within his to drag his thumb down my palm, sending sparks through my body. "I imagine I'll be keeping him extremely busy until Monday and well beyond, *Larissa*. Now if you'll excuse us, we need to eat so we can get home."

There's a long pause. I dare cast a glance up to see Larissa's mouth twisted with displeasure. "Well, best of luck to you." She holds her head high as she walks away at a brisk pace. When she disappears around the corner, I make a move to slide my hand out of Cain's but he traps it within his for a moment, studying it, before finally letting go.

"Sorry if I was being presumptuous, but she got under my nerves and I could tell you were annoyed. I figured pretending we were dating was the best way to get rid of her."

His brow spikes with curiosity. "How did you know I was annoyed?"

I hesitate for a moment, stabbing a chunk of steak from my salad. Should I tell him? Will he think I'm crazy? His expectant eyes on me make me finally cave. I gesture at his mouth with my free hand and explain, "You lick your top lip when you're annoyed."

"Have you been investigating me?" he asks playfully.

"Maybe," I admit, hoping he doesn't notice my ears reddening. "On my own, though. No hired help." A sheepish look flashes over his features, and I have to giggle. "I have a thing for body language and facial expressions. I used to do a lot of theater, and people-watching is a good way to learn how to play different roles."

"Drama . . . *hmm*." Cutting into his steak, he casually asks, "What else do I do?"

"Not much, to be honest. You're pretty guarded." Stabbing the air with my fork, I gesture toward his neck. "You rub your neck over that tattoo when you're anxious."

Cain nods. After a moment, "What else?"

"You clear your voice when you're uncomfortable."

"What else?"

"You ball your fists when you're really mad. I saw you do it that day at my old apartment." *And last night, with Bob.* "Sometimes I see you do it when Ben's around."

That earns a loud burst of laughter. "I know I do that. It's an old habit from my fighting days."

A little bread crumb, a little trace of info into the history of Cain. I greedily latch on. "Fighting . . . like boxing?"

He gives an almost imperceptible shake. "Fighting like the kind that you don't ever talk about. The kind that makes you a lot of money."

My eyes roam his face, as perfect as it is, and settle on the small scar above his left brow. And I wonder what kind of damage has been done to that beautiful body of his. "Were you ever badly hurt?"

"A few broken ribs, bruised knuckles, some cuts. That's all. So . . . no."

I glance down at his hands, which iced my cheek just twenty-four hours ago. Now I wonder what kind of damage they've also done. "Did *you* ever hurt anyone badly?"

Dark eyes lock on me as he admits, "Yes, I have, Charlie. *Very* badly. One of them never got up."

I'm not sure what reaction he's expecting from me, but that won't make me shy away. "Is that where you made this money you're talking about?"

"Who's being direct now?" By his tone, he doesn't seem annoyed. "Yes. I made most of my money fighting."

I clear my throat, deciding to steer the conversation in another direction. "How do you know Larissa?" Even her name makes my chest burn with jealousy. A startled look flashes across his face and I shrug. "You said you don't do small talk."

"I *got to know* Larissa during her last business trip to Miami and had no plans to connect with her again. Ever." He curls his lip in that playful way as he pushes my plate slightly, a reminder that I need to keep eating. "You saved me."

"I hardly think you were *in danger* with her."

His left brow arches drastically. "No, trust me. I was. That one is . . ." He shakes his head. When he catches me watching him—all kinds of awful lewd images flying through my thoughts, trying as I can to keep a straight face—his forehead furrows deeply. I think I see a hint of blush under that stubble but I can't be sure. "I'm sorry."

"Don't be." I pause and then dare add in a mock-sultry voice, "Mr. Investment Banker."

Cain's face brightens with a chuckle. "Women don't typically understand my choice in profession, so I'm not open about it."

He said *women*. Plural. *Dammit*. I was hoping she was it. "No, I suppose they wouldn't." I didn't understand his choice of profession, either. I still don't. He's so much different from any other club owner—and anyone else I've ever met. He almost doesn't seem real.

A morose look flashes across his face. "None of them know much about me at all. But that doesn't seem to bother them."

I feel a twinge of sadness in my heart. Plenty of women are loved and paid attention to only for their enticing exterior. But what about men like Cain? I'm no better than Larissa. I have used him in the same regard, while on the stage. That face, that body; they are distracting enough to not see the man that may lie beneath.

Ironically, I'm beginning to think that what is beneath that outer surface may be even more beautiful.

"Maybe you're dating the wrong type of woman," I say softly, my eyes holding his gaze.

"I don't date, Charlie. I've never done this. I told you that, yesterday."

"You also don't watch your dancers strip, right?"

I hear the light scratching sound of his hand rubbing over that stubble as he covers his mouth, hiding a tiny smile as he watches me with eyes that are suddenly sparkling playfully. "Only one."

Heat floods through my body. I wonder if he knows that he can do that with just a look.

By the time the waiter comes to clear the plates, my meal is only half-eaten, but I've polished off two-thirds of the wine and I feel it tingle through my thighs. Or maybe it's Cain's continued gaze causing that.

I let Cain lead me—slowly, reluctantly—to his Navigator. Opening the passenger-side door for me like a gentleman, he hesitates. His hand finds its way to the small of my back and the simple touch steals my breath away, as aware as my body is of him right now. "Do you want me to take you back to your apartment, or Penny's, or . . ." He lets the question hang, as if giving me the chance to decide if this night is ending or not. I have no interest in saying good night—and goodbye—to Cain yet. I know exactly what I want. By the way he's staring at my mouth, I think Cain does, too.

Swallowing against the explosion of excitement inside me, I settle a firm, unguarded gaze on him and slowly nod my head.

chapter twenty-three

■ ■ ■

CAIN

I keep my arm coiled around Charlie's taut waist as we pick our steps along the old pier. I could argue that I'm holding her so closely because it's dark, she's a bit tipsy, and the planks are uneven. But the full moon casts a healthy glow overhead, Charlie seems to have sobered up, and the planks are perfectly fine.

I was so close to driving us back to my condo.

So. Very. Close.

My uncomfortable erection reminds me of what I could be doing now, had I made a left turn instead of going straight.

But I can't. Not yet.

Not if I want to do this right. And dammit, I want to do something right. Driving Charlie home tonight so I can fuck her until the sun rises—when she knows nothing about the man I am—does not feel right. That's the kind of thing I do with Vicki and Rebecka. I won't treat Charlie like those other women.

I want more.

"So security just *let* us on here?" Her arm waves out around us, her heels dangling from her fingers.

"Sure. I'm a member here." The security guards at this private club all know me. I toss them money to look the other way when

I come out to the pier in the middle of the night. I've been doing it for years. It's my secret sanctuary. It's the only reason I joined in the first place.

I've never brought someone with me, though. I've never wanted to. And tonight, I tossed them extra to keep anyone, including themselves, off the pier.

When the server came to collect our plates tonight, I panicked. I wasn't ready to let Charlie go yet. I was enjoying myself too much. And that's despite Larissa showing up. Of all people to run into . . . *Fuck!* Thank God that woman had the decency *not* to bring up the explicit details of our time together. That weekend began with an innocent drink by the bar at the same restaurant we were at tonight and ended with Larissa, her very attractive twenty-three-year-old female assistant, and a bag full of toys.

That woman is into some weird shit.

I went along with it, but the guilt ate away at me later and I promised myself that I'd never hook up with her again. Larissa is a female version of what I hate, taking advantage of her power. Yes, she's beautiful and charming but she can be a coiled viper, like tonight, with Charlie. For a second there, I was sure she was going to proposition us for a foursome.

Something tells me Charlie has no interest in sharing me.

I grin, thinking about the smug smile touching Charlie's beautiful, full lips as she reached across the table and claimed me. It may all have been for show, but in that moment, there was nothing I wanted more than to be hers.

Tonight, the way she handled Larissa with class and grace and an edge of bitch was beautiful. Unexpected.

It made me rock hard.

Which is why I had to take her somewhere other than my home. Even now, I can't help but take note of how quiet and private this pier is. How dark it is. How easy it would be for me to get under that dress, something I've been fantasizing about doing for weeks.

We walk in silence, Charlie pressing further into me until we reach the park bench at the end of the pier.

"Do you come here a lot?"

"Every Sunday night, after Penny's closes. Always alone . . ." I guide her to the bench at the end and sit down next to her, stretching my arm out along the back to get as close to her as possible without pulling her onto my lap. Waves of her creamy floral perfume keep hitting me, making me inhale deeply.

"It's really pretty out here," she murmurs, tipping her head back to rest on my arm, her lips curled into a peaceful smile. "Serene." The moonlight shines over that pretty white neck of hers, exposed, and I find myself leaning in, fighting the urge to trail my tongue along it, all the way down along the full length of her body.

"Thank you for the flowers," she offers suddenly, adding more softly, "I never thanked you earlier. They're beautiful. The color is stunning."

I guide her face toward me with a finger at her chin. "Brown eyes are pretty, but violet eyes . . . I can't stop thinking about them." It's true. I haven't. I've been dying to see them again, since the day I hired her. "Why do you hide them?"

She pulls in her bottom lip, no doubt deciding whether she's going to tell me the truth or not. With a sigh, she says, "Because I need to be forgettable." The pain in her tone is unmistakable and it tightens my chest. Is this because of that douchebag Ronald? Or another guy like him?

I can't think about that guy right now. It'll make my fists curl, and Charlie will notice. I drove by his apartment building earlier tonight and almost stopped. Almost.

But I didn't. By the mediocre building, I'm guessing he wasn't showering her with money and gifts in exchange for sex at any point. I don't want to cause her more trouble and until I know what's going on, stalking the guy might not go over well. "You're a lot of things, Charlie Rourke, but forgettable is not one of them, violet irises or not."

When she opens her eyes again, there's a sad smile touching her lips. "Why do you come out here to think?"

Bittersweet nostalgia washes over me. "It reminds me of my childhood, back in L.A. My grandmother used to take my sister and me to the pier on Sunday afternoons when we were young." Despite raising the despicable man my father turned out to be, I remember my nan being a kind, soft-spoken lady who hugged us a lot. I think she did the best she could as a single parent, holding down two waitressing jobs to provide for them. I never met my grandfather. He went to jail for armed robbery years before I was born, where he eventually died of a heart attack. From the few comments that my dad made about his temper and how he "taught" my dad to fight, the apple didn't fall far from the tree.

On those afternoons, she'd treat my sister and me to hot dogs and an ice-cream cone each. We'd sit side-by-side on a bench much like this one while we ate, my sister's feet not even touching the ground, she was so young. I don't know that my nan could afford to treat us every week. But when I was young, I didn't think about things like that; I just took what was given to me. I don't remember ever saying thank you to her. To this day, I don't know if she ever knew how much I looked forward to those afternoons.

I wish I had told her when I had the chance.

"I don't remember my grandparents," Charlie says softly. "My mom said they used to care for me when I was really small. My mom had me when she was fifteen, so they helped while she was finishing high school. In my head, I see this older woman with blond hair and a red-checkered apron, standing on a big white porch, waving at me." She frowns. "But I'm not sure if it was real or not." Leaning in toward my body, her head nests itself in the crook of my arm. "What's your sister's name?"

"Lizzy." The painful lump that used to come with uttering that name has long since vanished, leaving only faint bitterness.

"Lizzy," Charlie repeats in a whisper. There's a pause, a slight hesitation, and then she confesses, "I would have had a brother, but he died during childbirth. My mom was going to name him Harrison. She said she always wanted a son named Harrison."

Wrapping my fingers around a strand of her hair, I start playing with it, marveling at its silkiness. "Harrison and Charlie?"

Her chest rises with a sharp inhale. "Where is your sister now?"

I pause to watch a ship sail by in the distance as I decide just how much I want to share with Charlie tonight. So far, she hasn't seemed at all put off by what she's learned. I can't help but want to just off-load everything and find out quickly whether she's going to reject me. Other than Penny, Storm, and Nate—and John, of course, who was the first officer at the scene *that* night ten years ago—I've never talked to anyone about my past. And no one but Nate knows the entire story. But do I really want to air all my shit in one night? I could end tonight's conversation very quickly by leaning in and kissing her. That would end all talking. I'm sure of it.

I feel Charlie's questioning eyes on my face and that's all it takes for me to relent. "She died ten years ago, with my parents, in a drug-related murder. The cops were never able to nail anyone for it."

Charlie's body tenses up next to me and that makes me hold my breath. Is this the part where she starts wondering if she really wants to get involved with a guy like me?

"What do you remember about your sister?"

Air hisses through my teeth. I'd expected her to ask how they were involved with drugs, if they were guilty. If I miss them. This is one question I didn't anticipate, and it somehow feels all the more invasive.

Charlie's hand loops around mine and settles in my lap. She pulls it to her, letting it rest halfway up her thigh, just below where her dress ends. Having my hand against her soft bare skin is definitely distracting.

My hard swallow fills the air. "At sixteen, Lizzy had a chip on her shoulder and an attitude that made you want to throttle her. She'd already been expelled from two schools, and suspended for fighting from another. She was into drinking and smoking pot. Older guys . . ." I shake my head.

Charlie's manicured thumbs work small circles around the back of my knuckles as she asks, "Did you get along?"

"Honestly . . . I couldn't stand her." It's painful even now to admit that, but it's the truth. "She wasn't the kid I grew up with. She changed. About three months before she died, I found out she was working for some douchebag strip club owner, giving blow jobs and God knows what else. She was working under the table and using the ID of a twenty-six-year-old Latina girl named Blanca who looked nothing like her. She was sixteen! The owner didn't care."

Exhaling heavily as if that act will release the guilt that still lingers ten years later, I continue. "And neither did I. Not enough." With trepidation, I glance down at that doll face and find . . . I don't know what that look is. It's unreadable. Not judgment, not disgust. None of the things I saw in Penny's eyes when I admitted this same thing.

It spurs me on. "I wasn't much better than her, believe me. I moved out when I was seventeen and spent a year crashing on friends' couches. I barely graduated high school. Then I started getting into the bigger fights. Making real money. Enough for my own car and an apartment. I let Lizzy come to live with me for a few months, but then I found out about the club and I kicked her out. She moved back in with our parents. I did nothing about the fact that she was selling herself. All because I couldn't see past the tough, bitchy exterior to the girl who was still somewhere in there, needing *someone* to watch out for her. I doubt she was so tough when they . . ." My teeth crack against the clench. "I'm sure she was more like the little girl I knew growing up, those last few moments of her life." At least, she always is in my nightmares, when the brutal and explicit details from the police reports come alive and I hear her screaming for me, for my help. For me to return the money that I'd stolen in the first place.

"And your parents? Did they know what was going on?"

Bitterness slithers through my body and, try as I might, I can't help but feel the tension coiling tighter. "My dad dealt coke and pot. My mother . . ." I heave a defeated sigh. ". . . dealt sex. They were scum. If they knew what Lizzy was doing, they didn't care. Fuck, for all I know, my mother was somehow getting a cut. Lizzy had no one to protect her from them."

Charlie's body turns rigid against me, reminding me of what she's probably had to deal with in her own life. Curling the arm stretched out along the back of the bench around her small frame, I pull her close to me.

The warm night air hangs silently around us as I wait for Charlie to say something. To tell me that it wasn't my fault, that I couldn't have known what would happen, that I shouldn't let the guilt eat me up. All the standard things I've heard from Storm and Nate, that don't ease my guilt. But she doesn't say any of that. Instead, she lifts my hand up to her mouth to kiss it softly before bringing it back down to her lap, where her dress has climbed up even higher.

"It sounds like she's not the only one who needed someone for protection."

I don't argue with her.

There's a pause and then she asks, "So, how did you end up in Miami?"

"After Lizzy was killed, I lost myself in guilt for a while. I . . ." My mind drifts back to those months after, when I was fighting more than I wasn't, and each fight was an all-or-nothing stakes, where I laid down every last dime to my name. It was high risk, high reward, and if I lost, I would lose everything. But I couldn't be beaten, because all of my opponents had the same face—mine. The brother who turned his back on his little sister. Not the sister who cussed and sneered and dropped to her knees for fifty bucks.

The little girl with hazel eyes, who sat quietly on that pier bench, eating her ice cream, gazing up at the brother who was supposed to always protect her. Lizzy became that little girl in my mind again. And it was that little girl who lay broken on the dirty, bloodstained shag rug in my parents' living room.

I pounded the shit out of myself for months.

Swallowing to keep the hoarseness from my voice, I continue. "I made a lot of money fighting. *A lot* of money." The hand I have curled around her shoulders flexes automatically, as it always does when I think of all those fights—all those ribs I cracked, noses I broke, guys I beat senseless. The guy I unintentionally killed the same night my family died. "Eventually, I got tired of it. I knew it wasn't going to make me feel better. So I decided to do something more . . . positive. I can't turn back time, but I thought if I could help other girls like Lizzy, maybe I'd feel like I'd be paying for my part. There's always going to be a girl who thinks she has no other choice and there are always going to be dirtbags like Rick Cassidy, who feed off their desperation and turn them into drug addicts and whores. I figured I could do something productive with my money, like open my own club. I needed to get away from South Central, though. I needed a change."

Charlie turns toward me, until I can feel her breath against my neck. As serious as the moment is, my blood instinctively flows downward. I don't know how much longer I can be a decent human being with my hand resting on her thigh like that and the swirl of raw emotion hammering in my chest.

"But why Miami?"

"Miami is known for its open-minded laws in the adult entertainment district. A lot of cities out there restrict nudity, or alcohol with nudity, or the types of dances you can get. Not Miami, though. In Miami, you can have a burger in one hand, a beer in the other, and a completely naked woman in front of you. I figured a city like this—with such liberal laws—would breed a lot of Lizzys. It needed at least one club owner who was looking out for the girls. Someone to balance out the worst of them.

"So, I opened up a small club called The Bank. It wasn't anything flashy or huge. I was just learning about the industry. Hell, I was too young to be opening up a club to begin with. But it did well because I put no restrictions on the girls, as much as I hated it. I still do. I let the girls do anything that is legal but nothing more, and I make sure they're safe." Damn, was there ever a painfully steep learning curve over those first few months of owning The Bank! Luckily, I'm a fast learner and I had a great source of information—a Vegas strip club owner. In exchange for one arranged fight—which I won and he made a boatload of money from—he let me essentially live in his club for a month, learning the ropes. He wanted to partner up with me when I left for Miami but I declined. Instead, John fronted the business as the owner, on paper, until I turned twenty-one. I knew I could trust him.

"So I try to do right by my employees, at least. Like I didn't do right by my little sister."

"So this is all about a second chance?"

"No. It's about trying to balance out the good with the bad. I don't believe in second chances, Charlie."

There's a long moment of silence and then she asks, "China reminds you of your sister, doesn't she?"

I nod slowly. "I get so much grief for keeping her around." With a sidelong glance, I admit with what I'd imagine is a sheepish smile, "I know she probably hasn't been great with you."

"That's an understatement." Charlie chuckles.

It's probably time I let her relax and stop slamming her with my shit. I know I can be intense. In one night, she has learned that I was bred and raised by criminals, that I'm no stranger to brutal violence, that I lie to women and then fuck them, and that I was the world's shittiest brother.

And she's curled up against me like she still wants to be here.

I can save the worst of it for another day.

She stands and walks over to lean against the railing of the pier, barefoot. If not for the full moon, I likely wouldn't be able to see much of her but thanks to it, I can enjoy the view of her silhouette with the ocean in the background. There's a breeze, just enough to send a few strands of her hair into disarray and the material of her short skirt swirling.

I miss her warmth next to me already. "Have you had enough of me tonight yet?" I murmur, and I hear the gloom in my voice. It's after three and I don't want to leave, but I noticed the dark circles under her eyes. I imagine she didn't get much sleep last night. Ginger told me she came home a few hours after the incident with her assailant with a tear-streaked face.

Turning slowly to face me, Charlie says, "I know you're telling me all of this to scare me away. But it won't work. Nothing you've told me so far makes me think badly of you."

An unexpected wave of relief crashes into me with her admission.

I watch her brow knit together as she hesitates, as if she's deciding whether she should say something. "What if . . ." Again, she pauses and I see her jaw tense. She suddenly looks away, blinking repeatedly. Are those unshed tears I see?

"Charlie?" Worry begins to bubble inside, all thoughts of getting under her clothes gone. "You can tell me, Charlie. Anything. I won't judge you. God, if you've learned anything tonight, it's that I won't judge you." Ronald Sullivan's name is on the tip of my tongue. I want to ask her, *Who is he to you? What did he do? Do you want me to get rid of him?* But I keep my mouth shut. I don't want to pressure her and I sure as hell don't want to send her running from me like I did yesterday.

Just as quickly, whatever it was—the fear, the indecision—disappears. The intensity of her gaze now reminds me of Charlie onstage. The bold temptress. My mind is still reeling with worry, but now my body is back on high alert.

Unavoidably, my eyes drop down to those tits that I've seen bared on twenty-two wonderful occasions and I inhale sharply. Yes, I've kept track of her shows. What I haven't kept track of is the number of times I've jerked off to the visuals firmly emblazoned on my mind, afterward. Just the thought has me adjusting myself before I can help it.

And of course she catches me doing it.

She smiles. The coy smile that she gives me as she's peeling off her top for me at Penny's.

I believe that I won't *ever* be saying no to Charlie Rourke.

I swallow as my blood begins pounding through my veins, as my breathing turns ragged.

As a spiderweb of tingles skitters over my skin.

I can't believe it. I've never felt this. Not even with Penny.

I'm actually nervous to be with a woman.

chapter twenty-four

...

CHARLIE

Would Cain understand?

Would he see my situation for what it is—that I continue helping Sam in order to survive? To give myself a chance to break free? Or would he see me as weak?

I was so close. It was on the tip of my tongue. But I just couldn't form the words. I couldn't risk it. What would he do? After everything I've just heard tonight, I don't know. Perhaps he'd help me because he craves fixing things, or perhaps he'd walk away because it's too much of a reminder of his past.

He can't fix this, though. He can only put himself in danger by trying. No, Cain needs to remain in the dark. And I'm leaving tomorrow, so there's no point shattering this illusion of me he has created—the abused runaway, looking for a fresh start. Half of it is true, in any case. Or will be, tomorrow.

Tonight is all about accepting that fate has brought a man like Cain to me. I think I may have stumbled upon a saint. I don't deserve him. Cain is a good man, hardened by too many wrongs in his past. Not his own wrongs, though it's clear he feels he needs to shoulder much of the blame.

He is as much a victim as his sister, from the sound of it.

As much a victim as I am, I sometimes believe.

Cain has put all of that behind him, though, and is doing something about it. I'm still in the thick of the wrong, and all I'm striving to do is run away and pretend that it never happened.

"I haven't told you everything yet," Cain offers softly, as if he's reading my mind.

I pause, wondering what else there could be besides the enormous personal tragedy he's just shared. In truth, I don't think I want to know. "You've told me enough."

And I've told you nothing. Half-truths, that's all. It's true that there's a tiny tombstone next to my mother's that reads *Harrison Arnoni.* I left out the fact that my mother died along with him, and that his father is a drug dealer who now manipulates my every choice, every decision.

And that memory of the blond lady in the red-checkered apron? That's real. Of course, I left out the part about the screaming match between her and my mother, who dragged me out by the arm, suitcase in hand, only moments later. I remember words like *Christian* and *sinner* coming from the blond lady's mouth. I remember a greasy-haired guy waiting for us in the driveway in a blue El Camino that reeked of cigarettes. I remember waving goodbye to my grandmother for the last time. I remember the tears streaking down her face as she waved at me.

For someone that young, I remember an awful lot.

But I can't share any of that with Cain now, because it would give away too much about my real self. Charlie Rourke is simply a bundle of lies with a few half-truths to appease my own guilty conscience.

And now I'm eager to silence my conscience entirely.

"Cain?" I take another step forward until I'm standing between his splayed legs.

"Yeah?" He's sitting, relaxed, with one hand stretched out along the back of the bench and the other resting casually on his knee. The tension in his jaw tells me he's anything but relaxed, though.

I wonder if he has any clue what's coming. He must. I've been rubbing up against him like an animal in heat for the past hour.

It's now or never.

"Are you always such a gentleman?"

A smirk touches Cain's lips. "No . . . I'm not. And you're certainly not making it easy on me right now."

Swallowing the conflicting thrill and nerves inside me, I ask, "And how would I go about making it impossible on you?"

Lustful eyes stare back at me and I catch something flash in them that I can't describe. There's a long pause, and then his hands wrap around the backs of my thighs. With a forceful pull, he directs first one knee up onto the bench, followed by the other. Before I know what's happening, I'm straddling his lap with my hands loosely curled around his neck and my dress pooled around the top of my thighs. Cain's hands have found their place around my hips, and he pulls them forward until they're flush with his, until it's impossible to miss his arousal against me.

Another wave of heat pools between my legs. I've been hot there since the second I woke up on his office couch, but the intensity has reached new levels. I wouldn't be surprised if I soak right through his pants.

"Are you sure?" His eyes are locked on mine, his lips—only inches from mine—parted, his breathing ragged.

I let my eyes skate over the masculine lines of his face, and my fingertips graze the light stubble along his throat. I inhale that delicious, clean, woodsy scent that I will always relate to him. I want to memorize every single moment of this, because no one has ever made me feel the way Cain is making me feel right now.

That what *I* want truly matters.

And in this moment, I want nothing more than Cain. Intentionally shifting my pelvis even closer to him, until his hardness digs into me, I let my lips trail against that strong jawline—something I have fantasized about doing every single night for weeks now.

I hear the hiss of air a second before his fingers loop around the thin straps of my panties and he tugs at them. His erection is straining against me. Just as quickly, though, he lets go, and his hands force their way up my back—beneath my fitted dress—to press my chest into his. I feel his heart pounding against mine as he catches my bottom lip with his tongue, beckoning me forward.

I accept the invitation, closing my mouth over his greedily, feeling his wet tongue connect with mine in a possessive dance. My hands find his face and urge him closer to me, relishing the light manly stubble beneath my fingertips. As much as I want all of Cain, I could just as easily do this until the sun rises; I love the way his mouth moves against mine, the way he tastes, the small groans he makes.

But I only have tonight, I remind myself.

Without his lips leaving mine, his hands emerge from beneath my dress to pull the zipper down. The material falls. With the skill of an expert, he has my bra undone in a second, exposing my breasts to the cool night air.

And to him.

His fingers waste no time finding their way to my bare flesh, splayed to stroke me, rubbing both hardened nipples with the pads of his thumbs simultaneously. Shivers run through my body. "Do you have any idea how long I've thought about doing this?" he whispers into my mouth.

"Weeks?" I tease, but my heart is racing. I can't help but begin rocking against him, his confession building my own desire to desperate heights.

He breaks free of the kiss with a groan, his hands sliding down to grip my ass. Guiding me up onto my knees gives his mouth easier access to my nipples. He takes full advantage, pulling one into his mouth. I inhale sharply against the almost painful suction, but he quickly counters it with a soothing tongue.

My arms instinctively wrap around Cain's head, squeezing him closer to me as my fingers wind through his hair. It's always styled so perfectly that I expected it to be stiff with product. I'm delighted to find that it's silky smooth.

I press my body closer to him. I can't get close enough.

"Fuck, Charlie," he growls, his thumbs sliding under the straps of my panties to yank them down as far as they can possibly go, until I hear the first tears of the elastic in them from being stretched too far.

I'm not quite sure how Cain maneuvers so smoothly, but in seconds he has me on my back, lying along the seat of the bench, as he stands over me. It's not the most comfortable thing to lie on, but right now I *really* don't care.

With proficient skill, he effortlessly draws my panties all the way to my feet and, removing them, tosses them casually to the ground. Gripping my legs by the calves, he gently bends them and pushes them back, making room to prop himself up with one knee on the bench and a leg on the ground, facing me. His hands land on my knees and begin their descent down the inside of my thighs. Heat rises in my lower belly.

And then he pushes my thighs apart. *Wide* apart.

Suddenly, the fact that I've been taking my top off on a stage for several weeks means less than nothing. I'm lying completely exposed on a pier bench in the middle of the night, for a man that every straight woman lusts after—that *I* lust after—and the very thought has tension suddenly jetting through my body. I don't know what I expected, but it wasn't this. Not so quickly.

Cain wasn't kidding about not wasting time.

He shifts himself to hover over me, the muscles in his neck and shoulders straining beautifully as he holds himself up. "You're nervous," he accuses with a tiny, teasing grin before he leans in and lets his tongue dart out to catch my lip.

"No, I'm not," I lie, feeling my cheeks flush.

"You tensed up," he pushes, nipping my bottom lip playfully before laying a gentle kiss on my lips. "You sure you're okay with all this? We can stop."

It is rather sweet of him to be so in tune with my body and concerned about me, but I don't want to stop. In response, my fingers wind through his belt buckle, unfastening it and making quick work of his buttons and zipper, my hand diving beneath his briefs to grasp his cock faster than I think he expected me to.

A low groan escapes Cain's lips.

And I smile. Ben was *so very* wrong. There's nothing Hobbit-sized or malformed here. Cain is *perfect*.

"What's wrong—you sure you're okay with this?" I tease, stroking his length, feeling the drops of moisture at the tip. Drops for me. I pull my hand out and make a point of licking my thumb as I peer up at him from beneath heavy lashes. "Are *you* nervous?"

He chuckles. Though it's not unpleasant, there's a hint of wickedness in the sound that I haven't heard from him before. "Is this a new game of yours? Okay, Charlie, you know I like to play your games." Shifting out of my grasp, Cain's hands work my dress down to my ankles and off. "I was going to let you keep this on, but . . ." Standing, he folds my dress into a neat pile and tucks it under my head like a pillow. Then, he resumes his perch on one knee, admiring my body without reservation. I don't doubt that the moonlight overhead is providing ample light for his perusal. I refuse to cower under his scrutiny, though this is both the most erotic and the most embarrassing thing I've ever experienced. "Does Security ever walk down here?" I ask, unable to mask the apprehension in my voice.

His hands move to my thighs. He pushes my legs farther apart, lifting one up to rest on the back of the bench while he urges the other one down, to dangle off the edge. Despite my attempts to act nonchalant, I inhale sharply, my body beginning to ache, searching for some relief, both from him and this compromising position.

"They won't tonight. I've made sure of it. I wouldn't do this with you out here, otherwise." I trust that he wouldn't, which makes me relax, marginally. With the high, thick wooden rails around us and the small structure that serves as a barrier behind us, we are invisible to everyone.

Still . . .

I don't know many guys who could just sit there and study a naked woman spread out like I am, especially given that I've just confirmed that Cain is rock hard and dripping. But this is what I get for trying to tease a man with the self-control of a machine.

I lie there, watching him—fully dressed—stare at me with a low, intense burn within those brown eyes for what is probably only a minute but feels like an eternity. Finally, that curl that I love touches his lips. "I'm not afraid to admit that I'm a little nervous, Charlie." I gasp as I feel a single finger trail slowly down my center, my body tensing up. "Can *you* admit that? Or are you going to continue lying?"

Cain is nervous? Panty-dropping hot Cain, who has women literally throwing themselves at him, is nervous about being with me? "Yes, I am," I finally whisper.

"Good. I know when you're lying, Charlie, so you may as well just come out and tell me." I feel the guilt trying to claw its way back to the forefront of my every thought, my every word, with his warning. But then his fingers slide over me a second time, through the increasing slickness, and the guilt instantly retreats. "Do you know how stunning you are?" My breath catches as I feel the welcomed intrusion, his fingers moving in a slow, circular motion as he watches my body respond.

I close my eyes just as his touch vanishes and the heat of his breath skates over me. I let out a tiny cry as I feel his tongue against me, replacing the work of his hands.

It's like nothing I've ever experienced before. My fingers once again find their way to his silky hair as I feel him moan against me, as his hands grip my thighs, as I bite my lip to keep from screaming out. All the intensity of those nights—the daydreams, the dances *for* Cain—combined with the reality that he is here now, with me, have produced a storm inside me that's ready to erupt.

Arching my back against the pleasure of his tongue—delving and sliding with expertise and specific intentions—I feel a familiar buildup in my lower belly. It doesn't take long before Cain's arms tighten around my body to keep me still as he finishes me off, and I have to grit my teeth to keep from giving the security guards a play-by-play.

There's no tension, no modesty left in me when I'm done and Cain's lips move up to trail kisses along my belly, my breasts, my neck. When he reaches my mouth, he doesn't hesitate to lay a gentle kiss, even though I can taste myself on him.

I've never tasted that. I've had guys go down on me before, but it felt like required foreplay before sex; it wasn't done half as well, and never to orgasm.

I've never orgasmed with a guy. Period. Though I don't think it's all that surprising; I *am* only eighteen. I'm getting the impression that I could experience just about everything with Cain if I had more time.

Sliding a hand beneath my shoulders, Cain pulls me up and onto his lap again, his erection digging into me, making it abundantly clear what he wants. What I'm willing to give him. As he leans forward to pull his wallet from his back pocket, my mouth affixes itself to the side of his neck—to that sensitive spot where the tattoo is—and my eager fingers work the buttons of his shirt to reveal the sculpted body beneath it. I've been dying to touch it again since that day in my old apartment. Now, I marvel at how hot his skin is as I press my own bare chest up against it.

When I hear the tear of the foil packet, I decide to help him out by pulling him out of his briefs, my warm hands quickly wrapping around his length to begin stroking. "Easy, Charlie. I'm about to explode," he growls as he lifts me up on my knees again. As he quickly frees himself of his pants by tugging them down past his thighs, I eagerly wait while he slides a condom on.

The agile, forceful Cain returns, grabbing my hips and moving them into position over him. He doesn't ask if I'm sure anymore. He doesn't ask if I'm nervous. He simply locks eyes with me as he pushes himself inside me smoothly—stretching me, filling me completely. He's almost too much for me and I have to breathe through the pressure.

When he's buried deep inside me, he stops moving and pulls me to his mouth, catching my gasp with his lips, stealing my air, my thoughts, my everything.

And then we begin moving against each other.

It's a slow cadence at first, his hands gripping my hips to dictate the speed he wants. I'm fine with slow because I'm still sensitive, and having him inside me is just plain overwhelming.

It doesn't take long for my body to accept him, though, and when it does, our momentum quickly accelerates, his thrusts becoming harder, his kisses hungrier, his size inside me swelling even more.

I finally break away from his mouth and push his hands away from my hips, locking eyes with him as I offer him a teasing smile as I take control of the rhythm, my own strong leg muscles working for him. He leans back, his lips parted, watching my body move beneath hooded eyes. His hand finds its way back and I'm about to swat it again, until I realize it's not there to dictate my movements. It's there to make sure I'm getting full pleasure from this as well.

"Charlie . . ." I hear the name in his whisper, the desire in it, and I truly wish it were *my* name he was calling out. Reaching up with his free hand, he curls his fingers around the back of my neck. He tugs my tongue into his mouth in a demanding kiss, smothering a deep moan as I feel his body stiffen, as I feel him pulsing inside me.

I did that for Cain. *Me. I* turned him on that much. That realization tears a second orgasm out of me almost instantly and I can't help but cry out.

Not until his hips stop and his breathing slows to a heavy pant do our lips break free of each other. I curl my naked body—

coated with a thin sheen of sweat now—into his chest, with him still inside me. Large, strong arms wrap me and I feel his lips pressed against my forehead. He makes no move to pull out, seemingly content to stay right where he is.

I marvel at this new version of Cain I have discovered. He's not the hard, aggressive man that I've fantasized about. He's not the emotional Cain I experienced last night.

He's aggressive *and* emotional. He's the best of both worlds. A guy I will crave incessantly when I'm gone.

"I promise, next time will be in a comfortable bed, Charlie," I hear him murmur softly. I fight to keep my body from tensing at his words but I can't, and I'm sure he feels it. Letting my mouth fall open against his neck, I greedily accept that I want a next time. I want it desperately. I want it now.

It was probably a mistake to let this happen.

- - -

The beginnings of dawn light the sky as Cain walks me to my apartment door. He casually suggested going back to his condo but I declined, barely able to get the excuses past the stabbing lump in my throat.

I have a dentist's appointment.

I need to go grocery shopping.

I need to take my SUV in for service.

Lies. All lies.

He didn't push, though, and I don't know if it's because the suggestion was not meant to be serious or because he took my excuses as a refusal of him. Or because he truly can tell when I'm lying to him and it pisses him off.

The car ride home was unusually silent and, as exhausted as I am after not sleeping for two days, as sated as I am, I almost fell asleep. If not for that sickness churning inside me the moment I pulled my dress on at the pier, I might have.

As I slide my key into the lock and push the door open, I

sense Cain's body step closer to me and I'm afraid he's going to invite himself into my apartment. Afraid because I'll have to send him away. Afraid because I would so much rather hold him close.

"Charlie?"

I grit my teeth for just a moment before I pull on a mask. Or try to. My adrenaline has finally worn off, leaving an empty shell of a girl who has experienced too many crippling emotions in the past thirty-six hours—both the best and the worst. I can't even think straight. Thankfully, I'm too tired to cry; otherwise I'd be bawling my eyes out now.

I'm exactly where I was yesterday morning, only now the ache in my heart is all the more pronounced.

Finally, I turn around to face Cain, to soak in those warm brown eyes that peer down at me, his apprehension poorly veiled within them. "Thank you for tonight, Cain," I begin, but I choke. Composing myself with a swallow, I manage to get out, "Thank you . . . for everything." *Why can't I keep it together? Just for a little longer, dammit!*

A deep furrow skitters across his forehead, but he smooths it over. "My friend Storm is having a small get-together at her house this afternoon. Kind of a celebration for her fiancé, Dan." He holds his phone up absently. "Just got the text. Anyway . . ." His voice drifts off as his eyes drift down to my mouth. "You should come."

I give him a pathetic attempt at a smile. "Sure, I'll think about it." *I'll think about it as I'm boarding the bus.*

Something that looks like disappointment flashes in his eyes and I balk at the swift kick of guilt to my stomach. "Okay, Charlie." He leans down to brush his lips against my cheek, close to my mouth but not landing there, as if unsure that I would allow it.

I don't hesitate to turn toward him to steal one last kiss, to try to convey with my body how much he has come to mean to me in a short period of time, how much I wish this could continue.

How much I will miss him.

A powerful arm coils around my waist as he crushes me against his body, matching and raising my level of passion with his own as he dips me back, forcing my mouth wide as his tongue dives in.

Cain doesn't seem to have any speed except "intense." Combining that with my own personal turmoil is a disaster waiting to happen. I close my eyes and let myself sink within his strength as I lose myself in him yet again, as the familiar burn begins to course through my body.

At some point, my knees buckle and I find I can't lift my eyelids. I barely hear the door close as I become weightless within Cain's arms. The soft cushion of my mattress is like a cloud as Cain lays me down.

"Charlie, where are your sheets?" I hear him ask, but I don't answer.

They're packed in my suitcase, which is sitting idly in the corner.

Waiting for me.

A moment later there's a hand smoothing the hair off my forehead. "Get some sleep."

"Okay," I murmur with a sigh, though I'm still fighting against the sweet pull of oblivion that beckons me to relent. I'm supposed to be leaving in a few hours, but I do need sleep. Just a few hours and then I'll go. "Goodbye, Cain." I can't drive anywhere right now . . .

■ ■ ■

Someone is pounding on my door.

My body feels like it's chained to my bed as I drag it up, reluctant to leave the comfort of sleep, even from a bare mattress.

"Charlie! Open up!" It's Ginger and she sounds frantic. Worry blooming inside me, I stagger out to the front door in a rush, throwing it open without caution.

"You're alive!" she exclaims, stalking past me into my apartment. The ties of her colorful bathing-suit top poke out beneath a red-and-white-striped sundress. "It's the fourth time I've come by today. I thought you were dead! Go and get ready."

"What?" I scratch my head absently, picking through my blurry memories. *Get ready for what?*

"It's after three o'clock and we're going to Storm's."

After three o'clock? "What?" I don't believe her. Dashing over to dig my phone out of my purse, I confirm with a rising bubble of panic that she's not lying. *No . . . I need to get to the bank and then sell my car and then . . . leave Miami. I won't have enough time!*

Ginger makes herself comfortable on my couch, remote in hand, twirling a hot-pink strand of hair. And I know that, short of agreeing to go with her, it will take a fire or a forklift to get her to leave. Her eyes drift over the flowers adorning my table. "Those are gorgeous. Who are they from?"

"No one," I mutter absently as I stagger back to my bedroom and shut the door. Falling back against it with a sigh, I close my eyes. *What do I do?*

I know that if I could shake Ginger, I could still make it work. I'd just be arriving in a foreign state and town in the middle of the night. I check the burner phone sitting in my purse, a twinge of anxiety stirring that I could have missed a call from Sam.

No missed calls. I release a sigh.

What if . . . could I stay for another day? I mean, is there *really* any danger in staying for just *one* more day? I have weeks before I can expect another drop request and Bob couldn't even get into Penny's if he wanted to cause me harm before then. And Sam is . . . I have to believe he wouldn't harm me on a whim or a hunch, even as paranoid as he is. I'm too valuable to him. I'm his unsuspicious pawn.

He'd come down here first. He'd visit me in person, see for himself. I have to believe that. After all, he *did* raise me. That has to account for something.

My resolve dissipates in seconds, as if it were never there. Or maybe it was, up until last night. The swirling nausea in the pit of my stomach finally relents to a burst of anticipation. Throwing open my suitcase, I quickly root through my clothes for my bathing suit.

Suddenly, I can't get to Storm's fast enough.

chapter twenty-five

. . .

CAIN

"Hey, stranger!" Storm greets me at the door, wearing an apron and a beaming grin. "I'm glad you could make it on such short notice." After claiming a tight hug, she rubs my biceps affectionately. Storm touches me a lot. I don't welcome the contact from others, but from Storm, I don't mind. I know it's a completely platonic gesture and, from her—one of my very best friends—it actually relaxes me.

Surveying her apron—one that reads *Warning: Woman Grilling*—I pat my stomach and ask, "What's for dinner?" Feeding people is Storm's passion and she's an excellent cook. They've joked about installing a revolving door for all the people who pass in and out of their Miami beach house on a regular basis.

"Homemade burgers and lots of other stuff. Enough for a crowd, and there seems to be one quickly growing around here." There's a pause and then, "So tell me . . . Are you or aren't you with this alluring new dancer?"

"Thirty seconds in the door, Storm. And I don't remember you being a gossip," I toss back. Inside, my guts are twisting. I don't know what the hell happened this morning. After what I can only describe as the kind of mind-blowing sex that sated every fiber of my body and soul in a way that no other woman ever has, Charlie shut me out.

I expected her to gladly accompany me to my place, to my shower, to my bed.

To eagerly continue where we left off.

But the only thing she seemed eager to do was get away from me. She started stumbling over her words, offering weak excuses. Practically begging me to drive her home.

Confusing the hell out of me.

In fairness, she *was* so exhausted that she practically passed out in my arms and was out cold within a minute of me laying her onto her bed. I know because I sat beside her and watched her drift off, pushing her gorgeous blond hair off her face, worrying that I should wake her up to take those damn contacts out, searching for pricey bedsheets that I couldn't find.

Still, exhausted or not, something didn't feel right about the way we left things. Maybe everything I told her started sinking in and she freaked out. Maybe I should have taken her back to my condo instead of letting that happen on the pier. I couldn't help myself, though.

I lay in bed for hours, analyzing every second, every word that escaped her mouth. Every moan . . .

And I still can't make sense of it.

God, I hope I see her today.

Ginger promised that she'd do what she could to get Charlie here. Now I guess I'll just have to wait. And dodge Storm's interrogation.

"I'm not. I'm a hopeless romantic. There's a big difference." She smiles, showing me her perfect white teeth. "And when it comes to the mysterious Cain's love life, yes, your friends are all *extremely* interested. I swear, Ben is infatuated. I don't remember him talking about one girl so much in my life!"

I hand her a gift bag with several bottles of wine, attempting to distract her as bare feet pad out from the kitchen. "Cain!"

Storm's mini-me barrels into me, her little arms coiling around my waist.

"Mia!" I chuckle to myself as I take a chunk of her golden-blond hair in my hand and give it a playful tug. She stares up at me with those innocent blue eyes, the same ones that pierced my heart the day she looked up and smiled as she toddled around the furniture in my office, enjoying her newfound mobility.

"All right, all right. We'll talk later . . ." Storm takes the wine with a secretive grin. "The guys are in the cave." Slipping her arm around Mia's shoulders, she gently swivels her daughter around and leads her back toward the kitchen. "Come, minion. Those vegetables won't wash themselves."

I head down the hall of their palatial Miami beachfront house. Storm moved in here three years ago with Dan, Mia, and their friends—sisters, Kacey and Livie. That was around the same time that Storm quit Penny's and opened up her own private acrobatics school. The day she came into my office to tell me—her fingers twisting the material of her skirt nervously, as if she wasn't sure how I'd take the resignation of the most popular dancer at Penny's—was the happiest day of my life.

Storm is my shining success story. She is why I do what I do.

Ben's obnoxious voice carries halfway down the hall. ". . . she was gone when I woke up, though, which sucked because *damn*, she had the most spectacular—"

"Cock?" I interrupt loudly as I step into the room, slapping Ben's shoulder as I pass by him. I'm not surprised to find the lot of them with beers in hand, playing video games. It's how I usually find them, while the women are hanging out on one of the many decks or in another room. Though Storm calls this room Dan's *cave*, there's nothing remotely cave-like about it. Light pours in through the wall-to-ceiling windows and, aside from the tan leather sectional and chestnut-brown cabinetry, everything's decorated in whites and grays.

"Boss man's here!" Ben yells as the guys burst out in a round of laughter over my well-timed interruption. "Just giving them the Mexico highlights."

"Embellished, I'm sure," I murmur, though I don't really doubt that every bit of what Ben says is true and happened exactly as described. Sometimes I wonder how his dick hasn't fallen off yet.

Dan rounds the couch with his large hand outstretched, a genuine smile stretched across his face. "Good to see you here, Cain."

"Congratulations, again. How's the head after last night?"

He cringes but then laughs. "Those guys are animals. Sorry I didn't get a chance to talk to you. It's been a while."

"I know. Crazy summer . . . Storm's doing well with the pregnancy so far?"

That light sparks in Dan's eyes, the one that always does at the mention of Storm. Now that she's marrying him and carrying his child, it's like a homing beacon. "Yeah, doing well. Should find out what it is soon."

"Girl," Trent—Kacey's boyfriend and a permanent fixture in the Ryder household—announces with a smirk, adding in a "hey, Cain," though his focus doesn't leave the intense one-on-one boxing round with Nate.

"Trent." I like Trent. I didn't like him so much when I found out who he really was, when everything about my bartender and Storm's best friend—Kacey—came to an ugly, explosive head. To this day, I thank God I didn't feel the need to have a background check done on him. If I had, I would have kicked his ass out of my bar.

And probably beaten him to within an inch of his life.

Dan casually leans over to flick Trent's ear for that comment before shaking his head. "God help me if it's another girl. I'm drowning in estrogen."

"Get a dog," Nate suggests, followed by a deep shout of "Yeah!" as Trent's player hits the ground in an exaggerated knockout screen shot.

"Why?" Ben snorts. "Storm will just have his balls cut off for humping everything in sight. Then, you'll *still* be surrounded by estrogen, plus you'll be stuck picking up a four-legged eunuch's shit twice a day for the next ten years."

Dan shoots a crooked grin his way. "Maybe not. Storm hasn't had *you* fixed for humping everything in sight yet, mate."

Another round of snorts and chuckles fills the room and I'm reminded of how much I've missed hanging out with the guys outside of Penny's. I've just let myself get too wrapped up with all things club-related lately.

I need to get a life. Ideally, one that includes Charlie.

"A drink?" Dan offers, already reaching for the bottle of Rémy that he knows I prefer. Normally, I'd never accept any of my friends catering to my expensive taste, but Dan and Storm can easily afford it and Storm won't have it any other way.

"How's the club doing these days?" Dan asks as he hands me a filled glass. "Ben told me about the metal detectors. You've got more scum coming in, now that Teasers is closed?"

"Yeah . . . It's an investment, but it's worth it." I take a sip of my drink.

He nods his head slowly, a curious look passing over his face, and I wonder where this conversation is headed this time. Conversations with Dan about the club tend to head in one general direction.

His voice lowers to say, "Starting to hear rumblings of someone new in Miami. From up north, bringing in pure street-grade heroin. Not one of these idiot gangbangers who we can usually take down in a few weeks. An organized operation. This could be big. They expect it'll lead to a turf war with the cartel." Dan studies me closely with his next question. "You haven't seen or heard anything?"

This isn't the first time we've had *this* conversation. I'm not the only one who had a background check done. After Storm quit Penny's, she admitted to me that Detective Dan had made inquiries and pulled some favors, suspicious of me. It didn't take him long to dig up my past. I may have—miraculously—avoided a criminal record for my own crimes, but I'm still tied to an ugly paper trail as it relates to my parents.

I was only involved in the drug and prostitution scene by relation. I guess good ol' Daddy didn't think mixing me up with that side of the family business was a smart move, when he could make so much money off my fighting. Dan's not stupid, though. He's seen his share of that world. He knows it's not built in silos— separating the dealers from the pimps from the thieves from the murderers. He knows that I've made all kinds of connections, whether I meant to or not. Hell, I still get approached by bookies once in a while for a big-ticket fight. Ten years later, all the way in Miami! And then there's the fact that I'm in the business that I'm in, where I'm constantly approached with illicit propositions.

Dan knows I could find out, *if* I wanted to get involved. *If* I wanted to risk being labeled a police informant, basically painting a target on my chest and putting everyone around me at risk.

"I haven't heard a thing, Dan. And you know those scumbags are not coming anywhere near Penny's. That's why I have the security that I do. That's why I'm selective with who I hire."

Dan nods his head once. "I know, Cain. But I told the guys I'd ask, anyway." With a heavy exhale, he quickly changes the topic, his tone lightening up. "So, tell me about this new dancer at Penny's."

"The one that's got Cain choking the chicken in his office every night?" Ben hollers, while furiously clicking keys to pummel Nate's player in the face. "Uh-oh. Look! He's pitching a tent already."

"Fuck off, Morris," I throw back with an annoyed chuckle. "I'm not . . ." I close my eyes and heave a sigh. There's no point defending myself. We're not at Penny's. That means the gloves are off and the jackass is just getting warmed up. Thank God he doesn't know about last night.

"That's how it's done!" Ben shouts, tossing the controller at

Nate's broad chest. "I mean, seriously, Cain . . ." Ben now turns to give me his undivided attention, shaking his head. "Such a travesty. You don't deserve to own a club. Fuck, you don't deserve to own a dick!"

I know Ben's just shooting his mouth off for entertainment purposes. We've had more than a few frank drunken-Ben conversations in the past, where he expressed his undying admiration for me for not taking advantage of my position.

Still, I toss a glare at Dan, who can't keep the smirk off his face. "Thanks, man, for bringing her up."

Dan lifts his hands in mock surrender. "Just surprised to hear the man of steel is finally hung up on a woman like the rest of us poor suckers, that's all."

"I'm not hung up."

The coughs and poorly muffled laughter from the couch area confirm that no one is buying that. Hell, *I'm* not even buying it. After last night, my thoughts are more firmly hot-wired to Charlie than they were before. Hell, she knows most of my personal shit! For ten years, I've kept everything closed in. One night with her and I'm spilling my guts like a prisoner in a torture room. Only I wasn't tortured. *Far* from it.

"Charlie might give you a shot, you know. If you'd stop your nightly jerk-off sessions already and ask her to yank your—" Ben's voice cuts off abruptly, his eyes riveted on something behind me. Dan and I turn in unison to find the subject of his crass banter standing at the entrance in a blue bikini, a veggie platter in her hands.

Ben's right. I *am* pitching a tent at the sight of that body. It's only that much more desirable, now that I've been inside it.

Now that I'm desperate to get inside it again.

But I'm ecstatic to just *see* her again. I must have a stupid-ass smile on my face right now.

Fuck it, I don't care.

I watch her stroll in, struggling to close my gaping jaw.

"Storm asked me to bring this to you guys," she explains, her bare feet soundless against the hardwood. *Of course, Storm did. Because I'm here.*

For a girl who had to have overheard Ben's crassness, given how damn loud he is, she's taking it rather well. No flushed cheeks, no mortified stare, nothing. I, on the other hand, grip the back of my neck to keep from lunging over the couch to pummel Ben.

"Hey, Charlie." Ben's big, dumb grin is in full force now. The guy's so smooth around women, he probably doesn't feel the slightest bit awkward. "When did you get here?" He certainly doesn't feel awkward about checking out her chest.

"Just now. With Ginger." Leaning forward, she offers her hand to Trent. "Hi, I'm Charlie."

There's a two-second delay in Trent's response, where he simply stares at her face before he calmly lays down the game stick and his beer, and reaches forward to accept her hand with that damn smile that all the girls at the club *still* chatter about every time he shows up there. "Trent. Hi."

The handshake lasts one, two, three seconds too long and I'm grinding my teeth, watching for any skin flushing or lip licking on her part. *Jeez . . .* I know Trent is head-over-heels in love with Kacey, so my jealousy is completely unfounded, and yet here I am, ready to pull them apart.

One night. Just one night with her and I'm done for.

"Hey, Nate." Charlie winks at the ominous teddy bear, who smiles at her before flashing a rare, wide, toothy grin my way. We connect every morning with a quick phone call or text. Today, he showed up at my door. He looked ready to beat the truth out of me by the time I finally confessed.

Rounding the couch, Charlie extends a hand to Dan. "I didn't get to officially meet you last night, what with my passing out and all."

"Charlie. I've heard so much about you." At least Dan has the decency not to stare at her.

"And who's been filling your head with lies about me?" she smoothly retorts, those beautiful wide lips of hers stretching into a grin.

"Cain never lies," Ben throws back with a smirk.

Her playful eyes flicker over to me, where they rest for several seconds—an amused light dancing within them.

I fight the urge to pull her in to me but I can't keep my gaze from dropping to those round tits and my mouth instantly parts, remembering the softness of them against my tongue. When I look back up, Charlie's eyes have darkened slightly.

"Good to know." With a wink and a firm, slow rub up and back down my arm, she turns to Dan and says, "Storm wanted me to tell you that she needs you at the grill. Tanner's out of control."

With a heavy sigh, Dan mutters, "Did he bring that spray gun again?"

"Yes." Charlie giggles. "And it's ridiculous."

Shaking his head, Dan smiles warmly down at her. "Okay, tell her I'll be there shortly."

With my glass to my mouth, my focus trails Charlie out the door, her hips swaying teasingly. She knows I'm watching. She must know.

"For what it's worth, I don't blame you, man. Wow." Dan's brow furrows. "A bit young, though . . ."

"Twenty-two."

He blows a mouthful of air out. "Well, if you were ever to give in to an employee, I wouldn't blame you for that one."

Too late. And I'm going to do anything I can to give in again. Tonight.

"Until then, do you want me to call Mercy to deal with your little *problem*?" Ben asks. "She's fantastic. And discreet."

I level Ben with a glare. "You'd better be fucking joking."

"Of course I'm joking! I haven't touched her . . . yet." His face splits into a wide grin.

"Good, because I'd seriously fire your ass."

"Well, then . . ." Ben slaps his hand on the coffee table. "Consider this my notice."

By the looks that exchange between me and the others, we're all wondering the same thing—is Ben serious?

He winks, then offers in a more somber tone, "I landed a full-time gig at a law firm in town. Just found out this morning."

"Seriously, Morris?" Nate presses.

"Yep." Ben's arms stretch out over his head, his hands nesting behind his neck as he sighs heavily.

I wasn't expecting to lose Ben so soon. "But don't you have another month before you get your bar exam results?"

He waves a dismissive hand. "Yeah, but I aced that. I'm not worried. They're not worried. I'll just be considered in a probationary period until I'm official."

My previous annoyance with Ben instantly vanishes. I close the distance as he accepts a congratulatory slap across the chest from Nate. I offer him my hand, which he takes firmly, a glimmer of satisfaction in those blue irises. "We're gonna miss you, buddy, but that's amazing. You've done well." He really has. After blowing his knee out and losing his shot as a star quarterback, Ben leveraged his brain—one most people wouldn't realize he had—to put himself through law school. Now, after years at Penny's, Ben is moving on.

The tactless brute bows his head, a rare, pensive look flashing over his face. I'll bet he hasn't bothered to mention it to his dad. The cranky old scrooge would somehow twist it into a failure. I think that's why Ben is such an easy, happy guy all the time. He's deathly afraid of ever being compared to his own father.

"Seriously, dude, don't go out there with that. It's embarrassing. I've got a picture of Charlie onstage that I can send to your phone, if you need it while you deal with your issue in the can."

The moment's over.

chapter twenty-six

. . .

CHARLIE

I shouldn't be here.

"Ahhh . . . this is the life," Ginger sighs, sinking back into her chair with a fresh margarita in hand. "If only we didn't have to work tonight."

I grunt in agreement, taking in the stunning stone patio area that overlooks an enormous, oddly shaped pool with several alcoves. The entire space is adorned with various tropical flowers. Sitting where we are, we're completely protected from the sun with a pergola and lattice.

"Thank God for the breeze," Ginger adds, and my eyes follow hers to the two oversized ceiling fans affixed to the beams above us, working overtime to circulate the hot summer air.

The sound of flames sputtering pulls my attention away to the far end, where Tanner—completing the "Cousin Eddie" look with a straw hat, black socks pulled halfway up his calves, and sandals—is demonstrating to Dan why his use of the two-handed squirt gun on a grill should be marketed. Alternating between head shakes and low chuckles, Dan finally gets Tanner to surrender his weapon and leave the grilling to him.

To the newly appointed DEA agent.

I shouldn't be here.

But I didn't really have a choice, I tell myself. Ginger was hell-bent on bringing me. When she admitted with a smile that Cain was hell-bent on her bringing me too, any hope for an argument died on my lips.

When Storm directed me to take a tray of veggies to a room down the hall, I didn't expect to be walking into a group of men talking about me yanking on parts of Cain. Coming from Ben's mouth, it's not exactly shocking, but still. I'm not sure how I kept the blush from my face. I was sure my knees would buckle for a moment when they all stopped to stare at me.

By the look on Cain's face, he was both surprised and *very* pleased to see me. By his blatant ogling, I'm pretty sure he wants more of what he got last night. That thought makes my entire body hum with excitement.

"You okay? You've been quieter than usual today." I turn to find Ginger watching me intently.

"Yeah, fine. Just tired," I murmur through another yawn. I feel like I could sleep for days.

"Late night?"

"Yeah." I help myself to a carrot. Tired and hungry. I haven't eaten all day. My body is all kinds of messed up.

"Hmm . . . So, did you finally break that stoic horse and work him in good?"

"Ginger!" My wide eyes dart over to Tanner. He's within earshot, but his back is to us and he keeps it that way. Given that he's avoided all eye contact with me since my near-nude fiasco with the deliveryman yesterday, I'm not surprised.

Thankfully, Storm passes through the doorway at that precise moment, balancing two bowls against her belly, exclaiming loudly, "Chow time!" Cain trails behind her, his strong arms laden down with more food. I noticed earlier that he kept a bit of the scruff on his face, shaving everywhere except the area around his chin and mouth.

I really loved the feel of that soft scratch against my skin.

My heart automatically starts racing and I catch myself smiling, memories of last night hitting me deep in my belly. All other realities fade into the background and my problems somehow become less urgent, less serious. That's what being around Cain does for me. He's a mental shield against all that is bad in my life. Even stripping onstage turned into something I could sort of enjoy—in a twisted way—because of him.

"Cain! We were just talking about you," Ginger chirps, relishing any opportunity to tease her boss.

"I'll bet," he mutters dryly, disappearing behind me to place the platters down on a side table. A second later, I feel cool hands curl around my neck and his index fingers slowly trace along my collarbone.

He must feel the hard swallow in my throat as I try to calm myself. *What is he doing? Does he* want *everyone to know that we slept together last night?*

Or . . . are we a thing now?

"Sorry to be rude, but the spawn demands food," Storm murmurs, not waiting to load a plate for herself. "Ladies, help yourselves before those rabid men come out. They forget their manners sometimes." Cain makes a point of pulling my chair out as I stand, his hands giving my waist an affectionate squeeze as I pass by, sending a thrill through my stomach. Storm happens to glance over her shoulder at that precise moment to catch Cain's hand on me and a sly smile touches her lips. I'm happy to see it's not a venom-laced sneer, like the one I'd expect from China.

Still, I wonder if they ever slept together. I wonder if he'd tell me the truth, if I asked. I wonder if I even want to know the truth. The idea of Cain with another woman—or women—makes me grit my teeth.

I just make it back to the table with a plate of food when the processional of large men files through the door. Cain's hands once again find my bare skin, his thumb rubbing up and down my spine, giving a light tug at the string on my bikini top, as if ready to untie it, as he pushes my chair in all the way. If I focus intently enough, I can still feel him inside me. I really shouldn't think about that right now.

I didn't expect this. I didn't expect him to be so open about whatever is between us.

I didn't expect to want it so badly.

My heart skips a beat as he takes a seat next to me, instead of at the outdoor sectional couch where Nate's already making himself comfortable. Leaning in, his mouth grazes over my ear as he whispers, "Sorry, but after last night, I won't be able to keep my hands off of you." It sends a shiver through me. "I hope you're okay with that."

By the smirk touching his face, he damn well knows I am more than okay with it. By the glance down at my bikini top, no doubt noticing the two tiny protruding bumps, he can now see proof of it, too.

I sit quietly as he pours a glass of water for me. "Tell me if you want something stronger and I'll get it from the bar for you, okay?" I nod but say nothing. Cain doting on me hits me deep in the chest, in an emotional wave that's both soothing and crippling.

"You serving women today, Cain?" Ginger calls out with an impish grin as she slaps Ben's muscular ass and cuts in front of him to load her plate. "Or just the one you're trying to impress?"

"He can be a smooth fucker if he wants to—" Ben's mutter is cut off with a sharp elbow to his gut from Ginger and a bark of "language!" from Storm. Ben's eyes instantly flash to the eight-year-old quietly hanging onto our every word from her seat next to Nate. He winces an apology to Storm.

"Here. Keep quiet." As if to prevent anything more from coming out of Ben's mouth, Ginger shoves three carrot sticks into it. He grins lasciviously at her but doesn't utter another word, busy chomping down like a horse.

"So, Charlie . . . Ginger told me you were a gymnast?" Storm says.

I nod slowly, wondering what else Ginger and Storm have talked about that involves me.

"You should come by my acrobatics school. I'll be looking for a part-time coach soon, given . . ." A manicured index finger points toward her waist as she spoons some pasta salad into her mouth.

"Oh . . ." I feel my brow knit tightly. "I don't know the first thing about acrobatics."

She waves a dismissive hand as she chews and swallows. "These kids need to keep up with basic fundamentals as well. I'll bet you'd be good with those. And I'd pay you, of course."

"Well, thank you for the offer," I respond, not sure what else to say. I'm not going to be here long enough to take her up on it, but it's nice of her to offer me a job. It makes me sick to think what she would say if she knew what I'm involved in. She certainly wouldn't want me within a thousand feet of her school and those kids.

"Poaching my employees, are we?" Cain remarks with a crooked grin.

Storm shrugs, throwing her own devilish smile his way. "I just figured you wouldn't want her on the stage anymore, now that . . ." Her eyebrows arch suggestively.

"Charlie won't be going back on the stage. At all." The answer is quick, firm, and without room for argument, I'm sensing. Not that I would argue.

At all?

A hand settles on my knee beneath the table, giving me a gentle squeeze before sliding up my thigh. Not too far. Just enough to remind me of last night. Thank God there's a colorful tablecloth hiding my wanton display as my legs part instinctively, earning a tighter squeeze and a slow hiss from between his teeth. I wonder if that's why he pushed my chair in so far.

Good God, does Cain think I'm into the public stuff? I mean, I *was* stripping for him . . . in public. Last night we had sex . . . in a public place, though it was deserted and dark.

My legs impulsively squeeze back together as a trickle of sweat—and not from the oppressive heat—rolls down the back of my neck. Cain doesn't move his hand. From the corner of my eye, I catch that almost imperceptible and downright sexy smile of his. Sexy enough to make me relax against his hand once again.

"So, Trent, I forgot to tell you that Charlie has your old apartment," Storm says loudly enough to be heard by the others, throwing a wink in my direction.

"Really?" Trent licks a spot of ketchup off the inside of his thumb before he takes another bite of his burger. He's a tall, attractive guy, with unkempt brown hair and a flutter-inducing smile. He's the type of guy I would have easily fallen for before I met Cain.

And now that I have met Cain, I think I'll be measuring all future men against him for years to come. Turning to take in a peripheral view of that intent gaze on his friends as he quietly eats, I wonder if there are more of him in the world. I wonder if I will ever meet anyone who will measure up, who will make me feel whatever it is I'm feeling right now.

Or if Cain is right and there are no second chances in life.

"Better tenant than you ever were," Tanner ribs with that goofy smile of his.

"That's because she's been spoiled with renovations and air-conditioning," Trent throws back, grinning at me.

"Hold on. Wait just a minute." Ben's hand is in the air. "When did you move in there, Charlie?"

"Just over three weeks ago," I answer, wondering where this is going.

Ben turns his sizeable body to face Tanner, who now has his head down and is inhaling his food as if it's his last meal. "I've been waiting for an apartment in that building for a year and you keep telling me there aren't any available, you asshole!"

"Ben!" Storm snaps.

"Can we wash his mouth out with soap, Mom?" Mia asks, an impish grin on her face.

"Forget soap. I think we need bleach," Storm mutters.

"I'm sorry!" Ben exclaims. "But the rent is ridiculously low for that place. Why wouldn't you give it to me, Tanner? No offense, Charlie."

I guess Cain has still managed to keep his ownership status somewhat private because Ben obviously doesn't know, otherwise he'd be riding his ass about it and not Tanner's.

"Tanner has strict rules against orgies," Cain answers for his superintendent.

Ginger and I barely keep our food in our mouths with the snort of laughter that ensues.

"What do you have against orgies?" By the expression on Ben's face, you'd think he was completely serious.

"What's an orgies?" All amusement cuts off as heads turn to take in the eight-year-old peering up with curious eyes at a frozen Nate—a raised brow and a fork heading for his gaping mouth.

Dan is on his feet instantly. "Okay! Mia, it's time to get ready for your sleepover. I'll drive you."

"But, Dan . . ." comes the whiny voice, though she stands and trails him sullenly.

"You two are on cleanup duty for that." Storm juts two fingers out, aiming at Ben and Cain, who both have the decency to look sheepish.

The little girl's disappointment at being forced to leave doesn't last long, though, as I hear her excited shriek from inside only seconds later. "Livie!"

"Hello, hello!" Two stunning young women step out onto the patio: one with bright red hair, the other with raven black. Both have the lightest blue eyes I've ever seen on a person, and anyone can see that they're sisters. Their windblown cheeks and wild manes make me think they were hanging out of a car, driving at high speeds down the autobahn.

The redhead makes a direct line for Trent to bend over and lay a borderline inappropriate kiss on his lips. Her black bikini shows off a solid muscular body, marked with white scars along one side. If she's self-conscious about them, you'd never know. Given her ass is angled directly in Ben's face, I'd say she's either oblivious or just *that* confident. I wonder if she stripped at Penny's, too.

"Are you intentionally torturing me with this view, Kace?" Ben mutters. That makes her break free of her lip lock with Trent. She turns to smack Ben's forehead playfully.

"Always."

The black-haired girl—I'm guessing the younger of the two—quietly places a box in front of Storm before reaching down to rub her pregnant belly.

"Oh! You picked up another key lime pie!" Storm squeals, her eyes lighting up.

"Kacey said we need to keep Genghis happy," the girl answers with an eye roll.

Storm snorts. To us, she explains, "Kacey swears the reincarnation of Genghis Khan is growing inside me and is trying to conquer the world by eating its entire food supply." Sitting up to eye the pie with wide eyes, she adds in a murmur, "She may be right."

The redhead—Kacey, I'm presuming—turns her attention to us, those haunting blue eyes scanning over the table, slowing as they pass over me, before settling on the man next to me. She walks over to pat his shoulder. "Glad to see you're alive."

"Good to see you two again." Gesturing toward me, he says, "This is Charlie. Charlie, meet Livie and Kacey."

I get a polite smile from Livie. From Kacey, a suggestive brow and, "*The* Charlie?"

I answer effortlessly, "*The* Kacey?" though I feel a blip of discomfort inside. I don't know how I should feel about being a topic of conversation among all these people that I don't know.

"The one and only," she answers with a laugh. "Tell me you didn't come with that schmuck over there?" Her chin juts in Ben's direction.

"No, but she'll be leaving with me. Right, Charlie?" His question is to me but his eyes and crooked smirk are on Cain, and I get the impression that he's intentionally needling his boss about something.

A deep chuckle erupts from the normally reserved Nate. I'm guessing he knows more than Ben does about what happened between Cain and me last night. That or Ben is really that obnoxious. Either is a possibility. All the same, I blush at the idea of Cain giving Nate too many details.

Ignoring Ben, Cain asks them, "What were you two up to today? You look . . ." His voice drifts off.

"Like we just jumped out of a freaking plane?" Livie's wide, stunned eyes tell me she's not kidding.

"And it was one helluva rush!" Kacey throws an arm over her sister's shoulders, her face beaming as she squeezes her tight. A small cheer erupts around the patio as everyone congratulates them on something I could never do, with my deathly fear of heights. Even the idea has a tremble running through my body. Of course Cain feels it and rubs my leg soothingly.

"Nice work, twisted sisters!" Ben calls out around a mouthful of food, sounding genuinely impressed.

Storm's eyes are positively twinkling as she gazes up at the two of them. "You didn't chicken out! Good for you, Livie. I'm going with you next time."

"No—no next time." Livie's head shakes back and forth adamantly.

"Oh, come on! It was fun! Admit it!" her sister prods.

"No. Not fun. Maybe fun later. Right now . . ." She takes a

deep breath and sighs. "I'm going to lie down for a bit. I need to unwind. And plot Dr. Stayner's death."

I wonder who Dr. Stayner is. It sounds like he had something to do with her jumping out of a plane.

"You want help unwinding?" Those deep dimples of Ben's are in full force.

"No thanks." The answer comes hard and fast, suggesting she expected his offer and had the rejection ready on the tip of her tongue. Still, Livie's cheeks turn crimson instantly. Spinning on her heels, she's gone in a flash.

"Good lord, Benjamin Morris!" Storm tosses her napkin on the table. "You are out of control lately. Do I need to have you fixed?"

Bellows of laughter explode from Nate and Trent. Even Ben and Cain start laughing. I'm thinking there's an inside joke that only the men are in on, because the women exchange puzzled looks and eye rolls.

I can't help but envy this group as I listen to the easy conversation flowing—the gentle back-and-forth banter and genuine laughs coating the atmosphere with warmth. There's a deep connection between everyone here, and I can't say I've ever experienced anything quite like it.

As much as I know I don't belong, all of them are doing their best to make me feel otherwise. And when the plates are empty and being collected, and people begin dispersing in various directions, a trace of sadness trickles through me.

"That was fantastic, Storm," Ginger exclaims, standing to stretch as a loud splash comes from the pool. Trent and Kacey, diving in together. "I'm going to go float for a bit before I'm forced to work by my slave-driving employer." She winks at Cain before sauntering off.

Ben's eyes trail her as if readying to follow, when Storm reminds him, "The kitchen is the other way." She flashes him a radiant smile as she banishes him to his punishment, adding sweetly,

"And make sure you rinse the plates well before you load them into the dishwasher. I had to get a repairman in here last time."

"Yes, ma'am." Ben is on his feet quickly, that grin of his still plastered on as he leans in over her shoulder and plants a kiss on her forehead. "And I'm sorry about earlier, with Mia," I hear him offer in an unusually soft tone. As much of an ass as he is, Ben isn't a jerk. Sometimes it's hard to remember that. Especially now, as I watch him steal a well-angled glimpse of Storm's cleavage, which is practically spilling out of her dress.

If Storm notices—which I'm guessing she does, because her hand reaches up to gently slap his face—she doesn't get angry. I don't think Storm is the type to easily anger.

"Thank you for the meal!" Tanner hollers, ambling toward the house. "Gotta get back to the apartment now."

"You're not going to stay for Dan's cake?"

Rubbing his protruding belly, Tanner mutters, "Oh, no. I need to get back to my, er . . ." His voice fades as he collects his water gun.

To your antisocial tendencies.

Storm just shakes her head and chuckles. "Glad you could make it, Tanner. Next time, why don't you bring that lady friend of yours?" Her suggestion only speeds his skinny legs as they carry him into the house. "He met someone online." Storm waggles her brows at me. "I'm trying to get him to bring her to the wedding."

The heat of Cain's hand suddenly vanishes from my thigh and a tiny whimper of disapproval escapes my throat before I even realize it. He never did try anything more, and that has left me both relieved and frustrated.

With a dark chuckle, Cain begins gathering up a pile of dishes. When I begin to rise, intent on helping, he urges me back in my seat with a push down against my shoulder. My eyes trail him as he follows Ben into the house, his arms filled with dishes.

"He's definitely a sight, isn't he?" A secretive smile touches Storm's lips as she breaks off a piece of piecrust with her fingers.

I clear my throat as a faint blush creeps into my cheeks. Storm can likely see that. Thankfully, she can't also see the spike of jealousy in my stomach. I don't want her looking at him like that, even if her observation is true.

When her soft, musical laughter fills the air, I realize she's teasing me. "Go on, Charlie," Storm instructs, shooing me away with a hand and a smile, her hungry eyes on the pie. "I'll join you shortly."

With a nod, I excuse myself, making a beeline to slip into the refreshing pool, conscious that the blue of my bathing suit is light enough to showcase any wet spots I may have acquired due to Cain's attention. My body revels in the slight shock of the cool water as it swathes my skin, taking my temperature down a few degrees. I wish I didn't have all this makeup on. I wish I could just stick my head in.

I swim to the other end of the oversized pool to discover a separate little spa, complete with jets to massage my tired, achy muscles. Hoisting myself over and in, I lie back and quietly take in the scene. Kacey is floating stomach-down on an air mattress, her attention glued to Trent, who is hanging off one corner. Ginger is chattering away at Nate, whose enormous body—solid with muscle—takes up two-thirds of the staircase.

Storm and Dan really do have a great life here. I can't help but feel like an intruder—accepting their warmth and hospitality, eating their food, laughing with their friends.

Keeping Dan employed.

Still, I could see myself living in this world—coming to barbecues, hanging out with these people, working for Storm at her school.

Being with Cain.

If only I could get away from Sam, truly put it all in the past. If only . . .

Twenty minutes later of jets massaging my muscles, as sleep taunts me between occasional hollers from Ginger, I hear the patio door open and close. I lift my head in time to see Cain's side profile exit.

My body instantly comes alive as I watch the muscles of that molded body—the body I was entwined with last night—shift with each step upon his approach. He changed into a pair of swim trunks that hang dangerously low on that sexy V-shaped pelvis that I knew he must have but am only now getting a good look at. As muscular as Cain is, he's in no way beefy. His frame is on the athletic side, complete with pectoral muscles that don't look more like breasts, veins that add dimension to his arms, and an exquisite eight-pack that is almost unreal.

I force myself to blink, hard, to relieve the sudden strain in my eyes.

His eyes lock on my location, and then Cain's sleek body vanishes into the deep end of the pool in an elegant dive. *Is there anything he doesn't do extremely well?* I fold my arms over the divide and rest my chin on them, waiting with heady anticipation as his long form moves underwater toward me, emerging less than a foot away. He folds his arms lightly over mine. He's so close to me that I would only have to shift slightly to kiss him.

"Relaxed?"

I'm not sure how to answer that, because I'm both relaxed and suddenly conscious of every nerve ending in my body. I dare maneuver a hand free and run a finger along his chin. "You look good with scruff," I remark casually.

With that dangerous gleam in his eyes that I saw last night, he leans over to whisper in my ear, "You look good, wet."

My breath hitches. I hadn't expected that level of brazenness out of him. After last night, I'm not sure why not.

He uses his powerful arms to hoist himself onto the wall. I shift back to give him room as he lithely slides into the spa with me. He loops an arm around my waist and pulls me onto his lap with no delay, reaching down to slide a finger under the material of my top.

I think I'm getting to see yet another side of Cain. A dangerously playful one that chills out with friends and takes what he
wants. And taunts me.

"Cain!" I hiss, more in surprise than anything else. I push his
hand away as I nod toward the others, though there's no way they
can see what's happening in the tiny spa, thanks to the little wall
and the sheer size of the pool. I doubt any of them would say anything, anyway. Except for Ben, of course, but he hasn't exited the
house yet. "Contrary to what you *obviously* think, I prefer privacy."

A flicker of amusement touches Cain's lips before disappearing. Stretching his arms out on either side of him along the
curved wall, he tips his head back and closes his eyes. "Don't
worry. I'm not a pervert."

His Adam's apple is jutting out at a sexy sharp angle and I
can't help myself. I reach up and slowly drag my finger along the
bump, feeling it move with his hard swallow. When I reach the
base of his throat, I don't stop, continuing down to begin tracing
his hard muscles and the patterned tattoos adorning his chest.

I fight the urge to slide my hand farther down, to see how
much this is affecting him. Knowing I can elicit such a reaction
from a man like Cain is as much a turn-on as having him actually
touch me.

His eyes open to watch me as I quietly study him. "I'm glad
you came today, Charlie. I thought maybe . . ." His voice drifts off
for a moment as I see his jaw clench. ". . . that was it." There's that
look—the same one I saw last night, when he asked me if I was
sure. If I was sure of being *with him*. As if there were any possible
reason anyone wouldn't be over-the-moon thrilled to have Cain's
affections.

His words feel like a punch to my stomach as a conflicting
swirl of emotions slams into me. Guilt because he's right; that
was *supposed* to be it! Anguish that I may have wounded him. Bitterness for the looming expiration date hanging over our heads.
Overwhelming desire to erase his doubts right here, right now.

Selfishness.

Pure, raw selfishness to grab hold of him and never let go, despite knowing I shouldn't. It's churning deep within my belly and it is impossible to resist.

How did this happen so fast?

My situation is impossible and, worse, I can't explain it to him. I wish I could, though. I wish I were confident that he wouldn't think less of me.

"Hey." One of Cain's hands lifts to close over the side of my neck, his thumb grazing my jawline soothingly. "Is everything okay?"

No, Cain. It's not okay. I'm hanging from a pendulum as it swings back and forth between a nightmare and a dream. Only the nightmare is real! When I'm with Cain, nothing else matters. And when I'm not with him, I'm acutely aware of how stupid I am for being here. How I'm so close to being free of Sam and the drugs forever, if I'd just let go.

"Yeah, I'm fine, Cain." The painful lump forms in my throat again. I duck my head because I'm afraid he'll see the lie in my eyes. I'm finding it harder to pretend around Cain. Taking a few deep breaths, I struggle to pull on a mask of calm. Or of playfulness. I settle on a mask of emptiness. I doubt it's a convincing one at that.

"Do you want to talk about it?" he asks quietly, evidently not buying my words.

I absently trace over the design decorating his shoulder, as a "no" flees from my tongue in a whisper. There's not much I can say without raising Cain's suspicion, and so I need to remain quiet.

Like the quiet little mouse that Sam taught me to be.

I'm surprised he hasn't asked about Bob. He hasn't even mentioned the other night, though my gut tells me it's on his mind. It's as if he's biding his time before bringing it up.

With a heavy sigh, Cain's head and arms falls back once again. This time his eyes remain open and I see the frustration in them. "Why do I feel like you don't really want to be here, Charlie?" I can sense rather than feel the tension suddenly channeling through his body.

"I do. Believe me."

There's a long pause. "You do realize that the things I told you last night I don't admit to just anyone, right?" He lifts his head again, his eyes pleading with me.

I can manage only shallow, ragged breaths. I *want* to be thrilled by Cain's words right now. So very happy that Cain is being so open with me, so honest. But I can't, and it's constricting my lungs painfully. I don't know how to answer, so I settle on, "Yes. I'm glad I'm here, too," because there's nothing more true than that.

That naturally furrowed brow creases further. "Did what happened last night bother you? Look . . ." I see the muscles in his jaw tense as he breaks eye contact, his gaze searching the water in front of us. "I know I can be really intense sometimes. And impatient. And maybe letting that happen out on a pier was less than ideal for you." Dark eyes flash to me. "Sometimes I'm less inhibited, when I'm not thinking straight." A hand lifts to play with a strand of my hair. "Maybe we should dial things back."

What? I feel the scowl form on my face. *No! Slow things down? When that damn clock keeps ticking away? No! No! No!*

He goes on, seemingly unaware of my internal panic. "I warned you that I don't know how to do this. Still—"

Cain's words die with a hiss the second I peel down the front of his trunks and grasp him tightly. He was already hard. "I have no desire to slow things down," I say evenly, holding his gaze as I begin stroking him.

He locks a steely gaze on me and I start to think I might have gone too far. But I don't stop. "Thank fucking God," he finally mutters, reaching down to pull my hand away from him with a chuckle. "But I don't think Storm will appreciate that in here." After a pause, he adds with mock seriousness, "Besides, I thought you preferred privacy."

"And I thought you didn't like wasting time," I throw back

and then shrug. "Maybe that was payback for the spectacle you made of me on the pier."

A raised brow is the only warning I get before my body is being moved, sliding off Cain's lap to land on the built-in seat, my back to the others and Cain's body between my legs, his knees bent and propping my thighs up, a wicked grin on his face. "You want a spectacle?" His eyes drift down over my vulnerable frame, easily visible beneath the water now that the jets have shut off. Heated eyes come back to weigh down on me, ideas circulating within them that I can't decipher but that make my body open up to him with anticipation. "You think *I* deserve payback? How about payback for the last three weeks?"

I snort. "What, are you going to pole dance on your stage for me tonight?" A visual slams into my mind and, despite how unbelievably masculine and striking Cain is, I can't help but burst out laughing.

Water starts splashing my face. "Stop!" I hold my hands up in defense, trying to protect myself through my continued fit of laughter. "All my makeup will streak!"

"Good," he throws back, his smile turning tender, his voice turning unbearably soft. "Then I'd get to see the real Charlie."

My laughter cuts off abruptly as I break from his eye contact. *Oh, Cain . . . the deception is so much deeper than eyeliner and tinted contacts.*

"Charlie?"

I struggle for a deep breath as I look up at him, risking a whispered question. "What if you don't like what you see?"

There's a long pause, where his serious eyes explore mine and I know he's searching for some truth, some reason for my fear, and then his hand slides behind my neck. "I don't care what you've done, Charlie. You should know that. Whatever you've been involved in to get by is in the past. Whatever your parents may have done. You're safe here and you can start fresh. Your slate is clean with me."

I believe him. If only it truly *were* in the past.

He closes his mouth over mine in a devastating kiss, wrenching the breath right out of my lungs.

From somewhere behind us, far away from this euphoric cloud I'm sinking into quickly, I hear Ben's voice suddenly boom, "When the fuck did *that* happen?"

■ ■ ■

"To my lovely husband-to-be." Storm stands with a glass of milk raised as sparklers dance over the cake on the table in front of me. "I'm so proud of you for chasing your dreams and for choosing a noble path catching scumbags, even when the path of luxury is easier and more appealing. Congratulations on becoming Special Agent Dan Ryder!"

Everyone lets out a cheer, including me, though I'm betting mine is the only one laced with gut-wrenching shame.

I wave away a slice of cake and quietly excuse myself to use the bathroom, grabbing my things on the way, in order to change. Nate and Ginger went ahead to open the bar but Cain held me back, so I'm basically at his mercy. Not that I'm complaining about that, though I'd rather be at his mercy elsewhere.

"Charlie?" *Speak of the devil* . . . I turn back to find Cain following me inside the house, his eyes on my ass before snapping back to my face. I don't know if he's just stealing those looks now or if he always was and made more of an effort to be covert about it. "What are you doing?"

"Just getting changed. Why?"

As he reaches me, I have to tilt my head back to meet his eyes. One hand lifts to settle on my shoulder, his thumb rubbing over it soothingly. "You were playing with your fingertips."

What? My face must say it all, because he smirks. "When you're nervous, you play with your fingertips. Not dramatically, but . . . I've noticed." A serious frown passes over his features. "What made you nervous?"

Damn perceptive man. "Nothing. I'm just not looking forward to a night of serving drinks." Trying to play off his worry, I joke, "I'm tired. Someone kept me up *all night.*"

After a long pause, a smile creeps along his lips. He lets his eyes rake over my body. "That's too bad. I was hoping you'd let me keep you up tonight, but . . ."

I rest my hand on my hips and school my face to seriousness. Meanwhile, excitement crawls along my skin like a quickly spreading flame. Another whole night with Cain. Just the idea is enough to weaken my knees. "Are you teasing me?"

His mouth twists with thought before he shrugs. "It's a nice change from the usual, wouldn't you agree?"

"What about the bar? Will Ginger be okay without me there?"

His eyes roll in response. I know it was a stupid question. Ginger was doing just fine before I got there. They probably don't even need three bartenders. As if to prove a point, he dips his head, his breath leaving a trail along the curve of my neck before he presses his mouth against my ear and whispers, "Do you *really* care?"

"No." *Oh God.* I sound all breathless and needy. Clearing my throat to force some composure into my voice, I add, "What will my *boss* say?" It's too easy to slip into this playful role with Cain.

Gripping my bare waist tightly, Cain settles a mock frown on me. "I've heard he can be quite the asshole sometimes."

I let a moment of silence slip, but then it becomes too much. "Okay." I hear the surrender in my own voice. Just like that, my need for money, what my future looks like, my various dilemmas . . . all are inconsequential next to time with Cain, yet again.

He removes his hands from my body and takes several intentional steps backward, until his back hits a nearby wall, as he attempts a discreet adjustment of himself. "You should get changed so we can get out of here. Now."

And I smile. I know for a fact, by the gentle nudges and hugs, that Cain has been at least semi-hard since the pool. Maybe even since I walked into Dan's den. Now he's struggling to control himself. I probably shouldn't enjoy it as much as I do. But I *am* enjoying it. Immensely. It's an instant adrenaline rush.

Maybe I'm an adrenaline junkie.

On playful impulse, I turn and swagger into the bathroom, making sure to sway my hips because I know Cain is watching. Sure enough, a glance over my shoulder confirms his eyes cast downward, his lips parted slightly.

He remains still, his body rigid, as I make my way into the open bathroom. "Did you need anything else?" I reach back to pull the strings, releasing my bikini top from my body. His eyes widen a second before I toss the material at his face. As he's catching it, I make quick work of my bottoms, yanking the side ties. I manage to toss the bottoms at him and slam and lock the door, a split second before he reaches it.

"Dammit, Charlie," I hear him growl from the other side. "Open the door. Now."

"Not by the hair of my chinny-chin-chin," I sing, pulling my sundress over my head. I purse my lips against the nervous giggle that demands to escape. After the afternoon we've had, I'm probably not in much better shape than he is, frustration-wise. I won't let him know that, though. This new game is too much fun.

Plus, there's no way in hell I'm having sex with Cain on DEA Dan's bathroom counter and if I open the door, that's exactly what's going to happen.

■ ■ ■

Cain lives in luxury. I mean, top-floor, double-story, panoramic-view-of-the-water luxury. The place is sleek and modern, sparse one may say, but the second I step into it, it feels like Cain.

"Come," he beckons, reaching out to take my hand gently. Cain has calmed down since I took my time, refreshing my makeup and fixing my hair, before finally emerging from the bathroom at Storm and Dan's.

He leads me through the kitchen, into a gorgeous living room. My stomach is a bundle of nerves and anticipation as we climb the stairs and he leads me into a plain all-white bedroom with a king-sized bed and a spectacular view through a complete wall of windows, the city offering enough of a glow within the room that there's no need for additional light.

I watch as Cain shuts the door, as his fingers flip the lock.

He walks over to his dresser. Without a word, he calmly unfastens his watch and places it down on the dresser's surface. Next come the contents of his pockets—his wallet, his keys, some loose change. He places rather than tosses each item. It's quite methodical, as if he does it every night, and though there's nothing particularly enticing about the steps, blood begins pounding in my ears as I watch Cain do it.

Grasping the hem of his shirt, he slips it up over his head.

I'm not sure if he wants me watching him like this. Am I supposed to be doing the same? I glance at the large, neatly made bed and I wonder absently if Cain has had women standing in this very spot, watching him do this very same thing. I wonder how often.

And then I squeeze my eyes shut against the thoughts, scolding myself, knowing that it's just my subconscious trying to sabotage my time with him. Or trying to protect me from falling any farther.

I'm beginning to believe that the depths to which a woman could fall for Cain are endless. To a deep, dark, infinite pit with no ladders to get away, no cushions to soften the impact.

No safety net.

No escape.

With a deep, calming breath, I open my eyes. Cain is standing in front of me.

chapter twenty-seven

. . .

CAIN

I'm not afraid of anything, yet I think I'm afraid of Charlie.

Not afraid *of* her.

Afraid of having her.

Of losing her.

To what, I don't know yet because she won't talk to me. But I can't ignore the sick feeling in my gut that Charlie is deeply conflicted and that I may lose her because of it.

She's hiding something. Herself, maybe. Some truth, most definitely. Hell, I'm not even sure I'm seeing the real Charlie half the time. Not many people surprise me anymore and Charlie keeps surprising me. In the past forty-eight hours, she has surprised me at least a dozen different times. One second she's shyly tensing against my touch, the next she's stroking my cock when there are five people at the other end of the pool. One second her lip is quivering as a silent, inexplicable battle goes on within her and the next, she's whipping her bikini bottoms at me with a lascivious grin.

And now, here she is in my bedroom, her eyes squeezed tightly shut. And I sense her mood has shifted once again. It seems to shift with the snap of a finger.

Sometimes I feel myself getting past the superficial exterior to the person underneath, only to question whether it's just another facade. Sometimes I wonder if I know anything about her at all. Sometimes I wonder if *she* even knows who she really is.

None of that scares me away. If anything, it's just pulling me in deeper. No woman has ever thrown me off balance like this before, made me feel like I'm losing control.

She's hiding *something* and I'm guessing it's something painful. I know I told her I don't care and I don't, but, fuck it, I want to know what it is. I'd rather just get it all out in the open and move on. She's clearly still afraid. I mean, if there was ever a chance for her to admit to something, wouldn't it have been last night, during my own purging? It should have been so easy for her to explain who Ronald Sullivan is to her, why he was ready to smash her face in. But she continues to pretend that it didn't happen.

I'm thinking of getting John here to tail that fucker until I get answers. I'm thinking of stopping by Sullivan's house and holding him down by the throat until I get answers, faster.

"What?" The question slips softly from her lips as her eyes slide over my chest. She hasn't stopped doing that all night.

I reach up to smooth my knuckles over her cheek, freshly made up after being in the pool. I wish she'd just wash it all off. I wish she'd take those damn contacts off, too. My mouth opens, the demand on the tip of my tongue, when she shuts her eyes and leans into my touch, her full lips parting slightly. I feel her hot breath against my skin, bringing a throb to my balls, reminding me how long today really has been.

What a single-minded asshole I can be, sometimes.

I really can't wait any longer.

With my help, her dress hits the ground soundlessly. She remains still, watching me as I unclasp her bra and peel her panties off without ceremony until, in less than thirty seconds, she's naked for me again.

I'm practically salivating.

Her fingers reach forward for my belt but I grab them and ease her down to sit on my bed. She watches as I remove my own pants directly in front of her, sliding my boxer briefs over yet another raging hard-on that Charlie has given me.

Her eyes flash wide for a second before she schools them. Even in the darkness—lit only by the city lights outside—I can see the blush.

The woman has removed her own clothes onstage in front of hundreds of men and yet she blushes at the sight of me, naked.

I fight the urge to laugh. What an unpredictable woman! It's frustrating, but . . . I also love it. "Give me a minute?" I ask, not waiting for an answer as I head out the door. I try not to run. She's still perched on the edge of the bed when I come back with a strip of condoms hanging from my grasp. "Sorry, I don't keep any in here," I explain.

A light frown curves across her forehead. "Where do you keep them?"

I sigh as I take in those creamy-skinned, muscular thighs, waiting to be pushed apart. I don't really want to explain this right now. *In the spare room . . . in the kitchen cupboard next to the fridge . . . in the side table of the living room . . . on my main floor balcony.* Everywhere that I fuck women.

I don't fuck women in my bedroom.

Tossing them onto the nightstand beside the bed, I stand naked in front of her, letting her take me all in for a moment. And she does, her lips parted slightly. I can hear her shallow breaths. Lifting her chin with my index finger until she meets my gaze, I explain in an even voice, "I've never invited anyone in here." As if that isn't clear enough, I add, "You're the only woman who's ever come near this bed."

I hold her gaze as I try to convey the truth to my words, feeling her hard swallow beneath my touch as a myriad of emotions begin whirling within those eyes.

The tension in the air is suddenly palpable as her fingers reach forward to slide along my stomach, up to my chest. She stands, leveling me with a calculating look of her own. One that says she's weighing the truth of my answer. "Why me?"

"Because you're all I've thought about for weeks."

"Is it because of . . . I mean," her eyes dart to my neck, "do I remind you of someone?"

Ginger told her about Penny, obviously. "You're not a replacement for anyone," I answer slowly, evenly. Truthfully. Charlie is so much stronger, smarter, more confident than Penny ever was.

A shimmer coats her eyes. I think she's beginning to understand . . . *this*. What the fuck is *this*? I honestly don't know. When did it truly start? Was it last night? Was it when she threw me that first wink onstage? Was it the second she walked through my door?

I sense a tremble in her body and I instantly pull her into my arms. A nervous giggle tickles my chest where her mouth sits. "It's all happening so fast. I just . . . When I took the job, I wasn't expecting *this*."

"I'm sorry, it's me. I warned you." The soft chuckle slides out of my mouth. "I don't like wasting time."

"Do you believe in fate, Cain?"

I hesitate. Something tells me that Charlie does. I'd hate to tell her that I don't. That I despise the very idea of fate because it means I was destined for this life the second I was born. And that I'd be a fool to think I have control over any of it.

Suddenly, she pulls away. Tilting her head in that playful way of hers, she sits and edges backward until she's in the middle of the mattress and lying on her elbows, knees bent but together, her back arched naturally. Like an alluring angel amidst a sea of bedsheets.

I can't help but gaze at her for a moment.

And then her legs fall apart and that coy smile curves her lips.

My hands are locked on her ankles and pulling her to me in an instant.

And I know in my gut that each kiss, each touch, each thrust tonight will sink me further.

Until there is no escape.

■ ■ ■

"What did I teach you?" His voice registers a split second before sharp fists bombard my chest, my ribs, my stomach.

My fifteen-year-old body—already hardened for a good beating—has come to refuse more than four hours of sleep at a time, always on guard. After all, longer sleeps only increase the odds of getting caught unconscious. I must have been exhausted, though, because this time he caught me in a dead sleep.

I spring out of bed in seconds and raise my fists, ready to fight. Dad's dark eyes—still red and glossy from whatever he'd snorted or smoked the night before—bore into me. "Always be ready, son. Every second counts."

My brain registers a weight against my chest and my eyes fly open. I'm a split second away from jumping into defense mode when floral perfume fills my nostrils.

I sigh. No one is attacking me. It's Charlie—her body nestled into my side, her head resting on my chest. And it feels fucking incredible.

"Nightmare?" I hear her sleepy voice ask. With the predawn light coming through the window, I can just make out her features. She's at peace.

"I'm sorry, did I wake you?" I apologize, pushing a strand of hair off her face. A glance at the clock tells me we've been asleep for a few hours.

Asleep.

Tonight was the first time I've ever fallen asleep with a woman.

I'm almost twenty-nine years old and I've never *slept* with a woman.

I've never even tried.

And now, feeling her silky skin against mine, her body relaxed and finding comfort molded into mine, I know what I've been missing. What I never want to miss again.

Her hand rubs over my chest affectionately. "Your heart is racing," she murmurs. It's almost like a purr.

"I'm fine." *Unless you break it.* The thought suddenly creeps into my mind unbidden, leaving me feeling like I've been punched in the stomach.

Charlie could break me. By the volcanic eruption of anxiety suddenly bursting, I acknowledge that she could shatter me worse than Penny did.

Permanently.

A second later, I feel her tongue dart over my nipple before her mouth covers it in a kiss. I groan, shifting to my side so I can face her. A tiny giggle escapes her but her eyes are still closed. I simply watch her, as her breathing slows and steadies, telling me she has fallen back to sleep.

chapter twenty-eight

...

CHARLIE

I've given up all pretenses that I'm leaving today or tomorrow. It might be in a week from now, or three weeks from now. But I'm not leaving until I absolutely have to.

I thought the night on the pier was intense, but last night felt somehow . . . binding. Cain showed me just how much more demanding yet gentle, how much more passionate yet considerate, he could be. Raw emotions—feelings I can't even comprehend, let alone verbalize—passed through each intimate touch, each time we surrendered ourselves to each other.

I don't understand how or why I've garnered Cain's interest, but I'll hold onto it as long as I can.

Every inch of me is sore. And yet, if Cain needed more of me, I would give it to him right now. I'll give him everything that I possibly can. Which doesn't feel like very much, especially compared to what he's so freely offered to me.

My heart aches with that knowledge. I don't know what to do. I don't see how this can go on indefinitely. And yet no part of me will allow the thought of leaving right now.

Perhaps he senses my presence because Cain suddenly turns to lock eyes with me, pulling a light gasp from my lips. His gaze drifts down my body, that deadly curl touching his lip. "I hope you don't mind me going through your dresser." My fingers stretch the plain gray T-shirt of his that I'm wearing as I make my way down the steps. I found it folded neatly in his top drawer and I couldn't help but put it on. It reaches my thighs, it's soft, and, though obviously laundered, it still somehow smells like Cain.

He places the cup in his hand down on the side table and silently strolls over to wait for me on the landing. By the sudden tilt of his head and his focus, I'm thinking the shirt isn't entirely long enough to cover the fact that I have nothing on underneath. When I reach the landing, his hand grabs onto the front of it, hiking it up around my waist as he pulls me into him. "I would prefer you without this." His hands slide down along my back to get a solid grip of my bare ass.

"What, like some sort of sex slave?" I tease as I inhale the scent of soap. Cain has showered. I, most definitely, have not. After last night's bedroom marathon, I'm regretting this fact right now. It doesn't seem to bother him, though. He pulls me into him tighter.

"I tried to wake you up this morning but you sleep like the dead," he says absently, a soft smile on his lips as his attention roams my face.

I scrubbed my makeup off before I came down. I also took out the contacts. I can do that much for him, at least.

"I could use a slave," he murmurs. Then he leans down and lays one of his knee-buckling, thigh-tingling kisses on me and I silently thank God that I at least used his toothbrush to clean my teeth.

"Hmm . . . I thought you said you weren't a pervert," I tease against his mouth.

His dark chuckle sends shivers skittering along my skin. And then suddenly I'm being turned and my feet are moving backward to keep my balance as his powerful frame overwhelms me. Before I know what's happening, my T-shirt is gone and I'm falling into the couch, just as Cain's track pants hit the floor.

The smirk on his face is downright dangerous. "I lied."

■ ■ ■

"I really like waking up to you in my home," Cain says as he slides a cup of coffee across the counter to me.

"I can tell," I murmur dryly, letting my eyes roll over Cain's arms, his chest, down his stomach—memories of what all those muscles looked like straining above me only twenty minutes ago firmly entrenched in my brain. With a glance up, I see him watching me with an amused smile, as if he knows exactly what I'm thinking about. I quickly distract myself with a fake itch on my thigh, focusing intently on it.

He *could* make it easier on both of us by throwing on a shirt. But he won't.

I think he likes me gawking at him.

It's not bad enough that Charlie Rourke is a drug trafficker and a retired stripper. Now I've turned her into a sex fiend.

With a chuckle, Cain states rather than asks, "You must be hungry. I've got . . ." He opens the fridge and peers inside. ". . . condiments . . . orange juice . . . bread." He sighs. "Sorry, Karina—my housekeeper—comes in twice a week to clean and replenish staples. I'm rarely here to eat a meal. But I'll get this stocked." Throwing the door shut, he pulls a piece of paper and a pen out of a drawer and asks, "What do you like?"

Cain is making a grocery list. For me.

I hesitate for a second and then grin playfully at him. "Frosted Flakes?"

I get an arched brow in return. "Really?"

"Childhood vice."

"Okay . . . children's cereal. That will spark Karina's curiosity, no doubt." A slow smile touches his lips as he jots it down. His penmanship is exceptionally neat. "Ten pounds of coffee . . . your own damn toothbrush, so you don't use mine again."

I feel the sheepish grin touch my face. By the wink he throws me, I *think* he's only kidding.

"Brass pole for my bedroom . . ."

"They have those at the local grocery store?"

His phone starts ringing as he adds while scribbling, "Ten economy boxes of condoms."

"What?"

He answers his phone with a chuckle and I use that opportunity to snatch the paper out from under him. He actually wrote that down.

"Nate," I hear him say as he dumps the rest of his coffee in the sink and places the cup in the dishwasher. "Yup . . . good." His gaze flickers to me. Listening for a moment, his eyes absently settling on my bare legs, Cain's face suddenly turns serious. He stands up straighter. "Seriously? Fuck . . . Why didn't you call me? . . . Yeah. I'll have to deal with her tonight." Another pause as he listens, his hand scratching his chin. Finally, he heaves a sigh. "Yeah, I'll be in by four. I've gotta take Charlie back to her place . . . Yeah." I can hear Nate's deep rumble on the other line but I can't make out what he's saying. "See you later."

I sense the atmosphere in the kitchen shifting as Cain's mood sours.

And I hate it.

"I should get you home, Charlie," he mutters, now focused intently on the granite pattern. I can tell his thoughts are elsewhere, moving out the door to head back into his own reality. Everything about him—his body language, his facial expression, his tone—feels like it's closing off. Shifting back to the Cain that I first met. It's as though he's pulling a door shut to leave me and whatever this is between us on the other side. Separated from that other part of his life.

Cain and I have a lot in common.

I dive for that doorway to wedge myself in. "What happened? I assume it involves Penny's?"

After a pause, "Yeah." He leans down onto the counter and I don't hesitate to reach forward and begin rubbing the muscles in his back, knowing that his body is tense again. I've noticed that the longer he's away from the club, the more he relaxes. "China and Kinsley were at it again last night, fighting over a customer like two alley cats." He shakes his head. "China threw a drink at Kinsley that accidentally hit a customer. Now the guy's threatening to sue."

"Shit," I groan, silently piecing together the conversation. "What does that mean? You're firing China?"

He scowls. "No . . . Kinsley." His eyes drift off toward the window.

Wow. I don't doubt that Kinsley is at least half-deserving, but . . . even with China physically abusing customers and putting his business at risk, he won't fire her?

His bottom lip pulls into his teeth. "I'm really starting to hate that place."

I lean in to press my lips against his shoulder, wishing I could help him somehow. "But you can't walk away from it."

"But I can't walk away from it," he repeats with a slow nod, more to himself. Breathing in deeply through his nostrils, he mutters, "I hate firing people."

"Want me to do it?" I offer casually, letting one hand settle against his chest while I gently run my index finger of the other hand down his spine. "I can pretend to be a mean-ass bitch boss for you."

I get a weak chuckle, but I'll take it. After a pause, he turns to look down at me. "I was serious about that management job, when I offered it to you. You want it?"

"I don't know, seeing as . . ." Should I be accepting this, given the situation? Or, the *situations*. Not only am I leading this secret life that will force me out of Miami eventually, now I'm having ridiculously hot sex with the owner of the club. A lot of it. And he clearly intends to have a lot more, based on the scandalous shopping list he's preparing for what I picture is a sweet old lady.

And better not be a hot young tramp in a French maid outfit.

I'll ask him about that later.

"Well, you've been giving me blow jobs for weeks every night before the club opens, so I don't see what the problem is," he teases dryly. *And those rumors will likely become reality* . . . "You're not going on the stage anymore, so it works out well for both of us. In fact," he says, suddenly standing up straight and turning to face me, "I don't want you behind the bar, either."

I frown at him, trying to figure out if he's joking.

Cain heaves an exasperated sigh. "Just because we haven't talked about that fucking asshole the other night doesn't mean I've forgotten about him, Charlie."

I avert my eyes but feel Cain's harsh gaze still on me. "I'm trying to respect your privacy and give you the chance to tell me about it when you're ready. That doesn't mean I won't do whatever I have to do to keep you safe."

Panic stirs as my brain processes his words. *What does that mean?* Swallowing the small scream in my throat, I ask in a decidedly shaky voice, "What did you do to him?"

Cain studies me—more likely, my reaction—for a long moment. "Made sure he knows never to lay a hand on you again."

"That's a little vague." It frightens the hell out of me. The last thing I need is a face-off with a vengeful Bob at a drop. *If* I do another drop. "Did you threaten him?"

He pauses as if deciding whether to answer me or not. "Nate can be an intimidating guy."

Something tells me there's more to this story. "What if he comes back and hurts you?" I'd die if anything ever happened to Cain or Nate because of me.

Cain's soft chuckle only increases my anxiety. "Don't worry about me, sweetheart. It takes a lot to knock me down."

I set my forehead against the bar. *Fantastic. Cain has a Superman complex.* And now I know for certain that Cain can't ever know anything about Sam. I can't have him and Nate tossing around threats if Sam were ever to show up unexpected.

Because Sam wouldn't bother trying to knock down Superman. He'd simply kill him.

"So?" Cain waits expectantly, though his tone has softened. "The job?"

"Can you afford me?"

"Oh?" He rolls on his elbows to face me, his smirk widening. "What's the going rate again?"

"A thousand an hour is what some are willing to pay."

"Right." Cain starts to laugh. "You're going to rob me blind, aren't you?"

I shrug. "Why else would I be here?"

Cain plants a kiss on each cheek, followed by one on my nose, and then he lays a deep one on my lips, pulling a moan out of my throat. "You'll be well taken care of, I can promise you that."

A twinge of guilt pricks at me. "How about we see how it goes. Temporary assignment, okay? We might not be able to stand each other after a week."

Cain shakes his head. "Sure, Charlie. But somehow I'm highly doubting that. Come on." I get a playful slap across the ass and I beam, silently commending myself for keeping that dark, broody Cain from shutting me out. "Let's get you some clothes and then we can go out to eat."

■ ■ ■

"Hey, Kyle!" The slightly awkward security guard offers me a crooked smile as I walk through the revolving door of the extended-stay motel, as I have every Monday morning for months now, a coffee in hand and a low-cut T-shirt on person.

"Hey, Charlie." He watches me walk up, his eyes appraising me. "I didn't think you were coming in."

Deliveries arrive by nine a.m. and I'm always here at exactly nine fifteen. Glancing at my clock, I note that it's almost ten thirty. It's the first time I've ever been late.

I had to get away from Cain, something I haven't done in

days. He's been within arm's reach the entire time and I've loved every second of it. Most of the time, we're either at Penny's or at his place. I've even started using the gym in his building.

I couldn't have him coming with me to pick up the latest burner phone, so I used the excuse that I needed clothes from my apartment. He told me to just pack my suitcase and bring everything over.

Cain was telling the truth. He doesn't know how to date and he sure as hell doesn't take things slow.

"I know. Traffic. Biscayne Boulevard is backed up with all the construction."

"Huh . . . that might explain it. Maybe the delivery guy is stuck in it too, because there's no package yet."

My stomach clenches. He can't be stuck in it because there isn't any construction on Biscayne Boulevard right now, as shocking as that is.

So, why isn't there a package for me?

Trying to appear calm, I let my eyes roam the lobby area, looking for something suspicious. Something dangerous.

Like Jimmy.

Or Sam. Would he break his rule and fly down here for me?

"Maybe. Oh well!" I give my best ditzy girl giggle as I hand him his coffee. What does this mean? I'm sure it means something. Do I still pitch my current burner phone? Do I call Sam? I haven't spoken to him since confronting him about the real Charlie Rourke and I have no idea what he's going to say.

Do I run as if the building is about to explode?

Suddenly I feel like an easy target, as if I'm standing in the middle of an open field with a slew of guns trained on me.

Kyle happily takes a sip of his coffee, oblivious to the danger and pretending not to be checking out my chest. I start babbling some nonsense about a party I didn't go to on Saturday, pretending not to notice.

All I want to do right now is get out of here.

I don't know that I can last the compulsory fifteen minutes. I don't know that I can last *five* minutes. Luckily, I'm not forced to find out, because the trill sound of the burner phone in my pocket starts to ring.

"I've got to take this, Kyle. I'm so sorry," I offer, abruptly turning and heading toward the revolving doors as I root through my purse. The second I step out onto the sidewalk, I'm scanning my surroundings, looking for some indication that I'm being followed. I see nothing. I've seen nothing for a week now and I've been watching closely for any signs of a tail.

On the fifth ring, I answer, clenching my muscles to avoid peeing my pants.

"Hello?"

"Hello, little mouse. How are things?" His greeting is much more pleasant than I had anticipated. It's as though our last conversation never happened.

"Fine. Except the delivery didn't arrive this morning."

"Yes, I know. I meant to call you earlier about that. I'm sorry if that worried you." This is odd. He's acting so . . . considerate. I see flashes of gymnastics trials and school plays, of Sam standing with armloads of flowers, garnering attention from parents as the doting stepfather. Of hoisting me up onto Black Jack's saddle with a twinkle in his eye.

The warmth of those memories spreads through my chest, reminding me that there was a time when nothing tainted our relationship. When I thought I was the luckiest girl on the planet.

"There are some issues with competition and we need to lay low for a while. Jimmy will sort it out, but until then, you just enjoy yourself. I see you've put a good dent into the money I sent to you."

"I bought a few new dresses," I lie. I went back to the bank last week to drain my secret account and a chunk of the one Sam knows about, dumping it all into a safety deposit box that I can access at any time.

"Good. I'll send you some more money to keep you busy. There won't be any more deliveries of any kind for a while."

There's dead silence on the phone as he waits for my response.

"For how long?" I dare ask.

"Months. Or longer. I may need to find another way in. It's getting risky."

Another way in? What does that mean? Another way in that doesn't involve me, perhaps?

No more burner phones, no more drug drops, no more deceiving Cain?

Could this *really* be happening? With my free hand, I pinch my forearm. I'm still here. My phone is still in my ear.

In the back of my mind, I can't help but wonder if there's something else at work. If it's not this easy, if Sam is in fact reacting to his suspicions about me. Either way, it sounds like I won't be doing a drop for a long time. Maybe ever again.

That life could truly be part of my past.

And then I could actually look at Cain as part of my future. I'll have to tell him about this one day, of course. But, by then, maybe he'll actually love me. Enough to be able to forgive me.

■ ■ ■

I don't walk through Cain's door.

I float. On a fluffy white cloud of shock and confusion and possibilities and hope that never existed before, I float through the condo, in search of a possible new future. I find it on the balcony, stretched out on a lounge chair with a book.

Cain looks up to see me standing over him. "Charlie?" He watches for a moment and then frowns. "What's wrong?"

Pushing the book free from his grip, I force myself onto the chair to lie on top of him, taking in his bewildered expression.

And the tears begin to fall.

Cain is beside himself, his body going rigid. "What's wrong, Charlie?" His hands, his eyes, begin searching my limbs as if searching for a physical injury. And still I cry, only now my laughter begins to weave in, sending me into a borderline hysterical fit of sobs, as I choke back the tears enough to say, "Nothing's wrong."

Cain must think I'm insane.

Maybe I am.

Or maybe this is what happens when you break free of a trap.

chapter twenty-nine

...

CAIN

Whenever I look at her, a hot burn fills my chest.

I don't know how I ever lasted a day without Charlie. Both work-wise and life-wise, I've never spent this much time with another human being. Not even Nate, who lived with me for several years.

I don't even mind coming into Penny's anymore. The place feels different. It's not just me anymore. Now I have Charlie at my side. And . . . those knots in my shoulders that never go away?

Fucking gone. Like magic.

Charlie magic.

She never explained what happened that day she came home and fell into a fit of tears on top of me. It took me a minute to accept that she wasn't hurt and she was actually happy, but when I tried to get answers out of her, she quickly shut me up by sliding her tongue in my mouth.

"Anything else you think we need?" Charlie asks, finishing off another week's schedule at my office desk. "I put the supply orders in as well. And we should have a beer delivery coming within a few hours." She knows the distributor customer service reps by name and we're somehow getting better service because of it, without any more of Ginger's shows.

All in all, Charlie is a quick learner and a hard worker. Fortunately for me, she hasn't learned not to wear dresses to work yet. "Perhaps." I dip down to close my mouth over that long, delicate neck.

"Whatever happened to your *rules*?" she teases with a giggle, throwing down her pen. "For such a stickler, you sure have done a one-eighty."

"New rule," I murmur. "You're not allowed to wear this yellow dress in here." It's the same one she wore the day of her interview, when she let it drop to the floor in front of me. From where I'm standing, I have the perfect view down the top of it. I'd rather have the full view. Before she has a chance to object, I have the straps pushed off her shoulders and her dress and bra pulled down, exposing those flawless tits of hers.

"Cain!" she exclaims as I reach around to cup each one, their weight perfectly balanced within my hands. I know her body very well.

"You shouldn't wear dresses if you don't want me to do this. Or this." In seconds I have my hands at her waist to hoist her out of her chair, kicking it out of the way. I press into her, letting her feel me so she knows exactly what's coming. "Lean over," I whisper, pushing all the paper on my desk to one side with a sweep of my hand.

"Everyone's waiting for us out there," she whispers breathlessly, but she follows orders and stretches her bared top half over the cool wood, looking over her shoulder at me with that devilish smile of hers that I love. Though she has accused me of being insatiable on several occasions, she never denies me. "Did you lock the door?"

"Of course," I mutter, hiking the skirt of her dress up around her waist. Round, muscular cheeks meet my gaze. I only lock it when she's in here with me. And when she's in here with me, it's always locked.

I hook a finger around the thin material of her thong and pull until it slides off and drops to the ground. Slipping a hand in between her legs, I offer her a smirk, which she accepts with a dark smile of her own. She's always ready for me.

I don't waste another second, unzipping my pants as I reach into the top drawer for a condom.

"Fuck," I mutter, slamming it shut.

She frowns at me.

"We're out." I can't believe I didn't notice that. I'm going to be left with a raging hard-on unless . . . I haven't been inside a woman, uncovered, since I was an idiotic seventeen-year-old. Feeling Charlie, skin to skin, would be ecstasy. Right now I'm thinking I don't give a fuck. But I know I will after. On my desk isn't how I want *that* first to go. "We need to get you on the pill."

I catch the wary expression flash over her features. It's the same one she gave me when I suggested she give up her apartment. I understand it. She wonders if I'm crazy. If we're moving too fast.

In my eyes, though, there's only one speed with Charlie. Now.

Standing, she turns to face me. Her fingers push their way down my hips, snaking under my briefs to chill my bare skin. She pulls everything down, letting my erection spring free. "It seems you have a problem, then," she says with a smirk. "Sit."

I do and she's on her knees in a heartbeat, positioning herself on the floor in front of me, between my legs. When both of her delicate hands curl around my length, I let my head fall back and I close my eyes.

And I wait.

I wait in agony, knowing what's coming, ready to explode with just the anticipation of her hot breath. She's so good at this. She's not nearly as practiced as Vicki and Rebecka are, but I'm happy about that because it means . . . she's not as practiced as them. And there's something about the way she goes about this that tells me that it's not a means to her own satisfaction. Charlie wants to do this for me. That thought makes me almost lose it.

When I sense the wetness of her tongue along my tip, I almost do explode.

It takes everything in me not to go off like a thirteen-year-old seeing a naked woman's body for the first time.

I groan when she takes me in completely, as she teases me with her lips, her tongue, her teeth. I let my hands fall around the back of her head, gently scooping her hair up and back so I can see her face. She must hear my raspy breaths, sense my buildup, because her mouth begins working quicker, more ardently.

Normally I would lie back, close my eyes, and drift. But I like to watch Charlie. I could watch her doing this every day for the rest of my life.

And I can't help but think that I'll never want anyone else's mouth on me ever again.

chapter thirty

• • •

CHARLIE

"The doors are locked!" Ben slaps his earpiece down on the bar in front of me. "Should I hand my piece to you, Miss Manager?" It's Ben's last shift at Penny's. He's putting on a big show of celebration but behind those blue eyes, I've caught a few glimpses of sadness. I know he's going to miss working here.

Shaking my head, I say, "Give it to Nate. I don't want to touch your wax-covered *piece*."

"No?" He shoves a pretzel into his mouth, his grin widening. "What about my latex-covered piece?" Ben apparently checked out of work about two hours ago and since then has been drinking by the bar, celebrating with the regular customers, so he's good and primed.

"Fuck off, Morris," Cain growls, appearing behind me to grip my hips and pull me into him.

Ben looks from me to his now ex-boss with a smirk, as if he knows what we were doing not fifteen minutes ago in his office. "Or what? You gonna fire me?"

"No, I'm going to ban you from Penny's."

That wrenches Ben's smile fast. "Well, fuck. I better get my fill, then," he mutters, running over to grab Mercy by the thighs to hoist her over his shoulder. She squeals and smacks his back, though there doesn't appear to be much force behind it.

With a chuckle and a shake of his head, Cain dips down to kiss the crook of my neck. I'm still shocked by his willingness to show his affection so openly. It's been a fast change but a dramatic one. And everyone seems to be accepting of it.

Almost everyone.

In my peripheral vision, I see China watching the display. I avoid her and she pretends I don't exist. It's the perfect level of interaction. I know Cain sees a side of her that I don't see. That no one else sees. Still, I don't trust her. I can't help but wonder, if she attacked me as she had Kinsley, what Cain would do. Would he make a choice between us? And would that choice be me?

I don't doubt that China has strong feelings for Cain. I mean, how can she not? She's known him for *years*. I've known him for six weeks—half of that intimately—and I already can't manage life without him.

For all that I hate about what I've done, there's one thing I can't regret.

It led me to him.

I don't know if things are moving too fast. I'm too ensconced in this Cain high to appreciate basic rules and he seems uninterested in slowing down. He's filling his kitchen with Frosted Flakes and every other kind of food I might like, talking about me moving in, giving me a key to his condo, practically demanding that I go on the pill.

Everything about him screams "future."

And I haven't heard a peep from Sam. Though I still keep my eyes open, always aware of my surroundings, it's not with the same level of trepidation as before. It's more out of habit than anything else.

"Bartender!" I hear Kacey holler, slapping her hands against the bar as if in a drum roll. Behind her, Trent towers, his hands around her waist, those deep dimples on full display as he winks at Ginger.

"Charlie." Storm strolls over, looking fresh and beautiful, even though it's the middle of the night and she should be sleeping. She doesn't hesitate to offer me a hug. "How's it going? How is being Cain's manager working out?"

"Less exposing," I answer truthfully and then can't help but smirk, because that's not really true. I'm just less exposed to the general population. Cain's "no sex in the workplace" rule has fallen by the wayside. Daily.

"Where is the jackass?" Kacey's eyes roam the club as Ginger lines up a row of tequila shots.

"Right here!" Ben hollers, seconds before he swoops in to lift Kacey's frame from behind into a big hug. Dropping her on the ground, he slaps Trent's shoulder in greeting and grabs a shot from the bar just as the overhead lights shut off and the stage lights flash on once again.

"Let's get this party started!" Terry's voice spills out over the speaker system, followed by "Lady Marmalade." A parade of dancers strut out from behind the curtain wearing an array of brightly colored burlesque costumes. Ben's face lights up like a kid at an ice-cream shop. Ginger told me they were planning something extra-special for their favorite bouncer's send-off. Though nothing is choreographed, it's quite the spectacle all the same.

"To Lawyer Boy. God help us all!" Kacey shouts and we all—including Cain—grab a shot and down it, the burn scorching my throat. Nate and a few of the other bouncers drag Ben, completely willingly, over to pervert row to enjoy the performance.

"All right, Dee!" Gingers exclaims, clapping her hands together. "We're gonna make Ben puke tonight. Trust me, he'll deserve it. Cain . . ." She bows. "Will you do the honor of the first drink?"

I watch with surprise as Cain pulls away from me to round the corner. I don't think I've ever actually seen him behind the bar, but I'd imagine years of owning one would give him plenty of opportunity to practice. He moves easily, not even reading labels before he's got four bottles lined up in front of him. He smiles to himself as he begins deftly measuring and pouring the gold tequila into three separate mixers.

Next goes the Jim Beam and the bourbon. By the time I see him tipping back the scotch, I'm pretty sure I'd rather light my tongue on fire than drink what he's making. Glancing over at Ben, lying shirtless on the stage with his arms nestled under his head, a dreamy grin on his face and both Hannah and Mercy dancing provocatively over him, I wonder if he should be drinking it either.

"It's going to be a shit show in here, really soon," I hear Cain mutter under his breath as he comes back around to take the seat next to me, pulling me into him once again.

"You do realize your strict rules are going out the window tonight, right?" Storm says to him with a giggle.

"Yeah." Cain's hands slide through his hair, sending it into sexy disarray. "I've already shut off all of the cameras. This is a private party, anyway."

Both Storm and Kacey turn to stare at me in unison. Leaning into my ear, Storm says out the side of her mouth, "Whatever you're doing to Cain, keep doing it."

Ginger is relentless with her concoctions. Cain doesn't even bat an eye as his premium liquor supply dwindles. Storm confiscates everyone's keys, just in case any partygoers get confused as to how drunk they truly are.

At some point, four dancers pull Ben back to a V.I.P. room. Or maybe it was only two dancers. I'm not quite sure because Ginger keeps giving me these Pepto-Bismol-pink shooters that she promises are mild. I think she's lying to me, because getting off my stool is proving to be a real challenge.

Hoots and hollers explode five minutes later as Ben struts out dressed in Mercy's green bikini and the smile of the Cheshire cat. What Mercy's wearing—or not wearing right now—is thankfully not evident because she has stayed in the V.I.P. room. The sight is both the funniest thing I've ever seen and the most unappealing, given his junk is hanging out the sides of the stretched-out bottoms. As attractive and well built as Ben is, no one can pull this look off.

Kacey hits the ground in laughter, half diving, half crawling for the phone in Trent's hand to snap pictures of her inebriated friend climbing onto the stage, giving everyone a very unpleasant view of him in a thong.

He clearly doesn't care, though.

"All right. Show's over for me. I'm exhausted and Dan's giving me grief about getting my pregnant butt home," Storm announces. "You going to be okay with this mess?"

Cain chuckles. "Yeah, don't worry about it."

"Okay, good." Turning to me, she smiles sweetly. "You're coming to the wedding, right?"

"I . . ." I hadn't really thought about it and Cain hasn't mentioned it. I know it's in a few weeks. I also know it is DEA Dan who's getting married. While I'd love to go, a part of me can't shake the feeling that it would be too disrespectful to them. That I could taint their marriage without them even knowing it.

"Of course she's coming." Cain's arm deftly snakes around my waist to pull me in close. "If she can get a night off work, that is. I heard her boss is a jerk."

"Yeah." I give him my best coy smile. "He's probably going to give me a *hard* time."

Cain's hand squeezes my thigh in response.

"On that note . . ." Storm leans in to give me a hug. "Good luck in the morning, Charlie."

"Well, that sounds like the kiss of death if I've ever heard one."

With a laugh, she stretches onto her tiptoes to drop a peck on Cain's cheek. "Happy birthday."

My jaw drops as the shock hits me.

By the wink she gives me, the devious Storm knew that Cain hadn't enlightened me. Judging by the scowl that flitters across his face after he catches my expression, Cain would have happily kept me in the dark.

"Today? As in, *today?*" I finally manage to get out.

"As in right now." Storm blows a kiss as she walks away.

"It's not a big deal," he mutters. Peering down at my face in earnest, Cain finally holds his hand out, beckoning. I take it and he leads me back toward the office. The air is so much cooler in here and I welcome it, practically falling into the black leather couch. Cain's desk lamp clicks on. It provides a nice, dim glow, much nicer than the harsh fluorescent lighting above.

"Here, drink this. It'll help tomorrow." Cain produced a cold bottle of water from the mini fridge. He takes a seat beside me as I chug back the entire thing.

"Is it just me or does your office spin after-hours?"

With a chuckle, he gently pulls me down until my head is resting in his lap. I can't help but inhale deeply, his cologne taking my intoxication level to where a boatload of shots could not. Fingers draw through my hair in a soothing manner and I moan responsively.

"Did you have fun tonight?"

"Yeah." I smile, a lazy giggle escaping me. "I really like everyone here. Especially Ben in a bikini."

Cain's hand stops abruptly. I accidentally smack myself in the forehead as I lift my hand to hit his, urging him on. "Keep doing that." I guess my request is coherent enough because his fingers start moving again, only now the index finger of his other hand trails up and down my cheek in an intimate manner. "Why wouldn't you tell me it's your birthday? I mean, we're . . ." I leave the rest of it unsaid. In truth, he doesn't know my real birthday. Or my real age. Or my real name. I have no right to be angry with him. And I'm not.

I'm hurt.

"It has nothing to do with not wanting to tell you, Charlie. I just don't care about my birthday."

"Because you're getting old?"

He snorts. "No, smart-ass. Because I never grew up celebrating them."

I frown, reaching up to loop my fingers within his. *Never celebrating your own birthday?* Even Sam—a ruthless, murdering drug dealer—always made sure each birthday of mine was special. We'd spend the whole day together and I got to pick the activities. It didn't matter what it was. He'd do it.

"What are you giggling about?" Cain suddenly asks.

I hadn't realized that I was. "Oh, just picturing the year I made my dad toboggan down a steep hill with me for my birthday." I snort as a visual hits me. "Sam fell off halfway down the hill and did cartwheels the rest of the way. I thought he was mad at me, but . . ." I remember that look on his face as he finally stopped tumbling. I was only ten but, for a split second, I was terrified he'd be angry with me for making him come out. ". . . he just laughed. He ended up doing three more runs before he complained that his old body couldn't handle it."

I sense Cain's muscles tensing under me. "Well, I guess you're lucky."

Now I feel like a complete jackass. I try to make amends by unfastening several of his shirt buttons and snaking my hand beneath to touch his bare skin. Cain seems to respond very well to physical affection. I'm thinking he didn't get a lot of it growing up. Then again, after my mother died, neither did I. My mom gave big squish-me hugs. But Sam was more about buying gifts and saying nice things than doling out daily embraces.

Maybe that's why Cain and I can't seem to keep our hands off each other. "I'm sorry, Cain. I don't know what kind of parents don't celebrate their children's birthdays," I offer softly. "I thought that was just a mandatory thing."

Cain's mirthless chuckle fills the darkness. "She celebrated one." There's a long pause, so long I turn to make sure he hasn't passed out. He's awake, his eyes intently on the side of the desk, his mind obviously far away. "On my fourteenth birthday, my mom introduced me to this girl named Kara. Said she was the daughter of a friend from out of town and asked me to take her out. The girl was hot and older and I had no plans, so I figured, why not?

"She picked me up in a van that night. We drove around for a bit, talked about nothing important, and then she pulled into an empty, dark parking lot. We started making out. Fuck, I wasn't going to complain. I was still a virgin and she seemed nice and into me. Things got heavy and before I knew it we were in the backseat. She was naked and pulling a condom onto me."

"Sounds like a fourteen-year-old's birthday dream come true," I blurt out, followed by a "sorry." *Those are the kinds of thoughts I'm supposed to keep inside my head.*

Cain snorts. "It was . . . until she dropped me off at home and I saw the tears running down her cheeks. I couldn't figure it out. She seemed so into it. When I got home, the first thing my mom asked was, 'Was she any good?' " I hear Cain's teeth grind together. "I had no clue what my mom was involved in at that time. A year later, a few buddies and me broke into the house where my mom ran her bookkeeping business—my grandmother's old house. I hadn't been in it for years. It was the middle of the night, we were drunk, and we just wanted a place to hang. Turns out that the bookkeeping business was more of a hobby, and a front for what was really going on inside that house. I found Kara in a room there with some old married guy. After I chased him out, she admitted that my mother had set everything up that night we were together. She wanted to make sure Kara could go through with paid sex.

"That's how I lost my virginity. At fourteen, to a prostitute, arranged for me by my mother." Cain's head falls back against the couch. "Kara ended up ODing a few years later," he offers vacantly.

"Oh my God, Cain." My chest tightens. So many of Cain's

childhood memories seem to end with sex, drugs, death, or a devastating combination.

Turning, I move to prop myself up on my elbow, intent on distracting him from his dark thoughts. But he quickly shifts out from beneath me, muttering, "I'd better go check on things out there." Without another look back, he leaves.

A prickly lump settles in my throat. Is this about his birthday? Or is Cain upset with me for something? I can't bear that thought. Maybe I shouldn't have prodded. I never prod. I shouldn't start now, slurring and dizzy from those stupid drinks. When he comes back, I'll shut up, wrap my arms around him, and hold him tight.

Until then, I'll just rest my eyes for a while. It feels so good to close my . . .

chapter thirty-one

...

CAIN

The place is a fucking disaster—empty glasses and bottles everywhere. Nate is sitting on the stage with his back against the dancer pole, hunched over. Focusing in on him a little more closely, I see that his eyes are closed.

Giggles from the V.I.P. room tell me that Mercy and others—likely Ben included—are still there, defiling the space. Aside from them, the place is empty. I hit the lights and grab some more water, then check the doors to ensure they're locked and security is set.

Charlie's snoring quietly when I return. I pull a blanket over her body and spend a long moment watching the woman I've come to care so deeply about.

And then I pull her file from my cabinet. I check the birth date to confirm that it's September 23. I've never been to Indianapolis, but I have a hard time believing they have enough snow to toboggan on in September. That's my first question. Maybe there's an explanation, though. Maybe they celebrated a few months late. Maybe they went to the North Pole for her birthday.

More important, though . . . who the fuck is Sam?

■ ■ ■

I know she's awake before she makes a sound or moves a muscle. I sense it in her body, the way it goes rigid against mine. I managed to slide in beneath her comatose frame last night and grab a few hours of sleep with her in my arms. "Do you know what time it is?" she asks in a croaky voice and I feel her swallow several times.

Reaching back to grab my phone that I placed on the side table last night, I flip it open to check. "Eleven."

She lets out a cute little groan. "God, I drank a lot last night. I've never drunk that much before."

"How are you feeling?"

"I may still be drunk."

I chuckle and then wince, the first sign of my own hangover making its appearance. I feel her swallow again and I reach back for a bottle of water. "Here, drink this."

She moans appreciatively, shifting into my groin. "Seriously, Cain?" She shakes her head.

"Sorry," I mutter. "It's the morning and you're lying on me."

"Hmm . . ." I watch as she eases herself up into a sitting position. I haven't forgotten what she said last night. I was drunk, but I wasn't *that* drunk. I know I told her that I don't care about her past. And I don't. But we've been together for weeks now. I'd like to know who the fuck Sam is and why she's referring to him as her father, when her father's name is George Rourke.

Or is it?

Standing, she wobbles a bit, using the wall for support as she heads toward the bathroom. "Yeah, I'm pretty sure I'm still drunk," she announces, pawing at the light inside before closing the door.

If I weren't me, I might not worry so much about this. But I *am* me and she still hasn't divulged a damn thing about herself, even after I laid my history out for her to judge. I lay awake beneath her for hours, trying to rationalize it, to tell myself that it doesn't matter to me. Still, I feel a sense of bitterness seeping in. A touch of betrayal that this woman doesn't trust me, or my word that I would never hold her past against her.

At the same time that the toilet flush sounds inside, her phone begins ringing. Normally, I wouldn't think to go through her things. Now, though . . . I don't hesitate. I unzip her purse. I pull her phone out.

And I answer it.

"Hello?"

There's a second or two of dead air and then, "Who is this?"

"This is Cain. You looking for Charlie?"

Another pause. "Yes. How do you know her?"

I don't like the calm, even tone of his voice. It sounds manipulative. "Sorry, I didn't catch your name?" The number is marked "unknown," so that doesn't help me.

A soft, condescending chuckle answers me. "That's because I didn't give a name."

This must be the same guy that Ginger spoke to. I don't have patience for this. "Well, then I guess you can go fuck yourself."

A sharp hiss fills my ear. "You don't sound like the kind of man I want my daughter with."

"Pardon me?" I did not expect that. And Charlie's father is in Pendleton, so it can't be true. "Who is this?" *Wait* . . . "Is this Sam?"

The line goes dead.

The phone is still in my hand when Charlie emerges with a freshly washed face. She freezes, her now violet eyes skittering from the phone in my hand, to her opened purse, to what I assume is a stony expression on my face.

"What are you doing?" She's trying to sound casual about it, but it's impossible. I can almost see the wave of shock as it ripples through her.

"Who's Sam?" I can't keep the bite from my tone.

She blanches, her mouth opening to tremble for a second.

"You talked to Sam?" Her jaw clamps shut instantly as if she didn't mean to say that out loud. There's undeniable fear in her voice and my anger wavers as worry courses in.

So Sam *does* exist. And she's afraid of him. "I don't know, Charlie. The man I just talked to said he was your father but he wouldn't give his name. So is your father Sam or George?" I can tell by her screwed-up face that she's trying to process the logic behind my words. I sigh. "You were talking about tobogganing with your dad last night. You called him 'Sam' but your dad's name is George. So . . ."

She averts her eyes to dart around the office, searching for something. An answer. Or an escape. Her eyes suddenly widen as panic flies through them. "Did you give him your name?"

"Yes, I did," I answer calmly.

Somehow, her face pales even more. "Why?"

"Why not, Charlie? Why wouldn't I?"

Her head shakes back and forth, ridding itself of panic and fear and . . . everything. "You had no right going through my things or answering my phone."

Standing, I gently place the phone back in the purse. "I guess not."

I turn my back on her and walk out to the club.

■ ■ ■

"Some people need sleep," John mutters groggily.

"Then don't sleep with your phone by the bed," I retort.

With a loud groan, followed by a coughing fit that leaves me cringing at the sound of morning phlegm in John's lungs, my P.I. demands, "What do you need?"

"Is there any chance that her ID is fake?"

"I assume you mean Charlie?"

"Yes," I snap with impatience. When I came back to my office after half an hour, Charlie was gone. She took either a bus or a cab, because she didn't have her truck here.

I have half a mind to drive over to her place and force the truth out of her. I can't bring myself to do it yet, though.

"It's damn solid if it is. She's got a valid passport, birth certificate . . . everything. Maybe it's a stolen ID. You'd need a ton of cash and major connections to pull that off."

"But it's possible." Is everything that I know about Charlie a lie? Has she been lying to me *all this time*?

His heavy exhale blows into the phone. "Yeah, I guess."

"Okay. Can you see what else you can dig up on Charlie Rourke? Old school pictures, gymnastics pictures, anything. And find out if there's anyone by the name of 'Sam' in her life."

"Will do."

I hang up. I stare at my phone, the lump in my throat choking. I want to call her. But, right now, I'm pissed off, too.

More, though, I'm something I haven't felt in years.

I'm hurt.

chapter thirty-two

...

CHARLIE

I knew it was coming.

I've sat on a park bench overlooking the water for hours, staring out at all the people who live their own lives, who worry about paying their rent and what bar they're going to go to on the weekend.

Waiting for my phone to ring. And now it's ringing, the display reading "unknown caller."

He's anything but unknown.

My stomach twists into knots as I answer.

"Hello, little mouse."

"Hi." I'm still shocked that he called my phone. It's registered under "Charlie Rourke" and I'm sure he's using a burner phone, but still, he's breaking one of his rules.

"How are things?"

"Good."

"Good. The weather's lovely at home." Small talk. Sam always did like to keep it simple.

"It's nice here, too."

"Good, good." There's a pause. "I need you to check your email."

My stomach drops.

"What?" No . . . I didn't hear that right. It's been only a few weeks. I was supposed to have months, or longer. Or forever. "I thought we were laying low."

"We were. The problem has been resolved."

What? "No!" I take a deep, shaky breath. I've never said no to Sam. Ever. "I mean . . ."

"Is there something wrong?" There's a long pause. "Is this because of Cain?"

He may as well have reached through the phone and torn my insides right out of my body.

Now Sam has Cain's name. How long before he has more? "No." My hand has never shaken as badly as it does now. I don't even have the steadiness to push it through my hair.

Why did Cain have to do that? Why? I had to fight the gasp from escaping my mouth today when I came out to find my phone in his hand and that strange, inexplicable look on his face. It was like a punch to my stomach.

And then he started questioning me, as I've dreaded him doing for weeks. I didn't know what to do, what to say, so . . . I turned it all back on him. As if *he* were to blame for all this.

I could tell he was angry with me. Worse, by the look in his eyes, I could tell he was hurt. When he turned his back on me and walked out, I did the only thing I could think of. I walked out to the street and hailed a taxi.

"Does he know . . ." Sam's voice trails off, deceptively calm.

"No!" That comes out strong and fast and unmistakable. "Nothing."

"Then how did he have my name?" Suspicion. I hear it dripping from his voice. He thinks he caught me in a lie.

"I was drunk. I let your name slip. It was something harmless, though, about birthdays and—"

"Nothing is harmless!" he snaps, and I flinch. With a breath, he adjusts his tone, though there's no mistaking the ice. "You are down there for a reason. You will do what I ask and you will follow the rules! And, if you don't feel that you owe it to me for giving you all that you have, then do it for your friend's sake be-cause, if I have to come down there, I'll make sure he isn't causing me any more problems. Do you understand?"

Dread seizes my lungs. Somehow I don't think a simple con-versation with a teenage boy—as he most likely had with Ryan Fleming—is what Sam has in mind now. "Okay," I manage to get out in a raspy voice.

"Good thing, little mouse. Right away." The line goes dead.

Quickly logging in to the Gmail account, I find the draft folder. Sure enough, the instructions are there.

Ten tonight. Eddie and Bob. *Fuck* . . . Bob. How is that going to go? I have to hope he realized his own mistake after he sobered up. Maybe he'll apologize?

Maybe I'm the biggest moron in the world.

I have to get out of work tonight. I wonder if Cain even wants me there anymore.

If Sam gets hold of him, he'll wish I'd never walked through his door.

■ ■ ■

I never noticed how heavy that black door at the back of Penny's is.

I could have just phoned Cain. Or texted him.

And yet here I am, walking toward it, aching to see him, ready to crawl on my knees to beg his forgiveness. I can't think much beyond right now, except that I need to see Cain. And that I'll be doing the drop tonight, to make Sam happy. To find some reprieve.

After that . . . I can't think about it. I know what needs to happen and I just can't face it right now.

On the third knock, the door opens and Nate's giant body fills the doorway. His face immediately splits into a wide grin when he sees me. Hope sparks. Maybe Cain doesn't hate me after all. If Cain hated me, Nate would know about it.

I walk down the hall toward Cain's office, butterflies stirring, preparing to give an award-winning performance on deathly female cramping—complete with hands pressed against abdomen and hunching over. That's the only thing I can think of and, given that my period is due any day now, it should work well.

I push open the door to find China, with her skirt hiked up around her waist, straddling Cain's lap on his chair, her lips locked onto his.

And the butterflies drop dead.

chapter thirty-three

...

CAIN

Fucking perfect.

I was one second away from forcefully removing a brazen China from my lap because she wouldn't get off voluntarily—after leaping on, uninvited—when she decided to plant her lips on mine, crushing my dismissal.

And of course that's the exact moment that Charlie would show up unannounced. Because that's the kind of luck I have.

By her wide eyes and hanging jaw, I can tell that Charlie is both surprised and hurt.

And I can't blame her.

In one quick motion, I remove China from my lap—trying not to shove her too hard as I push her off—and I stand, straightening out my pants. Charlie's eyes drifting down tells me that the bulge in my pants is noticeable. *Dammit!* That wasn't from China! That was because, while China was working on a basic math problem, I was eyeing the silver tie hanging on my door, remembering how I walked in to find Charlie wearing it—and *only* it—a few nights ago.

This is *exactly* why I should never have sex in my office.

Clearing her throat, her voice is strangely calm. "Sorry, I should have knocked. I came by to tell you I need the night off. I'm not feeling well."

Not feeling well. Bullshit.

Neither am I. *Fuck, China!*

I stall. "What's wrong, exactly?" *Stupid question.*

"Female issues." Her eyes avert to the floor and I know without a doubt that she's lying. But what can I say, except, "Sure, okay. I'll drive you back to my place."

"No. That's okay." She threw that one back fast. She begins to turn and my hand instinctively flies out, clasping onto her forearm. Not tightly, but enough to keep her there. "That wasn't what it looked like, Charlie. I promise."

She responds with a tight smile. Twisting out of my reach, she turns on her heel and briskly walks out. I hear the heavy exit door slam shut a moment later.

And that's when I explode. "What the fuck was that?" I spin around and settle a deadly glare on China, who has the decency to keep her eyes on the ground as she bites her lip. "What made you think that would be *okay*?" Picking up my glass from my desk, I swig back the last mouthful, those few seconds of emotion on Charlie's face replaying in my mind. "Dammit, China!" The empty glass is sailing out of my hand and toward a far wall before I realize that I threw it. It detonates into countless shards.

I've never lost my temper like this with an employee, but, tonight, I can't help it. I look like a more polished but equally slimy Rick Cassidy.

It takes me a moment to stop my shaking, and then I finally make myself turn around to face China again.

And my heart sinks.

There she is, backed into a corner behind my desk, trembling, her shoulders pulled in tight as she cowers. All color from her face has vanished. The China who works the crowd like she's got puppet strings affixed to their backs is gone, replaced with a pitiful young girl whose father used to scream and throw dishes at her. Right before he raped her.

My hand flies over my mouth as I realize what I've done.

Shit.

"Christ . . ." I start to rush over but when she shrinks farther back, I slow my steps, holding my hands up in surrender. "I'm not going to hurt you." I approach her with extreme caution, until I'm close enough that I can wrap my arms around her shaking body and pull her against me, all while the thickness in my throat grows. I smooth her sleek black hair back with my hand as her tears start to flow, dampening my shirt.

"I'm sorry," she offers between sobs, her voice so pitiful, so weak, so childlike. "I've only ever wanted to make you happy."

"I know." She needs to get back into therapy. She was doing so well. Then she started focusing on beating her learning disorder and she let the therapy part slip. She shouldn't have. I shouldn't have let that happen. China still needs professional help. And lots of it.

When she quiets but stays pressed against my chest, I ask, in as gentle a voice as possible, "What made you do that? We've already talked about this. I thought you understood."

There's a long pause, during which she reaches up to wipe away some tears. "I don't know."

"China." Playing clueless has never suited her.

"I just thought you needed it."

I heave a sigh and curse my fucking dick for starting this. The girl makes her money sniffing out hard-up guys with cash to burn. Hell, she's got erection radar.

"What I need," I say as I pull China away from me to look directly into her pleading green eyes, "is for you to accept that I will *never use* you like that."

She drops her gaze to my chest and nods. With pursed lips, she whispers, "Do you love her?"

Of course. I should have known that this is what it was about. I don't avert my gaze as I say very slowly, "I don't know yet. Maybe."

She can't keep the tears from welling in her eyes. "Why her, Cain? Why not me?"

Ahh . . . fuck me . . . I'm still angry with her but my pity trumps it. "I don't know. These things are beyond our control, sometimes." Pulling her to my body as she starts crying again, I mutter to myself, "I'm not sure it's going to matter either way, now."

I give her ten more minutes of my time.

And then I hand her off to Nate—who is not too happy about the prospect of a sobbing China on him—and I go after Charlie.

chapter thirty-four

• • •

CHARLIE

I so badly want to pick up that phone.

My hand falters, picturing the other end pressed up against Cain's stubble.

The slow but heavy rhythmic beat of my heart speeds up with thoughts of him, of what happened between us, of seeing him with China. He claimed it wasn't what it looked like—and it looked like China was giving him a lap dance while her tongue was down his throat. I almost buckled, the sight like a punch to my stomach.

I feel like a fool.

Has that happened before, between them? Has that happened since he's been with me? My arms curl tightly around my body at the crushing thought. Has he been lying to me this entire time?

Do I have a right to be angry with him, given all the ways in which I've lied to him?

Maybe Cain would be better off with China. Or a woman like China. Or anyone other than me, really. Anyone who wouldn't be putting him in danger as I have, by being so selfish, and so stupid as to believe I could have a future with him. My cluster-fuck of a life feels ready to explode, right here in this gas-station parking lot.

I didn't go home. I couldn't. Cain would track me down and then I'd fall apart into a mess of sobs. Maybe I'd even be brainless enough to tell him everything.

And that would put him in real danger.

I don't know how much more of this I can take.

chapter thirty-five

● ● ●

CAIN

"I hope you enjoy it," the young woman behind the counter offers, flashing me a teasing smile as she hands the key lime pie to me, intentionally grazing my fingers. She's pretty, but she can't be more than eighteen years old and that's way too young for me. Plus, I highly doubt I'm what she's looking for, unless she has daddy issues.

"Thank you," I offer politely. I don't recognize her, but I haven't been to this café in months. It has the best key lime pie in the city and I'm on my way to see Storm. I don't know what to do. Charlie's not at her apartment, she's not at my condo. She's not answering her phone. I'm going out of my fucking mind.

As I walk out the front door and pass by the patio, I note the newly occupied tables.

A pretty doll face catches my eyes.

It's Charlie's twin.

She has the same nose, the same big brown eyes, the same wide mouth. Only her hair isn't blond and curly, it's jet black and long, like China's. My feet slow of their own accord as I blink several times. *I've finally lost it. I've finally become so obsessed with Charlie that I'm seeing her everywhere.*

She's hunched over at a table, sipping a lemonade, opposite a large graying man in a red golf shirt. I can't see his face, but whatever he said must be funny because she tips her head back and laughs.

Just like Charlie does.

I know I should move on, but I stand there and watch as she slides that straw into her mouth for another drink, letting her eyes skitter over the tables around her, to a television up in the corner, to the walkway.

To me.

All the color drains from her face. Her jaw drops as recognition flashes in her eyes.

And I instantly know that I'm staring at Charlie.

chapter thirty-six

. . .

CHARLIE

This can't be happening.

Of all the places in the world for Cain to be right now, the goddamn café where I'm meeting Jimmy should not be one of them. This is beyond bad. The only thing that could make this worse is . . .

This.

My pulse begins pounding in my ears as I watch Cain step onto the covered patio. It takes everything in my willpower not to squeeze my eyes shut and pray. Pray that he'll keep walking. That this is all an illusion. That Cain's not really here. That I've finally gone crazy.

"Charlie, how are you?" His tone is so smooth, as if there's nothing at all unusual about this situation. That I'm not at a café, wearing a wig, clearly trying to disguise myself, instead of at home with a hot water bag and a bottle of Midol. He's used my name and there's no inflection, so there's no question. He recognizes me.

"Hi," I manage to get out, unable to pull myself together to act blasé about this entire situation. There's nothing blasé about this situation.

This could blow everything apart.

There's a pause and then Cain shifts his attention to Jimmy, who, though I can tell by his sudden shifting in his chair and his sidelong glance at me is uneasy, is not downright disturbed, as I am. Sticking his hand out, he gives Cain a toothy grin. "Hi, I'm Jimmy. Charlie's uncle."

Cain's eyebrows shoot up. "Uncle . . ." It's a moment before he accepts Jimmy's hand. "Nice to meet you. I'm—"

"Dylan." It comes out in a shout. When I speak again, I make sure that I adjust my tone. "Uncle Jimmy, this is Dylan." I hazard a glance up at Cain to see steely eyes on me.

Please go along with it.

"Yes . . ." Cain says, the word drifting off as his mouth twists slightly, his eyes never leaving my face. "Though some people call me Cain."

My heart spasms in my chest. I should have known. Cain is not afraid to give his name out. He's not afraid of anyone.

I wonder if he would be afraid of Sam.

Without prompting, Cain leans back to grab a chair from the table next to us. Swinging it around, he takes a seat. I finally notice the key lime pie in his hand as he sets it down on the table. It makes me think of Storm. He must be going to see her tonight.

"Do you live around here, Jimmy? Or are you in town for a visit?" Cain's voice is so smooth. He doesn't seem at all awkward and I don't know why, seeing as I want to peel my own skin off and run away right now.

Jimmy gives that jovial chuckle of his. "Oh, just in from New York for the week on business."

Nodding, Cain asks, "And what is it you do?"

"I own a construction company down here. Focused mainly on commercial sites."

I watch as the two of them casually chitchat back and forth, Jimmy fluidly lying to Cain and Cain accepting each lie without any expression at all, though I know he doesn't believe a word. I wonder if the real Charlie Rourke even had an uncle. I have no clue. But I'll bet Cain will find out, if he doesn't already know.

All I know is that this conversation needs to end now. I just don't know how to end it. Lying just isn't coming as easily to me as it used to. Not since I met Cain.

Jimmy is as aware of the clock as I am. The hotel drop site is ten minutes away and I need to be there in twenty minutes. There can be no delays. I don't want to give Bob another reason to be angry with me. He slurps the last of his lemonade rather rudely and then announces, "Well, it was nice to meet you, *Cain*."

Yes, Uncle Jimmy knows I was lying about the name. He's mentally sizing Cain up right now, noting his height, his weight, his hair color, eye color, the scar on his brow, the tribal tattoo on his bicep peeking out beneath the gray golf shirt.

Maybe even the one on his neck. If Jimmy tells Sam about *that* one . . .

That was a farewell from Uncle Jimmy if I ever did hear one. The problem is, Cain isn't accepting it. He slings his arm over the back of my chair and stretches his legs out, as if getting comfortable. If I didn't know any better, I'd think he was fully aware of the attempted dismissal and is politely giving Jimmy a "fuck off." I'm surprised he hasn't handed him a business card.

"Yes, it was nice to meet you too, Jimmy." He turns to look at me, his eyes rolling over my wig for a moment before settling on mine. As if he's letting me know that, yes, he's noticed my wig. In case there was any doubt. "Let me give you a ride back home?"

I'm going to be sick. I feel the blood draining from my face. "No, I'm good, I drove here," I answer in a clipped tone. I'm not even allowing myself to feel the sting of the China incident right now. I just need Cain to be gone. Him being here, talking to Jimmy, is enough to cause me a seizure.

"So, how do you two know each other, again?" Jimmy asks, cold, flinty eyes drifting between me and Cain's arm on my chair.

I clear my throat, scrambling to think of something. I can't give Cain a chance to answer. All Sam has right now is a name. He can't find out about Penny's.

"We have a mutual friend," Cain answers before I can cough up a lie. It's not a lie, but it's such an intentionally vague answer. Thankfully, Cain has no more interest in Jimmy knowing about him than I do.

"Oh, really . . ." Jimmy scratches his wiry beard as if in thought. "What's this friend's name? Have I met him? Her?"

And here we go. Jimmy is gathering information.

"No, you wouldn't have. Just a girl who lives in my building." To try and steer him away from any assumptions about Cain and me being a couple, I add with hesitation, "She's his girlfriend."

I feel Cain's cutting glare but I don't turn to meet it.

Jimmy's cheek puffs out as he presses against it with his tongue, taking the two of us in as he nods slowly. Deciding something, he glances at his watch and announces, "Well, my dear Charlie. I think we have somewhere we need to be." Making a point of standing up, Jimmy sticks his hand out. "Pleasure to meet you. Now if you'll excuse us."

Cain takes it. "Likewise, *Jimmy.*" He doesn't hide the iciness in his glare.

I follow suit, standing and collecting my purse and keys—the rental car keys—from the table.

"Charlie, a moment please?" Cain's tone is clipped.

I can see annoyance flash in Jimmy's eyes but he doesn't want to make a scene . . . yet. He pulls on the jovial voice and chuckle. "I'll be just over here, Charlie," he says, moving off no more than ten feet away, pretending to check his messages.

I know what he's doing. He's trying to get a picture of Cain. No doubt, for Sam.

I grab Cain's arms and swivel them so his back is to Jimmy. "What?" I whisper harshly. My level of panic has reached new highs.

"Charlie . . ." Cain's eyes roam over my face and hair again. I've experienced so many intimate moments with this man, and yet right now I couldn't possibly feel farther away from him. "Please don't do whatever you're about to do. I can't—" He cuts off abruptly, that jaw that I've had my mouth on countless times growing taut.

A painful lump fills my throat. He's figured it out. Maybe not entirely, but he knows it's something bad. "Can we talk about this later?"

I can see the internal struggle inside him. Will he even want anything to do with me later? Cain could do a lot of things *right now*. He could put up a fight. He could pull me into his car.

Or he could just walk away.

Finally, with narrowed eyes, he asks, "Are you in danger?"

"No," I lie quickly, my eyes flickering to where Jimmy stands, his head turned and tilted as if he's trying to catch the conversation.

"Charlie! We have to go. Your father is waiting for you," Jimmy calls out in a sterner voice than I've ever heard him use with me. Maybe that's his normal tone. I don't know anything about Jimmy. He could be a cold-blooded killer. He could be planning Cain's death right now.

I don't have to look up at Cain's face to know that there's a cyclic storm of unanswered questions brewing in his head. Is he wondering about the father that's in jail? Or the one who called today?

I don't need to look, and yet I do. My heart stops.

I don't miss the subtle shake of his head, the clenched teeth. The disappointment.

The anger, as he realizes that the woman he's been nothing but kind and generous and loving to is a liar.

I hear the agony in my voice as I whisper, "You need to let me go." *For good.* I'm no good for him.

"You want me to let you go? Fine." I see him swallow hard and then his face turns stony. "Consider yourself gone."

■ ■ ■

"What is this?" The guy flips a few strands of my black hair through his fingers. "A wig?"

"You want to borrow it?" I ask smoothly, letting my eyes shift pointedly to his receding hairline.

I get a cold, flinty glare in return. "You've got a smart mouth, don't ya?"

It's the only thing keeping me from pissing my pants right now. I bite down on my tongue to keep quiet and scan the small hotel room for anything important to note. It's a different hotel than before, but just as high end. Eddie and Bob are here—without any family as cover—but so is this new guy. He's on the heavier side, with beady eyes and a couple of days of dark scruff that camouflage the pockmarks on his cheeks. He calls himself Manny. Apparently he's Eddie's new partner. Maybe he is, but there's standard protocol and Eddie has clearly broken it.

Manny is not supposed to be here. The second I saw him sitting on the bed, I made a move to leave but Bob was there, blocking my exit, grabbing my purse before I could think to pull out my gun.

I knew I was trapped.

The pain in my chest instantly blossomed. There's nothing I can do except pray this isn't a setup, try not to lose control of my bladder, and get the hell out of here the second I have the chance.

Bob goes about his body search again. Thankfully it's silent and quick this time—with less groping involved—and I let myself breathe a tiny sigh of relief. I've received not a glare, not a word, not a flicker of an eye to do with "the incident." I can't help but notice that his nose looks somehow different. A bit swollen. And there's a lump on the bridge. I wonder if that was courtesy of Nate.

I remind myself that this is a business. A disgusting, illegal business but, as Sam rationalized before, everyone in this room just wants to make a lot of money. I just need to chill out and—

The sound of a small click is the only warning I get before the cool metal of a gun presses against my temple.

One heartbeat.

Two.

Three.

Each one slower, louder, harder. A strange wave of calm washes over me for a moment. And then my stomach drops out from my body, taking with it my ability to speak, to think, to breathe.

"So, what kind of fucking moron is this Sam guy, anyway? I mean, who sends a little bitch in for this kind of deal? You're good for shoving eight balls up your snatch and driving across the border. Did he really think we wouldn't put a bullet in you and walk away with the money *and* the goods? He's not the only one who can bring this in for us."

I fight against the shakiness in my legs as Manny drags the barrel of the gun along my cheek toward my mouth, to trail my lips. I can't stop my knees from wobbling. They're barely holding me up. "Not so mouthy now, are we?" He pushes the gun in slightly, just enough that I can taste an odd mixture of dirt and metal and salt and oil. The tiniest whimper escapes me. "Of course, a bullet is messy. I hate dealing with that kind of mess. It takes hours to clean up."

His words aren't missed. The promise in them stops my heart from beating altogether, as if someone has put his hand over the pendulum to stop time. My time, that is.

A calming numbness begins to swell through my body, mingling with the terror, and my thoughts drift morbidly away. I wonder how much of my blood will actually hit the gold-and-tan striped wallpaper. That *would* leave a lot to clean up. Will they do it here or somewhere else?

A loud click sounds in my ear. Not the safety, not the chamber loading . . .

The trigger.

Manny just pulled the trigger.

Cold rushes in a sudden wave from my head down to my feet, every part of my body paralyzed except for my eyes. They take in the hotel room, Eddie, Bob. I'm still here.

I'm still alive.

Maybe I didn't hear that. Maybe it was just my imagination.

Manny's mouth is moving again. It takes all of my focus to hear his words. ". . . or we could also cut this tight little body up into a thousand pieces and feed it to the gators." He shows me two silver teeth when he smiles. I stare at them, wondering how long he's going to drag this out, as he moves the gun from my mouth, sliding it down my chin, following the contour of my throat. I swallow hard as it keeps moving down my neck to my chest. The barrel of the gun tugs down the top of my shirt until it exposes the lace on my bra. "Of course, I'd make good use of this first. Such a waste not to."

My focus slides to his hands—big, rough-looking, hairy-knuckled hands. I'm sure he's not gentle. A single shudder courses through my body. I'm sure this is going to be ten times more horrific than what I lived through with Sal.

And I won't be walking away this time.

I wonder what will happen after I'm gone. Will Sam care? Will he seek revenge? Or . . . was this the plan all along? Botched drug bust that leaves girl dead in hotel.

Maybe Sam does truly love me.

Enough that he can't actually do the killing himself and so he's set Manny up to do it.

I wish I had kissed Cain today. Just one last kiss. Will he care that I'm gone? Will he even bother trying to contact me again? Will he figure out that I'm dead?

Now I can see the gun, see Manny's hands, see his finger on the trigger as it pulls. I jump with that clicking sound but otherwise stay still. Stay frozen. How? I don't know. How have I not lost consciousness now?

"Damn clip. Not sure how many bullets I have in here," Manny murmurs with a cruel smile.

"Manny," I hear Eddie call somewhere in the background. At least I think I do. My senses are sharper and at the same time feel completely unreliable. "Quit playing games. It's unnecessary."

"You are an odd one," Manny murmurs, ignoring his partner. "I have a few bitches bringing stuff in from Mexico. They drop to their knees for me as soon as I show them my gun, groveling and crying. But you . . ." His jaw offsets as he ponders me, his eyes shifting down to my chest. He pushes the metal harder against my chest . . . harder . . . harder . . . until I grit my teeth to keep from crying out in pain. "Trying to be tough. I'll bet you'd cry by the end. That's all right, though . . ." With the gun still pressed painfully against my chest, his free hand reaches down to grab hold of an inner thigh. I can feel the heat from his fingers as he squeezes my flesh painfully hard. "I'll make you scream one way or another."

The cool feeling deep inside me spreads wider and wider, fully taking over my senses now, as my breathing turns shallow.

And I know that shock has settled in.

Shock is good.

Shock will get me through this.

If anything can get me through this.

Eddie's still talking in the background. "This is good stuff, Manny. Don't burn this bridge for us right out of the gate." He's sitting on the bed, his hand over the suitcase, his face calm but his eyes full of wariness.

At first I don't think Manny heard him. But then I see his eyes tighten, and I can tell he's weighing his options. I imagine I know what they are: on one side of the scale is a valuable shipment of drugs that he could walk out of here with for free, but have to deal with a body and possible repercussions; and on the opposite side is a long-term business relationship. How long-term, really? Will it be two drops or ten before he makes good on his promise? I imagine it's only a matter of time.

"It's all good. All here," Bob says, thumbing through the multitude of vials. "Let's finish this up and move on. We don't need a mess to clean up."

"Just remember this moment if you ever think to come in here with the cops in your pocket." With one last long, hard look at my face, Manny drops his arm and steps away. I don't allow myself to take a full breath, even as Bob hands me the camera bag full of money, opened.

I struggle to keep my focus on the money as I flip through a few bundles, making sure they're not just newsprint or blank paper. Though, really, I don't see what the point is. If these guys want to rip Big Sam off, they easily can. If they want to rape me and chop me up into a thousand pieces for the gators, they can do that too. Manny's right. Young women are used as expendable mules across borders for small deliveries, not to complete massive transactions in hotel rooms. Sending me in here is just a disaster waiting to happen.

"We're good," I manage to force out, though my throat is bone dry. I throw the strap over my shoulder and turn, my hearing warped, my vision blurry as it focuses intently on the door.

"Look forward to seeing you again," Manny calls out with a wicked voice as Bob walks me to the door.

As I step out, a fist seizes my wrist. "Girl."

The last thing I want to do is talk to him, but I don't have much choice. He's leaning out the door, glancing over his shoulder, as if he doesn't want them to hear him. "If I ever see you again, I promise I'll make good use of that bed, do you understand?" He speaks in a low, fast, harsh whisper. "Get the fuck away from here and don't come back. I'm not taking the heat from your club friends *when* you turn up dead." He releases my wrist with a throw and slinks back, the door shutting quietly behind him.

Leaving me standing alone in a hallway with a bag of money, a bubble of vomit rising, and the knowledge that I was seconds away from dying tonight.

chapter thirty-seven

...

CAIN

"So . . ." Storm's arm is still linked around mine as we walk along the sidewalk, the oppressive summer heat making our pace extra slow.

"Are you sure we should be walking out here?" I ask, glancing down at her ever-growing belly.

She swats away my concern with her free hand. "Yes, I'm fine. And if I'm not, you can carry me back. Now, stop trying to change the subject." She peers up at me with that cute, curious stare of hers. "What made you show up on my doorstep tonight with that sad look upon your face?"

With a sigh, I mutter, "I don't know where to begin, Storm." Storm is the most nonjudgmental person I've ever met. I know I can tell her anything and not worry about her disapproval. Nor will she divulge anything. With my free hand lifting to rub the tension out of my neck, I give her the basic rundown of the last few weeks, ending in today's disastrous events.

She groans. "Oh, Cain. I'm so sorry. Fucking China." It sounds so off-kilter to hear Storm swear. Then again, no one would think she used to swing from a brass hoop above my stage only a few years ago. But if anyone can make Storm swear, it's China.

"I know. But China has issues. You know that."

"Everyone has issues, Cain. Stop making excuses for her," Storm scolds. "And if you have any hope of a relationship with Charlie then you know what you need to do."

I sigh, dreading the words. "China's got to go." Already, my chest is tightening, visions of the raven-haired woman kneeling on a dingy carpet in front of some asshole assaulting my conscience. *Fuck.* "But she's just so close to—"

"She's got to go, Cain," Storm says more forcefully. "We all make our own choices. You've helped her more than anyone ever has and probably more than anyone ever will. Now she needs to help herself." She stops and steps in front of me, poking my chest with a manicured finger. "And *you* have to stop living in your past or you're going to die a very sad, very lonely man. The thought of that breaks my heart." Stepping back, she gives my arm a gentle rub and then prods the conversation. "So you saw Charlie at the café, in a wig, with this uncle . . ."

I tell her the rest, including the phone call from the guy who's supposedly her father, "Sam."

"And it doesn't match up with what John's found out for you?"

"No." Part of me feels like I'm betraying Charlie by divulging this, even to Storm, but I don't know what else to do. I don't know what to think. With a hiss through my gritted teeth, I shake my head and admit, "I was so close to throwing her over my shoulder and walking out of there."

"I *am* surprised that Caveman Cain didn't make an appearance," she says with a giggle, her vision clouding over as her thoughts drift to the past, I'm sure to the time that I did that to her. I'll never forget it. The first day Storm came in with heavy makeup around her eye and a story about an unfortunate tumble into the wall, my gut told me to call John and ask him to do some research on her husband. When she came in with a fat lip a week later, my gut said fuck the research. Nate and I drove her home to find a coked-out asshole on the couch and a toddler crying in the crib. Storm started babbling about how he was stressed, how she'd said something stupid to him, that he'd never hurt Mia. All typical excuses used by an abused woman. I had heard it all before. That's why I scooped Mia up in one arm and, leaning down, hoisted a teary-eyed, scared Storm over my shoulder. In hindsight, I probably could have escorted her out on her own two feet but at the time, all I could think of was filling my arms so I didn't have a chance to beat that asshole senseless.

But I couldn't bring myself to do that tonight, to Charlie. I wanted her to make that decision on her own, to come home with me willingly. I didn't want to force her. I've never wanted to force her.

I need to know that she chooses me.

But she asked me to let her go, instead.

And I did. With my words, anyway. In those few seconds, I wanted her to feel the pain that I was feeling.

"Well, I'm sure you've figured this out, but it sounds like she's into something. The question is what."

"There are only a few things it could be." The very thought of her fucking another guy makes my fists ball up. But my gut says that's not it. She's not practiced enough to be doing that professionally. If not that, what else? Theft . . . extortion . . . drugs?

Shit.

Drugs.

"What?"

"Nothing." As I glance at Storm through the corner of my eye, her wrinkled brow tells me she may have come to the same conclusion on her own. Still, I won't voice this out loud. I can't put Storm in that position. I know her. She'd tell Dan. Not because she wants to get Charlie into trouble; she'd think she was helping. But Storm is naïve in that sense. Getting the DEA involved without knowing exactly what's happening could put Charlie's life at risk. I've seen this all before. They'll put her into a little room and drill her for information, and it will be up to her whether she wants to spend the next twenty-five years in jail or turn on whoever is making her do this.

Turning means testifying. Testifying means someone will want her dead.

I need to find Charlie. Now.

chapter thirty-eight

. . .

CHARLIE

I don't bother to smile at the valet this time when I climb into my waiting car. I don't even think about it. I don't race to the cash drop location. In fact, if the needle didn't tell me I was doing forty miles per hour, I'd believe my car was parked in the middle of the road.

Jimmy's clearance text on the burner phone he handed me tonight comes in and I do as expected, walking stiffly to my Sorento. When I'm safely inside it, with the doors locked and the key in the ignition, I have just enough time to grab and open the spare plastic bag sitting in the glove compartment before the entire contents of my stomach comes up.

I'm dry heaving when the burner phone starts ringing.

"Hello." I hear the emptiness in my voice.

"All good, little mouse?"

Did Sam know that Manny would be there? Did he do that to me on purpose, to scare me? Or is Manny the "other way in" that Sam was looking for? I'm not supposed to use names and give details, even though it's a burner phone and there can't be any wiretaps yet. Suddenly, I don't care. Of all the things I should be worried about, cops listening in on this conversation is not one of them. "Eddie has a partner. He was there tonight. His name is Manny. He put a gun to my head and pulled the trigger but the chamber was empty. Then he threatened to chop me up into a thousand pieces and feed me to the gators. He said he was going to rob you." The sentences come out choppy and without emotion.

Dead silence meets my words. I wait. I say nothing and listen, until I hear a sharp inhale. I picture Sam sitting in his cellar, smoking a cigar as he talks to me.

"Everything else went as planned?"

Sam doesn't sound like he cares that someone was seconds away from killing me tonight. But Sam is as hard to read as I am. I've learned from the best, after all. "Yes." *You got your money, Sam.* "I'm not doing this anymore. This was the last time." I set my jaw stubbornly against the urge to backpedal.

I'm not going back there.

"That's not an option. I have big plans for us. I was going to surprise you with this but I've been holding a cut for you, cycling it through some real estate ventures. One year with Manny and you'll have more money than you could dream of."

"*A year?*" My voice explodes into a shrillness I've never heard in myself. That I can't control. "I won't last a year. Didn't you just hear what I said? Manny's going to kill—"

Sam cuts me off with a sharp edge. "*I* knew he was going to be there. He was just making sure you were legit, that's all. Do you *really* think I'd ever send you in somewhere that I thought you'd get hurt?"

"You already have." My cold whisper is somehow harsher than the shrill voice a moment ago.

"That was a mistake that I made amends for. At great risk to myself, for you! Have you already forgotten?"

"I'll never forget what you did to him." Amends. Because executing a man is supposed to make me feel better.

"And have you forgotten *all* that I've done for you?"

I swallow the bubble of guilt trying to make its way up, fighting for dominance over my bitterness. But I say nothing.

"I'll take care of Manny, little mouse," Sam says softly, soothingly. "He was just keeping you on your toes, but I'll make sure he knows that you are trustworthy. Because you are, right?"

Sam is trying to appease me. Make me feel like he's actually doing me a favor. "I just want out. I don't care about the money."

In an instant, his tone is glacial again. "Really . . . the spoiled little girl doesn't care about the money. Will you care when you can't pay for your schooling? Or your fancy clothes and your car? I wonder if you'll care when you're whoring yourself out to make ends meet."

Too late, Sam.

How could you do this to me?

Sam has never spoken to me like that before. There's a long pause. "Let's talk tomorrow, when you've stopped being so irrational." The phone clicks, ending the call.

The near-death shock hasn't worn off but a familiar edge is beginning to find its way back in now: that familiar pain throbbing in my chest cavity, the difficulty breathing, the relief associated with wondering what it would be like to just fall asleep and never wake up again.

All the things I found a brief escape from with Cain.

But I was an idiot. There is no real escape.

Sam won't let me go. He'll never let me go.

"'I have big plans for us,'" I echo his words in a whisper as I wrap my fingers around the steering wheel, as I absorb the gravity of the situation. Those words are like a heavy steel door closing above me. Trapping me back inside this suffocating cage that is my life.

Somehow I kept the tears at bay while on the phone with Sam, but now that I'm alone they pour freely, burning hot against my cheeks.

Sam knows about Cain.

He has a name, a physical description. Perhaps even a picture, though he didn't mention it. How long before Sam finds him? If I stay here, I'm putting a target on his chest.

I can't put Cain in any more danger.

You don't do that to people you love.

Cranking my Sorento, I pull out onto the street, the lights and stop signs blurred by my tears.

With no destination, I drive.

I know where my selfish heart wants me to go. I don't even care about the China incident anymore. Given that I just had a loaded gun pointed at my head, it seems trivial. I don't know why China was on his lap. He says he had a good reason and I believe him.

But I asked Cain to let me go. And he did.

Which makes what I have to do easier.

I feel the freedom I had tasted fading away.

As Jimmy tails me.

I'm surprised that I even caught on. I wouldn't have, had I not looked in my rearview mirror at that precise second to see a black sedan three cars back make a left-hand turn, the streetlight reflecting off its shiny upgraded hubcaps.

It looked an awful lot like the same car I climbed into earlier tonight. Seven minutes and three turns later, I can't deny that it *is* the same car.

I pass by the entrance to my apartment building—quivering at how easily I could have brought Jimmy there, handing him yet another bit of information that could lead him to Cain—and I continue all the way to a twenty-four-hour diner on the other side of Miami.

Far away from everyone I've come to love.

chapter thirty-nine

...

CAIN

"Cain?"

The minimal hair that Tanner has left is standing on end as he answers his door, half asleep, the day's sports highlights blaring through his apartment in the background.

"I need a key to Charlie's apartment."

He frowns. "Well . . . er . . . the laws say—"

"Fuck the law, Tanner," I snap. "Either give me the key or I'll bust down the door, and then you'll be dealing with contractors to fix it."

Grumbling something unintelligible, Tanner reaches up and grabs the giant ring of keys that hangs on the wall beside the door. He reminds me of a jailer in that regard, but I don't say anything. Thrusting it forward with a scowl, I feel his eyes on my back as I march toward 1-D. Tanner's a fantastic superintendent.

"Charlie?" I call out as I step into the dark apartment. I'm almost positive she's not here because her car's not out front. Still, I know she has a gun and I'd rather not get shot tonight.

Silence responds.

She could be back any minute, so I don't waste time, heading straight for her bedroom. I don't expect to find much, seeing as my closet and dresser are overflowing with her clothes and her feminine stuff has invaded my bathroom cabinet. In fact, based on my cursory inspection of her bedroom, the room is empty, except for the sheets on her bed.

And the bottom dresser drawer.

I start rifling through the assortment of workout clothes packed within—shorts, T-shirts, yoga pants—until I come to one . . . two . . . three . . . I pull out five wigs buried beneath. Blond, brunette, short-haired, long-haired. The strands are silky between my fingertips. I'm pretty sure it's real hair, and if it's real, that means these wigs are expensive.

Suitable for high-end disguises.

And high-end crimes.

The curly brown one makes a thumping sound as I whip it at the wall in anger. How did I not have a clue? I've been sleeping with, working with, *falling for* this woman!

It has to be drugs. No wonder she's been so secretive. *Fuck!* Given who Dan is, my past . . . it's all adding up. I remember how she froze when she realized I had spoken to this Sam guy. It doesn't take a genius to figure out that whoever he is, he's controlling her—and she's terrified of him. Maybe he *is* her real father. That would mean she has assumed someone else's identity, because the one she gave me is real.

Someone went to a lot of trouble to hide who she really is.

Quickly searching the rest of the place, I find nothing of interest. And no gun. She must have it on her.

There's really not much left to do except sit on her couch—inhaling the faint scent of her floral perfume that it still holds. I slide my phone out of my pocket and dial her number. And wait. But . . . what the fuck am I going to say? Accuse her of dealing drugs over the phone? *Shit*. I should have given this some more thought.

With a heavy sigh, my thumb shifts to the "end" button when Charlie's sweet voice comes on to ask me to leave a message. But

I find I can't hit it. I can't break this connection to her. What if it's the only one I have left? What if this is my only chance to get everything off my chest?

"Hi, Charlie." My voice cracks with her name. It might not be her real name, but it's the only one I know. To me, she's Charlie. She's the woman who stole my heart right out from me before I even realized she had her hands on it. I chuckle into the phone, the irony not lost to me. I did hire a thief, after all.

Like a floodgate, the words begin pouring out freely and quickly as I try to beat the time limit on the messaging system. I explain what happened with China and how I'm firing her. I explain how I just rifled through her things and I know what she's into—or suspect what she's into—and how I don't care, as long as she'll let me help her get away from it. I'll do anything to help her get out of it.

I explain how I wish I had never said those words to her tonight, how I could never just let her go. How we can figure this out.

How I've fallen for her.

It isn't until the answering service cuts me off that I realize my entire body is shaking.

I lean back. I take a deep, calming breath.

And I wait for her to come home.

She's not leaving my sight again until she trusts me completely. Until I drag every last confession out of her beautiful mouth.

Until I get her out of this fucking mess.

chapter forty

■ ■ ■

CHARLIE

I won the showdown.

Four cups of coffee and two pieces of apple pie later, I watched the black sedan pull out of the parking lot and head left. He likely figured out that I was on to him. There's a good chance he's waiting in a nearby parking lot for my truck to pull out, so I watch the window for another two hours, until my eyes are heavy and I'm seriously debating curling up on the bench.

But I can't, because I still have too much to do, including the first unselfish thing I've done since the day I walked into Penny's. As soon as the plump middle-aged waitress comes back from her smoke break, I politely ask her for a pen and some paper.

■ ■ ■

I hug my knapsack to my body. There's fifty thousand dollars packed into it, so, naturally, I feel like a sitting duck with a sign over my head that reads "rob me of all that I have." It *is* all that I have, along with some basic supplies and a few articles of clothing that I picked up at the twenty-four-hour Walmart while waiting for the bank to open.

It took ten minutes to clear out my safety deposit box and

my bank account. When I went to sell my car to the dealership, they told me it would take a few days to cut me a check. I flirted, I yelled, I groveled. I pulled out all my best acting skills. Finally I asked them what it would cost to get them to take it immediately.

I walked out of there with ten grand in cash, knowing I had been cheated.

Not caring.

Now, as I sit on a bench, waiting for my bus out of Miami, there's only one thing left to do. Well, two things.

I'm not sure which is harder.

My burner phone rings. "Hello, little mouse. Feeling normal again today?"

Normal. What is normal? My quiet acceptance of all that Sam has trained me to be? Of his tainted love, with all the ugliness that comes with it?

I had an entire speech planned, about how he had taken advantage of me, how you don't put those you love in danger. How I don't think I can ever forgive him. But I'm tired and it just feels unnecessary. There are only two words I need to say.

They may come out wobbly, but they are unyielding. "Goodbye, Sam."

Shutting the burner phone off, I toss it in the trash as a wave of relief washes over me.

I am done with Sam.

That was the easy part.

Not wasting any time, I pick up my real phone. I take a deep, calming breath. And hit "send" on the text that I've struggled to type out for an entire hour. I know he called me last night—I see the notification of a message—and yet I can't bear to listen to whatever he said. Just hearing his voice might crack my resolve, which would be catastrophic. I've already set too many wheels in motion this morning. I need a clean break.

Cain gave me that last night.

The only reason I'm texting him now is because of that voice in the back of my conscience that says I don't want him to worry about me. Because, despite what he may think of me right now, he might grow concerned when I don't come to pick up my things, when no one hears from me again.

I wait for the indication that the message has been delivered, and then I quickly shut the power off, strip it of its memory chip, and toss it into the trash.

I wrap my arms around my knapsack and bury my face so no one sees the tears that begin pouring out.

Waiting for the second wave of relief.

The one that never comes.

chapter forty-one

...

CAIN

The chime of my phone startles me awake.

The words staring out at me from the screen turn my blood cold:

I hope you can forgive me one day. Please give my apartment to Ben and anything of mine at your place to Ginger.

It takes me another few moments to fully process what's going on.

Charlie is saying goodbye.

No.

Did she even listen to my message? She couldn't have. She wouldn't be leaving me if she had.

I rush to dial her number—number one on my favorites. It goes straight to voice mail.

Fuck. No.

With quick fingers, I punch out a message:

Call me. Now.

I get an error message back, saying the text was never delivered.

I try again.

I try ten more times.

Each time, the message bounces back. It's as if Charlie has disconnected her phone.

As if I'm never going to hear from her again.

The thought of that brings a sting to my eyes. *No . . . this can't be happening.* Checking the clock to see that it reads ten a.m.—I must have drifted off on Charlie's couch around six—I hit number two on speed dial. I don't even wait for John's greeting. The second I hear someone pick up, I throw out my demand. "Get your ass to Miami. Today."

■ ■ ■

"Still a fucking looker, I see," John booms, stalking into my office to slap his meaty hand against mine.

"And you're still not, I see," I retort with a wry grin, softly punching his substantial gut. "What is this?"

"The women love it!" With a boom of laughter, John turns to appraise Nate's size with a whistle. The last time they saw each other, Nate was still a scrawny teenager. "What have you been feeding this runt?"

Nate's face splits wide open in a grin as he takes John's hand in his own.

Nodding slowly, John murmurs, "Good to see you two again. I can't believe it's been so long since . . ."

"Nine years," I confirm. After *that* night, John seemed to make a point of swinging by my apartment weekly, offering any little bits of info on my family's murder. Bits that didn't add up to anything, but I appreciated it all the same because it meant the cops hadn't already dismissed it. He came around enough, saw enough of my black eyes and bruised knuckles, that he *had* to know I was fighting. He never questioned me, though.

The night that John showed up at my house three months after the murder with two mug shots was the night he earned my trust. Tossing them onto the table, he told me to memorize those faces and to run in the other direction should I ever see them.

They belonged to the men who the police suspected were involved and sometimes, especially in drug-related crimes that involved money, family members and friends become targets. If he knew anything about the money I stole, he never let on.

He warned me that the lead was circumstantial at best and wouldn't hold up in court but maybe, just maybe, they'd find concrete evidence. But he added that the police force was over-extended, that they had some high-profile cases on their desk already, that sometimes, despite knowing who the guilty persons are, those nails in their coffins could remain elusive.

Basically, John was telling me not to get my hopes up.

That was the last night we ever talked about my family's murder.

Tossing his duffel bag onto the floor—he obviously came straight from the airport—John takes a seat on the couch as I pour him a fresh glass of cognac. And he dives right into business. "So, her phone hasn't been used since an outgoing text to you at ten-oh-four this morning, eastern standard time. Looks like it's no longer operational. She must have pulled the sim card out. Banks accounts are drained. I've got her credit card being monitored and I'll get notified if it's used. I've got people searching the airlines out of here. But, if she took a bus and paid cash, we're S.O.L."

Nate and I exchange a serious look as John takes a sip of his drink. When I filled Nate in on everything earlier, I thought he was going to throttle me. He started to ask why the hell I ever let her leave with that guy, but he stopped short, knowing I was already beating myself senseless over it.

I'll never forgive myself for that.

"Oh, and that uncle you were asking me about?" John sets his drink down on a side table with a frown as he drags his bag closer. Pulling out a manila envelope that's tucked into a side pocket, he confirms, "His name is Phillip. Fifty years old. Mechanic. Here." He hands me a picture of a thin, brown-haired man, confirming one hundred percent that the man I met last night is not Charlie's uncle. Or that everything I know about her past isn't true.

Fuck, which is it?

"Cain, why the hell did you drag me all the way here to give you this information? I assume it's for something good. I mean, I don't mind seeing you." His hand gestures in the direction of the club with a knowing smirk. "I certainly don't mind visiting you *here*. But I could have given you all this information over the phone."

I pause to inhale the rest of my drink. "I've got another lead for finding her."

"Well then . . ." He moves with surprising agility for such a large, unfit man. "Let's get on with it."

Despite my sour mood, I smile. "Thanks for dropping everything to come out, John."

"All-expense-paid trip to Miami?" he snorts. "Why would I say no to that!" He takes the few steps around my desk to settle a heavy hand on my shoulder. "Besides, you know I'm a sucker for love."

chapter forty-two

. . .

CHARLIE

I wonder if someone actually went out of his way to cover this small, musty motel room in blue peacock wallpaper.

Maybe it was a special price that he couldn't pass up. Along with a discount on the cheap furniture, the puce shag carpet, and the mint-green floral bedspread.

Or maybe this is how all shady motels in Mobile, Alabama, are decorated.

It took one transfer and nineteen hours but I made it to my destination, care of the coin toss when I purchased my bus ticket. After spending hours looking for a motel that didn't require a credit card or an ID to rent a room, I finally found this one. All the scraggly-haired guy at the front desk seemed to require was an extra-tight T-shirt and cash.

Luckily, I had both.

I haven't slept in days.

I keep reaching into my purse for my phone, only to realize that I don't have one anymore. Nor do I have a driver's license or a credit card, or a Social Security number, or a passport. It's all gone, cut up into small pieces and burned.

I am no one.

I strip all the covers off the bed and pull on a T-shirt of Cain's that I had in my car, inhaling the fresh, woodsy smell until my lungs feel like they're about to explode.

Aside from my memories, this is all I have left of him. Even if I don't wash it, I wonder how long it will be before his scent is gone.

I burst out in a fresh round of ragged sobs at the thought, my arms clinging to my body as if the act will keep me together.

As if it will keep my heart from falling apart.

chapter forty-three

■ ■ ■

CAIN

"I've been on that guy for almost two weeks, Cain. I'm telling you, he's barely left his place. Aside from the hooker he picked up two nights ago and a trip to the grocery store for two steaks, one bag of jerky, two pounds of bacon, three dozen eggs, one pack of burgers . . ." John ticks off Ronald Sullivan's grocery list on his fingers to prove how good of a detective he really is, adding, "Oh, and a jug of OJ to round out his dietary needs. Aside from that, he hasn't left his apartment. I've got a GPS on his car for the times when I have to do things like use the can or grab some food. Or, dare I say, *sleep*."

I've been riding John pretty hard these past two weeks. He's staying at my condo, but he's rarely there. "Don't you think that's weird?" I say.

"Of course it is! But unless he leads me somewhere, he's useless."

"Cell phone?"

"One that he uses to phone his mother, upstate. If he's into what you say he is, then he won't use his own phone. Not unless he's an idiot." John shrugs. "You know, if Charlie is involved and she disappeared, they could be laying low for a bit, until they know their doors aren't about to be busted down by a raid."

He has a point.

"Yeah . . ." I sigh, just as a knock sounds on my office door. Ginger's head pokes in. She flashes John a wide, playful smile as she strolls in, her curvy frame in a pink dress holding his eye. "We've gotta go, Cain. The ceremony is in half an hour." Her voice has taken on an unusually soft timber around me since Charlie left. I don't know if it has more to do with feeling bad for me or feeling bad in general. The two of them had grown close as well. I haven't told her anything about my suspicions about Charlie and, surprisingly, she hasn't asked.

The last thing I want to be doing right now is going to a wedding. Right now, I'd rather climb into my car and drive over to Ronald Sullivan's house to knock the answer out of him. But this is Storm and Dan. I'd never miss this day.

"Come on, date." Ginger reaches out to help me out of my seat, pulling on my arm as I reluctantly follow. I was supposed to take Charlie with me to this and we both know it. I think that's why Ginger insisted on meeting me here and driving with me. I closed Penny's for the night. She probably figured I'd be at the bottom of my bottle by mid-afternoon.

I have to admit, the idea was tempting.

Her fingers reach for my tie, adjusting it. "You look dashing tonight, boss." She smiles, holding her arm out. I take it and let her lead me out with a knowing glance over my shoulder at John.

"You know where to find me," he mutters with a groan as he gets to his feet.

■ ■ ■

"Congratulations, man." I throw an arm over Dan's shoulders in a loose hug. I truly do mean it, despite my personal turmoil. Seeing Storm under that gazebo today, wearing a white dress and a beaming smile, gave me a moment of respite.

"Thanks," Dan offers with a chuckle as he glances over at his bride, posing with Kacey and Livie—her bridesmaids—out on the beach. It's just the two of us, standing off to the side, as a crowd of guests mingle and laugh. He pauses, as if he wants to say something, but he doesn't. Finally he asks, "Have you heard from Charlie at all?"

"No." They all know she's gone. Even Ben has gone out of his way not to antagonize me, and I doubt it has anything to do with trying to impress the cute date from his law firm with his good behavior.

No one knows *why* she left, and I'm sure as hell not telling my DEA agent friend.

"And John hasn't been able to find any trace of her?" Dan pushes.

I sigh. Dan came by the club the other day to check up on me and John just happened to swing by. I introduced him as an old friend, visiting, but Dan had him pegged as an investigator within two minutes. He also figured out that John probably doesn't use the most conventional, law-abiding methods to find the information he obtains for me.

"She's gone out of her way to make sure I don't find her, Dan. Not much I can do now." There is no trace of Charlie. She has quite literally disappeared.

Dan nods slowly. When I turn to look at him, he averts his eyes. It takes him beginning to bite his lower lip to kick my instincts into gear. "What do you know, Dan?"

Sliding a hand through his buzz-cut hair, Dan finally heaves a sigh. "I'll come by Penny's tomorrow afternoon, okay?"

I fight the urge to grab him by his lapel. "What do you—"

"It's my *wedding day*." Dan shakes his head firmly. "Tomorrow. Let's get into this *tomorrow*. Not tonight. Nothing I know will be of any use to you in finding her, anyway."

I watch him walk away, wondering how the hell he has anything on her at all. How much does he know? How *long* has he known? Did he know *before* me and not tell me? The silent barrage of questions are still assaulting me as my phone begins vibrating in my pocket.

"Is he on the move?"

"No, but . . . something has come up." A deep inhale into my phone tells me John has news for me and it's not good. I turn and begin walking down the beach, away from the crowd. "I just got a call from my buddy. Human remains were found six months back in a national park outside Augusta, Maine. Results just came in. Dental records match those of Charlie Rourke from Indianapolis. Died approximately four years ago from blunt trauma to the back of the skull."

My stomach drops. I suspected it, but . . . now I have the proof.

Charlie was never Charlie Rourke to begin with.

I'm in love with her and I don't even know her real name.

"They're trying to pin it on the father but so far, he's not admitting to anything. According to the reports, he seemed shocked when they started questioning him. Says he remembers being at work the night his daughter disappeared. They're checking into his alibi."

"So, Charlie . . ." I grimace. "*My* Charlie somehow ended up with the full identification of a dead girl."

"Yup. That's not easy to do, especially as doctored as it was."

I glance over at Dan as he lays a deep kiss on his wife's lips in front of a cheering crowd. What does he have on her? Will he even tell me? After all, I've never helped him when he asked for information. *Fuck*, I wouldn't blame him for not telling me a damn thing.

Tonight's going to be the longest night of my life. For a split second, I think about going to Vicki's house. I deleted her phone number but I know where she lives. I quickly dismiss that idea. I don't think I could even get it up.

And I have a better idea.

"John. When you see my Nav pull up, drive around the block until I tell you it's okay to come back. Got it?"

"Cain, that's not the best—"

"Got it?"

. . .

"What the hell happened to you last night?" Dan's face pinches together as he stares at me, his hand testing the now-empty bottle of cognac that sits on my desk.

"I didn't get married last night, that's for sure," I mutter with a dry chuckle, stretching my arms over my head. I assume he's talking about my black eye. Ronald Sullivan was faster than I'd expected. The fucker got one good hit in the second he opened the door. I probably should have made Nate stand out of sight. Then again, Nate shouldn't have been there in the first place. He saw me take off after dinner and jumped into my passenger seat as I was about to pull away.

Dan mumbles something unintelligible as he shifts my suit—strewn over the couch—and takes a seat. "Look, I don't have a lot of time and I sure as hell shouldn't be here in the first place. I could lose my job over this." With a heavy sigh, he reaches back to pull out a white folder that's tucked into the back of his pants, concealed. "Two weeks ago, I opened my front door to get my newspaper and found an envelope with my name on it, marked 'Confidential, DEA.'"

"Two weeks ago?"

"Yeah." Sheepish eyes flicker to me. "It was from Charlie."

I'm on my feet in a second, my voice suddenly blasting through my office. "You're telling me *now*?"

"Relax, Cain. Just . . ." His hand moves to rub the frown out of his forehead. "Sit down." As easygoing as Dan is, he knows how to pull his authoritative mask on. I do as asked because I can tell by the stubborn set of his jaw that he won't continue otherwise. "I didn't know what to make of it at first. To be honest, I was freaked out. I mean, who the hell is dropping off envelopes at my front door in the middle of the night? I only joined the DEA a few weeks ago. Eventually, though, I opened it." He pauses. "It was a note from Charlie to me, telling me I should be looking into a Sam Arnoni from Long Island, New York, because he's bringing large quantities of heroin into Miami."

"*Sam* Arnoni?" *The Sam that I talked to that day on the phone? Heroin?*

Fuck, Charlie!

"Yeah. There were some other names included. First names: Bob, Eddie, Manny. Street names, no doubt. Useless." He pauses. "But I started looking into this Sam Arnoni guy and . . ." Dan's head falls back. "Cain, you have the worst fucking luck in the world."

I feel my brow pull together tightly. "What is that supposed to mean?"

"'Big Sam' Arnoni has been on the FBI's radar for years, but they can't nail him." Rifling through the folder, he pulls out a small bundle of papers affixed together with a paper clip. He tosses it onto my desk without ceremony. "The guy has enough completely legitimate businesses—some inherited, some built by him from the ground up—to make it easy for him to launder his money and hard for the Feds to catch him. Plus, he's smart. Smarter than most of these lowlifes. He's kept his organization small. There's no grandstanding, no Godfather power-trip crap.

"Six years ago, the Feds thought they finally had an in. A guy by the name of Dominic was ready to turn. But he disappeared before they got any concrete information. Showed up dead a few months later. After that, this Sam guy buckled down even more."

Picking up the stack, I begin flipping through the pages. Mostly candid shots of a large, graying man in slacks and a leather jacket. "So, he's small-time mob, basically?"

Dan gives a half-nod, half-shrug. "Except I wouldn't say small-time. Not anymore, by the sounds of it."

I keep flipping, looking for something of value *to me*. "And how is Charlie involved in this? Are you saying she's—" My words die as I land on a picture of the same man with his arm around a young blond girl as they walk down the sidewalk. She can't be more than ten, and she's smiling wide up at the man, an ice-cream cone in her hand.

Dan pulls out a second stack of papers from the folder. "Sam Arnoni married a woman by the name of Jamie Miller twelve years ago. The picture on the top is her. She used to work at The Playhouse in Vegas."

The small hairs lift at the back of my head. That's where Charlie said *she* had worked. I study the picture of the woman in a skimpy silver dress and instantly see the resemblance—same blond curls, same wide mouth, same doll face, hidden by layers of heavy makeup.

Dan keeps talking, but I already know where this is going. "Jamie Miller died two years later giving birth to Sam's son, who also died. She had a daughter." I flip through picture after picture of Sam and the young girl. The two of them eating fries at a diner, him pushing her on a swing, him cheering her on as a medal is slipped over her neck, as she bows on a stage.

And Charlie is smiling in each and every one of them. As if she's genuinely happy.

"So, this Sam Arnoni guy raised Charlie as his own daughter."

Dan's mouth twists in a grimace as he pulls out the last stack of papers, handing it to me. "Her name's not really Charlie, Cain."

"I know." How many times had I cried her name out as I came? Did she even care that it wasn't hers?

My admission earns a high-browed stare but I don't elaborate, accepting the paperwork from Dan with a deep inhale.

What am I about to find out?

My hand falters on the first page—a candid color photo of Charlie coming out of the gym, her hair pulled back in a pony-tail, her face clear of makeup, her eyes shining like a meadow of violets in the sunlight. Just like she looked coming back from the gym in my building every morning, right before we showered together.

The painful lump in my throat that I removed earlier with physical violence and copious amounts of cognac is back with a vengeance. I'm about to ask Dan if I can keep this file when I see the copy of her driver's license.

The request dies on my lips.

"Is this real?" I close my eyes tightly and reopen them, hoping for a different outcome.

Fuck.

He sighs. "At least you know she's legal, Cain."

"Barely." I'm *eleven years* older than her? "What does this mean? That she just graduated *high school* a few months ago?" I don't remember high school; it was a lifetime ago. I don't know which shock is hitting me harder, though: the fact that she's only *eighteen* or . . .

"She was a good student. Quiet, smart. Focused on gym-nastics and acting. She was accepted to Tisch to start in the fall. Obviously the Feds had their eye on her but she was a minor, so tailing her was difficult. They mostly wanted to use her to gather information." Dan is watching me carefully as he continues. "It wasn't until the spring, after she turned eighteen, that they first suspected Sam of using her to deliver drugs. And then she just left. Apparently she had applied for a one-year deferral so she could travel to Europe. Her passport turned up being used at hotels in France, Italy, Germany . . . It looked legit. It seems Sam has really gone out of his way to hide her presence down here."

Someone must have tipped him off. He'd have to have an in with the FBI for that to happen. "So, someone is traveling around Europe under her identity, while she's down here, going by Charlie Rourke and . . ." I lock eyes with Dan, waiting for him to confirm my suspicions.

"She didn't admit to anything in the note, so I don't know her culpability. But she did explain how the drops are made, with fairly specific details." There's a long pause, and then I sense the air in my office shift. "How much did you know, Cain?" Dan asks slowly. "Did you know what she was doing when you brought her with you to my *home*? To my wife and unborn child and—"

"No!" I temper my tone quickly, because I have no right to yell at Dan. He, on the other hand, has every right to punch me. Repeatedly. "I didn't know." I sigh. "I started suspecting it the day before she left. And then last night—" I stop, deciding whether I want to share all of this with Dan. After what he's shared with me, though, I owe him this much. "There's a guy by the name of Ronald Sullivan who may be of help to you. With enough pressure, he'll talk. I have his address." It took a dozen hits and a few broken ribs to get him to tell me what happened the night I ran into Charlie in the café. How some asshole named Manny held a gun to her head, threatening to kill her, and how Ronald told her to run because she was going to get herself killed. Even thinking about it now sets fire to my blood.

"So, she's *really* gone? She never mentioned where she was going?"

I throw down the stacks of paper, hearing the accusation between his words. "I'm not hiding her, Dan! I wish I could find her, but she's *gone*. And do you blame her for running? She's probably given you all that she knows and you're looking to drag her in to interrogate her."

"Hey!" Dan barks as he jumps off the couch. "I'm on your side here. I haven't said a word about Charlie to anyone. No one knows she was working here, that she was dating you. If I had said anything, your life would be a circus right now." Clearing his throat, he adds, "I could lose my job over withholding this kind of information."

"Sorry," I mutter, pushing my hands through my hair. "I just can't believe she was doing this the entire time I was with her."

"You're not the only one. I can't believe I had a drug trafficker in my own home and I didn't have a damn clue." He exhales. "Who uses their sweet little eighteen-year-old daughter like that? And who knows how long he's been doing it! Things go wrong all the time with these transactions. Throw in a girl who looks like Charlie and it's guaranteed that they end up raped or dead. Or both."

Cold dread slides through my body. Had Charlie ever been raped?

"I wish I could help her, Cain," Dan says with genuine concern in his voice, his righteous anger fading. "But I can't if she's gone. If I don't know how much she really has on him. And if it's enough."

I tap the stack of information. "And if it is? Is there really any protecting her against someone like this? If he's what you say he is, if he likely killed his own best friend, what's to stop him from killing her? He obviously doesn't value her life. As long as this guy is in the picture, she's never going to be safe, is she?"

"Look, Cain, I know you haven't had the best experience with it, but you have to trust in the justice system. We don't know—"

"If it were Storm instead of Charlie, would you say the same thing?"

Dan hangs his head in response. That's all the answer I need.

And Charlie knows how much danger she's in. She's known all along, from the first day we met to the night she left.

I'm probably never going to see her again.

"This is serious shit, Cain. If this is the guy we've been hearing about around the city, he's moving some major quantities and he's pissing the cartel off. Anyone willing to do that is either really stupid or really dangerous. We already know he isn't stupid. You need to keep an eye out," Dan warns. "I don't know what she told him about you. I hope to God nothing."

Maybe not. But *I* did. I gave him my fucking name. And that "uncle" of hers got a pretty good description of me. For all I know, he also got a picture.

I'm not stupid enough to think they can't find me.

Or that they won't.

chapter forty-four

...

CHARLIE

"Love, do you mind bringing table seven an extra order of gravy on your way by?" Berta asks in that heavy southern accent of hers that I could listen to all afternoon. Especially when she addresses me with one of a myriad of pet names. My shift just started an hour ago and I've already been called "Honey," "Darling," "Sugar," and "Sweetie."

Some people might find it annoying, but I absorb each one of them like a flower yearning for sunshine.

Because none of them sounds anything like my old pet name.

"Sure thing!" I wink at Herald the cook as I scoop up the food-laden plates from the counter.

"Oh, Katie, you're such an angel," the heavyset brunette croons, patting my shoulder as she grabs three plates. "I knew my instincts about you were right."

Flashing my stage-perfect smile, I saunter over to the tables to deliver their orders. It was only two weeks ago that I sat at one of these very tables for hours, reading through paper after paper, hungry for any news coming out of Miami, wondering all kinds of things.

Was Sam there?

Was he looking for me?

Was he looking for Cain?

I hoped that the information I left for Dan on his doorstep, just hours before I got on the bus, was enough. It wasn't much, but it was really all that I had. If I had been smarter, if I had ever believed that I'd be stabbing Sam in the back, I would have saved the pictures of Bob and Eddie before they vanished from the draft folder.

After my third cup of coffee, the middle-aged waitress with a long braid reaching down to her ass and a name tag labeling her as "Berta" had asked me what a pretty girl like me was doing all alone.

I wasn't in the mood for idle chitchat or making up lies, so I very bluntly announced that I needed a job and a place to live. She asked where I was staying and, when I told her, her face pinched up with disgust. "Oh, that just won't do."

Now here I am, serving tables at Becker's Diner and renting out a room above Berta's garage, one block away.

It was almost too easy.

The room is small, but it's clean and safe and comfortable. Most of all, it's private enough that no one hears me cry myself to sleep every night.

Berta is sweet. She's a thirty-eight-year-old single woman who inherited the family diner and has been struggling to find good evening-shift help after a string of disastrous attempts. I don't completely trust her not to snoop, but my gun and my knapsack are hidden inside a vent, so I figure I'm fine.

And now I'm twenty-one-year-old Katie Ford from Ohio. I have a golden-brown chin-length bob, violet eyes, and I wear only light makeup. I have an ordinary family back home who is proud of me for graduating with a Humanities degree from Ohio State and who fully supports me while I experience life in the South. And I had my wallet stolen. *That's* why I have no Social Security number or other identification. Temporarily, of course.

I even went to church with Berta last Sunday morning.

I'm a new person. A good person who does good things.

Who hides her silent agony well.

"Here's your Philly steak sandwich, Stanley. Careful, it's hot." I set the plate down on the table in front of the regular—a forty-something-year-old hog farmer with orange hair and green suspenders who comes in at six forty-five every night and orders the exact same thing. I think he has a thing for Berta.

A lot of the customers here are regulars. It's nice. They make a point of saying hello, and that makes me feel not quite so alone.

"Hey, Katie!"

I turn around to find Will, Berta's nephew, hovering behind me with that goofy grin of his. "What are you doing after work tonight?"

"Oh, probably just heading home. I'm tired." I fake a yawn, knowing I can't make up an elaborate story with Berta on guard. She's hopeful that we'll start dating, promising that he may act like a hooligan but he's a good boy who could use a girl like me in his life, instead of those "floozies" he keeps bringing in here.

There's nothing wrong with him, honestly.

Other than the fact that he's not *him*.

Just the thought now brings a painful lump to my throat.

"All right. Well, if you change your mind, my friend is having a party tonight out on Copper Mill Road. Live band . . . kegs . . . You should come." His eyes shift down to my chest—only accentuated by the fitted "Becker's" T-shirt—before meeting my gaze and knowing he got caught. At least he has the decency to blush.

"Thanks, Will. I'll keep that in mind." I watch him as he makes his way over to join a group of his college friends at a booth. And it reminds me that I'm supposed to be in New York right now, attending Tisch, living my dream. Not serving burgers and sodas at a diner in Alabama.

Pining over a man I unintentionally fell in love with.

With a deep, calming exhale, I begin clearing a table of its dishes. Katie Ford from Ohio never enrolled at Tisch. She never stripped for a living. She never met a man named Cain.

And she also never dealt drugs, nor will she ever. I can't let that silver lining disappear within the suffocating black cloud.

A round of laughter erupts from Will's table as one of the girls playfully flicks his ear, the movement revealing a purple streak on the underside of her hair.

I smile at the bittersweet memory it triggers.

I wonder how Ginger's doing. I wonder if Katie Ford has any hope of ever making a friend like her. I've already reconciled myself to the fact that she'll never find a man like Cain.

I wonder what he's doing at this very moment. If he's out in the club or hidden in his office.

If he's thinking about me.

If he misses me.

Or if he has already moved on.

chapter forty-five

. . .

CAIN

It took Sam Arnoni exactly twenty-five days to find me.

"He's asking for you," Nate announces from my office entrance as John and I watch over the monitor the tall man in a charcoal-colored suit. I knew it was him the second I laid eyes on him. Dan left his files for me with the requirement that they stay locked in my safe at all times. I gladly followed the instruction, except for that one picture of Charlie, of course. That one, I folded up and tucked into my pocket, to pull out whenever I felt the need.

Turns out I feel the need at least forty times a day.

I memorized every detail about the man who turned his own stepdaughter into a drug trafficker. I know all about his many businesses. I know his approximate weight, height, birth city. I could describe the family crest tattooed on his chest if I had to.

Yes, Sam Arnoni is my enemy and I like to know everything about my enemy.

"Okay, I'm on my way," I tell Nate, adding, "Keep the girls away from him." I turn to John, who decided to extend his stay in Miami and turn it into a vacation. Apparently his vacation means watching from the shadows to see if anyone's tailing me.

"You want me to call Dan?"

"No," I answer quickly. Not until I decide what to do. "I need to know where I can find this guy at all times."

"I'm on it." Wheeling up the extra chair to the computer, he pans to the video feeds from the parking lot and begins rewinding. I assume it's to locate Sam's car. "You go wine and dine that scumbag."

"Thanks, John. And be careful."

"You too, Cain." There's a hint of something in John's voice now that I can't decipher. I wonder if he's thinking about the last time he got involved in one of these situations with me. He must be wondering what I'm planning now. How far I'm willing to go to protect Charlie.

I'm wondering the same thing.

I take my time, strolling out of my office with a glass in hand. Let the fucker stew. I know that Sam's not armed and I'm not worried about him physically overtaking me. I'm not afraid of him, period. Most people would have been waiting with trepidation for this moment. I'm actually quite happy that he finally found me. Now I just have to keep from killing him in my own club.

His large frame fills the wing chair at his table. I don't know who sat him in the V.I.P. section. If I had my way, the fifty-eight-year-old would be in the back corner, near the can. I watch as Mercy strolls by, her wide blue eyes flashing at the sight of him, but Nate quickly moves in to redirect her. I guess I can understand the appeal. The guy reeks of money and, with his natural gray streaks running through his dark hair, most women would consider him distinguished. Attractive, even.

All I see is a hungry snake among mice.

Intent on watching Cherry's performance, he doesn't notice my arrival. Or he wants me to think that he doesn't.

"You were asking for me?"

Steely eyes turn to settle on me. When he smiles, the mirth

doesn't touch them. "Hello, Cain." I can hear the New York accent roll off his tongue with those two words. He sticks his hand out and I take it. I take it and I fight the urge to break the bones within it.

"I'm sorry, do I know you?"

Sam's smirk puts me further on guard. He looks like the type who would investigate his enemies, too. I wonder how much he's managed to dig up on me. "Please, join me." He gestures at the empty chair and I can't help but chuckle. He's coming into *my* club, and inviting *me* to sit with *him*. Corking my annoyance, I accept the offer with a sneer. We sit in silence as Cherry finishes her act and Terry announces Levi as the next performer. Despite the situation, a blip of disappointment stirs in me, remembering that this used to be Charlie's slot.

It's the first time that I'm actually glad she's not here.

"I believe my daughter worked for you up until a few weeks ago," he starts, taking a slow sip of his drink. "Her name is Charlie."

"Your daughter, *Charlie*."

"Yes. Blond hair? Pretty girl." He takes another sip. "I believe you got to know her *well*."

I wonder if it bothers Sam that I was fucking his stepdaughter. If the monster in him is capable of being bothered.

I wonder if he ever touched her.

I beat that thought out of my head because I know nothing good will come of pondering it right here, right now, with his throat within reach.

I let my eyes roam over the club—spying Nate watching us without attempting to hide it. He's a good distance back, but he could climb over the railing in a split second if the need arose. "Yes, I did." I'm the master of holding my cards close to my chest. Now, though, I struggle. I'd love to verbally assault Sam with all that I know. But it wouldn't be advantageous, and so I keep my answers to a minimum.

"She's gone missing. I haven't been able to find her in weeks."
His brow knits tightly together. "I'm very worried about her."

I'm sure you are. I sip my drink, forcing it back between bared
teeth. "She left me a few weeks ago. I have no idea where she
went." I can feel his careful gaze dissecting me. I let him do it.
He'll find nothing but the truth.

She *did* leave me. It *was* a few weeks ago. And I have no
fucking clue where she went.

"Did she say why?"

I lock eyes with him now. "No, she didn't. She didn't tell me
a damn thing."

Sam shifts his attention back to the floor. "You know, you
were dating her and then she just up and vanished. If I were to
report her missing, you'd become a suspect very quickly. Things
could become . . . difficult for you."

"Please do." I can't keep that smirk off my face. "*I* have nothing
to hide." He's not going to report her missing and we both know it.

"No?" He tips his head back to finish his drink, an amused
smile on his face. "It looks to me like Cain *Ford* might have a lot
to hide. Especially from a girl like Charlie."

He's letting me know that he had me investigated. He's
trying to throw me off. Rattle me. Good fucking luck. "Charlie
knows everything there is to know about me." *Almost everything.*

"Oh?" He's trying to sound light, but I caught the slight crack
in his voice. "What about all of these people here? What would
they think of their righteous boss?"

"I honestly don't care," I throw out without hesitation, though
it's a lie. If my dirty laundry needs to get aired, *I'm* the one who's
going to hang it out. I can tell by his tactics that Sam is used to
threatening people and getting his way. It may have worked on his
teenage stepdaughter, but it's going to take a lot more than that
to get his way with me.

His body shifts until he's leaning over the table. "You don't
care that they know you're a killer?"

"Anyone climbing into that ring knew the risks," I shoot back, though my blood has turned cold. Is he talking about Jones? Or . . .

"Who said I was talking about *inside* the ring?"

Fuck.

How did he find out?

I hide behind my glass, never taking my eyes off him as he weighs my reaction. When I give him nothing, he continues. "Seems odd, doesn't it? That the two men suspected of murdering your family turn up dead six months later? *Beaten* to death?" Cold eyes glance down at my hands. "Rumor has it you were quite the fighter. Unparalleled in the underground world."

I struggle to school the panic in my eyes from showing. How the hell does he know about my family's killers? What kind of connections does he have? Who else knows? Surely he's not being fed this by the cops. Never once did they appear on my doorstep to so much as question me. If they had, I would have come clean. I would have told them how those two followed me through an abandoned warehouse one night after a fight.

How they threatened me. How they aimed a gun at my head. At Nate's head.

John was right. They came looking for the money that my dad rightfully accused me of stealing while trying in vain to save himself. Apparently they had been waiting in the shadows, knowing they could demand an exorbitant interest rate if they let me live to win a few fights first.

I wasn't going to give those assholes a dime, so I truly had only two choices in that moment: fight or die.

Nate knew . . . as soon as he saw my hands flex by my sides, he knew to dive for cover.

They might have had a chance of surviving, had I not seen the bloody crime scene photos, read the graphic reports.

Had I not known what they did to Lizzy.

I called John right away. He instructed me to go home, shut

my mouth, and he'd take care of it. I guess he did, because he never uttered a word to me about it again.

"I guess someone finally fought back," I answer, the hoarseness in my voice impossible to smooth.

"Yes . . . *someone* did." He scratches his chin as if pondering his next words, though I know damn well he already had this conversation planned out. "I heard they closed that case. Maybe, with the right anonymous tip, they'd reopen it?"

Dan said Sam was a smart guy. I see the evidence of that now. He may not know definitively what happened, but it's not hard to paint a picture with my face at the center of it.

"It'd be a shame to lose everything you've worked so hard to build here."

I want to reach out and choke the life out of this manipulative asshole. "What do you want?" I snap.

"I want my daughter back and I think you know where she is." All fluffiness in his voice has vanished.

"Well, I don't, so I'm of no use to you." Dumping the last of my drink in my mouth, I stand. "If you'll excuse me."

He jumps to his feet, and I can tell he's struggling to keep his composure. I know this kind of guy. He's not used to having people walk away without his dismissal. "You have a good club here. A lot of nice-looking girls," he muses, his eyes roaming the floor. To Cherry . . . to Hannah . . . to Mercy . . . to half a dozen other dancers. "I hear you like to keep them safe." Holding out a card with a phone number on it, he asks, "If you hear from Charlie, I'd suggest you call this number. And very soon."

I glare at it, silently willing it to burst into flames, but don't take it.

Finally, he places it on the table and I watch him stroll out.

I'm not stupid. I know what that offhand comment was.

It was a threat.

The rage fires through my body like nerve synapses, making my decision for me.

■ ■ ■

"You sure you want to do this?" Nate asks from beside me as we head toward the flashing neon lights, a beacon for the city's perverts.

I heave a sigh. "No, but I don't see any other choice."

"He's not going to like us showing up here," Nate mutters, but then his face splits into a grin. I have a feeling Nate wouldn't mind getting into a fight tonight. All this mess with Charlie has made me miserable, which in turn has made him irritable.

Sin City is almost double the size of Penny's. It's full of naked women, flat screens, and more private rooms than some motels. Each table comes equipped with a small monitor, where you can watch intro videos of each dancer. All in all, Rick does well for himself.

We skip the line and walk straight to the door. A big bouncer with a goatee removes the black rope and lets us pass with a wary expression. He knows exactly who we are. He came to Penny's looking for a job, four years ago. I almost hired him, until John found out that he has ties to a known drug dealer, who in turn has ties to the cartel. It doesn't take a genius to figure out that I'd be inviting the cartel into Penny's by hiring him. It's also not surprising that he's now the head bouncer at Sin City and that members of the cartel are known to frequent here on occasion.

Thanks to a few tips from my connections, I know that the man I want to talk to is here tonight.

While the bouncer may have let us in, he also made sure to flag us to Rick immediately. The hairy fuck is waiting for us as we step into the club, his arms folded over his chest. Even when the guy makes an effort to look presentable, he doesn't. His dress shirt is wrinkled and hanging out over a pair of ill-fitting pants, which have a prominent yellow stain on the lap.

"Coming for some real ass?" He smirks. "Or to steal more of my talent?" He's obviously still bitter about losing China to me.

If he knew that I let her go, I don't doubt he'd try to pull her in again.

"Rick," is all I can manage in greeting.

He sneers at me but keeps his distance. After the last time we met—in my club, when he called me a pimp and I broke his nose and knocked four of his teeth out—he knows better than to get too close.

Nate leans over to murmur, "I don't see him out here."

Dammit . . . that means I have to ask for help from Rick the Prick. "I need to see Mendez."

A scowl hits Rick's face and I can't help but think it's an improvement. "He's not here."

I don't have time for this. "Yeah, he is. So is it the champagne room or one of the private rooms?" Rick's mouth tightens but he remains silent. "Or do I make sure the cops crawl so far up your ass that you can't walk straight for a month?" The club was raided once before, but Rick has enough money and sense to hire good lawyers. Somehow, they couldn't find any really damning evidence to shut him down permanently, which makes me think he's not as stupid as he looks.

Swallowing hard, he mutters, "What do you need with him?"

"He's cute. I thought we could date," I throw back. Rick is the last person I'd ever trust with the truth.

After a long pause, Rick turns and, with a reluctant wave, leads us into Sin City's champagne room—a large suite decorated in floor-to-ceiling black. Black walls, black leather couches, black carpet. The only hint of color is the silver molding along the walls and trim on the couch cushions, and a few metal statues lining a bookshelf.

Three men sit around the oversized sectional couch, paired with girls in various states of undress, all of whom could stand to gain ten pounds. Off to one corner, a blond is on her knees, "earning her money" with a fourth guy.

I'm seconds away from knocking Rick's false teeth out for

allowing that. But doing so won't help my cause so I remain still, fists glued to my sides, as he lumbers over to a Hispanic man with short dark hair and pockmarks all over his cheeks. The voluptuous and naked Asian girl on his lap—who can't possibly be legal and whose eyes are glazed over in that doped-up way—doesn't even slow her grind as Rick leans in to whisper what I'd assume are introductions. My stomach instinctively tightens.

I can't believe I've stooped to this level, but . . . fuck it. This is what they do. I'm merely helping to speed things up.

Cold black eyes narrow as they settle first on me, and then on Nate. He's obviously not impressed, but his curiosity has been piqued. "Out," he instructs, giving his girl a light slap across the ass as she shifts off of his lap. The other girls quickly pull their scant clothing back on and scurry out. "You too," he orders, jerking his chin at Rick, and I can't help but smile.

No one trusts Rick.

When the room is empty, two guys come over to search both Nate and me, stripping us of our guns.

"What do I owe this surprise visit to?" Mendez asks, leaning back into the couch as if completely at ease. The repetitive twitching of his foot tells me otherwise.

I tilt my head toward the camera.

"Rick knows better." But after a moment's pause, he nods in assent and waves a hand to the guy on my left. Within seconds, the camera lens has been smashed. "I don't know why he even keeps those in here." He gestures to the chair positioned across the coffee table, facing him.

I take the proffered seat, while Nate stands back. He never sits. It makes him feel vulnerable and, in this situation, where all of these guys certainly have guns and are eyeing his looming figure suspiciously, we *are* vulnerable.

"So, the famous Cain Ford," Mendez begins, settling his arms behind his head. "My cousin watched you fight once, years ago, in L.A."

"Yeah?" I throw one arm over the back of my chair as I lean back. It's my own version of feigning relaxation. I may not be afraid but I'm no idiot. I'm sitting face-to-face with a cartel member, about to ask him for help. There's nothing safe or smart about what I'm doing. "Did he win any money?"

"No, he bet against you and he lost."

"I could have told him not to do that."

Mendez's low chuckle fills the room, the casual banter dispersing some of the tension. "Why are you here?"

I assume I have only minutes with him before we're kicked out, so I get right to it. "There is a man by the name of—"

"Haven't heard of him."

I don't let his abrupt cutoff deter me. It's probably wise that I don't say Sam's name out loud, anyway. "He's been taking a substantial chunk out of your business lately." There's no need to be more specific. I'm sure it's all Mendez has been thinking about. The sudden fire in his eyes is confirmation of that. He recovers quickly, though. "My paving contracts?"

I stifle my smile. They all have "legitimate" businesses in the forefront. Mendez will never admit to anything else. That's fine. I can dance this little dance with him. "He's in Miami right now. I don't know for how long." I reach into my shirt pocket and pull out the scrap of paper. On it is the code to locate the GPS that John affixed to the bottom side of Sam's rental car. Next, I pull out the folded picture from my back pocket. With an odd sense of calm, I unfold and toss both pieces of paper onto the coffee table in front of me.

Mendez's brow furrows for a second but he doesn't touch them.

"Feds have been trying to nail him for years and they can't," I add slowly. "It's like he's untouchable."

And as long as he's alive, Charlie will never be safe. There's no chance of her ever coming back to me. I desperately want her back. I'll do anything. Sell my club, walk away from what I do.

Set the cartel up.

That is, if Mendez takes the bait. I'm counting on his greed, his arrogance, his sense of entitlement.

I finally see it.

In those near-black eyes of his, the wheels begin churning. He knows what I'm expecting he'll do with this information. "Why?" It's a simple question. A fair one.

I sure as hell won't tell him why it matters to me. Information like that may cost me down the road. Standing, the only answer I give is, "Let's just say that we're both getting something out of this."

I walk out of Sin City, telling myself over and over again that I made the right decision.

That there was no other choice.

■ ■ ■

"Do I even want to know?"

I push my front door closed behind Dan as he stalks into my condo. He's never been here before. I'm guessing, by his overly calm tone, that he's not looking for a tour.

"I don't know. Do you?" I ask.

Dan stops halfway through the kitchen before spinning on his heels to settle shrewd eyes on me. "Sam Arnoni's body was found in his hotel room this morning by a maid. Beheaded."

I force myself to take a sip of my coffee, trying to hide the wave of shock that just crashed into me.

Twelve hours.

I walked out of Sin City twelve hours ago. I've got to give Mendez credit. He doesn't waste a second. The guy was probably on the phone with one of his "people" as soon as the door clicked shut behind me.

"Are you sure?"

Dan nods slowly. "I just left the hotel. Saw the body myself."

A prickle of guilt stirs inside me. "And no one else was hurt?"

Still watching me closely, he says, "No. Looks like a professional hit."

Passing by Dan, I make my way to my living room to look out over the bay in a dreamlike state.

Sam is actually . . . dead.

And I helped kill him.

"I'm . . . Did . . ." Dan begins to ask and then stops abruptly. "You know what? I'd ask you if you knew he was in town, but I don't think I even want to know that much."

"I was at Penny's until five a.m. and then at the gym until eight. You can check surveillance if you don't believe me. I'm not a professional hit man," I mutter dryly, adding, "or a murderer."

"I know you're not, Cain. And it's definitely a cartel hit, by the signature." We stand side by side in silence as we watch a sailboat pass by. It probably wouldn't take much for Dan to find out that I had been to Sin City last night. He could probably also demand to see my surveillance footage to confirm that Sam was at Penny's last night. *If* he truly wanted to know.

"With Sam gone, Charlie's free to come home, isn't she?" Dan finally asks. I wonder where he's going with this.

"If she knew that he was dead. If she knew she wasn't going to be arrested for anything, then . . . yeah, I suppose she could." I sigh. *Home.* Would she consider Miami home? Would she want to come back? "I don't know how to reach her, though. Do you think this will make the news?"

His hand scratches his chin. "Local news for sure. Maybe New York. I'll see what I can do. If she's in some small town in Alaska, she's not likely going to hear about this." He smiles. "I know a guy who knows a guy . . . who knows a guy."

chapter forty-six

...

CHARLIE

"See? Doesn't it look like he's wearing mascara?"

Berta has an obsession with a dark-haired reporter on our local news station.

"He probably is," I confirm as I count the money in my small waitress apron. On average, I'll make fifty bucks a night in tips. Seventy, on a really good night, Berta has promised. If she knew what I used to do, and how much money I used to make in one night, she'd have a coronary.

"And lipstick, too?" Her eyes squint as she studies the screen. "Yesterday, they were more peachy. Now they're red. What kind of man wears red lipstick?"

"The kind who deals with harsh lighting and high definition, I suppose." I quickly begin filling the salt and pepper shakers. The dinner rush is over, but it's homecoming weekend. Molly and Teena, the day-shift waitresses, are pulling doubles tonight in anticipation of a late rush.

"Doug's asking for you," Teena whispers with a playful wink as she floats by, though it's loud and raspy enough that half the diner probably heard her. Fortunately, the twenty-six-year-old mechanic is sitting in the far corner. Berta's fantasy of marrying me off to her nephew was short-lived. She forced me to leave work for an hour last night to watch the parade with Doug.

His smile reminds me of Ben—broad and dimpled. But he's not an obnoxious ass like Ben. He also kind of looks like him, with his blond hair and strong jaw. And he's polite. He was a perfect gentleman last night, walking me back to Becker's before it closed, offering nothing more than a "good night" head dip as he strolled away.

I wonder when this empty void inside my chest will shrink. It's been a month, and some days I think it's growing bigger. Isn't time supposed to heal all wounds? Shouldn't four weeks have given me some relief from the relentless pain and self-doubt?

I hold on tightly to the belief that I did the right thing. Still, the same regretful longing slams into me the second I open my eyes from a fitful sleep, coiling itself through my thoughts to linger throughout the day. It haunts me through the night, leaving dark circles beneath my eyes that concealer can't quite cover. It curbs my appetite, my body shedding weight it doesn't have to spare.

But the dreams . . . they are the worst. All variations of horror leading to the same outcome.

Cain, disgusted with me.

Cain, hurt by me.

Cain insistent on helping me, because of the man he is.

And ending up dead.

No . . . I did the right thing. The same cruel fate that brought us together was bound to rip us apart. It was only a matter of time. I knew it all along and yet I fell hard, all the same.

Berta's raised voice pulls me from my thoughts. "See, Katie? I told you that you're better off staying here instead of moving on to a big city." Berta is convinced that I should settle down in Mobile, Alabama, and work with her until we're both old and gray. "One of those movie-style drug murders. This time at a fancy hotel in Miami."

A cold shiver radiates from my chest as my eyes flash to the television, dreading . . . waiting . . . The reporter is going on and on, but the words aren't truly processing. "*Execution-style . . . cartel . . . turf war . . . heroin . . . drug dealer . . .*"

A picture flashes onto the screen.

I bite back a gasp. It's the man who took me to the park on Sundays, who hoisted me onto my horse, who cheered as I stood on the podiums for my medals, who shouted "encore" as I bowed onstage.

Who used me as a pawn.

Who turned me into a criminal.

Who put me in danger.

Who stole my life.

My stepfather—the man who raised me—is dead.

I can hear Berta talking somewhere in the distance, but her voice is blurred. I can feel her arm on my shoulder, half soothing, half trying to break my sudden daze as I stare at the screen, watching his name—"Big" Sam Arnoni—flash across the bottom.

"Katie!"

My eyes finally snap to Berta. She's staring at me with a wrinkled forehead. Without checking, I know I have the eyes of every single person in the diner on me right now. The feel of them turns my ears hot with embarrassment. "I'm sorry!" I finally manage to get out with a weak giggle. "I thought that was my high school English teacher for a second." I blow out a big gush of air, feigning relief. "That would have been weird."

Berta starts chuckling. "You scared the bezeejus out of me, girl. Go and get some fresh air. We'll clean up here." Glancing down, I see the broken glass and scattered salt all over the floor. The shaker must have slipped from my hand. I open my mouth but she's already ushering me past the counter toward the back exit, waving away my protests.

Thank God the back of Becker's is empty. I lean against the

deep red brick wall as a shaky exhale leaves my lungs. The fall air, though still warm by Long Island standards, is cooler in the evenings. It doesn't require a sweater but, all the same, I wrap my arms around my chest.

"Sam is dead." Those three words sail out of my mouth in a whisper. I let them hang out in the open, deciding exactly how I should feel about the sudden news.

There's no doubt I'm in shock right now. I mean, in my mind, Sam was indestructible. I, Cain, and everyone else was at risk, but nothing could stop Sam.

Could it be a ruse? Could Sam have staged his own death to lure me back out into the water? No. Sam would never allow his face to appear on the news with a label of "alleged heroin drug dealer."

Sam is dead.

I suspect that, at some point, maybe in an hour, or tomorrow, or next week, the reality of this will truly hit me, bringing with it genuine relief. Not relief that he is dead. Despite all that Sam had done, despite everything that he was, I must admit to myself that I never really wished him dead. No, it will be relief that I am truly free, that unfortunately his death was the only way that could happen.

Yet an underlying worry is working its way to the surface, bringing waves of nausea with it.

Sam came to Miami.

What if he found Cain? Would he have hurt him, even though I was long gone? Cain's death wouldn't make the Mobile, Alabama, news. I could be pining over a dead man right now.

Rushing back into the restaurant, I grab my purse. "Can you tell Berta I'll be about fifteen minutes?" I ask Herald and run out the door before I get his answer.

Now that Sam is dead, I'm obviously not worried about him finding me. But I don't know how Cain feels about me. I asked

Dan not to tell him about my note, but Dan doesn't owe me anything.

What if Cain hates me?

What if he wants me held accountable for my crime?

All possible, all reasonable.

Doing this is risky. Still, I need to know that he's alive.

The closest pay phone is four blocks down the street and I run the entire way, cursing myself for not buying a prepaid cell phone. I don't know how pay-phone tracing works, but I'm hoping it requires more than two seconds of air time.

It takes every last bit of loose change and three attempts, but I finally manage to accurately punch in Cain's cell number with my shaky hand.

It begins to ring.

I hold my breath.

A second ring.

A third ring.

A sinking feeling dips my stomach, knowing his voice mail will pick up by the fifth.

And then suddenly, "Hello?"

His deep voice steals the air from my lungs.

Cain is safe.

Sam didn't find him.

I reach for the telephone hook to end the call but my hand freezes. I can't will myself to pull it. To disconnect Cain from my life.

For just a few seconds, with this weak link, I feel like Cain is still a part of it. I can hear him breathing. I can imagine his phone pressed up against that hint of evening stubble that I've felt so many times against my skin.

"Hello?" he asks again, this time a touch of uncertainty in his voice.

My lips part just slightly as if to answer, but I can't. I can't even form a single word. And I still can't breathe. All I can do is listen to him as the tears begin to roll down my cheeks.

Another second passes.

"Charlie, is that you?"

My fist slams down on the hook a second before the ragged sob escapes my lungs.

■ ■ ■

"New customer at table fourteen, honey," Berta calls out, rubbing my back as she passes.

"Great!" By her grimace, I've failed miserably at sounding cheerful. I should just aim for content, even though I'm far from that as well.

There's a reason people say clean breaks are for the best. I *had* a clean break. It hurt like hell. And then I had to go and call Cain, to listen to his voice, to hear him acknowledge my existence. It was as if someone took a dull saw and hacked into my clean break to make it jagged and fresh. It's the kind of pain that makes you pass out.

The kind that feels irreparable.

That was three days ago. Since then, I've grabbed my knapsack each morning, taken the city bus down to the Greyhound terminal, and bought a ticket to Miami.

And sat on the bench, watching as the bus pulled away, telling myself that just because Sam is no longer a threat, it doesn't mean Cain wants anything to do with me anymore. That I should let him be. That I've brought enough trouble into his life. That the memory of those wonderful weeks with Cain will need to somehow fill the gaping void in my heart, because things can never go back to the way they were.

Of course Berta knows none of this, because I'm back in time for my shift every night, plastering on a weak smile.

I make my way over to table fourteen. There's a large man sitting there with graying hair and a round gut. Sliding a menu in front of him, I give him my best fake smile. "Hi, sir. Welcome to Becker's. What can I get you tonight?"

"Oh . . ." He pats his belly, never bothering to open the menu. "A black coffee and a burger."

"That's easy."

"I'm a creature of habit." He grins, and the smile reaches his eyes. "And please, call me John."

chapter forty-seven

...

CAIN

I can't believe we found her.

Given the life she used to lead, I can't believe she made such a rookie mistake. As I sit in my rental car and watch her take John's order through the diner window, I think about how fucking thankful I am that she did.

I owe Dan . . . I don't know what I owe him. A vital organ, perhaps. Through his connections, CNN picked up the murder story, sensationalizing it as part of a national drug problem piece. From there, it filtered out to a lot of smaller news stations.

After that strange call on my cell three nights ago, John had the number traced to a pay phone in Mobile, Alabama, within minutes. He was on the first flight out the next day. I would have been, too, had he not convinced me to stay. He figured she had used a random pay phone and it would take him weeks—or longer—to find her.

But she didn't. She used the one only four blocks away. And, thanks to John's weakness for local diners, he stumbled upon her within forty-eight hours.

She's cut her hair. It looks really pretty. It makes her look older, too, despite the light makeup on her face.

She still looks like a little doll.

Fuck, have I ever missed her!

It's taking every ounce of my willpower not to charge in there right now. I'm torn. I don't know why she hasn't come back to me, now that Sam is dead. I assume that's why she called when she did, but I can't be certain.

That makes me think that maybe she doesn't want to come back to me, regardless. Maybe she wants a clean break, with no memories of her old life. If that's the case, I don't want to make a scene in there and mess up all that she has going on. John confirmed that she's living above the garage of the diner owner—a nice lady with a criminal-free background, who closes the place to attend church early on Sundays.

And so I sit. And I quietly watch the woman I don't want to live without live a life without me in it.

chapter forty-eight

. . .

CHARLIE

My keys make a loud noise as they drop onto the dresser beside the door. My apron and purse follow, and then I kick off my shoes. It's my new nightly ritual. Next is a shower, to wash the greasy diner smell out of my hair. I never bother turning on the lamp because the fluorescent bulbs cast such harsh lighting and, besides, there's enough light shining into the window from the street.

I don't know how I missed him sitting on my bed.

"You just can't sleep without these fancy sheets, can you?"

I yelp out in surprise as I jump back, my back slamming into the wall. "How did you get in here?" I can barely hear my own voice, my blood rushing into my ears.

He stands and I instinctively take a step forward, toward that beautiful man who was mine for a short period of time, until reality caught up with me. But my feet stall, the truth of what I've done to him making me wonder if I should steel myself to defend against an emotional attack.

One that I deserve.

My breathing grow shallow with the rising panic.

Is he here to tell me that he hates me? That the cops will be here in minutes to arrest me?

Cain doesn't stop. He keeps moving closer and closer, until his overpowering body makes my knees weak and his stunning face makes me lean in.

And those dark brown eyes make me burst into tears.

He grabs my wrist and pulls me against his chest without hesitation, his arms wrapping me tight. "You know that I'm resourceful," I somehow hear him say over my sobs. He releases a deep sigh and I sense the tension in his body slide out. "God, Charlie, you've put me through hell."

"I'm sorry." I start crying harder with his words. "I didn't have a choice. It was—"

"I know." He eases his grip on me and takes a step back, tilting my head back with a hand on my chin. His fingers start smoothing away my tears. If he knew how many tears I've cried for him . . . "I know *everything*."

Swallowing the enormous lump in my throat, I echo, "Everything?"

With a sad smile, his eyes dip down to my mouth. "I know how your stepfather took advantage of you. I know what happened at that last drop."

I shudder with the memory of that gun against my temple.

"And I'm guessing you didn't tell me because you were trying to protect me." He pauses. "You saw the news, right?"

"Yes." I close my eyes, the smell of his cologne as soothing as it is intoxicating.

"You know that you're safe now, right?"

I stare up into those eyes that I thought I'd never see again. "Am I?"

Cain's furtive nod makes me believe him. "Dan's not going to say a word." His brow furrows deeply. "Is that the only reason you didn't come home?"

Home. "I didn't know if you wanted me there," I admit through a hard swallow. "I only called because I wanted to make sure Sam hadn't found you."

His arms seal me against his body once again—strong, protective arms that feel like they may never let me go again. I hope they never do. And he lets me cry against him without a word.

Until a strange thing happens. My tears begin to morph from sadness to relief to complete and utter joy, interspersed with little giggles.

As I realize that it's finally over.

Cain knows what I've done and he's here. And, I think, forgiving me.

It's finally, truly over.

"Your hair smells like French fries," Cain murmurs, and I feel his lips touch the top of my head.

"Sorry. I was just about to get into the shower."

"Really . . ." I catch the playfulness in his tone and my knees automatically buckle. I want nothing more right now. *But, wait.* I pull away, though I'm unwilling to release my grip around his ribs. "Cain. What about . . ." I exhale deeply. "Do you know that I used a fake ID?"

He studies me for a moment, as if deciding what he wants to say. And then that lip curls up. "You certainly have more talents than any eighteen-year-old I've ever met, though your dietary choices should have been a dead giveaway."

I duck my head slightly. "Are you okay with that?"

He chuckles. "Yeah, I'll survive." The backs of his fingers graze my cheek and I instinctively turn to catch them with my lips. "Besides, I never did live out my twenties like a normal person." Dipping down, Cain's lips brush mine as he whispers, "Maybe we can do it together." And then there's no more talking, as Cain claims my mouth as if no time has passed.

As if it belongs to him and him alone.

And it does. I should have known, from that very first kiss, I had fallen into another trap.

The difference is that this trap is one I have no desire to escape from. Ever.

"But . . ." He pulls back slightly and my mouth instantly feels cold. "I'm in love with a woman and I don't even know what name to call her by."

My breath hitches. Did I just hear that right? Pressing my fingers into his lean muscles, I take a moment to compose myself before I burst into tears. Again. "I mean, when Dan showed me a copy of your real ID . . ." His voice trails off as his eyes widen in exaggerated shock. What went through his head when he found out, I wonder. Did he immediately see it as I did? Fate playing its own strange little game?

He's watching, waiting.

"I think I'll always see myself as Charlie with you, but . . ." I begin, my fingertips tracing the ink on the side of his neck. So coincidental.

Or maybe not at all.

". . . I'll also answer to Penny."

epilogue

. . .

CHARLIE

February 14

All I can remember is that front porch.

But it's exactly as it was in my memory, right down to the ornate carvings along the tops and a set of stairs off the end. The house itself is a nice shade of blue. Black shutters frame the windows and the front door. Apparently it's a "shotgun" house, a style that is common to New Orleans.

And apparently I wasn't born in Las Vegas.

A strong, warm hand weaves itself through mine. "Are you sure you're ready?" I look up to see Cain's encouraging smile. He surprised me with a trip here. At the time, it was presented to me as a birthday weekend getaway. But then this morning, Cain explained the *real* reason he picked this destination.

John had helped him locate my grandparents. They're still alive and living in the same house that my mother grew up in.

And I'm about to see them again.

"Yes." With hesitation, I add, "Do you think they'll recognize me?"

Leading me until we reach the front door, he gently prods

me ahead of him. With a light kiss against my neck, he whispers, "Only one way to find out." His finger finds the doorbell.

I listen with a mixture of excitement and trepidation as the loud gong sounds inside. A moment later, the door creaks open, revealing a much older, grayer version of my mother in a simple white blouse and a pair of olive-colored trousers, a tea towel in her hands. "May I help you?" she asks, but her eyes are already narrowing as they scrutinize my features. Suddenly her hands fly to her mouth with a gasp. "Penny? Is that you?" After a pause, she cries, "It is you!" Without another moment's hesitation, she's pulling me into a tight embrace, just like I remember my mom used to, her cheeks instantly wet with tears. "Happy birthday."

■ ■ ■

"Just a quick stop in and then we'll head home," Cain promises as he shuts off the Navigator in the parking lot at Penny's. Leaning in to steal a kiss, he adds, "I'm looking forward to our own bed tonight."

"Yeah, I can't wait to *sleep*. Those old folks are exhausting," I reply with a playful wink.

We extended our plane tickets and spent an entire week with my grandparents. They insisted on us staying in their home instead of a hotel. I was afraid that might be too much for Cain to handle, but he and my grandfather seemed quite content to sit out on the porch every evening with a glass of that pricey cognac.

That first day was extremely emotional. They had no idea that their daughter had died. The last words spoken to each other were full of anger, fear, and later, regret. It was the day I remember. My mom announced that she was taking me and moving to Las Vegas to become a showgirl. They begged her to leave me with them—I was only three years old and didn't belong in Vegas—but she refused, for the simple fact that I belonged to her.

When weeks turned into months, and months turned into

years, my grandfather flew to Vegas. He searched every production house in the city, picture in hand, with no luck. No one with that face or name had ever worked as a showgirl in Vegas. So he moved on to the strip clubs. Finally, he found out from a dancer at The Playhouse that Jamie Miller had married some rich guy and moved away.

That was all anyone could tell him. I guess my mom didn't make deep friendships while she was there. My grandfather returned to New Orleans, heartbroken but hopeful that we were at least happy and safe. And that she would call. They didn't have money to hire an investigator.

They've been waiting for a ghost all these years.

They also asked me a lot of questions about my life. I tried to answer them as truthfully as I could, but some topics were impossible.

Like what happened to my stepdad.

And how I met Cain.

And why he calls me Charlie.

I didn't want to lie, so I answered as vaguely as possible. I think they finally caught on, because they shifted their focus to questions about my future. And those, I was very happy to answer. Truthfully. They know that I'm moving to New York in August so I can start at Tisch.

And that I'm madly in love with Cain.

And that he's moving to New York with me.

I've promised to Skype with them once a week and we're coming out to see them again in May, for a big family reunion. While my mom never had any siblings, she had plenty of cousins. In one day, I've discovered that I have an entire family.

A blood-related one, that is. I can't forget the other family I've come to know and love.

Cain clasps hands with me as we head toward that big black steel door. I struggle to remember that night last summer when I first saw the bright sign on top of this building with my name on it. I knew nothing else but that fate, in its twisted way, *must* have led me here and that I *had* to get a job here.

Apparently fate was also leading me to the man who would save me.

Two days after Cain found me in Mobile, he called Dan, who wasted no time hopping on a plane to meet us. It was beyond awkward at first. The three of us sat in a corner booth at Becker's, away from the prying eyes and ears, me suctioned to Cain's side while I waited for Dan to slap a set of handcuffs on the table.

But Dan promised that he would keep my involvement, my fake identity, my whereabouts—basically, my existence—to himself. He'd even help me get all of my real ID back. All he wanted in return was some help.

He managed to get me into a police station without causing a stir and we sat there for three days, surrounded by take-out boxes, scanning through mug shot after mug shot in a computer database. I was able to identify Bob—who Cain knew by his real name—and Manny, but neither Eddie nor Uncle Jimmy were among them. I'm not surprised.

Cain stayed with me for a week and then asked that I remain in Mobile until Dan could look into Manny and Bob, to make sure they wouldn't be a threat. As hard as it was to say goodbye to him at the airport, he was right.

And this time, I knew it wasn't goodbye forever.

A few weeks later, the cops nabbed Bob on a minor drug offense. I don't know if it was sheer luck or John-and-Cain-inspired luck. Truthfully, I'm not sure I need to know. According to Dan, Bob squealed like a pig facing the slaughterhouse, turning on Eddie, Manny . . . even his own mother and the small marijuana plant she grows in her backyard for medicinal purposes.

The Feds found Eddie hiding in Missouri with a distant relative, but they couldn't track down Manny. Unfortunately for Manny—and Jimmy, who it appears went into business with him—the cartel did.

The threat to me ended there.

It was mid-December when Cain pulled up in his Nav outside Becker's, and he hasn't left my side since.

Even now, as we step into his office, his hand is firmly entwined with mine.

We find Nate there sitting behind the desk, doing paperwork, and a fiery red-haired Ginger in a microscopic silver dress, muttering to herself about Cain's shitty organization skills and the lack of premium scotch in this place.

"What? Do you still own this place?" Nate's wink my way tells me he's not really mad about taking the burden on while Cain stayed in New Orleans with me.

Cain is handing the club over to him in August, but no one besides the four of us and Storm knows yet. He was going to just shut it down, unwilling to sell and have it turned into another Sin City, but Nate stepped in, expressing his desire to keep it going.

Cain thinks he's nuts but he has agreed, on the condition that Nate shuts it down the second he's had enough.

"You're back!" The hunt for scotch is abandoned as Ginger skips over to throw her arms around me. We picked up right where we left off the day I moved back to Miami. The only difference was that she wanted to know absolutely nothing about where I was or what happened.

Grabbing my left hand, she exclaims, "Oh, thank God. I thought you had betrayed me and eloped."

I roll my eyes as the heat crawls up my neck. If it were up to Cain, my legal name would already be Penny Ford. As much as I love the sound of that and as sure as I am that there will never be another man for me, I don't want to rush through life.

Not when I'm finally able to enjoy it.

"Just remember where your wedding is going to be," she reminds with a finger waggle in Cain's face.

Ginger bought a dilapidated old house in Napa Valley, which she is fully renovating. She had a lot of money saved, but not quite enough for her elaborate four-sided double-balcony design, so Cain and Storm are chipping in as silent partners to help her get on her feet.

Cain is actually venturing into the real estate market in a bigger way, investing in more properties and expecting a lucrative return. His latest purchase? A stunning and exorbitantly priced two-bedroom condo a few blocks away from my campus. Not exactly the life of a student, but, then again, nothing about my life has ever been ordinary.

And I have a feeling that with Cain, nothing ever will be.

But it will be different in all the best ways.

"All right, out!" Cain barks, but there's no bite to his tone.

Nate slams the books shut and rounds the desk, clasping hands with Cain as he passes. "Ginger," he says, wrapping a giant paw around the back of her neck, "I'm going to need a manager."

"And I'm going to need to set myself on fire," I hear her retort as they head down the hall. I catch the wink over her shoulder a second before Cain shuts and locks the door.

"Where were we?" Cain murmurs, pinning my body against the wall with his. Being in my grandparents' house limited our nightly "activities" somewhat. Cain has already promised that we'll be making up for it. By the feel of his hardness against me, I'm thinking he plans on starting right now.

I'm fine with that. I'll give Cain anything he wants, because he's given me *everything*.

There are no secrets between us anymore. He knows about every single one of my drops, and he knows about Sal Pal. I, in turn, know what happened to the two men who murdered his family.

I know how the cartel found Sam.

And I don't think any less of Cain for it. In fact, if possible, I love him more. We are simply two good people with equally flawed pasts, looking for perfect futures.

And I think we've found it, in each other.

ACKNOWLEDGMENTS

Writing books doesn't seem to be getting any easier. I thought this particular one was going to kill me. Thanks to some amazing people in my corner, it didn't. In fact, I came out a stronger writer because of it.

First and foremost, to all of my readers who have supported me over the years. Your words of encouragement and your love of my work is what keeps me pushing forward on the more difficult days and helps me celebrate the best of them.

To all of the bloggers who continue to spread the word and read my books, thank you. A million times, thank you. Your support behind Cain's book has been overwhelming.

To Heather Self, my crit partner, my U.S. term checker, my Texan friend. You know how much I struggled through this book (right down to the title). Thank you for your invaluable feedback to my ideas and challenges at all hours of the day and night.

To Autumn Hull, for being a fantastic blogger and friend. There's no one I trust to provide feedback on one of *those* scenes more than I trust you.

To K.P., I can't believe it's been a year since I first asked you to represent me for *Ten Tiny Breaths*. Man, has it been a wild ride? Here we are now, with a third book together. One day I will meet you in real life. On that day, I will give you an enormous hug.

To Stacey, what can I say, except that I am one lucky writer to have an agent who will meet me for coffee and sit through hours of random plot ramblings. And then go shopping at Target with me. Irrational fear of wasps and all, I'm so happy to have you in my corner.

To Sarah, you, more than anyone, know how much I struggled with Charlie and Cain. You were there with me through it all, reading the ugly first draft, answering my questions, and calming my worries while letting me write the story I was meant to write. Your talent and unfailing support made this book what it is.

To my publisher, Judith Curr, and the team at Atria Books: Ben Lee, Valerie Vennix, Kimberly Goldstein, and Alysha Bullock, for working so collaboratively with me to get this story into readers' hands.

To my family and friends, for tolerating my bouts of reclusiveness while in the depths of this book.

Special thanks to M and P, for your "expertise."